Jerusalem's Daughter

Jerusalem's Daughter

JENNA VAN MOURIK

NowGo Publishing

ISBN (Paperback): 978-1-7364392-0-3
ISBN (E-book): 978-1-7364392-1-0

This is a work of historical fiction. As such, some historical figures and events are represented in this work. Scripture may be quoted or paraphrased by characters to more accurately reflect how they would have spoken at the time in which the story takes place. However, all other characters and events depicted come from the author's own imagination. Any likeness to persons, living or deceased, is purely coincidental.

All scripture quotations unless otherwise indicated have been taken from the Christian Standard Bible®, Copyright © 2017 by Holman Bible Publishers. Used by permission. Christian Standard Bible® and CSB® are federally registered trademarks of Holman Bible Publishers.

Cover design by C. J. Graves.
Images licensed through Shutterstock.

"Palm Branch" chapter header illustration by C. J. Graves.

Printed in the United States of America.

First edition: March 2021

NowGo Publishing
www.authorjennavanmourik.com

DEDICATION

First and foremost, to my Grandma Shirley Graves, who first instilled in me the love for Bible study and the study of Biblical history.

To my "Imma" and "Abba" and all of my "Dodhs" and "Dodahs" who raised me. You have all been role models to me and encouragers of my faith since before I could even speak, let alone write words.

To Charissa, my cousin by birth and sister of my heart. Thank you for always going along with all of my crazy ideas and helping me turn my childhood schemes into grown-up passions.

To my husband, Brandon, who when I said, "I'm writing a book" simply replied, "Cool." Your praise from day one kept me going even through the tears and the writer's block (and your willingness to bring me coffee whenever I asked, and sometimes even when I didn't ask). You have always supported me in everything, and I love living life side-by-side with you. May our love be strong and our faith even stronger.

To God most of all, who writes all of our stories and weaves them together to reveal His glory.

NOTE TO THE READER

Dear Reader,

I vividly remember Easter Sunday in 2018. It was my first Easter with my husband. We'd moved away from our families after we got married so that we could both continue our schooling. I especially missed my family around the holidays, but I missed them during Easter most of all. It was the first major holiday where my parents couldn't visit. I spent the whole day decorating my house and cooking a festive feast for two, which I was very proud of at the time. I watched my favorite Easter films like the 1959 *Ben-Hur*, among others. As a long-time fan of Biblical fiction, these stories captivated me. I began to wonder more about what the lives of the common people who encountered Jesus might have been like. That was when, in all of my spare time, I began scouring the scriptures.

This story stemmed from the verse John 21:25, which reads, "And there are also many other things that Jesus did, which, if every one of them were written down, I suppose not even the world itself could contain the books that would be written" (CSB). I began to imagine what those "other things" might have been, and soon, the character of Shamira appeared in my head. She didn't so much appear as she did force her way in and demand her story be told, and I happily obliged. During the springtime as visions of palm branches, crosses, and Easter celebrations flooded my mind, I began writing this story.

It is my hope and prayer that you will be touched by reading this book, the book of my heart, and encouraged in your own faith journey.

—Jenna Van Mourik

GLOSSARY

Abba—Father
Ahav sheli/Ahava sheli—A term of endearment, "my love" or "loved one"
Bat—Daughter of…
Ben—Son of…
Chuppah—A Jewish wedding canopy
Dodah—Aunt
Dodh—Uncle
Hamud/Hamuda—A term of endearment, "cute one"
Hosanna—An expression of adoration or praise for a savior, meaning "help us" or "save us"
Imma—Mother
Ketubah—Marriage contract
Mezuzah—A small box traditionally affixed to the doorways of Jewish homes, containing a parchment inscribed with Hebrew words from the Torah
Mohar—Bride price
Pesach—The celebration of Passover
Pharisee—One who believed in strict adherence to Jewish laws, traditions, and religious practices
Sabba—Grandfather
Sadducee—One, usually a member of the priestly or aristocratic class, who differed from the Pharisees by interpreting scripture literally, rejecting oral law and tradition, and denying the coming of a Messiah
Savta—Grandmother
Seder—A special meal prepared during Passover
Shabbat—Sabbath, the traditional day of rest
Shalom—A greeting, meaning "Peace be with you"
Shofar—A trumpet-like instrument, usually made of a ram's horn
Tallith—A woolen shawl worn on top of the head, usually during prayer
Tanakh—The Hebrew Bible
Torah—The Law, or the first five books of the Hebrew Bible
Yeshiva—A Jewish school where scripture is studied

FAMILY TREE

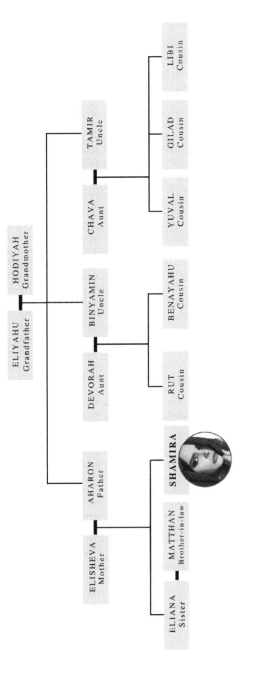

ELIYAHU
Grandfather

HODIYAH
Grandmother

AHARON
Father

DEVORAH
Aunt

BINYAMIN
Uncle

CHAVA
Aunt

TAMIR
Uncle

ELISHEVA
Mother

MATTHAN
Brother-in-law

ELIANA
Sister

SHAMIRA

RUT
Cousin

BENAYAHU
Cousin

YUVAL
Cousin

GILAD
Cousin

LIBI
Cousin

PART ONE

"A voice of one crying out: Prepare the way of the Lord in the wilderness; make a straight highway for our God in the desert. Every valley will be lifted up, and every mountain and hill will be leveled; the uneven ground will become smooth and the rough places, a plain. And the glory of the Lord will appear, and all humanity together will see it, for the mouth of the Lord has spoken." - Isaiah 40:3-5 CSB

"I rejoice greatly in the Lord, I exult in my God; for he has clothed me with the garments of salvation and wrapped me in a robe of righteousness, as a groom wears a turban and as a bride adorns herself with her jewels." - Isaiah 61:10 CSB

27 A.D.

Young Shamira squirmed from side to side in her seat. She raised her hands up to cup her face, overcome by a tingling sensation. It wasn't just nerves that made Shamira's muscles tense. There was something else. "Ah, ah, ah." Shamira struggled to control herself, fighting the itch that crept from the top of her head down to her forehead, behind her eyes, to the very tip of her nose, and finally: *"Achooo!"*

Turning to her left where Rut, her only *slightly* younger cousin and best friend sat, she whispered, "That stuff smells awful!"

Rut snorted in laughter, giving her away and startling the others in the room. Her blackish brown, tightly coiled hair bobbed as she giggled.

"Shamira!" Shamira's Aunt Devorah raised her hand to her chest as if clutching her heart. The woman, close to her mother's age, continued: "Look what you almost made me drop!" Revealing to Shamira what she had been cradling in her other arm, *Dodah* Devorah thrust the object so close to her face it almost hit her nose.

She felt the urge to sneeze again, but this time Shamira was able to stop herself.

"I am sorry, Dodah Devorah. I did not mean to frighten you, but something smells rotten!" While ten-year-old Shamira spoke her apology in earnest, her childish honesty gave way.

Devorah scoffed and continued walking toward Eliana, Shamira's sixteen-year-old sister, who was the reason all the women of the family had gathered in the upper room of their home.

"This does *not* smell rotten," Devorah scolded, waving her hand in the air. "This, as I'm told, is the most popular scent among noble women these days. It is meant to smell of fine spices, exotic herbs, and olive oil. It came straight from Rome! The wives of great soldiers and leaders anoint themselves with this very perfume. Tonight, Eliana will wear the same scent."

Regardless of the explanation, Shamira kept pinching her nostrils together with her petite, girlish fingers. If that was what the wives wore in Rome, she never wanted to go there.

Even without saying words, she could tell by the mischievous look in her cousin's eyes and the way her cheeks had gone red from stifled laughter, Rut was thinking the very same thing. They would likely spend hours giggling about this later.

Elisheva, Shamira's mother, turned her attention from her older daughter to her younger daughter. She bent to face Shamira at eye-level and whispered, "Shamira, if the smell bothers you then try to breathe through your mouth and not your nose, but don't hurt your Dodah Devorah's feelings, all right? That's a good girl."

Shamira nodded, studying her mother's warm honey-brown eyes. They were like Shamira's own, except for the small wrinkles that appeared on the outside corners when she smiled.

Obediently, Shamira lowered her hand to her lap and did the best she could to smile, albeit through gritted teeth. Shamira knew it was wrong to grimace and make faces in front of her Dodah Devorah who had worked so hard to purchase the ointments herself. However, no matter what she did, Shamira couldn't keep her eyebrows from creating creases of dissatisfaction across her forehead.

Her attempt at being well-behaved and well-mannered must not have been very successful, for she heard her sister Eliana snickering from across the room. Eliana was supposed to be happy that day, but not because of Shamira's antics. It was Eliana's wedding day; the day her long-awaited marriage to her betrothed, Matthan, was finally to begin.

Although Eliana was six years older, Shamira had always felt much closer to her than that. That is, until Eliana became betrothed. All she had talked of since the *ketubah* had been written up and signed was Matthan.

Eliana spent twice as much time in the kitchen with the older women, often joining them in the courtyard as they cooked over the fire or watched the bread rise in the clay oven. At first it had hurt her feelings that Eliana no longer had time to play with her like they had before, but at least she still had her cousin, Rut. She would have Rut for a long time too, because Rut was only six months younger, and neither of them would be getting married in the near future.

But now, with Matthan's imminent arrival, Shamira did not have much time left with Eliana. The sound of the *shofar* in the distance and the cheers in the street signaled to them the bridegroom's processional was beginning, and they only had a few moments left before he would arrive.

Devorah waved her hand in dismissal of Shamira's reaction and bent down toward Eliana. "Come now, Eliana. You are to be married today; allow us to help prepare you. Matthan will not be disappointed when he sees you and breathes in the luxurious scent of…"

Her speech paused while she pulled the ornate lid off the alabaster jar, smiling and ready to anoint her niece. Eliana reeled back, teetering on her chair. Even Devorah recoiled when the putrid smell permeated the air in the room. Shamira and her *imma* turned away while her sister and Dodah Chava pulled the necklines of their tunics up to cover their noses. Dodah Devorah ran—no, raced—carrying the jar with her, most likely outside to rid the container of its contents.

Dodah Chava turned to her toddler daughter, Libi, who was shaking her head back and forth. She stretched out her arms toward her little girl, but Libi only stepped farther backward, surprise in her eyes.

"My Libi, don't upset yourself! Dodah Devorah has taken the jar away. You do not have to hide from me, do you?"

Little Libi's gray eyes darted from side to side as she continued to wriggle and make faces of displeasure. Libi gestured toward the door, but Chava crept closer to her again, pulling her into an embrace. Chava demonstratively waved her hand in front of her own nose, and Libi mimicked her mother.

Elisheva offered her hand to her sister-in-law. "She is probably just frightened by all of the commotion. It's a very big day. I'm sure Libi will be all right in time."

Dodah Chava wiped a teardrop from her own cheek, blinked a few times, and morphed her sullen expression into a smile aimed at Eliana. "You are a beautiful bride, Eliana."

Shamira, although young, was not blind to her aunt's struggle. It hurt her caring heart to see her family so saddened. She vaguely remembered when Chava had labored with the twins, Yuval and Gilad, but she had only been six years old at the time. Chava had given *Dodh* Tamir, Shamira's uncle from her father's side, two fine sons, but she spoke often of the longing in her heart for a daughter. The joy her aunt and uncle had experienced when Libi arrived just over a year later was incomparable to anything anyone in their home had ever experienced.

Shamira remembered the cheers and the songs of praise by the women that day. Eliana, Rut, and Shamira had formed a circle and joyfully danced in celebration. Now there were four girl cousins, outnumbering the boys by one. They could not have been happier.

That was also one of the last days such glorious songs had filled the house of Eliyahu.

Now Libi was three years old. Other children Libi's age knew several words, and some could even carry on short conversations. Granted, they were often spoken in broken language or with speech impediments, but they could communicate verbally. At first, everyone, including Shamira, just thought Libi was shy or possibly a slow learner, but the gravity of the situation had begun to weigh on all of them. A wedding like Eliana's was not likely in Libi's future if she could not hear or speak.

Although Shamira didn't think there was anything really wrong with Libi, she knew others outside of their family did. It was clear every time they visited the temple to offer sacrifices, and when Shamira could overhear people explaining that her family was cursed. But how could they be cursed when they all loved God so much?

Devorah had returned to the room normally shared by only Eliana and Shamira. With her arms curled around her middle, Devorah meandered toward the back of the room.

Elisheva turned toward her sister-in-law. "Devorah—perhaps the perfume was ruined on the journey from Rome to Jerusalem. I'm sure if it had been fresher, it would have smelled just as sweet as you'd described."

Shamira's mother had a way of inspiring peace between other members of the household when they disagreed. Shamira had seen it enough times herself when her imma settled sisterly arguments between her and Eliana. She also had a special touch when it came to cheering up those who were hurting.

Devorah gave a half-smile, and then Elisheva turned back to Eliana.

Clearing her throat and blinking back the tears in her eyes, Elisheva spoke with the same tenderness that made her such a wonderful mother. "Eliana—your father and I have been praying for you and for this very hour since the day we knew we were expecting you. When you were born, we began to pray for your husband-to-be as well."

"We all have," added Devorah.

"Imma, I have had more support than any of the other young women I know. It is as if I have had three mothers instead of one! You, Dodah Devorah, and Dodah Chava. Each of you has taught me well, and I thank you. It is because of all of you that I do not fear marriage, for you have all been such wonderful examples to me." Eliana, ever the cheerful and kind older sister, smiled at her mother and aunts.

Shamira was often jealous of her sister's ability to be so amiable and good-hearted all the time. No, that simply wasn't right. An ability was something you learned. Eliana didn't have to learn how to behave properly; it was just a part of who she was. A trait Shamira most definitely did *not* share, but deeply admired.

Elisheva took a deep breath as if to savor this moment before she spoke. "I am happy that is how you feel, Eliana. Still, once you are married to Matthan you will be a part of his household. I am sure we will see each other as often as we can, but it will not be the same as it is now."

Elisheva continued, "I am so glad you feel well prepared for this new part of your life, but before Matthan arrives, I must be sure—do you have any more questions? Are you certain about… well, what I mean to say is, are you fully aware of your *other* wifely duties?"

Shamira noticed her mother's olive complexion turn crimson as she asked the question. Why on earth would her imma be embarrassed or concerned? Eliana was a fine cook and wonderful housekeeper; Imma had nothing to worry about. Shamira shrugged off the confusion.

"It's not fair!" Shamira blurted out. "I don't want Eliana to go!" Shamira confessed what she'd thought a hundred times but had never before spoken out loud. She couldn't hold back her tears any longer—not with the reality that her sister would be leaving soon confronting her.

"Shamira," her mother reprimanded, "do not cast such disappointment on today, your sister's wedding day. This is to be the happiest day of her life and you should be happy for her."

Elisheva tilted her head down toward her youngest daughter, raising her eyebrows. Imma was beautiful and full of grace, but she was also a strong woman who demanded authority with just a simple glance. Shamira recognized the look and knew she needed to comply, but her heart was still torn.

"But Imma, I don't want Eliana to go! I will miss her too much! Won't everybody?" Shamira's petite lips began to quiver as she pondered what life would be like without her sister. She had slept side-by-side with Eliana for years, whispered secrets under the stars, shared the same chores, and escaped misadventure after misadventure. How would life go on as Shamira had known it without her older sister there to experience it with her?

When Eliana stood, the rich blue fabric of her dress flowed

down her curves, swirling like river water with her movements. The linen swished on the ground, making sounds like a small waterfall as she crossed the room. She took Shamira's hand and said, "Shamira, it will be a good thing for me to be married, and Matthan is a good man who comes from a wonderful household! I will visit you as often as I can. *I promise.*"

Shamira, while slightly encouraged, still cried out to her imma. "But why must she go to live with Matthan? Why can't Matthan come to live here? We're a wonderful household too! What's so special about him and his household?" These questions seemed quite logical to her as she considered this option.

Shamira saw Chava and Elisheva muffle laughter behind their hands, but her Dodah Devorah was not as easily charmed. She glowered at Shamira, an expression of annoyance Shamira almost didn't notice, for it was an expression Devorah almost always bore.

"It is just the way things are, child. Soon enough, it will be your turn to get married. You will not be so upset then," Devorah chided and then, with a knowing tone that made Shamira cringe inside, added, "Indeed, give it a few years, and you'll be begging for your father to make such a match for you!"

Devorah was right on two accounts. First, at ten years old, Shamira's mother had already told her about the many changes her body would face. She knew within the next couple of years, she would experience her first red flow. And just a few years after that, if Eliana was any example, she would either be betrothed or already married. Shamira didn't want to think about marriage yet—she still wanted to run in the fields with her cousins, laughing, playing, and singing the day away.

Second, Matthan was a good match by all standards. Shamira had overheard many times that Eliana could not have found a better husband and that she would want for nothing once she joined his household. Even so, Shamira couldn't bring herself to care about his wealth, or her sister's good fortune, or how lucky the two of them were. All she knew was that Matthan was going to take her sister away. For that reason, and possibly a few others which may or may not have had more to do with his physical appearance than anything else, she was decidedly unenthused about the whole occasion.

There was actually nothing wrong with Matthan's appearance; he looked like many other men. Shamira just didn't understand why Eliana had to carry on about him so much. He looked nothing like their beloved *abba*. Shamira was sure her father was the most handsome man in Jerusalem.

"Oh no," Shamira explained. "I will never get married. I want to stay here with all of you, forever!" All of this change was too much, too fast. To everyone else, Shamira knew she was still a child whose opinions were disregarded. Eliana was the only person older than Shamira who had ever really listened to her. Shamira clung to her older sister, burrowing her tear-stricken face into the intricately embroidered tunic which had been made just for this occasion.

"You will always be with me, Shamira. I will pray to God for you every single night, and you will never leave my heart." Eliana continued to hold her little sister as silence fell over the room, and Shamira calmed down in her sister's arms. Whatever happened, they would always have this bond. A bond that didn't need words.

Even Devorah smiled at the two sisters' shared embrace.

Suddenly Shamira could hear shouting in the streets. No— chanting. Music. Understanding dawned on her quickly, and she pulled away from her sister. Backing away from Eliana and making a dash toward the other side of the room, she shouted, "He's here!" just seconds before they heard the knock on the door. "I'll get it!"

She had nearly made it to the stairs when her Dodah Devorah blocked her path, steadying Shamira with a tight grip on her small shoulder.

"No, you won't, Shamira! Your father will get the door." Devorah turned around. "Eliana, we must put your veil on."

"I still want to go see!" With Dodah Devorah's interest being focused on the bride-to-be, Shamira's excitement got the best of her, and she charged out of the room. Rut followed shortly behind, but at a much more reasonable pace.

Tumbling down the stairs, Shamira skidded into the main room and butted head-first into Matthan's side. Falling back onto the ground, Shamira's face turned scarlet red as she clambered up onto her own feet and brushed the thick waves of hair out of her face.

"Pardon me, Aharon, but this was not the daughter I was expecting," Matthan quipped.

Shamira's abba, Aharon, cleared his throat. Tittering, he replied, "My apologies for Shamira, she is young and quite easily excitable." He smiled at Matthan, but his sideways glance reprimanded Shamira.

"*Shalom,* Matthan," she said, with shakiness in her voice.

Shamira looked up at Matthan quizzically, wrinkling her nose and trying to judge what he was thinking. She didn't think Matthan was very handsome, but then again, she didn't think any boys were very handsome. His face caught her attention when his expression shifted from expectance to awe. She wondered what could possibly be so distracting, and then she turned around.

Eliana had just entered the room, followed by her mother, aunts, and cousins. When Eliana descended the steps and came into the light, Shamira was rendered speechless. Even from behind her veil, Eliana radiated joy and love.

For a few moments, Shamira forgot all about the changes she was about to face. She forgot about Matthan, about her sister moving away from home. She even forgot about how she knew she would probably be scolded later for her abrupt entrance—all she could think of was how gorgeous Eliana looked.

Shamira was confused by her mixed emotions as the procession through the streets began. Moments ago, she had shed tears at the thought of Eliana leaving home. Yet when her bridegroom arrived, Shamira felt so excited that she could burst. Now seeing her sister's exquisite appearance, she was overcome with pride and gratitude to have been blessed by God with such a beautiful sister both inside and outside. Shamira wanted to be just like her.

And then Matthan took her away.

Shamira and her family had followed the crowd to the house of Matthan's family. She held her mother's hand the whole way. The women and children maintained a respectful distance from the head of the parade, giving Shamira an opportunity to offer an apology for her earlier outburst.

"Dodah Devorah," she whispered. "I'm sorry that I said the ointment had a smell; I didn't mean to be hurtful."

Her aunt patted her softly on the head and thanked her young niece. With a sense of peace, Shamira took a deep breath as they walked on, seeing the gates to Matthan's courtyard in the distance. There would be a feast in honor of the bride and bridegroom, and all of Eliana's friends and family were meant to be present.

The smell in Matthan's courtyard, which was many times larger than Shamira's own, was an aromatic blend of sweet flowers used for decoration and savory meats prepared to satisfy the crowd. The couple was seated at a table in the center of it all. As was the custom, Eliana had been crowned with a wreath of flowers that rested on top of the golden-brown waves of hair daring to peek out from beneath her bridal veil.

The presentation of the food penetrated all of Shamira's senses, and her mouth began to water. It seemed Matthan's family had spared no expense, and this was to be an elaborate dinner with all manner of celebration.

Shamira stood amid the crowd with her arms crossed, examining the scene. She saw her imma visiting with other women, helping to serve and beaming whenever someone stopped her to mention what a beautiful bride Eliana was. Shamira narrowed her eyebrows disapprovingly at the sight of some of the guests who were singing, dancing, laughing, and making all manner of noise. They seemed more like children than grown-ups. Her *Savta* Hodiyah had told her earlier that some may have had a little too much to drink.

She didn't understand adults at all—did they really find this fun? Shamira might have seen the fun in it too, if it wasn't making her head hurt so much. Wine flowed freely into the cups of the men present, and between the musicians hired to aid the festivities and the hoots and hollers of the guests, Shamira could scarcely hear herself think.

Shamira heard a boy chuckle behind her, and she almost didn't notice him. *Almost.*

But she had noticed him, and in an instant, she whipped her

head around to face him. "What are you laughing at?" she confronted him, suddenly embarrassed and a little defensive. She wasn't sure why, but something about this boy made her feel uneasy. Planting her hands on her hips in a way she hoped would make her seem more confident, she wrinkled her nose from side to side.

"You've got a funny nose!" He suppressed his laugh but didn't hide the goofy smile that had spread from ear to ear.

Shamira instinctively brought her hand up to her face. Unable to ignore him, she countered, "My nose isn't funny at all! And you're one to talk—you've got funny hair!" She stood up straight, refusing to allow this boy to humiliate her at her sister's wedding feast. Though she was small in stature and otherwise harmless, she shot a glare at him she could only hope would drive fear into the heart of any unsuspecting boy.

Going red in the face, the boy stepped backward. He raked his fingers through his hair in a feeble attempt to smooth out the dark, wild curls that grew in all directions.

"I'm sorry," he whimpered, as if it physically pained him to apologize to her. "I didn't mean to offend you. May I ask your name?"

Shamira brought her hand down to rest again at her side as she observed the boy. Outside of her family, she had rarely ever spoken to boys. This one was taller than her and maybe a year older. Still, as she made note of his slight frame, she was certain she could take him in a fight if it ever came down to it. Assured that he was probably more talk than anything else, she found no harm in the introduction.

"I'm Shamira *bat* Aharon. This wedding feast is in celebration of *my* sister."

She made sure she emphasized the last part, because for some reason in her ten-year-old mind, she believed it would intimidate him. At the very least, she hoped it would. She certainly didn't want him to know the strange fluttery feeling in her stomach.

Normal color returned to his cheeks, and the boy smiled. His stance relaxed, and he replied, "My name is Asa *ben* Avram. Thank you for not being cross with me, Shamira."

"I never said I *wasn't* cross with you." Just because she could make polite conversation, didn't mean she wasn't holding back a fire inside of her just waiting to be stoked.

Asa ben Avram was puckish in a way that simultaneously interested Shamira and made her feel anxious.

"Well, you haven't cried for help or told me to go away yet, so you can't be that mad." Asa's deduction seemed reasonable.

Shamira nodded her head, irritated that she couldn't come up with a better response, and even more irritated that despite his other flaws, Asa ben Avram was right in this regard. Her feelings continued to surprise her as she realized she was glad he had not walked away after her outburst.

"So, are you happy for your sister?" He raised his bushy eyebrows in question, moving two steps closer to her.

She moved two steps farther away from him.

"Happy? Why should I be happy?" Shamira scoffed at the question. She scraped her foot back and forth, creating patterns in the soft dirt beneath her. She was looking for anything that would distract her from the conversation she didn't want to have, especially not with a near stranger.

Asa tilted his head to one side. "Do you disapprove of the match?"

"It has little to do with 'the match,' as you call it, and everything to do with the fact that I don't understand why she must get married at all." Her tone of voice may have come off a little bit stronger than she'd intended, but she didn't mind. It seemed to have the desired impact on Asa.

"Don't you want to get married when you're older?" His voice cracked. Was that disappointment she heard? "Have children and raise a family?"

Of course a boy would have no problem with the idea of marriage. They had the easy part. They didn't have to leave their home. The thought of being away from her abba and imma was more than Shamira could bear.

She stood on her toes to meet him eye to eye, but still fell short several inches. "If I got married, and that's *if,* not when, I wouldn't want to marry someone I barely knew." She softened and shrugged. "I don't want to leave my family. Shouldn't that be my choice?"

Asa shook his head and turned away, muttering, "What do you know? You're just a girl."

Shamira leapt around him and halted him in his path, digging her heels into the ground like a lioness ready to attack. "I'm not just a girl. I'm ten years old and nearly a woman!"

"Well, you're the shortest 'woman' I've ever met."

He had a point. Compared to him, and probably everyone else, she was more of a lion cub than a lioness.

Shamira bit her lip and countered, "Well, that doesn't make me any less of one!"

This time, Asa ben Avram went silent. There were no quips, jokes, or hasty remarks. He just smiled down at her, his dark eyes reflecting the flickering light of the nearby fire. She began to teeter back and forth on her heels unsure of whether to run for her mother or ask him what in the world he found so amusing.

Out of the darkness, a large hand crept over Asa's shoulder and gripped his arm. "My son, what are you doing? Your mother and I have been looking for you." The voice was stern and angry sounding.

"I w-w-was, I was just talking to Shamira."

Had she heard him stutter just then? What about his own father would make him stutter? Shamira had never been afraid of her father, no matter what kind of trouble she had gotten into, and she'd had her fair share of trouble over the years.

"She's the sister of the bride," Asa explained.

Shamira had to lean her head all the way back to get a good look at the man, who was obviously Avram, Asa's aforementioned father. She recognized him as one of the priests from the temple.

"Ah yes, another one of the shepherd's flock," the man said through bared teeth.

Shamira didn't understand his meaning at all. Her family was responsible for a good portion of Jerusalem's sheep and livestock trade. Even so, she somehow sensed what he said had not been meant as a compliment.

"My *Sabba* Eliyahu trades some of the best livestock in the city." She lifted her voice at the end of her sentence, almost as though she were asking a question. In a way she was. She had been puzzled by Avram's response—what was wrong with being a shepherd?

"Yes, yes, I'm sure." He nodded, but he seemed to be looking straight through her. "Asa, go and gather up your brothers. There is no need for us to stay here any longer."

Asa nodded respectfully and started to leave, but not before bending down slightly to whisper in Shamira's ear. "Maybe I'll see you around, nearly-a-woman."

Shamira spun around, ready to set the record straight. How dare he use her own words to mock her! Yet, when she opened her mouth to scold him, he was no longer there. He seemed to have vanished into the crowd.

"Asa?" she called out, but he was already gone. His father had disappeared too, and once again, Shamira was left standing in the courtyard by herself. "Asa?" she called out his name again, barely above a squeak. Disappointment hollowed out a hole in her heart where the boy had been, a place that felt cold, that had never felt cold before.

The racket was getting louder, and more people had begun to cheer and shout. Shamira realized the wedding feast was fast approaching its end, at least for this evening. She turned her attention to the front of the house where Eliana stood hand in hand with Matthan underneath the four pillars and festive floral arrangements of the *chuppah*. She flailed her arms in all directions, trying to get her older sister's attention so she could say a proper goodbye. It was no use, Shamira couldn't see anything behind Eliana's veil.

She watched, feeling somewhat useless and largely ignored, as Matthan led her sister through the arch and into the dark house, closing the door behind them. The noise swelled to an almost deafening volume, and Shamira felt her mother's presence beside her.

"Come along, my dear girl. I think it's time we went home." Imma patted her on the shoulder.

"But I want to stay, Imma. Please?" Shamira begged despite the fact that she knew there was no point in staying any longer. Her sister was now a married woman and she would be spending several days alone with no one but Matthan before she would be seeing anyone else again. Shamira's mother was right; it was time to go.

"You mustn't beg so, my child. You're the oldest now. It is up to you to be a good example to your younger cousins. They will all be looking to you. Come, let us go find your abba and we can all walk together."

The oldest of all of her cousins? She wasn't sure how she felt about that fact, but she wasn't altogether displeased about it either. Shamira did not object to her mother, but acquiesced, taking it all in stride. The whole way home, she felt somewhat strange. She wanted to ask Eliana about Asa and why he had made fun of her. She wanted to talk to her about the delicious food and laugh with her about Dodah Devorah's earlier misfortune with the perfume.

Shamira waited until there was enough distance between them and her other extended family members before she spoke. "Imma?"

"Yes, Shamira?"

"Imma, I'm so confused. I'm sorry I wasn't my best today. I didn't mean to bring sadness." Shamira shivered as she tried to hold back her tears. Her mother's arms encircled her, comforting her and making her feel safe.

"I understand, Shamira. You feel things so deeply, *hamuda*, so full of passion and so protective of your family."

"Why does it all have to change, Imma? I liked things as they were so very, very much. Why can't things stay just as they are now? I don't know if home will still feel like home anymore. Not without Eliana."

Imma smiled. "Can I tell you a secret, Shamira?"

Shamira's eyes widened. She didn't know if Imma had ever told her a secret. "You can trust me, Imma."

Imma's voice was very soft. "I feel a hole, an empty spot, as well." Shamira felt her imma's arms squeeze even tighter around her. "I know it can be scary to grow up, especially when it feels like everything is changing. But Shamira, the Lord will help us both, and He will never forsake us."

Imma began to sing softly, a lullaby she'd sung often to Shamira when she was very young. Shamira felt much better by the time they entered their courtyard.

She went to bed willingly that night. It had been a very long day, both physically and emotionally, and she was utterly exhausted. However, one last nagging thought kept her awake, pestering her and reminding her of its presence each time she turned her head on the pillow. What did it mean to be the oldest, and a woman at that?

She was going to have to take on a lot more responsibility from here on out. Her cousins would depend on her. Shamira knew she could be stubborn, but her abba had told her another quality that went hand in hand with stubbornness was determination. Perhaps she could use this quality for good.

She determined, as vehemently as ever, to rise to the challenge; to be the best older cousin she possibly could be. She would help her mother and aunts whenever and wherever possible, and try to put away all childish things—well, most childish things. She was a grown-up now, a woman, or "nearly-a-woman" as she had told Asa. She was going to have to start acting like one.

As determined and excited about growing up as she was, there were still a few things about it that sent fear into her heart. Growing up meant more change. Her whole family would change. Eliana had only just left, and Shamira had already made it very clear she never wanted to leave her family. Still, it seemed to her that women had little choice in the matter, and Shamira was not so keen on having a ketubah written up and signed as Eliana had been. She shuddered to think that as the oldest, she herself might even be the next one to get married. Would she have a voice in that decision?

Once again, tears forced their way out from behind Shamira's eyelids, and she concentrated all of her energy on holding them back. On a night like this she longed for nothing more than to whisper her thoughts to her sister and confidant; she had never felt more alone. Shamira suddenly had an idea and tip-toed out of her room.

"He protects his flock like a shepherd; he gathers the lambs in his arms and carries them in the fold of his garment. He gently leads those that are nursing." - Isaiah 40:11 CSB

Shamira yelped in pain as Rut's knee slammed hard into her stomach. Startled out of sleep and with her eyes now open wide, she grunted at the realization that Rut was still sleeping peacefully, completely unaware she had just made an attempt on Shamira's own life. Shamira stretched out her arms and locked her elbows, pushing Rut off her mat and back onto her own. She was beginning to rethink her decision to ask Rut to come and stay with her last night; if it was going to mean more nocturnal warfare, it definitely wasn't worth the risk. However, the room seemed so empty without Eliana's presence in it, and truthfully, Shamira couldn't manage to fall asleep without her. She had asked Rut to stay with her in the little room she once shared with Eliana so she wouldn't have to be alone. Dodah

Devorah had frowned for just a moment as she'd thought over the request, but then with a tentative smile she had given Rut permission to join Shamira. Now though, in light of the recent murderous act, Shamira was starting to see the positive side of being in solitude.

Shamira never had this problem when Eliana shared the room, but Eliana was gone now, and Shamira needed to accept that. She was now the oldest in the house and, at this rate, also the most at-risk of an early death. She tried to ask herself what Eliana would do, and she knew instantly Eliana definitely wouldn't be so dramatic.

Rut yawned loudly. "What's the matter, Mira? Why did you wake me up?" *"Mira"* had been Rut's special nickname for Shamira since they were toddlers. She'd come up with it after struggling to pronounce the "sh" sound in Shamira's name, and now all of her cousins called her that from time to time.

"I didn't wake you up—you woke *me* up!" Shamira buried her face under her blanket, whisper-shouting. "And now I'm going back to sleep!"

"Hm," Rut groaned.

Shamira could hear her rustling around the room, making up her bed, and getting dressed for the day. Just because the sun was up, didn't mean Shamira was ready to rise as well. She was still exhausted from staying out late at Eliana's wedding. Shamira tried to block out the sounds of her cousin's footsteps going back and forth.

"Who's that?" Rut's footsteps stopped and light penetrated the room. Shamira's eyes burned, even from underneath her blankets.

"Who's who?" she muttered, still trying to convince her mind to fall back to sleep.

It wasn't working.

"There's a boy outside of our courtyard."

"A boy?" Shamira shot straight up. She wondered if it was Asa, and in the same breath, questioned why she cared.

"He's just sort of standing by the gate," Rut croaked out the words. Her eyes barely above the windowsill, she stretched up on tiptoes, bracing against the wall.

Shamira may have only been a few months older than Rut and of small stature herself, but she was several inches taller. Cocooned in her blankets, she wobbled toward the window, stepped behind Rut, and pulled the window covering back even farther.

From her room on the second story of the house, she had a perfect view of the street below them. She had often come here to watch the world go by when she was particularly upset or if she just wanted to hide; like the time she'd knocked over the pot of stew her mother had spent all day making, or when she thought she might help the other women spin wool and instead made a terrible, tangled mess of it.

"That's the boy from Eliana's wedding!" *Asa ben Avram.* So it was him.

"What boy?" Rut squeaked. "Mira, you spoke to a *boy?*"

Shamira didn't even bother to answer, but moved quickly about the room, hurrying to tidy things up. "Quick! Help me make up the beds and get dressed! I'll tell you about it later."

She had only one thing on her mind: finding out why that audacious boy had come to intrude on her home uninvited. As a woman, and as the eldest, she would do like her mother would and turn the boy away herself.

Shamira did her best to hurry through her chores, not bothering to explain to her mother why she was in such a rush. With a clatter of dishes and a leaping of feet, she bounded back and forth from the table to the kitchen. She was determined to see if Asa still lingered, and if so, get answers. When she had finished, she started to run outside into the tiny courtyard.

"Shamira," her mother called out as she leapt over the threshold. "Aren't you forgetting something?"

Shamira turned on her heels to face her mother. Her bed was made, the dishes had been cleared, her sandals were tied… What had she missed?

Elisheva pointed a finger at the *mezuzah*, the small decorative case affixed to the house's main doorway. It was the most ornamental part of their home, and rightly so, for it contained a parchment inscribed with the holy words of God. "Remember, Shamira, to take time to pray to God in your haste. Every time you go through the doorway, you must touch your hand to the mezuzah and thank Him for His goodness. It is how we show our respect and devotion to Him: by putting Him first before our own wants or needs."

"Yes, Imma," Shamira stretched up on her toes to place her fingers on the ornate container, praying to God, thanking Him for her family, and asking Him to help her get answers from Asa ben Avram.

She had to force all of her body weight onto the old, creaking gate in order to get it open. Finally, when it had cracked open just wide enough for her waist, she slipped through and let it slam shut behind her.

"What are you doing here?"

"Do you remember who I am?" he asked, as if she could have forgotten in a single day.

"Of course, I do!" She rested her hands at her sides. "You're Asa ben Avram, the boy with the crazy hair."

He guffawed. "And you're Shamira bat Aharon, the little girl with the funny nose." He shook his head and turned as if to go. "I don't know why I even came here anyway."

"I'm not a little girl!"

"Oh, yes. Certainly, how could I forget?" He smirked. "You're nearly-a-woman."

"Why are you here?" She had no patience for him and his teasing. The boy shrugged his shoulders, apparently having no good reason for gawking outside of Shamira's family home. "Don't you have your own family who needs you? Chores? Something else more important to be doing?"

He shrugged again. Could this boy be any more impossible? He was like most boys, she supposed. She straightened her back, making an effort to stand and appear a little bit taller than she really was. Despite her best efforts, she was still completely enveloped in his shadow. She turned her chin up in a way she'd seen her imma do many times before. It had only been a day since the wedding, but she would prove to this boy that she was in fact a woman now.

"Well," she said, drawing out her vowels and deepening her voice. She hoped it made her sound more mature, but she couldn't ignore the way Asa's lips twitched as if he were holding back laughter. Inside, her confidence plummeted, but she remained staunch and serious on the outside. "As you see, we are very busy here and can't be bothered."

Suddenly a high-pitched scream sounded from inside the house. Shamira jerked and wobbled on her feet, nearly falling into Asa, but catching herself, she turned on her heel and reached for the gate. She pushed on the gate, adrenaline helping her force it open so she could see what on earth was the matter. She was caught off guard when little Libi went barreling past her into the busy streets of Jerusalem, which were only growing more crowded as the day went on. People were beginning to open up their businesses, and the stalls in the marketplace were being filled by merchants and customers alike.

All the air in her lungs escaped her, and she screamed, "Libi!"

Her stomach sank to the ground. What had she done? She knew the rules—the gate was always meant to be closed and latched for Libi's sake. If she ever wandered out, there'd be no way for them to call out and find her because she wouldn't be able to hear them.

The family inside the house barely had time to react and realize what had happened. Libi had run away! Chava was in the doorway, tear-stricken and clutching her arm. For whatever reason, Libi must've had some kind of a fit or perhaps she had become frightened at something. It didn't matter. Whatever it was, it had sent her fleeing. She saw her uncle and father running toward them, but Asa reacted much faster.

"I'll get her!" he shouted and ran.

"Not without me, you won't!"

Not stopping to think, Shamira turned on her heel and raced to catch up to Asa. He didn't know anything about Libi, and she was Shamira's cousin after all. As the oldest, it was her job to take care of Libi, not this stranger's.

Shamira noticed Asa was very agile and had a way of anticipating the movements of the people ahead of him. Under, over, and side to side, he dodged through the people, carts, and wagons. She could hardly keep up with him at this rate.

"Libi! Libi!" he called out.

"It won't do you any good!" she said as loud as she could, hoping he could hear her.

"What do you mean?" he called back, straining his neck toward her but keeping his eyes focused on the streets as he ran ahead.

"Libi—she can't hear you! She's deaf-mute!" Shamira was on the brink of tears, but she bit her lip hard to fight them. She had to be brave now for Libi, and if nothing else, she refused to cry in front of a boy. *This* boy in particular.

Suddenly, Asa veered off to the right into a small alleyway. Shamira pressed through the chaos. The crowds were like a wall of people, and she was too short to look over them. Perhaps this tall, gawking boy actually was a blessing. She raised her eyes heavenward to pray, begging the Lord to help them find Libi.

Nothing about this was particularly unusual. Libi was prone to tantrums when the family was unable to understand what she needed or was trying to communicate. She would often find places to hide if she was upset, but she never left the house. If she had tried, the gate surrounding the small courtyard would keep her from getting any farther; she was always safe. She had never been strong enough to open the gate herself, but Shamira had swung it wide open for her. If anything happened to her youngest cousin, Shamira would never forgive herself.

"Ugh!" She slammed into Asa and fell backward into the hard-packed dirt. "What are you doing?" she shouted, shaking the dirt off of her dress and wiping her sweaty hands across her chest as she felt her racing heart. "Why are you stopping?"

He motioned toward a group of barrels positioned just at the end of the alleyway. He moved very slowly toward them, placing one foot in front of the other. The barrels and crates teetered back and forth. Something, or someone was hiding among them.

Shamira narrowed her eyes and that was when she saw Libi's eyes peering at them warily from the cracks between the barrels. Libi's wide, beautiful, gray eyes.

"Libi!" Shamira jolted forward, halted by Asa's arm which flew out in front of her face, nearly sending her backward again.

"Don't frighten her," he cautioned. "If she can't hear you, she might think that she is in trouble." He continued to move closer to her, and Shamira watched in anticipation. If he had any hope of earning Libi's trust, he would have to make a spectacular first impression.

Libi sat shaking with her knees pressed up against her chest. Shamira wasn't sure if Asa would know what to do next. How could he? He didn't know Libi. He had only just found out about her condition. Usually, when people found out Libi couldn't hear or speak, they eventually began to ignore her. Sometimes they would even distance themselves from the entire family, as though being deaf-mute was somehow contagious. The whispers and gossip would slowly follow. *"What sin could their family have committed for their daughter to be punished like that?"* Asa had yet to say anything of the sort, but then again, he hadn't exactly had the chance. Shamira was still holding out on that matter.

Asa reached out his hand to Libi, an open offer for her to take his arm. He smiled at her, whispering, "You can trust me, Libi."

Shamira saw him enunciate every syllable and make steady, cautious movements. She marveled at his actions and the way he seemed to be mindful of how Libi would perceive them. He didn't look scared or upset. His face was actually surprisingly calm. Libi may not have understood words, but she knew what facial expressions and emotions were, perhaps better than anyone else. She also understood body language along with some basic gestures and hand movements.

Miraculously, Libi reached out and took his hand. He pulled her from her hiding place and picked her up. She was very petite for a three-year-old. Easy enough for a boy—no—a young man to carry.

Some unknown emotion bubbled up inside Shamira. Was it

respect? Admiration? Or just thankfulness and nothing more? She looked into his eyes, expecting to see him demanding her thanks for being a hero and for saving her cousin. Rather than promoting his act of kindness, he simply smiled at Libi.

"She's all right, Shamira," he whispered.

Something about the way Asa grinned made Shamira feel uneasy, *again*. Her stomach curled, making her feel just the way his smirking had made her feel the night before. Perhaps she should not have skipped breaking her fast that morning. She felt herself blushing and looked away, increasingly embarrassed.

"Shamira! Libi!" voices called out at the end of the street. Shamira recognized them as her abba and her uncle, Dodh Tamir.

"Abba!" She ran toward her father. "Asa was standing outside of our house and—"

"Thank you, young man." Her father interrupted her. "Without you, we might never have found my niece. Our family will forever be grateful to you."

"*Ahava sheli!*" Dodh Tamir rushed up to Asa, collecting his daughter into his own arms.

Asa shrugged his shoulders. "I'm happy that I could help. I found her hiding behind those barrels over there. I'd hate to think what might have happened if somebody else had found her first."

"Yes, yes." Shamira's father gripped Asa's hand and shook it. "You have done a very kind thing for our family. You must come back to our home and allow us to share what remains of our morning meal with you. It is not very much, but we must honor you somehow. Libi could have been lost forever without you!"

Shamira wasn't so sure about this. If Asa had not been at the family dwelling, the gate never would have been open. As grateful as she was for his act of valor, she was still troubled it had happened at all. If only she had ignored his presence, but instead she had practically run to him. It was clear from her father's invitation Shamira wouldn't be getting rid of him for a while, and for whatever reason, she wasn't nearly as annoyed by that as she thought she should be.

"Imma, may I attend a special meal with the household of Eliyahu at week's end?" Asa asked his mother without trepidation. He withheld Shamira's name, knowing that might be too obvious to his family.

"Hm?" his mother replied, turning her head toward him but not looking directly at him.

Asa knew she'd heard his voice, but he suspected she wasn't really listening. While he disliked taking advantage of her like this, he also knew he never had to fear her. She seldom said no to anything he asked. If he asked her, she might let him go, and then he would never have to bring the invitation to the attention of his father.

"The family we met at the wedding we attended earlier this month. The young merchant's wedding," Asa answered the implied question, deliberately choosing to emphasize Matthan's standing in the community, rather than Shamira's own family.

"Oh, the shepherd family?" Her eyes were glazed over, and her expression had an emptiness to it. She paid little attention to what Asa or his brothers did with their spare time. From the time they were old enough to begin learning to read and write and study under their father, she had distanced herself from them. From everyone.

"Sons belong to their fathers," she had said when Asa had asked why she didn't play with them anymore or sing to them at night. *"And if I'd had any daughters, they wouldn't belong to me either, but to the men who would eventually be their husbands."*

Asa nodded. "Yes, they've invited all of us to a meal."

"Us?" Her whole body stiffened. Asa knew she disliked being in public, especially with his father.

Something about the upturn in her voice made Asa nervous too. He knew that tone of voice meant his mother was afraid of something, and he didn't like it when she was frightened. He hadn't meant to tell his mother the invitation was for the entire family, but this time it had just slipped out. For the most part, he was usually allowed to do whatever he pleased as long as he had finished the studies his father had given him and could give a report on what he'd learned at *yeshiva* each day.

"Since it is an invitation for our household, you will have to ask your father."

Her words came out cold and emotionless. Asa knew she was right. His father would be displeased if she made a decision on his behalf.

"Ask me what?" a deep voice asked, reverberating and echoing off of the high stone walls of their house.

Asa cleared his throat and straightened his back. His father hated when he seemed anxious. If he wasn't quick enough answering one of his father's questions about the *Torah*, or fast enough at repeating a passage he was supposed to memorize, it always cost him something. A thump on the head, a blow on the cheek, a shove that might send him to the ground. The first proverb Asa had memorized was: "The one who will not use the rod hates his son, but the one who loves him disciplines him diligently." His father seemed to believe that was the only form of love.

"Abba, the house of Eliyahu has invited us for dinner." Asa turned on his heels to look his father directly in the eye, something he noticed his mother refused to do. Was it sadness that kept her from engaging? Fear of some kind? More than likely, it was a combination of both.

Asa knew his father was fond of punishing him and his brothers for any manner of disobedience or perceived deviance, and although he had never seen his father strike his mother, he'd seen her crying more times than he could count. Even though he had been a young child when he had first noticed her trying to hide the tears on her cheeks, he had still been able to sense there was something more going on beneath the surface.

Now that he was older and nearing twelve, almost a man by society's standards, he could fill in the gaps in his memories enough to know what happened between his parents, and why his home would never be as full of the same kind of love that filled Shamira's home.

"Eliyahu? The shepherd family? Ha!" His father chortled.

"They aren't just shepherds, Abba. They are responsible for a fair amount of livestock trading. They sell fine wool in the marketplace after the shearing season is done, and they even use the milk to make butter and cheeses!"

Asa's voice rose with excitement as he shared what he had learned from observing Shamira's family and the way they made ends meet. His endless hours of Torah studying had made him a quick thinker, and he'd picked up on the processes easily. Sometimes he wondered what it would be like to spend all day working with his hands for something more than just inscribing letters and symbols on parchment.

"Yes, yes," said his father through gritted teeth. Asa could tell he wasn't impressed as he waved his hands in the air in dismissal.

"Well, Abba, they want us to attend a special dinner in their home…" —Asa was losing what little confidence he had and could barely bring himself to finish the sentence— "in my honor."

"Your honor?" His father balked even louder. "Well, I suppose it can't be that difficult to impress a family of simple shepherds."

"No, father," Asa objected, before amending his statement and tone. "Abba, I mean. I helped rescue one of Eliyahu's granddaughters. They want to thank me."

"Hm, the outspoken girl I saw you speaking with at that wedding?" Avram reclined on a cushion and stretched his legs. He turned his head toward his wife. "Bring me a drink," he ordered before turning back to face Asa.

"No, not Shamira," said Asa, placing just a little bit of extra emphasis on her name, "Libi, the youngest one. She's deaf-mute."

At that, his father's almost-black eyes widened. His mother interrupted in a voice that was barely above a whisper. "Perhaps it would be better not to go, my husband. Surely, God does not see these people favorably."

Asa watched as his mother said the words as though she had rehearsed them, handing his father the drink she had poured with shaking hands. He took it from her, and then waved her away.

"You've practically spilled half the cup. Is there nothing you can do right?"

"But, Abba," Asa attempted to divert his father's attention. He didn't like seeing his mother cry. "Would it not be rude to refuse their invitation? After all, it is very considerate of them to offer to share what they have when they have so little in comparison to what God has given us. They would also be putting a great imposition on themselves, having to all wash and take time away from their work. The invitation is for all of us— you, Imma, myself, my brothers…"

"I do not think that is what your father would think was best, Asa." His mother spoke again, and Asa realized his mother was trying to protect him from the wrath of his father. Instead, she had only incurred his wrath on herself.

"Quiet!" Avram snapped, causing his mother to tremble. "I will say what I think is best!"

Asa bowed his head respectfully, hoping his father would calm down and not lash out at either of them.

"Actually, as it happens," his father began, tempering his anger, "I think this would make a wonderful teaching opportunity."

"Yes, Abba?" said Asa, already mentally scanning the Torah scriptures for answers to questions that had yet to be asked.

"What is our purpose as Levites?" he asked.

"God appointed the Levite tribe to serve Him, setting them apart from the other tribes of Israel. Levites became the mediators between God and His people, serving in the temple as Priests and teachers of the Law," Asa replied.

"And what does it mean to be mediators?"

"To communicate God's will for His people. To oversee worship, perform sacrifices, and teach the Law."

"Yes! Teaching the Law. It is important that we keep an eye on these lesser peoples. We must ensure they know the Law and are keeping it to the letter," Avram explained. "That is why I think we should, in fact, attend this small dinner. To ensure that

Eliyahu and his family are indeed following the will of God."

Something about the way his father spoke the words made a knot form in Asa's stomach. He was getting the feeling his father's intentions were more sinister than purely educational or administrative.

"Yes, Abba," agreed Asa, wishing he could trade his family for Shamira's family, where they spoke more about how much they loved each other and less about how the laws applied to each and every situation.

"Zilpah," Avram turned his attention back to Asa's mother, "You will see to it Asa and his brothers are prepared for the meal, dressed appropriately, and on their best behavior. I do not expect you to make conversation with these people—I know you can't. Just keep quiet and see to it I will have no cause to be ashamed of you or my sons."

"Yes, my husband," she said as she exited, leaving Asa alone with his father in the cold sitting room.

"If anything goes wrong, Asa, if you dare speak out or object to anything I say—well, you know what will happen when we arrive home."

Asa gulped. "Yes, Abba."

He waited on his toes for whatever his father would say next, whether he would keep talking or dismiss him. He wanted his father to be proud of him for saving Libi, to encourage his friendship with Shamira's family, to show any kind of love at all toward him. Was he pleased with his oldest son in the slightest, or did he, as always, have more important matters to attend to than his family? Shamira's father and uncles spent more time at home and with their families after long days of hard work. Why couldn't his father?

"Good, I'm glad you understand," his father stated bluntly. Was it really true? "Now come closer to me. I want you to recite the passages you were meant to be memorizing this week, and then tell me what they mean and why they are important."

As though nothing had ever happened, his father went back to discussing scriptures and scrolls, lengthy passages and lists of laws. Or had he ever stopped talking about such things? Regardless, Asa did as he was told, reciting each passage perfectly, careful not to add a single stutter.

"Well done for today," grunted Avram, after Asa had finished.

"Thank you, Abba."

His father continued without pausing. "Remember, soon you will come of age, and after that you will be consecrated to God and set apart for the holy appointment which I already hold. Keep up in your yeshiva studies. They're only going to get harder. Soon you will not have time for such distractions as shepherds and dinner invitations from the poor. It will be your job to keep them in line."

The pronouncement hung over Asa's head like a thundercloud, ready to burst open and drown him in a flood at any moment. He knew it was the truth, and his studies up until this point had taught him it was his inevitable duty, but why did his father talk about Shamira and her family like they were as low as the dirt beneath their feet? Asa liked being around them. Sometimes he liked it more than studying, even if studying would earn more satisfaction from his father than spending time outside of the temple walls and beyond the border of the upper city.

Although his father had implied on more than one occasion that people like Shamira had less and were less than themselves in every way, he couldn't help but feel that Shamira had always and would always have more than he did.

*"In the same region, shepherds were staying out in the fields
and keeping watch at night over their flock. Then an angel of
the Lord stood before them, and the glory of the Lord shone
around them, and they were terrified." — Luke 2:8-9 CSB*

Several weeks had passed since Eliana's wedding, and Asa's
subsequent invasion of their family. Shamira shifted on the
cushion as she listened to her sabba sing songs of praise to the
Lord. Caught up in the music, she moved to the rhythm of his
song. Her mother placed a steadying hand on her shoulder,
silently cajoling her to sit still out of respect. Shamira had never
been very good at sitting still or being quiet. Doing both of those
things at the same time drove her wild inside with all the
trapped, pent-up energy. Her mother's arms around her kept her
from moving anymore, so while her body stopped fidgeting, her
eyes continued to dart back and forth.

Asa had been staring at her all throughout her grandfather's
song. She wrinkled up her nose at him, irritated as any girl

would be at the unwanted attention of a boy—no, young man. She'd stopped calling him a boy after he'd saved Libi's life. He'd earned her respect that day, and her family had gained a friend. Hopefully by the end of this meal between their family and Asa's, their entire families would be joined in friendship as well.

Ever since Asa had started coming around their house, Savta had been encouraging him to bring his family; the invitation had been accepted only recently. It was unusual for a temple priest to dine with a common family, and even more unusual to share the *Shabbat* dinner together. It seemed everyone, Shamira herself included, hoped the evening would progress smoothly.

At the closing of the song, Eliyahu pulled his *tallith* from his head. leaving it resting on his shoulders. He cleared his throat, and announced, "Come, let us break bread."

The bread was passed from person to person, a piece torn off and placed on each plate. Shamira's mother tore off a piece for her, and Shamira recoiled at the fact that her portion was half the size of what the adults were eating. Her family had spared no expense with this meal, putting out everything they had to offer in the hope that it would please their guests. Shamira, Rut, her mother, and aunts had spent the entire week cleaning the house from top to bottom and making preparations. Her father and uncles had not set foot in the fields for days to ensure they remained clean according to the Law.

Now, the day they'd been waiting for had arrived, and their honored guests sat just across from Shamira and her parents. On the table before her was a delightful spread of fruits and cheeses. Clusters of grapes and figs colored the table. Large bowls nearly overflowing with lentil and barley stew were placed in the center. Perhaps if she could not have any more of the bread, she would be allowed generous portions of those foods instead.

"Imma, I'm hungrier than that," she said softly, or so she thought. Apparently, spending the whole Shabbat day sitting still in thoughtful prayer and reflection took a lot out of Shamira, thus making her starved by the end of her *difficult* day of rest.

She stared at the feast longingly but found herself startled by the sound of pompous laughter which seemingly surrounded her. She turned her head all around, trying to figure out who was laughing so hard, but no one in her family was smiling. She looked across from herself where Asa was sitting, smirking as usual, and then she looked directly to the side of him.

On the right was his mother, her face pale and fear stricken. On the left was Asa's father. Aside from the fact that he was literally shaking with laughter, his demeanor remained otherwise unchanged from how Shamira had observed him at Eliana's wedding. A haughty smile spread across his face, and his eyes sharpened into slivers like the eyes of a snake. Before Shamira's mother could respond to her, Avram interrupted.

"Really, Aharon. You let your daughter speak out like *that?*"

"She is only a child," Shamira's father replied.

Shamira was grateful her father had defended her, but she saw a shadow of disappointment pass over his face and that single expression left her feeling low and guilty.

"She is not much younger than my son, and I know very well what I would do to him if he ever spoke to me like that, especially in front of guests." He looked down at Asa, whose back straightened. Next to him, his mother shuddered, and the two little boys to the other side of her who were, of course, Asa's brothers, all followed suit. "Indeed, *my* sons know their place."

"I assure you, Rabbi, she is learning all the skills which will be necessary for her to make a good wife and homemaker someday. She helps her mother and aunts with the household chores every day, save the Shabbat, and loves and respects her elders. She is simply… growing up."

"Helpfulness does not excuse outspokenness," Avram barked. "The child must learn restraint, and you must discipline her when she does not exhibit it."

She felt horribly awkward for speaking as she had; she had meant no disrespect. She wondered what Avram meant when he said Asa knew his place, and later, when he heavily implied that she ought to as well. What *was* her place?

Before Aharon had time to respond, Savta Hodiyah entered the conversation with a calm and collected tone. "Avram, it is a great honor to have a teacher like yourself sitting at our table on this night. While we visit the temple often for prayers and offerings, we have never been so blessed to have someone of your influence seated with us."

Savta smiled at the man who would otherwise deserve none of her kindness if not for the fact that his social status was considerably higher than that of the humble shepherd's wife.

Even so, Savta was a good hostess. She could easily steer the conversation in any direction.

It was all because of Savta that Asa had even brought his family to their home in the first place. Ever since Asa had made himself a regular guest to their household, coming and going as he pleased, she had constantly been pestering him to bring his family for dinner. At some point, it became inevitable Asa comply, or he would risk being deprived of anymore of the delicious dates Savta had begun setting aside especially for his visits.

To others it may have seemed that Asa received some kind of special treatment, but Shamira knew her savta was just that way with everyone. No one who appeared at her door ever longed for anything that she had the ability to give, whether it was conversation, food, or love.

At Savta's compliment, a tight-lipped smile crept across Avram's face. "Yes, well, I believe it's important that myself and other priests remind lesser people of our presence, otherwise you might all forget to bring your offerings to the temple!"

Just as he finished, he started up with the laughing again. Was that supposed to be another joke? Shamira did not understand his sense of humor at all, and now her ears were beginning to hurt at the obnoxious, boisterous sound of his cackling fit. She narrowed her eyebrows at him and made an expression that had gotten her into trouble with her imma many times before. Even though it was wrong, Shamira was grateful her imma sat beside her and not across from her where she could see, otherwise she would have been sent away at once.

What did he find so amusing that he had to sit in a fit of laughter throughout their entire shared meal? No one else in the room laughed, so Shamira thought he must not have been very funny to anyone. Shamira tried to stay still but every ounce of her small, slight frame flamed with heat and anger. This was a moment when she knew to stay silent and learn from her elders whom she so very much wanted to honor.

"With all due respect, Avram, we never forget *any* of our offerings," Shamira's Sabba Eliyahu said. "But tell us more; how are things otherwise at the temple? It seems the crowds have been bigger than ever in recent days."

"Now, now," he began, waving a finger back and forth in their faces, "you know I am not permitted to discuss any official matters, but I will say things would be a lot easier on all of us if the zealots would quiet down their messianic rumors and take their fanatic ideals elsewhere." He waved his hand as though dismissing something or someone.

"Do you not believe the time of the Messiah is near?" Eliyahu leaned forward, his brows knit together.

Shamira noticed her own father shift on his cushion as he watched the fragile conversation unravel like the wool her mother and aunts spun during the day. He looked as though he were about to be sick, but Shamira was fairly certain it was not because of the food.

"Eliyahu," sighed Avram, "it would be foolish of me to say I did not believe the Messiah was coming, but look at the times in which we live! We are ruled by the Romans, and as good as they are to us, provided we abide by their laws, Caesar is no Messiah. Aside from fanatics, I know of no *serious* efforts in Jerusalem to regain political power, and it would be wise for all of Israel if no one did."

He continued to stuff his face with an obscene amount of food. Did he have any idea of how much that would cost their family? They weren't struggling by any means, but food was dear to them with so many mouths to feed, and Avram seemed to eat for three.

"Perhaps the Messiah will not come from a place of power, Avram. Perhaps he is already dwelling among us?" Eliyahu suggested.

"Ha!" Avram mocked, food nearly spilling out of his mouth. Shamira saw her Dodh Tamir and Dodh Binyamin bury their faces in their hands. "I would sooner believe the Messiah was in the company of the sinners and the demon possessed than born of such a lowly birth as this."

"But you are wrong." Eliyahu's voice cracked, and his face shook with passion.

"I beg your pardon," coughed Avram, pulling back from the table in surprise. "Perhaps, shepherd, you would like to explain how you've become such an authority on these matters?"

His face snarled into a ferocious, twisted grin; the kind of grin Shamira imagined lions exhibited just before they attacked their lowly prey.

"I'm waiting." His voice was demanding, if not threatening.

"When I was a young man, I was shepherding a flock in the fields just outside the city of Bethlehem. One night, not so very different from this one, an angel appeared before me with a message. Suddenly, there were more angels than any of us could count. Angels! Truly I say unto you, I was just as surprised as you are now. It was deafening and peaceful, terrifying and exciting, wonderful and emotional, all at the same time."

"Preposterous," Avram muttered.

"I am not lying to you, Avram. Would I lie about such a thing? They proclaimed the birth of the Messiah!"

"I should hope you are not lying, Eliyahu, for to spin such a tale is nothing short of blasphemy. You're mad to even suggest such a thing!" He rolled his eyes. An imaginary cord was pulling the room apart, the tension growing more and more dangerous with every spoken word.

"I am telling the truth! That very night, angels appeared before me and my eyes beheld the glory of the Messiah, brought forth humbly to this earth and laid in a manger."

Tears filled Eliyahu's eyes. Shamira knew the story well, and she'd never tired of hearing it, but she had never seen her sabba so upset in all her life. Her breath hitched. Normally, she enjoyed imagining what the angels must have looked like in all of their glory, but something about the surrounding conversation made her anxious.

"Enough! You could be killed for such blasphemy, Eliyahu." Avram swung his fist down onto the table, crashing onto the hard wood and sending an ear-splicing sound echoing across the room.

Killed? Was it really so? Shamira put down the bread she'd been holding. She didn't think she could eat anymore, not when there was talk of death at the table.

Avram shook the table as he rose to his feet. He steadied himself with a violent, jerking motion, nearly overturning the entire table with his force. Fruits, bread, and lentils slid from their place. Whole trays and dishes knocked into each other, their contents spilling over and mixing together, spoiling the entire meal.

In the flicker of the lamplight, Shamira saw Asa's mother biting back tears, but otherwise, she sat so still—it was as if she was familiar with such outbursts.

Asa himself, normally always bearing an impish grin, had hardened his expression into a blank, unreadable stare. His boyish features were chiseled away with the clenching of his jaw. It was barely a moment before Shamira herself realized why he seemed so terrified. The dim light cast ghastly shadows on his father, whose near-black eyes seemed to turn into holes. He looked like a monster—the kind that chased Shamira in her nightmares. Only this was not a nightmare, and Shamira could not pinch herself and will Avram to disappear.

"Avram, my father is old. Surely you would not charge him with such a crime as serious as blasphemy in these, his last years. I beg your forgiveness," Aharon said.

Shamira watched as he tried and failed to coax Avram to cast his father's comments aside and rejoin them at the dinner table, however much of a mess it might have become. She saw her Savta Hodiyah's arm reach out to her sabba, physically trying to keep him from speaking again.

"Yes! He knows nothing about prophecies or their interpretations, as I'm sure you do," Savta whispered.

The room stood still, and Shamira had to remind herself to breathe. Her imma pulled her closer to her chest, and Shamira could feel her mother tremble in rhythm with her heartbeat.

Shamira had heard Eliyahu's story almost every night. He retold the tale with such passion and vigor; she had never thought to question it. Now, she questioned why he told it in the first place, if the threats made by Asa's father were true. She did not know much about the adult world, but she knew enough to know what the punishment for blasphemy was.

Avram breathed out heavily, his nostrils flaring as he did so. His back straightened a little each time he inhaled. When he finally seemed to relax, he announced with an eerie calm: "My family and I will be leaving now; we'll show ourselves out."

The first to rise from the table were Asa's little brothers, who bolted from the room in mere seconds. Closely following was his mother, who walked with her gaze affixed to the floor and took small but rapid steps after her younger sons. Shamira looked to Asa, anxiously watching to see what he would do. Curious to her, he did not immediately rise as his mother and brothers had done. He seemed to remain frozen in his seat. That familiar hand fell on Asa's shoulder. His fingers clenched so tightly his knuckles turned white. Shamira imagined it must have hurt a great deal, maybe even bruised.

Asa didn't even flinch.

"Come, my son. We're leaving. *Now.*"

Asa raised his head ever so slightly to meet Shamira's gaze. She probably wouldn't have even noticed if she hadn't been paying close attention, and surely no one else would have been able to see it either. His lips parted ever so slightly as he mouthed something to her, but it was so quick she wasn't able to interpret it.

Her brows furrowed, and he leaned forward toward her as though he were about to say something else or possibly try again, but he was instantly jerked backward and upward by his father before he had the chance. He turned toward the exit and Avram gave him a push in that direction.

"Thank you for your generosity," Avram added, not turning around. "I am sorry our time together ended under such unpleasant circumstances. Nevertheless, I am sure our paths will cross again the next time you come to the temple to give your offerings."

Somehow the way he said "offerings" no longer sounded like a gift from the heart to Shamira; it felt dirty and tainted.

"Shamira, take these dishes outside, please," Elisheva requested.

With shaky hands, Shamira pressed the stack close to her body, walking slowly and looking down at her feet to make sure she didn't trip. What was left of the disastrous meal with Asa and his family had been salvaged and finished, and it was now time to clean up. The house was growing dark and while the younger children were being tucked into bed, the adults were settling in for a quiet evening of rest. Holding her breath, she tiptoed across their home. All she had to do was deliver an assortment of bowls to the kitchen where they would be cleaned and stored by someone with hopefully better coordination than herself.

"Shamira!" a voice whisper-shouted in the darkness of the kitchen.

Shamira heard the crash of the dishes on the floor before she knew she had dropped them. Fortunately, nothing broke—this time.

"Who's there?" she said, her lips quivering.

"Calm down, Shamira." As the voice spoke, Shamira began to recognize its owner. "It's me. Asa."

Shamira let the tension fall from her shoulders. "Asa? What are you doing here?" She kept her voice soft and low, unsure of whether or not to alert the others he was there, if they were not already concerned about the crashing sound just moments before. Although, with all of the discussion happening inside, and everyone else busy with their own tasks, they probably hadn't even noticed.

She knelt down to pick up the dishes, and Asa did the same. "Here, let me help. It's my fault that you dropped them."

Shamira wanted to say it wasn't his fault, and she probably would have dropped them anyway, but she would have rather just let him take the blame instead. Inwardly she chided herself for such a petty feeling. Asa had done so much for her family and the way that his father had treated him was an unpleasant memory that still burned in her heart.

Their hands brushed up against each other, and she instinctively jerked back. "I can handle them myself, if you please," she said, wrinkling her nose and staring him down until he moved back.

"All right, all right." He raised his hands in retreat, and then muttered, "Girls..."

Shamira set the empty dishes on the table to her right. "What do you mean 'girls?'"

"I came to apologize to you, and you can't even be bothered to hear me out."

"Apologize?" She placed a hand on her side and raised a questioning eyebrow at the boy, whose face was only lit by the pale moonlight streaming in through the high-up window on the other side of the room.

"Yes... For my father."

"Your father asked you to apologize?" She hoped her disbelief wasn't obvious. When Asa rolled his eyes, she knew she'd failed at being discreet. She turned aside, embarrassed for the first time in front of a boy so near her own age.

"No, I came on my own. He was rude to you and your family, and I just couldn't let it happen without doing something about it."

"But you didn't do anything about it," she pointed out.

Shamira looked at the way Asa gingerly leant to one side, awkwardly shrugging his shoulders and grimacing with each movement. She realized he had done something about it, and he had already paid the consequences. Her heart softened, and she was willing to listen.

"Maybe that's because I've learned my lessons, unlike you, who is clearly ungrateful for anything that I try to do," Asa grunted.

Still, looking at the way he favored one side over the other and seemed to move ever so cautiously of his garments and his surroundings caused a lump to form at the base of her throat and made her feel sorry. "I'm not ungrateful," she whispered.

"You're not?"

"You probably saved Libi's life that day." She recalled their first real encounter, the day after Eliana's wedding.

He waved it off. "No, all I did was run after her."

"But you ran fast! Faster than I could have. My family will always be grateful."

Asa smiled, but didn't respond. What else did he want her to say? Shamira didn't like the silence that had settled between them. "Won't you get into trouble if your father finds out that you're missing?"

"He won't miss me for a while." Asa sighed, then straightened. "But I wouldn't want you to get in trouble, Shamira."

She didn't say anything in response because she didn't understand why she would get in trouble. All she had done was drop the dishes, and she'd cleaned those up. He brushed his shoulder with his left hand—was that how his father always punished him? Shamira suddenly felt something was very wrong. Her father had never laid a hand on her, except a gentle one out of love. Had Asa never known any different?

"I'll go before anyone finds me here. I only came to say that I was sorry."

He turned to leave, but something deep down in Shamira made her lurch forward. "Wait!" He turned back. "Don't go yet," she sighed.

"Why not?" he said, his bushy eyebrows moving closer together.

"I just want to know why you apologized."

"I told you. My father was rude to your family and—"

"No." Shamira cut him off. "Your father says my sabba could be killed for his beliefs. Why would you, the son of a priest, come here to apologize for something that your father believes is right?"

He smiled down at his feet. "I had no idea you could talk so much."

"That's not an answer to my question," she insisted, holding her ground as she'd learned to do with her younger cousins. Asa may not have been a young child placed in her charge, but she knew she could get him to comply, if only for the fact that he seemed to inexplicably comply with all of her other requests.

"All right then! Maybe I don't believe everything that my father believes."

"What do you believe?"

He shrugged in answer to her question, so she pressed on.

"Do you believe what my sabba said? Do you believe that the Messiah is coming? Or maybe that he already has?"

"Do you?" he countered.

Shamira thought for a moment and narrowed her eyes in pensive concentration. It was all she had ever known; all she had ever heard and been taught. When she saw the passion in her grandfather's eyes each time he told the story, the light that seemed to radiate from within him made her wonder how she or the rest of her family could ever believe anything different.

"Yes, I do."

Her heart beat a little faster after she said the words. What if Asa reported her to his father? Would she be killed? She put that thought aside. Even though she hadn't known him long, she felt she could trust him.

"Then I suppose I do too," he said.

"Suppose?"

"Well, if my father found out that I truly believed it, there'd be a much worse punishment waiting for me when I get home then there probably already is now."

He grinned, with a flicker of fear passing briefly across his otherwise amused countenance. Was he actually joking about punishment? Shamira's eyes widened at the thought, her own heart petrified on his behalf. She could not imagine being struck by her abba, or any of her family for that matter, much less making light of it.

"But why do you believe it?"

"Why do you?" he countered.

"Well, because my sabba says it is true, and I know he's not crazy like they say. I know it!"

He smiled again and answered for himself. "Well, I may think you're strange, but I don't think you're crazy either. If you believe it, I'll believe it."

She turned her head, wondering if she should trust him. Was he being serious or was this just another way for him to tease her?

Almost absentmindedly, Shamira opened her mouth to speak, letting the words slip out as she daydreamed, forgetting her circumstances. "What do you think the Messiah will be like?"

"Well, the *Tanakh* says that he will be many things."

"But do you think he'll be kind? Do you think he'll care about us?"

"Of course, he will! We're God's chosen people. The Messiah will be a powerful leader."

"Powerful?" Would the Messiah be powerful enough to heal Libi? To restore peace to her family? If Libi could hear, Dodah Chava wouldn't have to worry about her running away again. She would be safe. Other people wouldn't look down on her or their family. Perhaps Dodah Chava and Dodh Tamir would even be happy again, like they used to be when Dodah Chava was still expecting Libi and before they learned of her condition. Then everyone would be happier and there would be no more need to argue or be sad ever again.

Shamira's imagination ran wild with ideas about what the Messiah would be like and how things would change when he finally arrived. Would she be there to see it?

She hoped so.

Her silent thoughts were interrupted by a call from somewhere else in the house. "Shamira, come upstairs. It's time for bed!"

"There, you see. I should be going," he said, gesturing to the door behind her.

He walked toward the table positioned directly below the window.

"Wait."

"I've waited long enough, don't you think?"

"Here," she said as she gathered whatever leftover scraps from their meal she could. "Savta would be furious with me if she knew you'd visited and hadn't been fed while you were here, even if we just had dinner."

Shamira held out her hands, offering to him the meager bundle she had wrapped up in a small cloth. He smiled. "Well, I'm only taking this so that you don't get into any trouble on my account with your savta. I've seen her when she's happy beyond all comparison, and I'd hate to see what she's like when she's upset!"

"Thank you," she whispered.

The door behind her creaked, and Shamira jumped around to face whomever it was that had come in. "Imma!" she shouted with surprise. "I was just..." She scrambled trying to think of an explanation for Asa's presence in their home.

"You were just clearing the plates, I see. You've done a wonderful job, my dear girl. Now go on upstairs to bed. Rut has already settled down, and I don't want you tripping over her in the dark after she's blown out the lamp that Dodah Devorah sent up with her."

"But..."

Shamira turned around and suddenly realized why her mother was so calm about finding her and Asa in the kitchen together. It was because he wasn't in the room at all. Shamira didn't have time to wonder how he'd managed to escape so swiftly, and through the window no less! Even if she were standing on the table, Shamira knew she couldn't reach it. She wouldn't have been able to crawl through it without falling or breaking something, and Asa had done it with an injured shoulder!

Her mother was already turning her back around and sending her upstairs with hugs and kisses goodnight.

As she laid her head to rest on her mat, she wondered if Asa would be all right, or if his father really would punish him severely so soon after a punishment already delivered. Despite her concerns, she didn't worry over it for too long. The day's activity had tired her body and fatigue overtook her. Her last conscious thought before falling into deep slumber was that she knew she would see Asa again very soon, and if Rut could see in the dark, she would have seen Shamira's final thought sent her to sleep smiling.

Without anything left to plan or prepare for, Shamira's daily life had become just as dull as it had been before Eliana had become betrothed, only Eliana wasn't there, and Shamira missed her with all of her heart. As much as she disdained Asa—well, as much as she thought she disdained Asa, even his presence would be a welcome change of pace from the repetitiveness of daily life. But of course, household chores and activities demanded her attention. They were the kinds of things which Shamira loathed, not because they were loathsome tasks, but because she was so very bad at completing them. She was always dropping things, mixing up the wrong ingredients, or creating a general mess. One such mess lay right before her, in several pieces.

"Bring the water over here," Dodah Devorah had demanded.

As much as Shamira tried to lift the heavy jar, it was still far too big for her, and she couldn't see where she was going. Seconds later, a cacophonous crash halted all progress in the kitchen. The jar now lay in pieces on the floor, floating like little islands above the water which had been poured out and wasted. Shamira knelt in front of her mess, her hands breaking her fall and just barely missing any of the ceramic shards.

"I'm sorry," was all she could manage to whisper through the suffocating embarrassment that hindered her every breath.

"Now we will all have to go and draw more water! And what of the pot?!" Devorah threw her hands up in the air.

"Shamira," her mother rushed to her side, "That bit of the floor needed washing. Thank you for your help; now you've saved me the trouble." Her imma smiled at her, not raising her voice a single tone higher or lower than it had been prior but remaining perfectly calm.

"But Imma, I broke the jar..." Shamira fought against the tears that welled up in her eyes. The only thing she was thankful for was the fact that she could not see Dodah Devorah's disapproving looks through the blurriness of her watery vision.

"It is only a jar, my dear girl, and an old one at that. We can find another." Keeping her left hand on Shamira's back, Elisheva began gathering the ceramic pieces with her right, carefully moving each one into a little pile.

"I ruin everything, Imma." Teardrops slowly began to trickle down her puffy cheeks. "I'll never learn my place!"

"Learn your place?" Elisheva drew back, raising her eyebrows at her younger daughter. "Where did you come up with a thing like that?"

"That's what Asa's father said before they left! That I should learn my place." She couldn't help herself now. The tears rolled down her cheeks, enough to refill the entire water pot and still spill over. That is, if they still had a water pot.

"Oh, Shamira," she said. "Come here into my arms. You are too sensitive for this world. Have you ever heard your father or myself use such a phrase? No, of course not. Because your place is right here," she placed her delicate but worn hands on her chest, "In our hearts. You can never disappoint us, and certainly not by a few harmless household mistakes. Do you understand?"

Shamira kept sniffing and sucking in short, sudden breaths, her chest rising and falling faster than her lungs could handle. Her mother pulled her into her arms and embraced her in that special way Shamira was convinced only mothers could. In her worst moments, none of her aunts or even her savta could make her feel as loved as her imma. Maybe her abba, but there was just something special about her mother's love.

"Would you like to do something else for me?" she whispered. "I can finish cleaning this up myself."

"I'm not sure..." Shamira hesitated, curling her fingers up into fists and rubbing the tears from her eyes.

"This is something only you can do, Shamira. The others and I are all busy preparing for this evening's meal, cooking, washing and what not. Why don't you run along and look after the younger children for us? Do you think you could do that? It would be a great help to us, and you're the only one who isn't busy here in the kitchen."

Shamira wrinkled her nose, red from her sniffling, as she contemplated her mother's request. She was right. Her aunts and Savta were all busy with other tasks like spinning wool, washing linens, and cutting and cooking all kinds of delicious foods to make into fine meals. Someone had to watch the children, and Shamira felt herself to be a very good option, all things considered.

Slowly and tentatively, she nodded her head in agreement, all her hesitations dissipating from her mind with each deep breath she took.

"All right then, you will be in charge, and if they don't believe you, just tell them you have our permission. Now run along and see what they're all up to!"

"Yes, Imma." She smiled, having forgotten her earlier accident completely.

"Oh, but one more thing," said Elisheva, rising to her full height and turning just slightly to the side. "Chava? Chava, why don't you let Shamira play with Libi for a while? That way you can rest."

"I'm not tired, Elisheva," she said. She may have claimed not to be tired, but the dark circles weighing down her eyelids gave her away, even to Shamira.

"Then come and help me with the food. There's far too much for me to do on my own and the others are busy."

Slowly, Chava rose from her seat, tugging Libi along as she walked across the room. Chava placed Libi's hand in Shamira's, stiffening as she did. The last time she'd let Libi out of her sight, Libi had nearly been lost forever. Shamira refused to let that happen again. She looked down at Libi and the two of them exchanged smiles. Shamira would never let any harm come to Libi again. She was the oldest now, and she would protect her cousins, no matter what.

She would be more than satisfied doing just that for the rest of her life, and as long as she lived, she would never let someone like Avram say a single bad word about her cousins, her family, or herself ever again. She didn't need to learn her place, for her place would always be where her heart was. Not bent over a fire, not standing silent in a dark corner out of sight, but with the people she loved. As for whether or not she still wished to spend time with the mysterious Asa ben Avram… She was unsure.

PART TWO — SIX YEARS LATER

"When all the people were baptized, Jesus also was baptized. As he was praying, heaven opened, and the Holy Spirit descended on him in a physical appearance like a dove. And a voice came from heaven: "You are my beloved Son; with you I am well-pleased." As he began his ministry, Jesus was about thirty years old and was thought to be the son of Joseph, son of Heli," — Luke 3:21-23

"Comfort, comfort my people," says your God. "Speak
tenderly to Jerusalem, and announce to her that her time of
forced labor is over, her iniquity has been pardoned, and she
has received from the Lord's hand double for all her sins." -
Isaiah 40:1-2 CSB

33 A.D.

Shamira paused a moment, making sure not to trip on her skirts.
As she had grown taller, her hem had grown longer and longer
with each passing year. The way it seemed to hinder her every
move flustered her. In truth, she could do her chores much faster
without all of the swishing and swooshing that came with every
turn. Then Dodah Devorah would only have half of the reasons
to complain.

Just as the thought crossed Shamira's mind, her aunt's shrill
voice broke through her thoughts. "Hurry up, Shamira!"

The blazing sun shone down in her eyes, disorienting her. It took a moment to collect herself before she ran up the steps to join the rest of her family. First, they walked through the Court of the Gentiles. The noise rattled her brain, and everywhere she turned there was someone trying to sell her something. With her whole family surrounding her, they pushed forward into the masses. Aside from the fact that her Sabba Eliyahu and Savta Hodiyah were not present, there was nothing else out of the ordinary about the day.

Her family regularly visited the temple to worship and offer sacrifices and tithes. This time, her sabba and savta had elected to stay behind. Both were growing numerous in years and getting from one place to another was becoming strenuous for them. It would have been even more challenging with crowds like the ones they were experiencing on this particular day. The closer it came to *Pesach*, the more the streets of Jerusalem thickened like a swarm of locusts during harvest.

Shamira, seeing her dearest cousin close by, reached out for her and caught her dress. "Rut, it is not even time for the Pesach celebrations, yet there are so many people!" Amazement filled her heart at the sight of the crowds.

"Perhaps some of the people have arrived early to be with their families and are simply taking advantage of the opportunity to worship in the temple." Rut spoke quickly and quietly under her breath, rationalizing their presence away before Shamira could continue. Shamira continued on anyway.

"And all the others are taking advantage of the opportunity to make more money?" Shamira raised an eyebrow at Rut, who was more like another sister than a cousin. At the very least, they could pass for sisters at first glance.

They both had the same olive skin and dark features, although Rut's spiral curls were much more defined than Shamira's loose waves, and where Shamira's nose turned up at the end, Rut's was straight. Rut also had a full hourglass figure and deep-set eyes, and Shamira often found herself admiring Rut's beauty, selfishly wishing they shared more of the same characteristics.

They had lived under the same roof all their lives and shared practically everything together, and the bond between them only strengthened as they grew older together. Shamira tightened her sash just above her hips, the only visible sign of her womanhood. Her figure had otherwise remained what she considered to be shapeless.

"You mustn't say such things, Shamira."

"Really, Rut?" She pouted her lips. "Why ever not?"

Rut sighed, and Shamira could tell her persistence bothered her.

"Shamira, we both must learn to hold our tongues; this kind of conversation isn't becoming for young women like us. That is what your abba and mine would want."

"But neither your abba nor mine would sell in the temple, Rut," Shamira pressed, hoping reason would persuade Rut that it was worth speaking about.

"It isn't our place to decide such things."

Bending her head down in shame, Shamira felt the chill of the words that had haunted her since her childhood. "Rut" —her eyes widened, and she spoke in earnest— "where is my place?"

Rut offered no immediate answer. Shamira tried to guess whether or not her silence was due to the fact that she didn't hear her, or because she thought the question had been rhetorical.

Shamira still wanted an answer to her question but knew not to persist. She was a woman. A young woman, but a woman even still.

Women were meant to be quiet. Although she had heard what "her place" was before, and she had heard her mother assure her a thousand times that she was worth more than just her ability, or lack thereof, the message of her society had grown clearer and clearer every day.

It had grown clearer when she had to stop climbing trees because her skirts made that impossible. It had grown clearer when she'd been disregarded in public places and when her words went unheard by men—men who only answered to her father or uncles. It had grown clearer when her monthly red flow arrived for the first time, and her aunts rejoiced that she was now of an age to marry and bear children.

She had one place in the eyes of the world, and although it

was the only place for her, she wasn't sure if she fit into it.

Breaking the silence that had fallen between them, Rut interrupted Shamira's thoughts. "I believe this is our place, Mira."

However small, a smile breached Rut's otherwise serious and refined face.

Shamira couldn't help but share in that same joy. They continued through Gate Beautiful and arrived at the Court of Women, where the children and their mothers could worship. Shamira saw her Dodah Devorah and Dodah Chava along with her mother all join each other in song and prayer. The men continued on, farther and deeper into the temple.

"Come and forget your troubles with me."

Rut smiled once again and began her own melody. Rut's voice was beautiful and light, making Shamira wish her own voice was not so especially deep for a woman. Her melodies would never be as charming as Rut's, but they would be just as passionate.

Humbling herself, Shamira also raised her voice unto the Lord. It may not have been beautiful, but her praise was jubilant. Rut was right. In this moment, this was the place they were both meant to be. How good it was to worship the greatness of God.

Out of the corner of her eye, she saw something which troubled her. Now distracted from her worship, Shamira turned her head toward the Nicanor Gate, where her abba, Aharon, entered the next court accompanied by her uncle, Dodh Binyamin. Six or seven paces behind them was her Dodh Tamir.

Tamir had been curt with everyone over the past few days, and the dark circles under his eyes were becoming a constant feature. His attitude wasn't unusual, but Shamira felt as though he was carrying heavier burdens as of late. His back bent forward as he carried a sacrifice toward the altar.

Shamira looked back to her Dodah Chava to see if she showed any of those same signs of grief and shame. Dodah Chava bore a stiff upper lip, her mouth moving only slightly with her song. She did not glance in her husband's direction, but rather kept a firm grip on Libi.

Libi.

In the dark hours of the night and through the thin walls, Shamira could often hear her dodh and dodah going on about Libi from her own room. Those arguments had only become more frequent, and sometimes it seemed as though Chava blamed Tamir for Libi's affliction. She would beg and bargain for him to make more sacrifices.

"This is all we can afford!" Tamir would say.

"Your family are shepherds. You deal in livestock. Can't any of those be spared?" Chava would argue.

Regardless of the walls that separated them, Shamira could always distinguish the way Dodah Chava's voice would crack with desperation. Silence usually came next, when neither one of them would relent.

Chava seemed to believe that if they could just offer more sacrifices, Libi would be healed. It was probably only because of her frustration that Tamir spent so many nights sleeping out in the fields, a job mostly reserved for the hired shepherds her Sabba Eliyahu had found once his sons had all begun families of their own.

Sabba expressed it was important that his sons spend time with their own children, especially since the boys were still not old enough to shepherd themselves.

Shamira's heart ached when she would hear her aunt and uncle fighting, and she often cried herself to sleep when their silence spoke louder than their words. Even in her pain, she could only imagine what Dodah Chava must have felt. She wished so desperately that Libi could be healed, or at the very least, that God would heal the wounds tearing her family apart.

Shamira looked back at Dodah Chava one more time before focusing her thoughts and prayers back toward God. She looked on only long enough to see the single tear dripping down Chava's cheek and onto the top of Libi's head. Whatever sacrifice Tamir was offering now, Chava had fought hard for it. Shamira prayed it would turn out differently than all of the other times her family members had offered sacrifices on Libi's behalf. While she knew in her mind such a positive outcome was not likely, a little stirring in her heart made her hope against hope that this time things would be different.

Asa had spent the morning assisting at the temple, following his father, listening to his interpretations of the Law, and engaging in scholarly debate with his father's colleagues and other young men his age. He had spent the last six years debating the same passages over and over again. He knew all the possible arguments and the scriptures that supported some stances and destroyed others. He could answer any question by quoting passages from memory, yet he still found that none of the answers he'd been trained to give were right. At least not for him.

While his quick recall of the Torah scrolls seemed to give his father deep satisfaction, Asa had felt that after so long, the practice had grown tedious. But how could it? This was his destiny. It was what he was meant to do for the rest of his life.

"It's very simple," said one of the other Levites his age who was also working toward becoming a priest. "The Torah is the Law. It is meant to be applied strictly and literally. There is no conjecture about it."

"But the Torah was written over a thousand years ago. My father says that we, as Levites, are now meant to interpret the Law as we see fit for the times in which we are living now. Surely the meaning can change across hundreds of years," argued another Levite on Asa's right.

"Asa, what do you think?" said the first.

In truth, Asa wasn't really listening well enough to their discussion to be able to form an intelligent reply.

"Hm?" he asked, distracted by the light shining in his eyes.

"Asa, the Torah. How is it meant to be interpreted? Do you believe in a literal interpretation, or that its interpretations can evolve?"

Asa bit his lip, trying to force his mind back into academics. He turned away from the direction of the sun, and that was when something even brighter caught his attention.

There at the other side of the outer court, near where the offerings were given, was Shamira and her family. Strands of her long waves of dark brown hair turned a brilliant golden hue in the sunlight. She was gesturing toward her cousin Rut and wrangling the other children with her as they made their way out of the temple. His heart leapt inside of him—he'd nearly missed her!

"Asa, are you going to answer?"

"What? Oh, I'm sorry. Please excuse me." Asa was already parting from the group as he spoke. "There's someone here that I have to see."

He dodged between worshippers and those waiting to offer sacrifices, quickening his pace with each step until he was right behind Shamira.

"Beni, come on!" Rut nodded toward the exit.

The scrawny boy, who wasn't much older than Asa had been when he had first met Shamira, rolled his eyes and complained. "My name is Benayahu! I'm not that much younger than you, and I'm nearly as tall. I shouldn't have to do what you say."

Asa saw Shamira shake her head at Rut. She still hadn't noticed his presence.

"Rut," she said firmly. "If he'd rather stay behind and face a stern lecture from your imma then let him."

Together she and Rut continued to walk with Libi and her two brothers, Yuval and Gilad, in tow.

Asa saw Libi turn toward him, and her wide grey eyes lit up when she recognized him. Asa held up a hand to his face, shook his head, and pointed to Shamira, trying to tell her not to alert her older cousin to his presence just yet. She smiled and turned around, and Asa was grateful the girl hadn't given him away.

"She won't be happy that you chose to stay behind, Beni," said Shamira with a focused and determined gaze. Asa always admired how she could be both charming and strong at the same time.

"That's right!" said Asa, joining the conversation and making Shamira jump. He laughed knowing he was still able to surprise her even after all these years.

She reached up behind her and pulled her covering tighter

around her hair, gasping. "Asa! What are you doing here?"

"I practically live here, remember?" He raised an eyebrow to tease her, even though it was more of a reality than a joke.

Asa ran his hands through his hair in a vain attempt to keep his dark brown curls out of his face, and then turned his attention toward the nearly-twelve-year-old boy going on twenty in front of him. He lowered his voice as he would to talk to any man. "Benayahu, your sister and cousin are right, and you would be wise to listen to them! I don't think Devorah would like it very much if you left the girls alone."

"Alone? Them?" Benayahu laughed.

Crossing his arms in front of his chest, Asa continued. "But of course, them! Two young ladies and a group of children, defenseless without their guardian."

Benayahu tilted his head, still looking confused. "What guardian?"

"Asa?" whispered Shamira. She flashed a look at him, and he could tell she thought he'd gone crazy. "What are you talking about?"

Asa continued without hesitation. "Why, you! Benayahu ben Binyamin, the eldest grandson among the grandchildren of Eliyahu. Haven't you been paying any attention? The temple is busy today and someone needs to escort the women and children safely home. Why else would your mother send you with them?"

Benayahu smiled. Apparently, he found the title of "guardian" too tempting to refuse.

"Of course, she would!" Benayahu cleared his throat, lowering his voice to match Asa's tone. Asa smirked but tried to hide it from Beni, whose newfound confidence was growing with each step he took forward. "Come ladies, we must be moving along now."

Beni leaned closer toward Asa. "And as for you, I'm not entirely sure it is proper for you to be speaking so casually to my cousin Shamira. It would be better for you to come calling more formally next time."

With a nod of his head, Beni marched forward with Yuval, Gilad, and Rut following close behind. At the rate he was growing up, they wouldn't be able to keep calling him "Beni" for much longer.

Rut took Libi's hand from Shamira and walked ahead to give them just a moment alone together. Asa was grateful, not knowing how many of those he would likely have in the future.

Together, both Shamira and Asa laughed at Beni's antics, but neither of them said anything. Asa had spent a lifetime studying the poetry and prose of King David, but just one look from Shamira's honey-colored eyes could render him speechless. Instead of talking, they settled into a comfortable quiet, placing one foot in front of the other and continuing to walk forward but without breaking eye contact. What did one say to the love of their life, when it seemed like everything stood in the way of them being together? He wanted to reach out, to touch her, to show her how he felt when his words failed him, but he couldn't do that either.

Rut called out in the near distance, "Mira, one of me and three of these children is hardly fair! Are you two going to keep laughing with each other throughout the entire walk home or are you eventually going to come back and help me?"

For a young woman to speak like that in the presence of any other young man would have been unacceptable. They had all known each other for so long, however, that Asa fit into their family like another brother, instead of the son of one of the most respected temple priests. For that he was grateful—in their family, he could just be himself.

"Coming, Rut!" Shamira called out.

Both of them quickened their steps as their time alone together came to a close. He'd had but a few seconds with her, and he'd wasted them without saying anything of value or importance. He couldn't let her go yet.

Shamira moved to join her cousin where she ought to be. She hadn't realized how far she had fallen behind. Rut was struggling to keep the two little boys in line, while still trying to keep Libi by her side. If Yuval and Gilad had it their way, they'd have run off and gotten lost in the crowd a long time ago. At ten years old, both of them were so active and energetic, it was a wonder they'd never gotten lost before.

Asa's hand on Shamira's shoulder stopped her from getting too far ahead of him, but he quickly withdrew it. Shamira was stunned into silence and froze in place, not because she disliked his touch, but because she very much *did*.

"Can I see you soon?" He lowered his gaze to meet hers, completely earnest.

Truth be told, he had started following Shamira and her family nearly everywhere after Eliana's wedding. She had scarcely been able to get away from him for more than a moment when she was small; now she didn't want to. As the years went on, his father insisted he spend more and more time studying the Law and observing the sacrifices in the temple than frolicking through the fields with shepherds' children. Apparently, a Levite had better things to do.

Furthermore, as Shamira had come closer to a marriageable age, it had become harder for her to make up excuses that would allow her to spend time with Asa. Unless he was planning to offer a bride price to her father, sneaky conversations like this might be all they had. Still, her father was a reasonable man and liked Asa for who he was. He had a long history of friendship with their family, and as they had all become close to each other, it would be nearly impossible for him to refuse Asa the occasional social call on the family.

"You're seeing me now." Shamira bit her lip and then abruptly changed the subject. "I have to help Rut."

Asa stepped in front of her, his tall frame towering over her. He was not particularly muscular. As the son of a temple priest, he spent very little time doing hard labor. Despite this, he had a presence about him which could not be ignored as well as a wingspan Shamira could not get past.

"You know what I mean." He bent his head downward,

lowering his voice.

"Walk with us if you like. You can speak to my father when he joins us." Why couldn't she speak for herself? In her heart she wished she could share all of her thoughts and feelings, but in this, she knew to respect her abba.

Suddenly, Shamira realized what she'd always known but had been too afraid to ever admit, even to herself. Since the day she had first laid her eyes on him, she'd always felt betrothed to Asa. She knew it was an impossible situation: the son of an important leader and the daughter of a lowly shepherd, albeit a very successful family of shepherds. Despite that small fact in her favor, it could never be. It would take a miracle—miracles—for such a match to be approved.

That is why the day they met was consequently the day she had sworn she would never marry anyone. What she had tried so hard to bury all those years ago was springing up within her now, overwhelming her with emotion greater than she could contain.

Every time she thought of marriage, it pained her to do so. Her heart wanted nothing more than to be with Asa, but then she would think of all the traditions surrounding marriage. She would have to leave her home and make a new home in her husband's household away from all she had ever known.

She didn't know Asa's family very well, but she knew they were very affluent. She was fairly certain she would never be invited to their home. Even if she were, she knew their household was most certainly bigger, and more would be demanded of her when it came to keeping the house and helping with the food preparation. Untalented in the kitchen as she was, she would be a disappointment to them all.

In addition to chores, there were heavier concerns that kept Shamira awake at night and often turned her heart to prayer. Asa had not said a lot on the subject, but she'd seen bruises and observed stiffness enough times to know their home was not like her own.

After Eliana had gotten married, Shamira had scarcely seen her. Matthan worked very hard to provide for her, but his home was on the other side of the city. Shamira couldn't visit unescorted, and Eliana had new duties in her husband's house. She had meals to prepare and aging family members to care for. They saw each other often enough, but it was never the same. Never the same carefree roaming among the sheep in their family's pastures, never the same casual chats, never the same jokes, and never the same spilling of the most secret of secrets. Shamira missed her terribly. Maybe if Eliana were here now, she would know exactly what to say that would make everything clear. Without her, Shamira's emotions stayed tangled up in a knot like poorly spun wool.

Shamira pondered the thought of leaving her home and specifically her cousins—that had been the part of marriage she'd feared the most of all. Would Rut be just as lonely as Shamira had been? Or would Rut be like Eliana, eager to wed?

She had never even considered that before. All of her "little" cousins would eventually grow up and get married. Shamira didn't want to be left behind, but she didn't want to lose them either. Every day reminded her she was not a child, and soon they wouldn't be either.

The burden of change seemed to push and pull at her like a shepherd's crook. Shamira was like a sheep wanting to go her own way and wander from the rest of the flock, but the rod of change and the hook of time kept nudging her back in line, guiding her in ways she was afraid to go.

These were not new feelings for Shamira; she talked about it often with Imma in the kitchen, with Rut as they fell asleep at night, and sometimes with her abba when she walked with him to the fields. Change had just never been easy for Shamira. She loved life with her family just as it was.

Shamira, catching up to Rut, offered to hold Libi's hand. Rut did not object and passed her younger cousin's hand from one arm to the other, making sure Libi understood what was going on. With her right hand, Shamira made a walking motion with her fingers, and then pointed to herself.

"Libi? Would you like to walk with me? Then we can wait for your imma outside of the temple." Shamira didn't wait for a response, but when she smiled at Libi and Libi smiled back, Shamira felt the familiar feelings of love and joy take hold over her heart.

"Yuval, Gilad! What game are we playing today?" Asa called to the two boys, Libi's older brothers.

"Yuval took my shepherd!" Gilad cried out, reaching for his brother's arm. Gilad was still too small in stature to compete with his twin brother, who was already coming close to their father's height. Yuval took after his father, Tamir, in being so tall for his age.

"I did not! I was only borrowing it!" Yuval kept the little wooden object hoisted in one hand while placing his other hand defiantly at his side. Between caring for Libi and keeping her two very competitive boys in line, it was no wonder Dodah Chava was so often exhausted by the day's end.

"Yuval, give your brother what belongs to him." Asa's voice was soft but firm. The boys respected Asa because they had known him for so long, and also because they associated him with their older cousin Shamira who was so often put in charge.

Reluctantly, Yuval lowered his hand to give Gilad the toy, but not without making him struggle a bit. Yuval kept a tight grip on the little wooden shepherd, and Gilad had to pull at it several times before he finally let go. With a grunt, he retrieved his toy and nearly tripped. He quickly went back to playing, seemingly happy his belonging had been returned as he knocked one of his wooden carvings against the other.

Asa placed a protective hand on Gilad's shoulder. "Tell me, Gilad, what is that one?" He gestured toward the other carving in Gilad's right hand, a smaller carving with a round top.

"That one is me. I'm helping my abba, the shepherd, with the sheep," Gilad boasted, his face beaming. Although he never *really* was much help to Tamir, it was endearing to watch how he followed his father everywhere and tried to mimic his every move. That is, whenever his parents were on good terms and his father was actually around.

Shamira watched the conversation, always amazed at how well Asa fit in with her family and how good he was with children. Based on what Shamira had seen of his family, he hadn't had a loving example in his father, but the way Asa was so kind and considerate to everyone just made Shamira want him to be a part of her family even more—permanently.

She dared to imagine what a life with him would be like, if it weren't for all of the fears holding her back. In her mind, she conjured up a world where she and Asa could do whatever they wanted without any regard for societal differences or class. But she knew in her heart that if Asa even wanted to marry her, it would be highly unlikely his father, Avram, would ever let his son, a Levite, enter into such a union. She might have meant the world to Asa, but to the world all she would ever be was a common shepherd's daughter.

Shamira could hear the voices of her older family members slowly approaching behind them, getting louder and louder the closer they got. Their little group had not been moving fast enough, and the adults were catching up. To be fair, a large group like theirs rarely moved quickly.

Suddenly, without warning, Shamira halted in her tracks. "Rut, wait..." she said, instructing her cousin to do the same and signaling to Benayahu. They each pulled the children surrounding them close and turned to see what was happening. The usual cheerful banter of their family members had sharpened into what seemed argumentative.

The voices of her Dodh Tamir and Dodah Chava were not pleasant, but sharp and cutting. Libi might not have been able to hear what was going on, but Shamira felt Libi press closer to her body, trembling a little, gripping Shamira's skirts.

"Please! There is nothing we have not told you. There must be something else we can do!" Dodh Tamir's pleas were broken as he cried out for help, their two groups finally joined together as one.

"There is not a prayer which remains unsaid, nor a sacrifice which has not been offered." The priest raised his empty hands in the air. Shamira recognized him immediately as Avram, Asa's father. Asa must have seen what was happening as well, for she could feel him tense beside her, pulling away and leaving a cold, empty space between them.

"We have given everything we have to give to the Lord," Dodah Chava cried, tears staining her garments in large damp circles on her chest.

The priest dismissed her as if he had not even heard her speaking. Turning to Dodh Tamir, he continued. "Whatever sin you or your father or your family is hiding cannot be hidden from God. He will punish you as he chooses until you confess and atone."

Shamira's spirit was one of the few things that had remained unchanged in the years since Eliana's wedding. Willful as she was, she could not stand idly by and watch her family be publicly shamed and rebuked, *again*. She felt her pulse quicken and a lump settle in her chest. She lunged forward, but Asa caught her arm in a futile attempt to dissuade her from bringing any shame on herself.

Shamira fought Asa's grip until she was able to pry his fingers off of her. Lurching forward and pulling Libi alongside her, she cried, "Please, no!" Asa tried to stop her again, but she jerked away from him. "My family has not harbored anything or done any evil in secret. We have kept nothing from our Lord. Libi is innocent!"

"God punishes those as He sees fit!" Rabbi Avram towered over her with fire in his eyes. A kind of fire Shamira's own glare reflected. "Your family ought to punish you as well for your own temper and sinful ways! Perhaps then you'd have a better understanding of authority!"

Shamira was a protector, a defender. Although fear held her back in many other instances, her temper often propelled her forward when she should have otherwise remained still. Why couldn't the shepherd's rod which propelled her forward in appropriate moments, also hold her back from making mistakes?

Shamira was ready to open her mouth again but was interrupted by the appearance of yet another familiar figure. Aharon had stepped in front of Shamira and blocked her view. "Please, sir, my daughter is very close to Libi. She spends much of her time looking after her younger cousins, and sometimes she lets her emotions get the better of her. She spoke out of turn, and I'll see to it she knows that, but her actions were motivated by love and nothing more. I beg your pardon for her."

The passion of emotion she had felt moments prior vanished,

replaced by the weight of regret on her shoulders. Shamira shrank down behind the tall, strong form of her father. She would be reprimanded later, and she knew it, but she also knew her father loved her and in whatever way he could, he always understood her. At the very least, he made the effort to.

"Avram, I beg of you, do not let her youthful will impact your discussion with my brother and his wife."

Seemingly appeased by her father's response, Avram straightened his back as a snake-like smile spread across his face. "I am glad we agree; your daughter's actions must be kept in check. Rest assured, she has had no impact on what I have already said about your family's… *situation*. Furthermore, she will have no more impact on my son. Asa! Come here at once!"

Shamira whipped her head around just in time to see Asa's reaction. His jaw clenched and it was clear to her that he was angry. She could see the veins protruding from his neck and arms. Her head covering had fallen to her shoulders and her curls were now free, a problem she didn't have time to care about. A part of her heart had just been torn in two.

Had her foolishness cost her this relationship with Asa— whatever kind of relationship it was?

Asa was her oldest friend outside of her family. He was also her *only* friend outside of her family. She was more than grieved to think the trouble she had caused had brought them to this parting. Perhaps it was for the best. It was inevitable that he would marry someone else; she wasn't fit to be his wife. The disgrace she'd brought on her family had just proven that. Inside she prayed again that God would forgive her temper and help her to control her tongue.

"Father, we have been friends with the house of Eliyahu for a long time. Destroying such a relationship would be unfair to everyone involved." Shamira had never seen Asa openly object to his father, but she had seen him try to reason with Avram discreetly.

Shamira listened as he paced himself. Unlike her, Asa was not as likely to let his emotions get the better of him. He had inherited his father's diplomacy, and Shamira was grateful that seemed to be the only part of his father he had received.

"My son," Avram said. As good as Asa was at speaking and spinning words into persuasive speeches, his father was better. Insults from him sounded like sweet honey, and threats sounded like lullabies. "I am merely suggesting you devote more time to your studies. Soon you will start a family of your own, and you will need to be able to provide for them. It is important now that you put away childish things for the good of your education. You are a Levite, and it is your duty. That is all I mean."

Asa moved to join his father on the other side of the temple, gazing back apologetically at Shamira. Both men turned to leave, but Avram stopped suddenly as if he were feeling... regret? Remorse? No, it was neither of those things, and to tell the truth, Shamira wasn't sure if she even believed he was capable of showing those kinds of emotions.

She had seen this particular expression before, many times, on the faces of the people who would stop in the street and stare at her family. Shamira knew that emotion as pity.

"One more thing, Tamir," he said, one eye cast over his shoulder. *"Ha-Makom yenahem etkhem be-tokh avelei Ziyyon vi-Yrushalayim. Ad bi'at ha-go'el."*

A fire of rage blazed within her, burning her cheeks, for just as she knew what emotion was written plainly across his face, she also knew exactly what those words were. They were a common enough phrase, reserved for those in *mourning* and usually grieving the death of a relative or loved one.

"May the Lord comfort you among all mourners for Zion and Jerusalem. May you live until the coming of the Messiah."

Apparently, Avram now considered her aunt and uncle's quest for the healing of their daughter a lost cause, at least as long as Israel lived under oppression and without a Messiah to rule over them.

Looking down at Libi, Shamira began to cry warm salty tears that flowed from a broken heart. She didn't believe most things Avram said, but this time a part of his words had been embedded with truth. Their only hope was finding the Messiah.

"Abba, I don't think that was entirely fair to them," said Asa.

"I don't have to give you an explanation unless I choose to," his father said, still fuming about the interaction. "But because you seem unable to let it go, I'll give you one. Those people are cursed by God."

"Father!"

"Quiet, son! This is what you asked for. The Law isn't always about making people happy or giving them hope. The Law is about upholding the truth and maintaining order. There is something that family has done to anger God. That is why that child remains deaf-mute, and that child will be their shame as long as they live. No sacrifice will ever change that unless they atone for the sin that caused this child to be born deaf-mute."

"They haven't done anything. Shamira was telling the truth, there is nothing they have not confessed." Asa had known them for long enough to know they were good people. Why was his father so convinced they were not? Just because of their status?

"That may be what they say, but I assure you, there is nothing that can be kept secret from God. And that girl, Shamira, is just as much of a disgrace to them as the deaf-mute one."

Asa bit his lip and continued carefully. "But did you have to give them a mourner's blessing? Take away all of the hope they had left? Can we really know that God will not look mercifully on them?"

"As I said, the Law isn't about hope. It is about the truth. Those who live their lives outside the Law will get what they deserve, and we know from the history of our people that God always sees to that."

"But—"

"Don't question me on it any further. Get back to your studies." His father turned on his heel and stomped toward the door.

It was true. The history of their people had proven that

anytime the people of Israel strayed from God's plans for them, punishment and misfortune always followed. But Asa couldn't help but wonder if it wasn't also true that God's actions were motivated by love? Didn't God desire for His people to be close to Him, not just to reign over them but to be united with them as it had been in the Garden of Eden? Wasn't that why God had promised them a Messiah in the first place?

"Abba," said Asa, walking after his father. "Do you really think the time of the Messiah might be near?"

"Ach, not you too," his father groaned. "Please do not talk to me about Messianic rumors. There is enough talk of that as it is between the zealots and the new radicals who believe one charismatic Nazarene is the promised leader of our people. Nazarene! Can you imagine?"

Radicals? What radicals? Asa would certainly get back to his studies, but not before finding out what his father was talking about. Then, his studies would be focused solely on Messianic prophecy.

JERUSALEM'S DAUGHTER

"The shepherds returned, glorifying and praising God for all the things they had seen and heard, which were just as they had been told." - Luke 2:20 CSB

Shamira walked through the familiar wooden gate into her family's shared home. The house, built in the traditional four-room style with two rooms on either side of the courtyard and two other rooms opposite the gated entrance, was not grand by any means. The courtyard was barely large enough for cooking, and the walls had been repaired and added onto many times to accommodate their family as they had grown. What the structure lacked in width, it made up for in height. Ladders and stairways both inside and outside connected the additions and rooftop levels. Shamira looked up at her own window, which faced out over the courtyard and into the street, longing for nothing more than to disappear behind that curtain for the rest of the day.

Shamira was still holding Libi's hand when their Savta

Hodiyah rushed out from the house in a hurry with her arms wide open, stopping only to press a hand to the mezuzah and say a prayer. With declining eyesight and excitement all wrapped up together, she seemed to overlook Shamira's tears.

"Oh, my girls! Where have you been? It seemed like you all were gone unusually long today, hm?"

Savta Hodiyah kissed each of their cheeks, a habit she would never grow out of, and squeezed them tightly in her arms. Her Savta's warm embrace would always make Shamira feel safe and secure, no matter how unsettling that day's events had been, or how many times Shamira had made mistakes and felt like a failure.

"We have just returned from the temple, Savta. If we took too long, blame it on the boys or the crowds. The temple was unusually busy today, and the boys were... well, *usually* rambunctious."

Shamira tried to mask her feelings of guilt and shame with a laugh. She could have told Savta Hodiyah about everything that had really happened at the temple, but she was still too angry to even discuss it. She also knew it wasn't entirely her story to tell. If anyone were to discuss what had happened, it should be Chava or Tamir, because they were the ones who had been wronged.

"Well," Savta smiled, "At least you're back now. Come inside, come inside. The meal is already prepared. I've been keeping it warm for your return—Oh! Rut! Beni! You're back as well!"

As quickly as Savta had approached Shamira and Libi, she ran toward her other grandchildren. Shamira smiled. It seemed as though her grandmother had an endless well of love, constantly overflowing and never running dry. Regardless of what had happened earlier, Shamira was glad she could come home to such a warm environment. In the back of her mind, her thoughts and heart were with Asa, knowing his homecoming would not be like her own.

Libi tugged on Shamira's sleeve, and Shamira looked down at Libi's wide, gray eyes. Did Libi understand what had happened? Was she all this time aware of the rift between her parents? Did she know what had caused the breakdown of their relationship? Shamira prayed to God it was not so, but looking at all the questions swirling around in her little cousin's eyes sent shivers up and down her spine. Whatever Libi felt, she didn't need words to express it.

Trying to put on her bravest face, Shamira said to Libi, "Come on, let's go inside. Would you like me to braid your hair for you before we sit down for dinner? You'll look like a queen then, and we can pretend that you are our honored guest at a royal banquet." She tugged at her own hair, plaiting a few strands and making a crown-shape with her fingers.

Libi nodded enthusiastically in agreement.

She gave Libi a reassuring smile, pressed a hand up to the mezuzah, said a fervent prayer, and entered the house. She was looking down at Libi to make sure she did not trip or stumble when Shamira herself bumped into her grandfather, nearly bringing both of them down with her.

"Sabba! You startled me!" Shamira placed a hand over her heart, which was skipping beats with shock.

Leaning back, Eliyahu chuckled. "Am I so old you've already confused me with a ghost?"

Shamira giggled, embarrassed. "No, Sabba! Never!"

Eliyahu placed a hand on Shamira's shoulder. "Tell me, granddaughter, how were things at the temple today?"

Shamira took a moment to think of a response, wrinkling her nose from side to side. She knew she didn't have to hide things from her grandfather, but she also wanted to be tactful. Her words had gotten her into enough trouble already. Before she could even open her mouth to give him an explanation, Sabba interrupted her thoughts.

"Shamira… What did you do?" His voice had lowered. It was his way of being stern, which he only ever did out of love, and her wrinkled-up nose must have given her guilty feeling away.

"The temple was crowded today. There were many people there. Lots of things were happening all around!"

"As there usually is this time of year, so close to the Pesach, but I don't think that's what you really want to tell me."

Dangling her head low in sadness, Shamira sighed. "Oh, Sabba. Asa's father, Avram—the priest—he said things about Libi. I couldn't help it. I had to say something in her defense, and he... he... he..."

Breathing deeply, Sabba reached for her, pulling her close to his chest. He must have filled in enough of the gaps in her telling of the story with his own imagination, and for that Shamira was grateful. She deeply inhaled the musty scent of sheep and earth which he still somehow bore even years after he'd officially retired from working in the fields. Shamira, unlike most girls her age, didn't mind the smell. It was a comforting reminder of her family and heritage. She would never get tired of it—it was the smell of home.

"Oh Shamira... I'm not blaming you or punishing you; that is up to your father. I might have done the same thing myself when I was your age, but I am not a boy anymore, and you... you are no longer a little girl. You must learn to control yourself; you could cause great harm to yourself and to our family if you do not guard your tongue. You are too impulsive, Shamira."

"I know, Sabba... I know."

She was grateful her sabba had not forced her to recount and relive the day's events all over again, but his reprimand, as kindly as it had been delivered, still stung. She was foolish; she had been foolish, and she had been told she was a foolish girl a hundred times before. Perhaps not in those exact words, but they might as well have been.

Was her sabba right? Perhaps if she were a wiser, quieter, or even silent young woman, things would be better. It would have at least been better on this day. Was silence truly what God, who had given humans the ability to speak, required of her? Or did He have a different purpose in mind?

"Shamira, I see in you many of my own qualities. That is why I must tell you that what I'm saying to you, I'm saying for your own good," her sabba replied.

Shamira mentally prepared herself to hear those ever-present words about knowing her place and being a proper, respectful young woman. She closed her eyes, because maybe it would be easier to hear if she didn't have to look at the person saying it and see the shame in their eyes.

"Shamira," continued sabba, "your words are *powerful*. That's why you must be careful. There's no telling how many wars a person could start—and finish—with their tongue."

"Powerful?" Shamira blinked in surprise, letting the word settle in her mind.

Troublesome.

Problematic.

Outspoken.

Those were all words she had been called before, and noticeably, there was one word absent. *Powerful*. Never in her life had she ever considered that the words she spoke could be powerful. Powerless and useless, yes, many times. But powerful?

Never.

She wanted to ask Sabba what he meant. She'd seen the problems her words could cause, but how could they be powerful in a good way? However, she could tell Sabba had said all he was going to say on the subject.

"Come now, Shamira. I believe I heard you promising to braid our Libi's hair. You wouldn't want to break that promise, would you?"

"Of course not."

"Good! Then get yourselves upstairs. I will speak to both of your parents about what happened today."

She smiled, nodding in understanding and knowing sabba meant well. Surely, he could sort everything out just as he always had in their family. Always.

Shamira took her seat at the table and motioned for Libi to sit down beside her. Her mother and aunts had long since given up asking Shamira to help them serve, unless they were in the mood to scrape the meals off the hard-packed dirt floor, which was never the case.

Anyway, it was far better that Shamira keep Libi company. She always felt that the inability to hear or speak was too great a burden to bear for her sweet and beautiful younger cousin, but at least she did not have to bear it alone. Libi had her whole family around, supporting and loving her, and Shamira was grateful the Lord had given her the ability to serve Libi well. Since Shamira often spoke too much, and Libi couldn't speak at all, they were both considered different by others' standards. Because of that, they understood each other with or without words.

Shamira still felt remorseful for how her words had caused her family to have such an unfortunate altercation with Avram in the temple. She was also still upset that in his rage against her, Avram had denied her family any hope for Libi's healing. But while those feelings lingered, so did the longing in her heart for the Messiah her sabba had spoken of so many times before. If they truly were living in the time of the Messiah, he could set things right. He could heal all things—surely, he would have the power to do that and more.

With all of these thoughts running through her mind, she turned to look at Libi, who smiled from ear to ear, perfectly content. Her hair was in delicate little plaits that weaved all around her head. Libi was obviously enjoying being treated like a queen, and Shamira was happy she could give that gift to her, even if it only lasted a few hours. Plaiting hair was a good distraction from her problems, and on this particular evening she had many problems from which she wanted to be distracted.

Once everyone was seated and after the prayers had been said, the long-dreaded discussion began. She had managed to avoid Rut's pointed gaze for most of the meal and had ignored much of what the adults were saying, until she could refrain no longer.

"And then, just as he was turning to leave, he insulted our family by giving them a mourner's blessing! A mourner's blessing!" Dodh Binyamin was just as vocal as Dodah Devorah, especially on this occasion.

"He actually said those words to you?" Eliyahu's eyes

widened at the opposite end of the table.

"Abba, it was humiliating."

Thankfully, no mention of Shamira had been made in her uncle's retelling of the story. Shamira doubted it would come up again in front of the family, but she was sure her father would be addressing her in private. At least her father wasn't the type to single her out in front of the others.

"'May you live until the coming of the Messiah,' he said. The Messiah! Ha! When the Messiah comes, He shall strike such a man down swiftly. He will free us all from oppression, and even from the oppressors who disguise themselves as His servants," Dodh Binyamin continued.

"If the Messiah comes..." Tamir grunted.

Shamira saw Dodah Chava sitting awkwardly on her cushion, leaning forward with her brows knit together, just before she opened her mouth to join the debate.

"The Messiah will never come! God has forgotten us. He has forsaken us all, even the innocent!" Chava shouted.

At this, Shamira and the other women gasped, for even Shamira knew Chava shouldn't have said such a thing. Chava gathered her skirts, as if to leave the dinner table upset and her food untouched.

"Stop it!" Eliyahu brought his hand down on the table hard, smacking the surface and rattling the dishes strewn across it. "I will not hear any more of this talk!"

After Dodah Chava sank back down into her seat, her head down, Eliyahu continued. "Is the faith of my sons and daughters so weak? So easily forgotten? You talk of the Messiah like He is a myth or a pagan legend. Have you forgotten? I have seen the Messiah!" Eliyahu shook as he spoke. He repeated the words, but softer this time with a gruffness that was the product of his overwhelming emotion. "I have *seen* the Messiah!"

Those were powerful words, and Shamira reveled in each one, repeating them over and over again in her mind.

"Abba... Not this again." Shamira's own abba pleaded with Sabba. Shamira waited on the edge of her cushion for Sabba to tell the story again.

"Do you not believe me? What makes my testimony any less

valid than yours?"

"Abba, I didn't mean that I didn't believe you. But you know what could happen if—"

"Aharon!" Savta snapped. "Let your abba speak." While her sons may have grown old and become fathers themselves, they always listened to their mother. Especially when Savta Hodiyah gave them *that* look.

Shamira watched with trepidation as Sabba drew in one long breath, pausing for just a moment before letting it out. Behind his closed eyelids, his eyes darted back and forth as if he were seeing it all over again. Creases appeared on his forehead and around his nose, and Shamira's heart beat faster as she waited for him to recount the story. The story of the Messiah.

When Eliyahu's eyes opened, they were not focused on anything or anyone in the room. They were staring at something far, far off in the distance. He smiled slightly, and his eyes brightened. The starlight from that night seemed to have been permanently captured in his gaze.

"There was… a great light in the heavens that night. I was not much younger than Tamir is now. You boys couldn't have remembered it; you were all too small when we lived in Bethlehem. The other shepherds and I saw something in the sky. Something…indescribable. It was blinding, deafening, terrifying, and peaceful all at the same time!

"There was a moment where we thought our lives were over and that we were dying. We fell to the ground, scared for our lives and trembling in the presence of such glory. That's when we heard… a voice. The voice belonged to the angel of the Lord, and he spoke to us. He said, 'Don't be afraid, for look, I proclaim to you good news of great joy that will be for all the people: Today in the city of David a Savior was born for you, who is the Messiah, the Lord. This will be a sign for you: You will find a baby wrapped tightly in cloth and lying in a manger.' Suddenly, these angels appeared all around us. I've never heard such a glorious sound!"

Sabba reached out with both hands as though he were reaching for those same angels among them.

"What happened next, Sabba?" Gilad interrupted.

Sabba Eliyahu smiled and chuckled softly, patting Shamira's cousin on the head.

"*Hamud*, I have told the story often enough. You should know! But I suppose you should also know I never turn down the opportunity to tell the story again.

"Well, as I was saying, when the angels had left us, the other shepherds and I were amazed at all we had just witnessed. A great light, all the heavens opening up, angels appearing in our midst and all at once disappearing into a single star. I remember feeling… so unworthy. Who was I but a humble shepherd, who could barely support his own family?

"We were not welcome in town because of our stench. We spent most of our time tending to livestock, and we were often unclean due to the nature of our work. We were not important by any means, so why were we given this great news with no one of good repute there to witness it? Only us? Sometimes I still question the Lord's reasoning behind it all.

"Regardless of whatever fears I might have hidden in my heart, it was an easy choice to make. Unanimously, we set out in search of this baby, and lo and behold—there he was. The hope of the entire world, lying in a manger of all places, just as the angels had said he would be! This baby… although he had just been born, had such a presence about him.

"Looking upon his face was like looking upon the angels all over again. It was like nothing I'd ever experienced before, nor that I am likely to ever experience again."

Shamira saw the tears dripping from her sabba's eyes, as they so often did at this part of the story. Savta reached out for his hand, tucking it between hers.

"We fell to our knees and we worshipped him, this newborn who was proclaimed our Savior."

Sabba tilted his head back toward the heavens. "So, what then, my sons, is so hard to believe about a Messiah in our midst? What makes such a thing so impossible, you will not even believe the testimony of your own father?" The old man fell back into his seat, gasping for air and placing his hand over his heart.

Shamira glanced around the room waiting for someone to

respond, waiting for anyone to say they believed her sabba— that they believed the Messiah was coming. Better yet, that he was here! She waited for someone to apologize to him and assure Sabba their faith had never wavered. Instead, Dodh Tamir and Dodh Binyamin turned their heads away from him. Shamira looked to her own father, certain he would not deny her Sabba Eliyahu. He was his firstborn son, after all.

Running his fingers along his jaw, her abba opened his mouth as though he was going to respond and closed it again, seemingly lost for words. When he opened his mouth a second time, words did not fail him. "Abba, you have seen what none of us have seen. Do not blame us for not recalling something we ourselves have not experienced."

Sabba shook his head. "I do not blame you for not remembering. I blame you for not having faith in God's promises. To not have faith in my words, I can excuse. To not believe His words..."

Shamira watched the heated exchange with bated breath. Such tense conversations were few and far between in their home. She had never before known her family to fight or disagree like this. She looked at her younger cousins who were eating and oblivious to the adults' cutting discussion. The exception of course was Rut, who was also wide-eyed and biting her lip at the scene playing out before them.

Perhaps this was not as rare as Shamira had previously believed; perhaps with maturity she was simply more aware. Had she been the only one who had taken Sabba's words as unfailing truth all this time? Was she the only one who shared his faith? More and more, Shamira was becoming aware of many things of which her child-self had been ignorant. Parts of the world which her innocence had hidden from her were now exposed, and every day the sun seemed to shine a little less brightly than before.

"Very well, then. It is time for me to take my leave; I am excusing myself." Eliyahu withdrew from the table. Savta stood, nodding to her children and grandchildren with a look of disappointment, and dutifully followed her husband.

In all of her sixteen years, Shamira had never seen her

grandparents leave the dinner table before the meal was finished.

While the rest of her family seemed to move on, Shamira couldn't help but wonder… Was a Messiah on the way? Avram had been right on just one thing—only a Messiah could save Libi. If there was such a person, as her grandfather sorely believed there was and as Shamira had always agreed, she would have to find him. It was the only way she could help Libi and restore peace in her family.

"Shamira, let me clear the table," Elisheva, said, gently prying the stack of dishes from her hands, going against her customary after dinner routine—one of the only kitchen chores for which Shamira was responsible.

"Imma," she sighed in return. "I haven't broken dishes in years! I'm much more careful now than I was back then!" She smiled at her mother, only slightly embarrassed.

"I know that, but your abba would like to speak with you." Imma's voice was serious, and Shamira bowed her head, avoiding eye contact.

"Oh." Of course, he wanted to talk to her. Everyone seemed to have had something to say after her outburst.

Elisheva set down the load in her arms and placed a firm hand on Shamira's shoulder. "Shamira? He's waiting outside."

"Hm?" she hummed, distracted and confused. "Oh, yes. I shall go to him at once."

Shamira nodded in obedience and turned to leave the room, taking small but quick steps. The little conversations that were taking place inside the house faded into a low murmur the moment Shamira crossed the threshold, brushing her hand over the mezuzah. She stopped for a moment to pray for peace. She observed her father who was standing straight with his arms folded across his chest and his head tilted all the way back toward the stars. She was like her father in many ways and this was one of them.

She approached her abba quietly, not wanting to distract him from his thoughts. Once at his side, she tilted her head back too, curious to see what he saw in the heavens.

Looking at the stars, she wondered what it must have been like to be her sabba, and to have seen a light as brilliant as he described it. The stars were beautiful and stunning, so she knew whatever he had seen must have been even more so. Even with all of her imagination, she couldn't begin to picture what it must have been like to be in the presence of angels.

"What are you looking at, Abba?"

He turned suddenly, looking surprised to see her standing beside him. Had he not heard her approach? Shamira smiled at the thought, for perhaps she wasn't as clumsy as she believed.

"Shamira, I didn't hear you coming."

"Had you expected me to trip and fall at your feet?" She laughed nervously, ignoring the tension that loomed just overhead. Her stomach churned.

"*My* daughter? Never!" He started to smile, and then suddenly his face became very grim. Her quip was worth it, even if it had only made her abba smile for a moment. His admonishment would have to come eventually, and she couldn't distract him forever.

Shamira bit her lip as his gaze returned to the stars above them, only this time looking far less peaceful.

"I came as soon as Imma told me that you wanted to speak with me. What troubles you, Abba?" She knew exactly what it was that troubled him, and she knew it was her fault, but the question seemed like a good way to usher in the inevitable.

"You are the light of my life, Shamira. Of course, both you and your sister are and always have been, but with Eliana married I am left with only you to dote on." He paused to look straight into her eyes. "You know how much I love you, don't you?"

"Abba!" She wrinkled her nose from side to side, curious that he could ever question her on such a matter. She had known it every day for as long as she could remember. "You would have to love me very much to put up with all of the trouble I have caused you and Imma to endure!"

"Trouble?" he laughed. "I only remember the smiles your mother and I would share after we had wiped your tears and sent you off to play elsewhere. No child was ever more drawn to tears and despair than you."

He grinned from ear to ear as he reminisced over those early days of her childhood. Those were the days when all her problems were easily solved by a quick hug or kiss. Now the world was changing quickly, and things were far more complicated.

"Must we relive those days?" she asked. She felt her cheeks blush.

"Don't be so embarrassed. You kept your mother and I young in this way. In keeping us so busy we hardly ever had time to realize we were growing old. We only had time to keep chasing after you." Stretching out his arm, he pulled her closer to his side and held her tenderly with all the affection a father could give his daughter.

Shamira didn't want the moment to end. She loved being held by her parents and being their little girl, but as she felt his chest rise and fall beside her, she knew every day the time was drawing nearer where she would no longer be their "little girl." But it was during moments like this that Shamira felt truly safe. Someday she would likely not be theirs; she would be married and would belong to her husband. She shivered thinking about it—the thought of belonging to any man who wasn't Asa left a lump in her throat. It was yet another reason why she prayed relentlessly that she would be spared from a loveless match.

For too long the happy quiet had hindered her abba from saying what he had intended to say before she had joined him in the courtyard. She knew it was difficult for him to admonish her—it always had been. He did it anyway, and each time, Shamira's cheeks became saturated with tears because of the grief she'd caused. She would never remove the stain of guilt on her conscience until she apologized and tried to make amends, and she believed he knew that by now. Although she no longer cried at every predicament, this night was no different.

"Abba, if I had done nothing wrong, then we would not be having this conversation," she reminded him.

He looked at her, tears filling his eyes and making them glisten in the moonlight. "When did you grow so wise?"

Aharon was a good and gentle father. Sometimes Shamira felt like she didn't deserve such loving and forgiving parents.

"Unlike the days of your childhood, I can no longer get rid of your sad eyes as easily as I would like. Very well then, have it your way. Sit down so we can talk properly." He gestured to the rough-hewn bench beneath the tree. Even from under its branches, she could still make out some of the stars. She delighted in their silvery beams of light which danced with the wind through the leaves above her.

"You know, many years ago the Lord promised Abraham descendants as numerous as the stars. Each of us has a star in the heavens that is our star, Shamira. You and your sister are the brightest stars your mother and I have ever seen. You have been such blessings to us. The light you brought into our world is more extraordinary than all the stars in the sky combined. I would hope one day when you are older, married, and with children of your own that you might understand this.

"Nothing has brought your mother and I more joy than having you two stars in our lives. Your savta would say the same thing about myself and my brothers, although we may have been considerably more difficult to raise than you or your sister. Still, knowing you, raising you, and loving you has been an experience unlike any other. If I could make it so every two parents had a star in their lives as bright as you, a child in their lives as extraordinary as you, I would do it."

He paused, and Shamira wondered if he would ever get to the part of this conversation when he would admonish her. He began again, "Shamira. I can think of no two parents more deserving of a star like you, than your aunt and uncle. Tamir and Chava love Libi with all of their hearts, but you must understand their love for Libi goes hand in hand with their pain.

"When Libi cries, they cry. When her heart is broken, their hearts are broken. When she is in pain, they are in pain tenfold.

They won't hear her voice. They show Libi every day that they love her, but she won't be able to actually hear the words. They won't sing songs together as you girls and your mother used to. Shamira, Tamir will never be able to have conversations like *this* with his daughter. They would do anything for her, even making countless sacrifices at the temple if there was even the slightest chance it might heal Libi."

Shamira straightened. "But father, they have confessed their sins! Dodh Tamir and Dodah Chava are good people. No sacrifice, especially a sacrifice performed by someone as hypocritical as Avram, could ever save Libi from a punishment that none of them deserve."

"Shamira!" Aharon raised his voice. "For once, think before you speak!"

Shamira shrank back and away from him. Because he rarely ever raised his voice to her or to anyone, she knew this time she had gone too far. Despite her personal feelings, Avram was still a person of authority who demanded respect, and sacrifices were still a part of the Law which had been given to them by the One True God. Those kinds of things were not meant to be tossed aside lightly.

Rising to his feet, he took several paces back and forth before continuing. "You must understand my frustration, Shamira. My worries and anxiety! People have been put to death for saying less!" Tears filled her father's eyes, shattering Shamira's heart into a thousand shards. "I do not want my brightest star's light to go out."

Weakened, she rebutted, her voice trembling with nervousness. "But, Abba, what about what Sabba says? About the Messiah? He could save Libi! I know it!"

"Your sabba... is an old man. You mustn't believe everything he says." He bent his head in dismay, and Shamira briefly wondered whether or not he was ashamed of his father or himself.

"But weren't you there? In Bethlehem?"

"I was but a child at that time, Shamira. I believed every story I heard and got in trouble because of it." He stopped for a moment, hesitating. "I would love to believe what he says is true. That there is a Messiah among us, that there is a just God who will right all the wrongs in our world, heal the afflicted, pay the debts of those who are indebted. But Shamira, I was not there that night. I was asleep by my mother's side. I did not see the angels, nor did I hear their message.

"Binyamin and I were children, and Tamir barely more than a toddler. What I did hear were the horrid rumors about my father and mother when people whispered behind their backs. What I saw were innocent lives lost because of these rumors."

Shamira turned away from him to wipe the salty tears from her own eyes. She wanted to ask more questions, to understand his pain, but her own heartache was too overwhelming. He let out a long, tired breath, and Shamira rose from her seat. As she gathered her skirts, she prayed he would give her permission to retire. Shamira had troubled him and upset him, and she wished to trouble him no longer.

"Shamira, wait."

"I am truly sorry, Abba. I shamed our family today, and now I have upset you. Please let me go inside before I upset someone else. I just want the sun to set on this day and to not have to live in it anymore."

"Let me finish what I have to say," he countered.

She obeyed and sat back down beside him, still barely able to look him in the eye.

"Shamira, ahava sheli, my bright shining star—your faith is admirable. You believe in something which you have never seen, that you were not even alive to have been able to see. You believe the darkness will end. You believe in the future, and you are full of hopes and dreams that some of us wouldn't even dare to have. These are all incredible qualities. You are also passionate and full of love. This is an incredible quality too, but one I fear gets you in trouble more often than not.

"All I am asking is that you consider whether or not your words, however true they may be, may hurt more people than just yourself. What if your actions at the temple today, speaking out against Avram, a respected priest and teacher of the Law, meant Tamir and Chava would only receive more harsh treatment? I know to you, kind-hearted Shamira, this seems ridiculous and irrational. Indeed, it may be so. But in the future, consider how your actions affect others before you do something so brash again, all right?"

She took a few deep breaths of her own. She had never thought her words might have consequences for Dodh Tamir and Dodah Chava. Nobody talked about it, but everyone knew their marriage was strained. If she had added anything to their list of problems, she would regret it all the days of her life.

"Yes, Abba. I promise I will try to be more considerate. All I want is to honor our family and God. Words are powerful," Shamira said. "Will you forgive me, Abba?"

"Shamira, you have already been forgiven... There is no punishment I can give you that would be greater than the punishment you will give yourself. The real question for you is will you be able to forgive yourself?"

After that, Aharon excused her to finish her chores and help settle the children for the evening. Shamira was grateful her father had not demanded an answer immediately, because in truth, she couldn't provide one. At the end of the evening, she retired to her room. It was no surprise to her to find Rut already there. She'd likely been waiting to speak to her ever since the evening meal.

"Shamira, are you all right?"

Shamira nodded in the shadows.

"Rut, I must learn to control my words; I could do our family great harm if I don't master my own tongue." Shamira joined her cousin at the window, looking out at the deceptively peaceful city. Jerusalem was at war beneath the surface, with the need for reconciliation battling the desire for retribution against Rome. It was the kind of internal conflict Shamira knew all too well.

"You could also do great good," said Rut, in a clear attempt to offer comfort. "I am sorry about what happened with Asa though."

Shamira nodded. "I'm sorry too. I'm afraid that tonight Asa will not sleep comfortably. His father was so angry, I could see it in his eyes." She paused. Silent tears trickled down her cheeks as she thought of Asa and the damage she had imparted on him and potentially their relationship. "What if I don't get to see him again?"

Rut shook her head. "I don't believe that, Shamira. Asa will find a way—he always does."

"I hope so," Shamira whispered.

"And Jesus increased in wisdom and stature, and in favor with God and with people." - Luke 2:52 CSB

Shamira stumbled a little, balancing the basket on her hip while she bent halfway over trying to see and avoid stepping on any more rocks. Her feet were already blistered enough from previous, less graceful attempts at bringing lunch to the shepherds in the pastures. Shamira and Rut didn't always deliver meals to the shepherds, especially now that most of them were hired boys from Jerusalem. She had been told things were different before she and her cousins were born. When her abba and uncles watched over the flocks, her imma and aunts would bring meals often to lift their spirits. They were young, in love, and carefree.

Shamira loved hearing stories about those days and imagining what her parents must have been like when they were her age. Those happy days of youth were gone now. While love still filled their home, they had responsibilities and were occupied in different ways. The children kept their mothers busy at home, and the men had cultivated the business side of things.

Savta, with loving interference, insisted Shamira and Rut take Beni and Tamir's boys with them when they delivered the midday meal, expressing her dislike of how much time Tamir spent away from his children, saying by their age, they should be preparing to learn a trade. Gilad especially admired Tamir, always playing with his wooden carvings and pretending to be a shepherd right alongside his abba.

Yuval was growing restless, and his streak of wildness showed the need for his father's hand and guidance. So, every so often, if Tamir was out in the fields with the sheep and they were not too far from the city's gates, Shamira and Rut took the children to the pastures to deliver food. They often joked with each other that they were actually shepherdesses and the children were their sheep.

"So other than the conversation last night, they never punished you?" asked Rut.

Shamira shook her head. "No... Abba said he could not punish me more than I would punish myself."

"I don't disagree with him on that regard," Rut replied.

Shamira couldn't decide if she was grateful her father had spared her punishment, or if she still felt guilty. She felt like she needed to be punished in order to truly be forgiven. She bit her lip, unsure if she wanted to proceed with the conversation. Then she decided she couldn't go on unless she discussed it with someone, and there was never anything she couldn't discuss with her best friend.

"Rut, what do you really think about what Sabba says? Do you think there is a Messiah in our midst? It is all I can think about. Well... almost all." In the back of her mind she was seeing a tall young man with twinkling eyes whom she missed very much.

Rut sighed, "I don't know. But it's not up to us to decide such things, Shamira. No one would listen, we're just girls."

"Young women," Shamira corrected.

"Either way, what we have to say won't matter."

"Yes, it does. Words have power, Rut. God can use them for great things." Shamira's mind suddenly drifted away to what her sabba had said to her before.

Rut smiled. "Oh, Shamira! If only everyone could think the way that you think. Then—"

"Wars could start and end with a single word," Shamira whispered, echoing the sentiments shared by her Sabba.

"Where do you come up with these things, Mira?" asked Rut, craning her head to one side.

"Never mind that. My point is that what you say does matter. At least it does to me, and I want to know—do you believe what Sabba said?"

"I believe that Sabba is telling the truth when he says he was visited by angels that night."

"But do you believe that the angels were proclaiming the birth of the Messiah?" Shamira knew Rut was usually quiet about things like this, but Shamira pressed her anyway. There was nothing they couldn't share with each other, no matter how hard it might be to say.

"It's hard to know, Shamira. We weren't there. We weren't even born yet! I can't help but wonder why, of all people, the Lord would have chosen to proclaim the birth of the Savior to mere shepherds. I'm not like you Shamira, this kind of talk—it frightens me."

"But don't you agree that the Messiah is coming? That he is coming soon?"

"I think… I think that he might be. But to claim such a thing borders on blasphemy, Shamira. You're willing to stake your life on this?"

"Stake your life." Those were powerful words, so powerful that they stopped Shamira's heart for a moment after Rut had said them, but she would not be made silent by them.

"Yes, I am."

"Mira… I wish I were as brave as you."

"Maybe you don't. What you call bravery, our parents call recklessness," Shamira warned.

"No wonder you're always getting into trouble." Rut laughed.

"Sabba didn't seem upset when I told *him* what happened outside our home. It was as if he somehow already knew."

"Well maybe that's because he's grown accustomed to your outbursts."

"My outbursts?" Shamira said, now feeling somewhat offended. "Am I always going to be the troublemaker in our family?"

"Maybe." Rut's sincerity almost made Shamira jab her elbow into Rut's side. "But then we'll always be getting into trouble together!"

At this, both of them laughed. From the moment they could talk, they'd begun devising plans together. Naturally, Shamira was usually the instigator of their mischievous schemes, but Rut had played along all the same. Perhaps the reason they were so close was because they had spent so much time being scolded together.

As they had gotten older, Rut had tried to keep Shamira from pursuing every single whim. When Shamira was unstoppable, as she usually was, Rut always went along, and Shamira knew it was usually for no other reason than to make sure nothing truly terrible happened.

"Don't make me laugh so hard," said Shamira, her words staggered. "I'm likely to drop my basket!"

"Well, it's a good thing we're here, isn't it?"

"What?" Shamira raised her head up and sure enough, she was surrounded by sheep. "I hadn't realized... I was just trying not to trip."

"Well perhaps if you kept your head up more instead of always looking at your toes you would have noticed all the sheep, or at least you would have noticed Asa."

"What?" Shamira exclaimed. Her heart seemed to flip over Rut's mention of him.

"Abba!" cried Gilad as he ran in between Shamira and Rut, creating a gust of wind in his wake.

"What are you talking about Rut?" Shamira ignored her younger cousins.

"Be careful not to startle any of the sheep, boys!" Rut called after Tamir's sons.

"Rut—what do you mean?" sighed Shamira, exasperated.

"Asa, he's standing over there," said Rut absentmindedly.

She was already unpacking the food and preparing their midday feast. "Beni, come here and sit for the meal."

"I don't want to sit. I don't have to do what you tell me to do, and I don't like being called Beni! I should be working already anyway," Benayahu stormed off in another direction, calling back over his shoulder, "I'm going to talk to the *men*. Don't wait on me."

Rut took a deep, slow breath. "I don't know what's the matter with him lately. Everything I say is somehow twisted into sounding like an attack on his character. It's not my fault Abba and Imma haven't let him take a job outside of the house yet. They just don't think he's responsible enough."

"Never mind him, Rut. Asa is here?"

"Mhmm," Rut mumbled as if not even surprised by the appearance of the boy they'd know all their lives, who was quickly standing out as a fine young man. "Again, if you weren't so focused on me, you would have noticed him by now."

Rut pointed a finger, and Shamira turned her head in its direction. There he was—the mysterious, handsome, and elusive Asa ben Avram. Shamira hoped he would be as happy to see her as she was to see him. At the same time, she was concerned that like her abba, Asa would also be disappointed with her actions.

"What's he doing here?"

"Herding sheep?" said Rut in jest, giving Shamira a sideways glance as she arranged the loaves and fruits they'd brought with them in neatly wrapped individual servings. Rut was such a good hostess. Shamira always admired the way she could make a simple meal look like a banquet.

Shamira began to fiddle with the bit of hair at the end of her braid, plaiting and unplaiting. "Should I... Should we... What about the..."

"Oh, just go talk to him already," Rut laughed. "You're not helping me any by just staring at him and whispering half-sentences to yourself."

"Are you sure it's all right?" said Shamira.

She was ready to run to Asa's arms in a heartbeat, but she restrained herself for two reasons. The first being it would have been wildly inappropriate for her to do so, and even if it wasn't, Asa had never actually opened his arms to her. The second being she felt like she was often leaving her work for others to do, and Shamira didn't want Rut to feel overburdened.

"There's hardly anything to do here Shamira. Just don't stray too far and be sure to invite him to eat with us! Even if Beni doesn't like sitting with me, he always enjoys spending time with Asa."

"All right," said Shamira, already too far gone for Rut to hear.

He saw Shamira's slight, elegant frame walking toward him and smiled, laughing in spite of himself. He knew if Shamira could hear even half of his thoughts, she would throw a fit. Never in a thousand years would she have described herself as elegant, but then, Asa didn't really care how she would have described herself. He was so sure she would be his one day; nothing anyone said or did to dissuade him would keep him from pursuing her. From the moment he first saw her when they were children, his heart had been inexplicably and irrevocably bound to hers.

"What are you doing here?" she asked in a practical, focused tone. Could she really pretend not to notice the emotions they shared? Age had made her shy, but Asa knew the fiery spirit he had first admired was still inside of her somewhere. It's what attracted him to her so much.

"I'm working!" he said, proudly raising the shepherd's staff he'd found discarded in the fields high up in the air. Although it wasn't the truth, he enjoyed the look of shock and disbelief on her face far too much.

That caught her attention. *"Working?"*

When she crossed her hands over her waist and wrinkled her nose in that most adorable way unique to Shamira and Shamira alone, he couldn't keep his secrets from her any longer. He also knew she was probably irritated with him and his lack of direct answers, but regardless of that fact, he still found her irresistible. Maybe even more so than usual.

"Alright, I'm not working." He lowered the shepherd's staff to his side. "I was outside of your house when I heard you gathering the children to come here. Rather than wait, I thought I'd hurry down some side streets and try to surprise you." A wry grin spread across his face as he watched her go from being utterly shocked to something further beyond that. He had always loved surprising her when she least expected it, ever since they were children.

"What about your father?" she asked, her mouth agape.

"What about him?" He forced himself to chuckle, masking how he really felt.

"Asa! You know very well you can't just show up here after what happened at the temple without explaining. At least not to me." She snatched the rod out of his hand, grabbing his arm with the crook of it and stopping him from escaping her questions. He relaxed, letting her think she'd won this battle.

"All right, all right, shepherdess." He smiled at her, gently removing himself from the crook of the staff and removing the staff from her surprisingly strong grasp. "My father dismissed me from my studies early today and told me to go home, but he didn't say to go straight home, and he still won't be finished at the temple for several more hours. I wanted to see you."

"Are you sure you will not get into more trouble on my account?" She lowered her voice to a whisper, her eyes widening.

"He can't object to what I do with my free time, so long as I always do what he says during the rest of the day." He took a long, deep breath.

Her eyes kept darting back and forth, searching his. "Why are you here?"

Asa had already answered that question, but he knew that wasn't what she meant. She was asking why he would take such a risk to see her.

He looked down at her, completely losing himself in her

wide honey-brown eyes. He admired the way little wisps of her hair fell, framing her face and blowing back and forth in the gentle breeze. She took his breath away, and he could barely speak.

"Isn't it obvious?" he whispered.

He wanted to see her. He *had* to see her. She was the light of his life. If only he could work and earn a real wage, then he might be able to offer a *mohar* sooner rather than later. Although his father would look down upon them, Asa envied the shepherds in the fields who chose their own paths and earned their own money. Asa's paths would always be directed by his father, and his father would never approve of him taking on another job if it would distract him from his studies. On top of that, he was certain his father was unlikely to contribute to a bride-price, particularly if Asa wanted to marry Shamira. Because of that, he saved what coin he was allotted, but it could take him a long time to earn the money on his own.

Still, he would take that chance—it was all he had, and Shamira was worth waiting for.

"Would you like to join us for a meal?" she began. "Rut and I have brought some food for Tamir and the others. Since you work for my father now, I suppose that includes you."

He could tell the timing of the invitation was an attempt to divert his attention to something else. Asa looked away, feeling somewhat embarrassed at the effect Shamira's mere presence had on him.

"Of course."

They took a few steps together in unison before Shamira stopped abruptly.

"Asa, I want to say something," she announced, avoiding eye contact.

"I can tell." He smiled, halting just a few paces ahead.

"I wanted to… First, I wanted to say thank you for talking to Benayahu at the temple. He hasn't been acting himself lately and—"

"Oh, he's acting like every other boy his age. Wanting to become a man overnight, feeling as though the passage of time has made him a man, and being frustrated the rest of the world hasn't recognized it yet. He just hasn't realized there is more to becoming a man than age. Don't worry about it, it was nothing." Asa smiled down at her. Truth be told, there was nothing he wouldn't do for Shamira's family. They felt more like kin to him than his own father and brothers.

"And" —she drew out the word— "I wanted to thank you for trying to keep me out of trouble. I made a fool out of myself, and I deeply regret that it cost so much for all of us. I just wanted you to know that I am sorry. I do appreciate you; we all do. I hope you will forgive me?" It was likely the boldest she'd ever been in sharing her true feelings. Her voice lowered, but he heard her words loud and clear as she spoke again. "I was fearful I would never see you again."

Asa wanted to reassure her she had nothing to be sorry for, that she had not made a fool out of herself, and that he loved her and her passion for her family more than anything or anyone else in the world. Such things would have been very inappropriate for two young people alone, but he knew no matter what, nothing could stop Shamira from speaking her mind, especially where her family was involved, even if it got her into trouble. He thought it was her best quality.

"It's all right, Shamira. My abba was in a disagreeable way; that's not abnormal. I'm just sorry it happened at your family's expense." He raised his hand up to his head, scratching his forehead and pushing the wild blackish-brown curls out of his face.

"What had him so upset?" It was a silly question, since Asa's father was nearly always upset about something.

"It's just that… there have been… *Rumors.*"

"Rumors?" asked Shamira.

"From Bethany. A teacher there has reportedly raised a man from the dead." Asa spoke carefully. Each word felt like a war within himself, with two sides pulling him apart. His father's piety and narrow-mindedness fought against his own curiosity and conviction.

*"*The dead? They say this man can raise people from the dead?"

Asa continued to explain. "It's not the first time my abba has had dealings with this man. He is called Jesus of Nazareth, and they say he has performed all kinds of miracles. According to my abba, he is nothing more than a wicked blasphemer who claims to have the authority to forgive sins. Apparently, he is planning to return to Jerusalem for the Pesach. My abba and the other members of the Sanhedrin have been very busy trying to… decide what they will do."

"Miracles?"

Her whole body lunged forward. She seemed more interested in hearing about this man than she'd ever been about any of Asa's temple-related anecdotes, and he knew exactly why. She was the only girl he knew who was more interested in Messianic prophecy than ketubahs and wedding plans.

"What do you think?" she asked.

Asa studied her and marveled at how she hung on his every word, but he questioned whether or not she was more interested in what he had to say about the Nazarene than anything *he* actually had to say. He didn't mind though; he was happy to converse with her on any subject.

"He has a great following. People have been making large claims about him. Some say he may even be the Messiah."

"The Messiah!" Shamira exclaimed, "I knew it!"

"That's what *people* say," Asa reminded her. He wasn't aware of any definitive proof, and he didn't want Shamira to get caught up in something even worse the next time she encountered his father. He could tell she was already far too interested for her own good.

"What do *you* say?" said Shamira.

He had to answer her. There was no way he could deny her. Asa knew Shamira was well aware of that fact as well, which was why she pressed him.

Asa bit his lip trying to come up with an adequate response. To say yes would give Shamira hope and joy, but it would also be in direct betrayal of his father. Even if he didn't agree with his father's practices, could he really betray him?

Instead, he compromised. "I think I would like to know more of this man before I come to a decision."

"But do you think he *could* be the Messiah?"

Asa chuckled. "Why so many questions, Shamira?"

"I just need to know, Asa."

The stern tone in her voice and the way she narrowed her eyes at him told Asa she was being completely serious. Besides, he knew exactly why she needed to know. He didn't need to hear the answer out loud.

He sighed. "It is hard for me to believe God wills the continued persecution of the poor and the oppressed by our leaders and those in power. I've witnessed it first-hand. I think if the Messiah were here, in our midst, right now..." Asa was beginning to drift away, lost in his own thoughts. "I think that is exactly where he would be: with the poor and the oppressed, like this Jesus of Nazareth."

"Oh!" Shamira spun around, nearly tripping on her own feet.

Her laugh was contagious, and Asa couldn't help but join her. He admired her smile and the way her dark hair took on different shades of rich brown and honey when the sun caught it. He had always found the little lines that appeared around her nose when she laughed so endearing, and today was no exception.

Certainly, she had played at being stubborn and disinterested in him since they were children, but he knew he could never care for anyone the way he cared for Shamira.

"Asa, I need you to find out more about him. For me, Asa. For me, *find him.*"

He looked down at her, finding it difficult to respond for possibly the first time since he realized he was in love with her. Conversation with her had always been easy before, but this was no ordinary conversation. To seek out this teacher would go against everything his father so firmly believed and taught. To dismiss the teacher as his father had would go against everything that anchored Asa: that God is a God of love, not hatred, not oppression, not harsh judgment.

Asa didn't understand everything about God, and he doubted he ever would, but if there was one thing he did understand, it was love. He would do anything for the impulsive, brown-eyed girl in front of him because he loved her.

So, he tentatively reached out and brushed Shamira's

shoulder. It was an unexpected touch, maybe even too bold for him. Looking into her eyes past his own reflection, he could tell that every fiber of Shamira's being was counting on him to find Jesus of Nazareth.

Equally consumed by adoration and trepidation, he whispered, "All right." He cleared his throat and then quickly added, "Whatever you ask of me, I will do it," before walking forward. He had surrendered to her, whatever the cost to himself. They took a few steps together in unison back toward her other cousins, who were waving them over to hurry for the food. As they walked, he continued, emphasizing each word so she knew the truth of them.

"And Shamira, no matter what happens, I will always find a way to see you again."

"Then the eyes of the blind will be opened, and the ears of the deaf unstopped. Then the lame will leap like a deer, and the tongue of the mute will sing for joy, for water will gush in the wilderness, and streams in the desert;" - Isaiah 35:5-6 CSB

"Boys!" Shamira cried out, distressed at the scene she saw playing out in front of her. The two boys ran in circles, making wild motions with their hands, shouting, lunging at each other, and playing rough. "Stop this at once!"

"Shamira, we were only playing," Yuval said as he rolled his eyes.

"You're getting old enough to know the difference between playing nicely and taunting others."

"Gilad and I were having fun, Shamira. No one was getting hurt."

The way Yuval continued to talk back to her set her on edge. She often thought if their father were around more often as an example, they might not have been so disrespectful to the others in the house, but she would not say such a thing out loud. That was between Dodh Tamir and Dodah Chava. It was their marriage and children. Shamira was only their cousin after all, but even as their cousin, she was permitted to discipline them in a few ways.

Resting the bowl she had been carrying on her hip, she admonished them. "I'm not talking about Gilad." She pointed her eyes in the direction of one very frightened nine-year-old little girl, curled up in the corner.

The boys were playing a familiar game. One of them would pretend to be a wild animal, usually a mountain lion, preying upon defenseless sheep. The other would play the shepherd and would do his best to fight off the attacker. But Libi didn't have that context. All she saw was her brothers fighting against one another. She looked horrified.

Gilad lowered his head and apologized. "I'm sorry, Shamira."

"Don't apologize to me; apologize to your sister."

"But she can't—" Yuval began, cut off by his older brother's hand hitting him smack in the middle of his face.

"Apologize." Shamira commanded them.

The boys walked toward their sister, dragging their feet and saying in unison: "We're sorry, Libi."

"It was only pretend," said Yuval, crossing his arms and shaking his head in an attempt to show Libi it was not true.

"We're not really mad at each other," said Gilad, reaching out a hand to Yuval, demonstrating that they were on peaceful terms.

When they had finished, they turned to Shamira, their eager eyes seeking approval. While she might have tried to be a little more creative when giving an apology, or at least a little bit more sincere, she couldn't fault them for being children. The simple apology was enough, and Libi was already relaxing.

"Do you see? She understands you."

"May we go play now?" Gilad whined ever so slightly.

Shamira, who had been trying to be disciplinary, shouldn't have laughed at him, but she couldn't help herself. All Gilad and Yuval wanted to do, and probably all they could think about was having fun. She wouldn't take that from either of them. They both still had a few more years ahead of them before they would be considered young men. Meanwhile, these years were meant to be played away.

Shamira smiled and said, "Yes, you may go play." She ran her hand through his curls, messing them up and making them twirl in all different directions. Gilad shook it off and turned to go. Shamira called as he ran: "But play in the courtyard and out of the way of the others, all right?"

Shamira didn't bother to listen for an answer. They were already halfway down the stairs, leaving her alone in the upper room with Libi. Shamira cleared Libi's mat of her brothers' cast-off belongings and took a seat there for herself. She motioned to the space next to her and beckoned Libi to join her. The girl smiled in understanding, and her wide eyes lit up with excitement and anticipation.

Shamira placed the bowl she had been carrying between them and Libi leaned over its edge, gazing upon its contents, which would not be unfamiliar to her. Some time ago, Shamira had started getting Libi to help her make the bread by kneading the dough. It was a simple enough task, and the way it made Libi's gray eyes shine like silver showed Shamira the girl very much enjoyed being involved. She imagined Libi's existence would have been very solemn otherwise, since most things were done for her. It wasn't intentional that Libi was so often left out of helping. On the contrary, everyone was always trying to involve Libi in daily activities, but Dodah Chava often kept her close.

Somewhere along the line, kneading had become a sort of secret task between Libi and Shamira. She did the hard work of grinding the grain down to flour and Rut the more precise task of measuring the water, salt, and just the tiniest bit of leaven. When it came time to knead the dough, Shamira would enlist Libi's help.

Libi looked up at Shamira, blinking her long, dark lashes several times as though she were asking for permission. Shamira nodded her head and lifted up her hands, curling and uncurling her fingers to make the motion of kneading. Then, she took

Libi's hand and placed it in the bowl to begin the process.

Libi's lips spread into a wide smile. Little by little, she pulled, squeezed, and rolled the dough until it couldn't be kneaded anymore. Shamira was grateful for the help, and truth be told, Libi's speed and dedication had begun to rival Shamira's. No one, save Rut, knew about Libi's hand in the breadmaking, so nobody ever noticed how Libi beamed so much with pride when the bread was presented at mealtime. The fact that it helped Shamira get the work done twice as fast was a mere afterthought, quick and fleeting.

"Libi?" Shamira whispered. "May I tell you a secret?"

Libi slowly raised her head to read Shamira's face. Shamira's movements must've drawn Libi's attention to her, because despite the fact that she knew better, it was almost as if Libi had *heard* her whisper.

"Yesterday, Asa told me about a man. A teacher who has been travelling the land, speaking about the Lord and the forgiveness of sins." She paused mid-thought, glancing up to make sure no one was nearby. It had been risky enough, pressing Asa for more and more information. She didn't want to risk getting anyone else involved.

After a while, she continued. "They even say he has healed people from their afflictions and raised the dead to life!"

Chills ran down Shamira's spine just thinking about it. She pondered the Lord's promises of deliverance, redemption, and a Savior for all people.

"Libi?" she leaned in closer. "I believe that man is the Messiah." Shamira said it somberly, knowing that in saying so she could very well be accused of blasphemy. But she knew she *had* to tell someone, and a very peculiar thing happened when she did.

Libi smiled.

An indescribable feeling of hope swelled inside of her. Everything in her life was about to change, and she wanted to remember what it felt like to have so much faith in a man she'd never seen, to see a light in the darkness that few others could see, and to be on the very precipice of it all, waiting for God to answer the prayers of countless generations. At that very moment, it was highly possible that His lips were parting to form the answer. Oh, how she looked forward to hearing those words.

How powerful they would be.

Shamira arose to take the now thoroughly kneaded bread back to the kitchen. The next step required the bread to be separated into what would become loaves after they had been left to rise and then baked in the clay oven. Before she could do so, Shamira was distracted by a call from downstairs.

"Sha-mir-a!" a familiar voice called out from somewhere in the main part of the house. It was the voice of her mother, who sounded strangely giddy for this time of day, usually the most grueling hour of work. "Shamira, come at once! Eliana is here!"

Eliana!

Shamira could scarcely believe it. It had been so long since she had seen her older sister; sometimes they went months without meeting. Shamira had no real right to intrude on the home of Matthan's family. To show up unannounced would have been abusive of their hospitality. So, their meetings usually waited until it was planned, or when Matthan had business to conduct with their family, buying wool from her sabba for their linen trade.

Not bothering to take proper care, Shamira hoisted her skirts high in the air and charged down the stairs, skidding to a halt when she'd reached the group of older women. She'd nearly dropped the bowl she'd had in her hands, but gently set it down once she'd collected herself.

Eliana rose to her feet, mirroring the joy Shamira felt herself. "Shamira! You never change, do you?" Eliana laughed. Shamira imagined she must've been a sight to behold, red in the face and panting for breath. Shamira's mother or aunts might have scolded her for making such an entrance, but Eliana would never. "I'm so happy to see you, Shamira!"

"Me too, Eliana! You have no idea how happy!" Shamira embraced her sister, and they clung to each other for a very long time before pulling apart.

Libi, of course, had followed Shamira. She tugged lightly on Eliana's sleeve.

Eliana bent down. "I am so very happy to see you too, Libi." She pointed to herself, then back to Libi, then to her own smiling face. She gave her petite cousin a gentle hug and then looked around the room. "And where is our Rut?"

"She'll be along very soon," Dodah Devorah promised. "She is just finishing up the wool project she has been working on. She hardly stops spinning it these days, but she has real talent. Her nimble fingers are perfect for the work!"

Shamira wondered how long it had been since their last reunion and how long it would be until the next. She shook her head and determined not to let such thoughts spoil the special occasion.

"Come, Eliana," said Dodah Devorah. "You were just about to tell us how things have been in your household. What news have you of Matthan and his family?"

"Oh yes," Eliana said, blinking rapidly and dabbing the corners of her eyes with her little fingers. Shamira watched as Eliana gracefully took her seat on a nearby cushion and then did the same herself. "Things have been... normal."

Shamira noticed her mother lean forward. Eliana and Shamira had their fair share of secrets, but their mother could almost always tell when one of them was holding something back in conversation. Their mother placed a supportive hand on Eliana's shoulder, and urged her forward.

"Go on, tell us what has happened since we last spoke."

Shamira watched as the tears welled up in her beloved sister's eyes and then fell in painfully large drops one by one down her cheek and onto the hem of her dress, and a beautiful dress it was.

"Oh, Imma, with every year it gets harder and harder. In the early days of our marriage, we were so happy, but now the pressures of the other family members have caused tension between us. I'm not sure I can stand it, and even worse, I'm not sure if Matthan can either."

Elisheva took the bit of cloth she kept tucked between her belt and her dress and gingerly wiped away each and every one of Eliana's tears.

"Now, now… it can't be as bad as all of that. Why don't you tell us all of the details, and we'll see if we can't work it out, hm?" Their mother half-whispered, half-spoke with all of the same tenderness she'd had when Shamira and Eliana were younger and had fallen and scraped their knees or gotten a fleeting, but painful sickness. Their imma could fix anything with a whisper and her gentle touch.

"I fear the other wives in the household despise me, and Matthan's mother does little to help the situation. She merely reminds me of my continuing failure at what she sees as my one duty: to give Matthan a child."

Shamira's own heart ached at how painful she imagined it must have been for Eliana to say those words aloud. For whatever reason, God had chosen to close her sister's womb at this time. Shamira knew what a man like Asa's father would say about such things and felt anger stirring inside her heart. She chided herself for being upset over a conversation that had not even taken place, but perhaps she was really upset at the countless similar sentiments she had heard expressed over the years. She breathed in a prayer asking for peace to calm her emotions as her sister poured out her heart.

Elisheva's back straightened. "But Matthan loves you, does he not?"

"Regardless of whether or not he loves me, Imma, the situation is not easy for him. I only meant it is hard for any man to continually return to his home, only to discover that no peace exists within its walls. I hope I didn't frighten you all! Do not fear for me; Matthan is a good man. He's a *wonderful* man. He is only weary and tired of the perpetual nagging, just as I am."

"Eliana, sometimes the Lord does things we don't understand for reasons that we can't comprehend. But Eliana, there is always a reason."

"Is there, Imma? I see no reason in this."

"Have you forgotten why I gave you your name, Eliana? When your father and I were married, I couldn't wait to have a child. I prayed every day for you, and when I conceived, I declared that I would name you Eliana if you were a girl, for God had answered my prayers, and He answered them again six years later when He gave us Shamira. Sometimes He doesn't answer us right away."

"Perhaps sometimes He doesn't answer us at all," said Eliana, the tip of her nose red from sniffling.

"He always answers, Eliana. The answer may not be what we expect, but you must keep your focus on Him. Only He can bring you joy," Elisheva advised. Eliana's frown lifted into a soft smile.

Shamira watched and listened as both Devorah and Chava also offered Eliana their sympathies and encouragement. Unlike the uneasy situation Eliana described, the women in Shamira's own home were more than friends. They had become true family. Shamira wondered if she would have such strong relationships with the family of whomever she would marry. More importantly, she wondered if that family would be Asa's.

Quickly realizing what she was thinking, Shamira drove the thoughts out of her mind. Marriage? If it meant going through everything Eliana was enduring, she would rather not. Besides, if she left her home in favor of another, who would be there to watch over her cousins? What if something happened to her family and she wasn't there to help when they needed her most? Shamira didn't want to think about leaving any of them, or any kind of change at all, but her heart still tugged at her mind, reminding her she was in love with Asa.

"Even if we never had children, I think I could learn to be happy. We were happy for so long when we were first married, but how can either of us be happy with things the way they are? The stress? The pressure? Day after day I do everything that is required of me, yet it brings no fulfillment. I feel *so empty* inside all of the time."

Shamira's blood was boiling as she thought of all the ways in which Eliana had been mistreated by that family. How they had taunted her for something that wasn't her fault. Worse, how they estimated her value upon it.

She leapt up from her seat and groaned, "I wish you didn't have to go back to that house. It isn't right for you to be treated so harshly over things you can't control."

Judging by the ghastly looks on the faces of those around her, Shamira knew she'd been a little louder than she'd intended to be.

Elisheva turned her attention to her younger daughter, who had now realized her error and was shrinking back sheepishly into the corner. "It is the way of things, Shamira. You will see soon enough."

The foreboding way her normally calm and uplifting mother had spoken made her feel uneasy. What if she didn't want to?

Or… What if she did?

JERUSALEM'S DAUGHTER

"Acknowledge that the Lord is God. He made us, and we are His - His people, the sheep of his pasture." - Psalm 100:3 CSB

The afternoon visit continued, and Shamira tried not to interject anymore into the conversation while the older, more importantly, *married* women talked among themselves. They had more in common and better advice for her dear sister's plight than she was able to offer. The sun gradually lowered until it was nearly gone completely behind the tall Jerusalem buildings. At that time, Eliana excused herself, and went to join Matthan who was waiting just outside to escort her to their home.

Shamira seized this as her opportunity. Just as Eliana had begun walking out into the courtyard, Shamira ran out the door in haste, stumbling before turning back to place her hand on the mezuzah and thank God for the unexpected blessing of Eliana's visit. Then, without skipping a beat, she jumped ahead and down the narrow path to meet her sister at the gate.

"My, Shamira! Do you ever walk like a lady?" she teased. "Imma always used to say that you never did learn to walk, you just sat up one day and started running. I'd say you never stopped!"

Shamira normally would have laughed with her sister, but a sinking feeling in her stomach at the sight of her leaving prevented her from doing so.

"Eliana... I've missed you so much."

Restraining herself no longer, Shamira wrapped both of her arms tightly around her older sister, dreaming that perhaps as long as she held onto her sister, she could hold onto the moment they shared, preventing time from passing altogether.

"Shamira, don't do this to me or we'll both end up crying all over again!" she said, half-smiling, half-tearing up.

Shamira pulled herself back, despite the fact that it caused her great pain to do so. "I'm sorry... did I ruin your visit? I didn't mean to be so rude and short, it's just that..."

"Shamira, hear me when I say this. I once had the same thoughts you have about marriage. It terrified me, and if we're going to be brutally honest, sometimes it still does. But it has good parts as well, so don't close your heart off from love so soon."

"You? You thought marriage was terrifying? You were completely in love with Matthan from the first moment that you laid eyes on him. You hardly talked of anything else." Shamira rolled her eyes. She was saying it playfully, but it was based on truth.

Tilting her head to one side, Eliana answered, "I may not have voiced my concerns, but I had them all the same. I think every girl has those doubts at least once before her marriage."

"Then why—how—did you ever get married?" she whimpered.

"Because... I love Matthan."

The answer rolled off of her tongue easily and effortlessly, like she didn't even have to think about it. Regardless of the many things she was uncertain about, Shamira knew Eliana could always count on Matthan. He was her constant. He kept her going, he kept her heart full even in the darkest of times, and

Shamira knew Eliana was facing her share of dark times.

Shamira didn't need to try to understand how Eliana felt about him; she already knew because of her own feelings for Asa. She just couldn't admit them out loud.

With Shamira's outspokenness and tendency to jump into things without really thinking about them, people would assume she would have no problem committing to spend the rest of her life with Asa. However, it was the one thing, besides controlling her tongue, that she truly struggled with at her very core. The uncertainty of it all, and the idea that she could lose everything that made her "her" in marriage, the way Eliana was no longer Eliana, but Matthan's wife.

"But don't you love your family here? How could you... was it difficult, leaving us?"

"Of course! You have never left my heart or my prayers—not for a single day. But Shamira, you must understand, my being married and living away doesn't mean I ever forget about you. Ever. It just means my situation has changed. My lot in life would be easier if I still lived at home. You all are so much more supportive than Matthan's family, but you have known me my whole life.

"Even as much as I would have enjoyed staying, it simply isn't the way of things. I made sacrifices to be with Matthan, certainly, but I made them because I love him, and I wanted to be married to him. I wanted to spend the rest of my life with him." Eliana cleared her throat. "I really must be going, though. I'll try to come and see you again soon though—I promise."

"You better keep that promise, sister."

"I will, and I will keep praying for you as well." Eliana finished, smiling as she walked toward Matthan who was just outside with their abba.

After all of their conversations, Eliana had every right to be selfish, but even after everything, she was still concerned about praying for others. That was who Eliana was. Shamira wished she could be more like her, but in the meantime, she was just glad she had Eliana in her life at all. As she pushed the creaking wooden gate closed, Shamira whipped around on her heels, startled when she came face to face with her savta, nearly knocking her over.

"Savta! How long have you been standing there?" Shamira placed a hand over her chest, taking in a few deep breaths to steady herself.

"Long enough, child." Hodiyah smiled. Her eyes twinkled with youthful mischief even after all of her years. Shamira wanted to correct her and say she wasn't a child anymore, but in truth she didn't mind the endearment one bit coming from her grandmother.

"Oh," Shamira sighed. "Well, I'll just be heading inside now. I'm sure that there is still a lot of work to be done for this evening's meal, and I don't think I ever finished making the bread. Imma will be very cross if I don't return soon and take it to the kitchen to rise."

Hodiyah grasped Shamira's elbow, keeping her from running off. Her grandmother's grip shocked her, and to her surprise, Shamira could not escape.

"Not so fast. I think it's about time you and I had a little talk."

"Savta—"

"No objections, you're always running around, Shamira. Talking to Rut, your grandfather, looking out for Libi and the boys. Stop running and talk to me, your dear old grandmother." She grinned impishly.

Hodiyah led Shamira over to the bench beneath the tree in the courtyard. Shamira could remember back when the tree was not much for shade, when it was just a sapling she and Eliana often played beside. Now it was big enough that Chava's boys could hide behind it in a game, which they were doing now.

"Yuval, Gilad. Go inside," Savta directed.

"But Savta…"

"Just while Shamira and I talk. Perhaps you can ask your imma if she will let you sneak a few of the dates I've set aside for dinner, hm?"

Savta gave them that very special look that was uniquely her own, and they obliged, hopping down from the branches and running inside. Then Savta claimed the shaded area for herself and Shamira.

"Now we can really talk."

"What if I'm too weary to talk?"

Shamira had just about had enough talking. Every time she opened her mouth it seemed like she did something wrong, and she was exhausted of that feeling. If Sabba was right and her words had power, then why had she yet to do anything good with them?

"Then let me talk." Savta patted Shamira on the back. "You know, I was around your age when I married your sabba. We lived in Bethlehem back then. He had approached my father about my hand in marriage when we were quite young. My father saw it as a good match. Eliyahu was a distant kinsman. He had a steady job, and he could provide for me in all of the ways my father expected him to. They had arranged a meal so we could meet and see if we were compatible. Little did any of them know I was already very well aware of who Eliyahu was."

A wry smile stretched across her face, creating new lines between the ones that were already a part of her.

"You were?" Shamira's eyes widened. She didn't want to talk necessarily, but she was always in the mood for a good story. She had no idea there was more to her grandparents' love story, and she waited on bated breath to hear the tale.

"I was," she half-whispered. Savta's eyes glossed over as she continued. "I would suspect every young girl in the town was aware of Eliyahu. He was not so much older than the rest of us, but he certainly looked it. He was taller and much stronger than half the young men his age, and such a hard worker too! I think all the girls in the village pined for him, someone dedicated to their work and all."

"Are you sure it wasn't his appearance? So *tall* and *strong?*" Shamira teased, over-exaggerating each word as she said it.

"Shamira," said Savta Hodiyah while laughing. *"That* was a very long time ago!"

"Well, it must have at least been a part of it!" She smiled, her heart bubbling as she imagined what their budding romance must have been like.

"All right, all right, I admired him very much. But it takes more than physical attraction to make a relationship last as long as ours has. It takes hard work, and occasionally, sacrifice. However, if you truly love the other person, then it is more than worth it for the wonderful life you will get to share."

"I know that, Savta."

"Then why do you recoil every time you hear the word 'marriage?'"

Though they were not unkind words, Shamira felt a sting. Did she truly appear to abhor the idea of marriage so much it was readable on her expression? That wasn't what she meant at all. It wasn't that she was closed off to love; she was closed off to the idea that if she was married, she'd be leaving behind everything she'd ever known. Would it be worth it?

"I do not think that is it, Savta..."

"It is that you care so much for your family, you're not sure how you could part from them. It is that you are afraid of change because until recently, every day of your life has been relatively the same, but as you've grown up you've had to face all kinds of unwelcome changes. It is that you are such a *strong* girl, you aren't sure about being vulnerable to another person."

Shamira wanted to ask her grandmother how she possibly could have known and understood all of that, when Shamira herself barely even understood it, but Hodiyah was already opening her mouth to speak again.

"Shamira, marriage is hard for every girl. Leaving my brothers and sisters on my wedding day may have been the hardest thing I've ever done. I couldn't imagine not seeing them every single day as I once had, but it was not a very long distance. I saw them often enough, and if I'm being perfectly honest, in those first few months I don't think I minded the distance at all, if you know what I mean... But there came a time when your sabba had decided it was time to move on from Bethlehem. There were many contributing factors to that decision, having our three sons was one of them, but mainly, it was that night out in the fields."

Shamira had never once considered what her sabba's miraculous story would have been like for her savta. It seemed erroneous now that she thought about it, to have never considered her grandmother's perspective.

"What was it like, Savta? The night that Sabba saw the angels?" Her heart began to race at the mention of the angels, the miracle, the prophecy, and the idea of Jesus of Nazareth.

"Well, Shamira. To be honest, for me it was confusing. I saw no angels; I received no special proclamation. When your sabba told me about everything that had happened... I am ashamed to admit that it made me angry. Not just with him but with God. It didn't even matter to me whether or not I believed him. All that mattered was that it had happened to him, not me."

"Did you believe him?"

"I don't think I did right away... It was difficult at first. Nobody in the village believed him! They called him crazy, said he was mad, a downright lunatic. That's when things started to get worse for us in Bethlehem. That story drove us away from his family. It drove us away from the whole town! Eventually, people stopped speaking to me, and then they stopped letting their children play with ours—your abba and uncles, that is. I considered taking the children and leaving, returning to my father's house, in the hopes he might come to his senses. But he didn't 'come to his senses.' I did. I knew I couldn't leave him."

"So, you *did* believe him?"

"I left with him. Life in Bethlehem had become... difficult. It was difficult leaving my family, but it wasn't as difficult as it would have been if we'd stayed there. We were making arrangements to leave Bethlehem and begin a new life somewhere else when... this may be difficult for you to hear, Shamira. The king at the time, King Herod, had heard of this rumor that a king had been born in Bethlehem. This little story I thought your grandfather had just made or possibly dreamed up had made it all the way to the ears of King Herod! But the king wasn't very happy about the idea of a new ruler. Shamira— he ordered the slaughter of all the boys in Bethlehem under two years of age."

Shamira turned a ghostly shade of white, and her heart fell into the pit of her stomach. Her father and Dodh Binyamin would've been older by then, but that didn't mean her family had been untouched by such horrific acts. "But... what about... Tamir?"

"Tamir is our youngest boy, but he had been a toddler when it all happened. By the time the execution was ordered, he was even older. By God's grace, he was spared."

"Praise the Lord!" she sighed deeply.

"Yes, praise Him for all of our sakes. But there were many others who were not so blessed that day. The Lord gives and takes away, and for your sabba's brother Zevulun, your great-uncle... He took away."

"Sabba's brother... that would mean—"

"Your father's cousin was one of many boys slain that day. He was small, but they had played together often. Before it happened, our families all used to be so close. We thought we would raise our sons together. Zevulun's son was named Asher. They'd had many daughters, but Asher was their only son, and Zevulun had been taken with him since the moment he was born.

"When Asher... when Asher was killed, it put a divide between Zevulun and Eliyahu that neither would cross. We were grieved for them; they had lost a son, and we had lost a nephew. But that didn't matter. In their eyes, your sabba was at least in part responsible, and even that small part of responsibility was enough to make Zevulun vow never to speak to Eliyahu again. We tried to help them. Many times, I visited and tried to bring food. We did everything we could.

"Eventually, Zevulun's heart grew too hard for even the love of a brother to break through. It was more than just his anger at losing Asher—it was his jealousy that our boys were still alive. He threatened Eliyahu, and said he never wanted to see any of us ever again."

"Oh, Savta!"

"Their father had hoped one day they would manage the sheep together, but I think even he understood such peace between us was nearly impossible. Regretfully, he split the livestock between your sabba and Zevulun. We packed our things, took what little we had, and of course all the animals entrusted to us, and made way for Jerusalem. It wasn't a long journey, but it felt arduous. Mind you, I was still very angry about having my entire life uprooted! I was moving away from Bethlehem, where I had spent my whole life. I would be even farther away from my brothers and sisters, far away from everything I had ever known. Aharon and Binyamin were coming of age, and Tamir was growing up so fast. My heart ached that my parents would no longer get to see their grandsons regularly. They would miss so much, and I would miss them.

"One of the first nights after we left Bethlehem, I remember walking away from our tent for a while, out into the open with the sheep that were still grazing under the moon. Amid all my other angry thoughts and selfish prayers, I remember wondering what possible satisfaction Eliyahu could have gotten, tending those sheep day after day, night after night. He had to lead that flock from place to place, make sure they were fed, protected, always had enough water to drink. He had to make sure they thrived—those helpless animals. A thought came to me. A thought I most assuredly do not believe was from my own mind but had been placed on my heart by God Himself. In His eyes, I was just like those foolish sheep. I needed to be wrangled in every once in a while, or I might get lost. I had to be taken care of, or I might perish. *Sometimes*, I even needed to have my entire life uprooted so I could *thrive*.

"You see, when the sheep have eaten all the grass from one part of the field, they need to uproot and go somewhere else, or they will starve and stop growing. I suspected God was trying to tell me I had grown all I could in Bethlehem, but He wanted me to keep learning, to keep growing, and to keep thriving, so He sent me to Jerusalem! I could have remained in Bethlehem, the silly, foolish, and selfish girl I was. Or, I could have taken my sons to Jerusalem and become the woman I am today, a grandmother with wonderful grandchildren, just like you. Do you understand?"

"I am beginning to," Shamira said, speaking softly.

"If I'd allowed fear—fear of leaving my family, fear of getting married, fear of the unknown—get in the way of living my life and following God's plan for me, I don't know what would have happened to me. If I had refused to follow your Sabba, Aharon would never have met your beautiful mother, and I would never have met you! The same with all of my grandchildren, and all of my many blessings. Shamira, God was keeping watch over me. He is keeping watch over Eliana, and He will keep watch over you, wherever He may guide you."

"Wherever?"

"Wherever." Savta smiled. "Whether that's into a beautiful marriage with a strong, godly man. Whether that's into a strange adventure you experience all on your own. Whether it's both of those things, and maybe even more. God will always be watching over you, like the shepherds watch over the sheep."

Shamira stared for a long while at her grandmother. She could not imagine a world where her Savta Hodiyah was not the strong, leading matriarchal figure she had known throughout her entire life. A world where she was not a role model to her, a world where she herself did not even exist.

Furthermore, she couldn't imagine what she must have been through. And Asher, the baby boy who had been killed—was he the reason her father and uncles were so averse to Sabba's beliefs? Which reminded her, Savta had never answered her question.

"Did you—do you believe Sabba now? About the Messiah and about everything he saw?"

"Like I told you before, I didn't believe him for a long time. I thought something was terribly wrong, just like the rest. But Shamira, we both saw children slaughtered. We saw parents bury their infant sons. After that, I was sure he would give up and admit he didn't know what he was talking about. As horrific as all of it was though, your Sabba's faith in God—in what he believed he saw—never wavered. Not once. I was sure when Zevulun threatened him, he would give it all up to make peace with his brother, but he couldn't. He wouldn't. As much as it pained him to see his family members in mourning, he still believed what he had witnessed. I knew then in that moment he couldn't have made it up. He was willing to risk his life for his beliefs. How then, could I not believe him? He was passionate, like you."

Shamira turned red, but as moved as she was, she still had more questions. "What about the baby? Not Asher. What happened to the one Sabba believed to be the Messiah?"

"They disappeared one night. Just up and vanished... no one

ever saw their family again."

Shamira didn't know what to think now. She had just heard so much. She had *learned* so much. She was too stunned to speak, she just stared at the sky in wonder.

"Come, let us go inside. You were most definitely right earlier when you said there is still a lot of work to be done before the evening meal," Hodiyah said, hoisting herself up. She started toward the house but turned back and added, "But Shamira?"

"Yes?"

"You could get the day's work done in half the time if you let Libi help you more." Hodiyah winked and walked into the house, with an added spring in her step. Shamira's jaw dropped.

Savta had known what they'd been up to the whole time. Had it ever been a secret?

"Mira... Can I ask you something?" Rut propped herself up on her mat. After Eliana's visit, there had been much work to do to finish the evening meal, and even more to do with taking care of the children. Now, late in the night, they were just getting ready to sleep, rest, and awaken with replenished energy for the next day. It was one of Shamira's favorite times, often side by side at their small window, sometimes stretched on their mats, but sharing and talking together, even as they drifted to sleep.

Rut's question didn't wake her; Shamira could hardly call what she was doing sleeping. She had been tossing and turning since her head hit the mat. Her mind was captivated by thoughts of the mysterious Jesus of Nazareth. Shamira wondered what he was like. Was he full of light as her grandfather, Sabba Eliyahu, had described? Was being in his presence as humbling and awe-inspiring as he had said it was? She wondered what other things he had done, beyond raising the man from the dead in Bethany.

Her first thought went to Libi. Could Jesus of Nazareth restore her hearing?

"Anything…" she said, yawning as she answered Rut's question. She stretched her arms over her head and rolled onto her side to face her cousin.

"Do you love Asa?"

"Rut!" She tossed a cushion at her cousin. "What makes you ask that?"

"Shamira, I think it's obvious to everyone that you feel *something* for him, except maybe you," she whispered, throwing the cushion back. "But I wonder if you know what we see."

Wrinkling her nose, she looked away from her cousin, avoiding eye contact as much as possible in their small, shared space. She loved having Rut so close by, even if she did ask petulant questions sometimes.

"What does it matter if I do? I hardly have time for such dreams," said Shamira defensively.

Rut took in a sharp, quick breath. "Why do you act that way all of the time? As if marriage is a frivolity not to be bothered with?"

Tossing her head back onto the cushion in defeat, Shamira groaned, "I don't think that, Rut…"

"What if I wanted to get married? How would you feel about that? Because that's all I want. To have someone look at me the way that Asa looks at you—someday." Rut was asking difficult questions.

"I…" Shamira began, struggling to voice her feelings. "I would be very happy for you, if that's what you really wanted."

"Is it not what you want?"

"I don't know. I mean, I do. But it seems so impossible. It could never be."

"Why not?"

"Why is it so important to you right now?" Shamira redirected the discussion and hoped it wouldn't come back around.

"It's not!" Rut crossed her arms. "We used to talk about everything together. I don't see why things would start being different now, but if you truly don't want to discuss it, just say the word, and I'll never bring it up again. I promise."

Rut was not just a cousin; she was a good friend and Shamira was blessed to have her in her life. Rut's words hit their target directly in the middle of Shamira's heart. She winced at how sharp and short she had been. They *had* always talked about everything; what was it that made her feel so defensive about this particular topic?

Perhaps, as Savta had said, it was the fear that if she admitted she had feelings for Asa, she could never take them back. If a betrothal ever did come, then there would be a wedding and a wedding meant two things: the union of the bride and groom, which was a joyful thing, and the separation of the bride and her family, which terrified her.

Then came children.

What if she couldn't have children? Would she be cast aside? Or what if she did, and by no fault of their own, they were born deaf or blind or mute—and Shamira was blamed? What if none of that happened, and she carried many healthy, beautiful children into this world, but only girls and no boys? Would she be considered a failure? A commodity with no real purpose, except to bear sons, which she might not be able to do?

If she married, what would she be giving up? Shamira wasn't sure she could endure any of those things. Still, to keep her thoughts from her dearest cousin meant a kind of separation worse than the one she already feared. A loss of their friendship entirely.

"I'm afraid."

It was barely a whisper, but Rut heard it all the same. Shamira had never been very good at admitting she was afraid. She had always seen herself as the strong, independent one. Others had seen her as the confident one who was often saying too much. Admitting she was scared took its toll on her pride. She didn't think that she could ever be considered the protective, older, wiser cousin if others knew that she had all of these fears hidden away in her heart.

"You? Afraid?" Rut gasped.

"Rut, you can't possibly understand. You're just—"

"What? Too young? We're practically the same age, so you

can't use that argument on me like you'd use it on the boys. And Shamira—just because you're the oldest doesn't mean you have to put all of this pressure on yourself. We're cousins by blood, but sisters in our hearts. You don't need to protect me or be an example. You can share things with me. I'm your cousin after all, not your daughter."

Shamira could hold herself together no longer. Instead, she let everything out, crying: "I never wanted to fall in love! The very night of Eliana's wedding, I promised myself I would never marry. I was just a young girl, and I wanted to be with Abba and Imma forever. I suppose I might have grown out of it, but I've seen Eliana suffer so much. You heard her story, Rut. You know how Matthan's family treats her. She's lucky that Matthan is so gracious and loving to her; not all men are so kind. What if I were to be trapped in a marriage and was not so fortunate? A loveless marriage where every day, each of my failings and shortcomings were made known to me. The same night I promised myself that I wouldn't marry, was the night I met Asa…"

Rut pulled Shamira's shaking body into her arms, inching their mats even closer together. Shamira continued to tremble as a few rebellious tears trickled down her cheek, but she found much comfort in the reminder that she and Rut did not have to be so separate from one another. Maybe it was because she was always busy watching the younger children that she hadn't noticed the incredible woman Rut had become right beside her. She was loving, patient, and kind, but stern when she had to be.

"Oh, Mira."

Rut was always good at providing comfort and solace to the younger children, and Shamira was at this moment no different from them.

"Shamira, look at me," she said, leaning back and straightening herself. "I am in the same position you are. There is nothing different. I am a young woman of a marriageable age. I know your fears and concerns, but I look forward to marriage as a blessing. Who is to say we cannot both marry men that we love, and men who love us in return? That's my prayer and I know it is yours too, but you still haven't answered my question," Rut reminded her.

"What question?"

"Are you in love with Asa ben Avram?"

Shamira sighed. "He is a good man. He has been kind to our family for years, and the children love having him around."

"But do you love him?" she repeated.

"I… I still don't know what I want, Rut."

Rut yawned and fell back onto her own mat. "You don't need to know what you want in order to know what you feel."

"It would be impossible for us to marry."

"Why?" Rut growled into her blanket. "Why do you think it's so impossible?"

Shamira could barely even begin to organize all of her reasons into a single answer. "He is the son of a priest! A very important priest, at that. They are a part of Jerusalem's elite. Who am I? A girl from the lower city with no advantages, nothing that would make me a 'smart match' for a young man of his standing. Eliana was lucky to be married to Matthan. They are a wealthy family, with business ties from here all the way to Rome. But me…wed Asa? It would be impossible. I'm no one."

"Mira… Has Asa ever, *ever* said anything like that to you?"

Rut was right and Shamira knew it, but it didn't make believing it any easier.

"No…"

"Because he cares about you. Not your status. The only thing that seems impossible to me is the idea that Asa would ever marry anyone *other* than you. You're the one who won't let the relationship get any further," Rut sighed. "And to be honest, if you really believe such things about Asa, then maybe you are right to not want to marry him. It would seem like you don't know him at all."

That hurt. Shamira knew his heart like her own. She knew Rut was telling the truth. She knew Rut had every reason to say the things she'd said. That didn't make hearing them any easier. Why was she doing everything in her power to convince herself there was nothing between them?

"I do know him." It took courage for her to speak the words out loud.

"I've known both of you for years now. You're both stubborn people. You're stubborn because you won't let yourself even entertain the thought of marrying the man of your dreams. He's stubborn because he wouldn't let anything get in the way of marrying the woman of his. Not social status. Not money. Not even his abba's expectations. Mark my words, Mira. Asa will have no one, except you. You said yourself that words have power—use your words to pray to God and ask Him to make all things right in His timing."

"Mark your words?" Shamira questioned.

"Mhmm." She nodded. "I have a good feeling..." she said with a smirk.

"What do you mean?" said Shamira, now completely engaged in the conversation.

Rut chuckled low and under her breath. "Goodnight, Shamira."

"Rut? Rut?" Shamira whisper-shouted into the darkness. It was no use. Rut had rolled onto her side and had made it very clear she wouldn't be saying anything else.

What could she have meant? Shamira would definitely need the Lord's mercy and comfort tonight. There were so many questions whirling through her mind, she felt as though she would never get to sleep without divine intervention. At least one question had been answered: Shamira loved Asa ben Avram, and she could admit it. What she needed to do now was learn to trust in the Lord, as Rut had said, and wait on His timing. That brought another thought to her mind—she couldn't wait for the Messiah to come.

"Six days before the Passover, Jesus came to Bethany where Lazarus was, the one Jesus had raised from the dead." - John 12:1 CSB

"Ach!" Asa shouted. Another rock had found its way into his sandal. He bent down to remove the impediment and toss it back on the road behind him. When he touched his sandal, the wretched thing completely fell apart and down to the ground in pieces, pesky pebble included.

The sandals he owned were not meant for long walks, especially on rugged terrain. Neither was his clothing. His attire was more ornamental than it was functional. He tugged at his collar and wiped the sweat from his brow. He wished he'd had more covering from the blinding sun beating down on him, but his clothes were made for display, not for practicality. They reflected his father's future for him, as he was destined to sit in the temple for hours at a time studying the Torah. This garb was not for travelling, and especially not his sandals. It was only a

127

matter of time before they were both broken.

He picked up the broken sandal to inspect it. It was useless now. To repair the damage would require the services and tools of a leatherworker. He had others at home, but he wasn't going home. He was going to Bethany.

It had been a difficult task managing to convince his father he would be spending the day with a friend. Asa didn't have very many friends, and the people his father called his friends were more like acquaintances. He only knew them from yeshiva, and rarely talked to them about anything except for their schooling. But it hadn't been a complete lie. If everything went according to plan, hopefully the people he was seeking out would become his friends. In any case, he was at least doing all of this *for* a friend, and that was close to the same thing.

When Shamira had asked him to investigate Jesus of Nazareth, he didn't want to agree, but at the same time, he had to for both her heart and his. If he didn't, he would have let Shamira down, and he never wanted to do that. With or without shoes, he would be pressing forward in the two-mile journey.

He bent down and took the other sandal off as well, seeing no sense in wearing only one, which was liable to succumb to the same fate as the other.

The walking gave him time to think, even if the majority of his thoughts were about the terrible heat. Everything he was doing right now would be wrong in his father's eyes. He would be punished without a doubt if his father ever found out.

But *why* was it wrong?

All his father ever said was that Jesus of Nazareth was a public nuisance, a blasphemer, and a threat to God's chosen people. Avram seemed to feel about Jesus the same way Asa felt about the rock caught in his sandal; they were mere obstacles to be removed. But why? Every time Asa asked the question, his father would change the subject or give him an answer that didn't really explain anything. He would remind him it wasn't his place to ask such questions, and that whatever Jesus of Nazareth did pertained to the chief priests and the chief priests alone. That made Asa curious. Curious enough to agree to a ridiculous plan and walk to Bethany. It wasn't a long walk even at a relaxed pace, but it was beginning to feel like the longest journey he would ever have to take.

Asa knew what his father wanted. He wanted his son to follow in his footsteps. To advance as a scholar, work at the temple, and serve God from within the priesthood. Nearly every day of his life had been spent in observance of the priests and their rituals. But seeing how his father treated everyone—Shamira's family included—didn't exactly make Asa feel inclined to do the same thing.

It wasn't about beliefs—or maybe it was. Asa believed in God. He believed in keeping His commandments and following the examples left in scripture, but he wasn't sure he believed in God the same way his father did. His father believed in the Law, first and foremost. In fact, sometimes it seemed like the Law was the only thing in which his father believed. But Asa had read more in the scripture to imply that God was not only a God of justice, but also a God of love. Love was something Asa wasn't even sure his father could feel. Regardless, it made Asa wonder. Were judgment and sacrifice the only components to a relationship with the Most High? Was that all there was? The Torah he was studying seemed to proclaim so much more.

"Ouch!" Asa stubbed his toe on a sharp rock.

Not having any sandals was starting to take its toll. He looked down at his foot, which was blistered from the terrain. Thankfully he wasn't that far from the town. He could find Jesus of Nazareth or one of his disciples once he was there, preferably after he found a leatherworker to mend his shoe. Then his journey would be near an end, and he'd either have one of two answers. Either Jesus was just another blasphemer, as his father claimed, or he was something more, as Shamira believed and as Asa was beginning to hope. Would he know for certain if this was the Messiah whom Shamira so desperately longed for?

"Shalom! Are you all right?" someone called out in the distance.

Asa squinted up, still bent over inspecting his foot. All he could see was a black shadow overcome by the brightness of the sun.

"Shalom," he replied. "I'm all right, thank you, just a broken sandal. Nothing more!" He hoped his response was dismissive enough so he could avoid conversation and get on with his business. He didn't have time for hospitality. He had to find the teacher from Nazareth, and then he had to get home before his father started wondering where he was.

"Do you need help?" This stranger was persistent. Too persistent.

"No, thank you!" he replied. Asa noticed the stranger coming closer. "I'm all right, just in too much of a hurry."

"What happened to your shoes?" Now the stranger was right beside him.

"Useless things, they weren't made for walking. One of the fool sandals fell apart some distance back." Asa didn't make eye contact, he just kept brushing the sand off of his feet and inspecting them for any other wounds.

"Ah, I see. Why don't you come with me? You can wash your feet, and maybe we can even find you another pair of shoes for the rest of your journey. That is, if your journey doesn't stop here?"

Asa could see no other option but to agree with the man. After all, he was going to need better shoes if he planned to make it home in a timely manner. "Very well. I can't see any good reason why not."

"All right then! My friends call me Peter. What is your name?"

"My name is Asa," he said, stretching out a hand to shake the hand of his new friend. He was a tall, burly man with weathered hands. He could tell from his physique he must've been a laborer, perhaps a carpenter or a fisherman.

"What brings you to Bethany, Asa? Did you travel far?"

"I'm from Jerusalem, so not very far. I have actually come in search of someone else… There is a teacher I'm looking for. My abba says—I mean, everyone I know says he's…different. They say he is a miracle worker who comes in the name of God."

"I see," Peter began. "And you have questions for him?"

"I don't know if I have questions *for* him, but I do have questions about him."

"What kind of questions?" Peter asked. "An hour's walk under this sun is a long way to come just to satisfy curiosity."

"I don't know," Asa muttered. "Nothing important I suppose."

"Try me," Peter insisted.

Asa sighed. There was no stopping this man. "Well, for starters, who is he really? Is he truly as powerful as they say he is? Can he really perform miracles? Is it true he claims to be the son of God? Did he really raise someone from the dead?" Asa found once he opened his mouth, he couldn't stop asking questions.

"Ah-ha, so you have a lot of questions then."

"See? I told you that you couldn't help me." Asa paused and then politely added, "Beyond my shoes, of course."

"I don't know about that."

"What do you mean?"

"The teacher you're looking for—the man called Jesus of Nazareth. I'm one of his disciples."

"You're—wait. Where are we going?"

He chuckled. "My master and the others are staying with some friends here in Bethany. That's where I'm taking you actually, if it's all right with you."

Asa was stunned. "All right? It's an answer to my prayers. Thank you!"

He was overwhelmed with the feeling that this could not have been a coincidence. This was a miracle in and of itself and hope was springing up in his soul. He had just so happened to encounter a disciple of the very man he'd set out to find, and he was now being taken to that man. God was leading him to answers, whatever answers they might be.

"Well then, come on," Peter replied, quickening his pace.

Asa didn't care how sore his feet were, not when he was so close. If he did this for Shamira, it could change everything between them. If he could give her everything she wanted, would she finally admit to her feelings for him? If he could give her what she was seeking, would it be enough to win her heart?

Even if he could win her heart… Would that be enough to sustain them?

It was a small home, but it was filled with a lot of people. Too many people for the size of the room. From what Peter had told him, Jesus of Nazareth had twelve disciples, in addition to his many followers. There were also some women who occasionally travelled with him or hosted him. Asa had been introduced to a woman called Martha, and briefly to her sister Mary when he'd first arrived. Martha had been in a hurry and hadn't stopped to say anything more than a simple greeting, and to ask Mary to set another place for him.

At first, Asa felt quite out of place, as though he were intruding on a family meal or entering someone's private home without invitation. In a way he was, but none of these people seemed to mind. In fact, they were very kind to help him and had already welcomed him, washed his feet, given him water to drink, and put out food to eat. Curiosity, and his sore feet, had compelled him to stay.

"That man over there—that's the one you serve? That's Jesus of Nazareth?" Asa gestured to a man at the end of the table, who commanded the attention of everyone in sight.

Peter looked up and nodded his head. Asa observed Jesus. He seemed to be a very pleasant man, gentle in nature. The people he was talking to appeared at ease, but then again, it didn't appear they had any reason to not be. Asa wondered what he had expected to find. A brutish man ready to lead an army into Jerusalem? Some kind of raving lunatic who couldn't speak coherently, let alone converse? By all accounts and outward appearances, Jesus was just an ordinary man, except for his alleged extraordinary abilities.

"So, Asa, tell me about yourself." The room was buzzing with people and conversations. Peter's voice was low, but Asa heard this demand loud and clear.

Asa grimaced a bit. This was the part of the conversation where Asa would have to reveal his identity, and then he'd probably be asked to leave. He at least hoped he would be asked to leave. He half-expected them to just throw him out.

"I don't really know what there is to tell." Asa stalled. "I live in Jerusalem. I heard about your teacher and decided to come here to see if the rumors were true. That's all."

"Yes, yes. You've told me why you're here, but you still haven't told me anything about yourself," said Peter, giving him a sideways glance. If he was suspicious, he had every right to be. As a disciple, he probably wanted to make sure his master was safe. Asa was a stranger to all of them. He couldn't accept their hospitality without at least being honest in return.

Seeing no way out of the conversation, Asa asked, "What would you like to know?"

Peter cleared his throat. "Well, I saw your sandals, or what's left of them anyway. They're good shoes, not for walking though. What do you do? Are you a working man?"

"I'm... training under my abba."

"What does your abba do?" countered Peter, raising an eyebrow.

He dropped his food onto the plate in front of him. "He's a priest at the temple in Jerusalem."

There. He said it.

Peter wanted a direct answer, and now he had one. Asa stood up from the cushion to leave. "I'm sorry to have taken advantage of your hospitality, and I thank you for bringing me here. I shall be going now."

"Going? Where?" asked Peter. His brow furrowed. "You haven't finished your meal yet."

"You'd dine with me, knowing my father sees your teacher as a threat to thousands of years of tradition? You can't possibly be blind to the way the priests question your teacher. They think he's mad."

"Ha!" Peter chuckled, a little bit too loudly for comfort. Asa was trying *not* to attract attention, but Peter's outburst had thrown any chance of that back onto the road to Bethany like a stone in one's shoe. "Young man, we have eaten with lepers, prostitutes, the sick, and the poor. Sitting down at a table to dine with the son of a priest will not be a challenge."

"But I...you are...but Jesus..." Asa's face reddened.

"Jesus is a teacher, and you are a student, correct?"

"Yes, technically, but—"

"Asa, Jesus wants to know you. Not who your father is or what your father has done. He would invite you to be a student of him, if only for a day. Eat a meal and see what you can learn while you're here."

Asa took a deep breath. He would not be thrown out of the house; that was a relief. Asa was still left with questions. "What about you? Who are you?"

He chuckled. "I am *really* a nobody. A fisherman from Galilee."

"Galilee? You're a long way from home then."

Peter nodded his head.

"May I ask why?" Asa continued.

"Because he asked me to."

He said it with such solemnity Asa was taken aback. Peter didn't even pause to think about his answer. This man had convictions. Convictions and beliefs Asa had yet to understand. Peter must have seen the look on Asa's face, because he stopped eating and continued on, telling the story and animating it with his expressions.

"He called me out from the shoreline. I was tired and not in the mood for conversation, if you can believe that. We hadn't caught any fish, and, as you can imagine, that was a problem. In the middle of all of that, this man, Jesus, came up and asked us to push our boats out to sea so he could teach the crowd on the shore. We were tired, hungry, and we wanted to go home. But I sensed this man wouldn't leave us be until we did as he asked, so I humored him. When he was done, he asked us to go back out to sea and let our nets down. I thought he'd gone mad. You can't catch fish at that time of day! In my own mind I planned to prove him wrong. But we did as he asked, and then... and then..."

Peter started to laugh so hard he could barely finish his sentence. "And then our boats started to sink, because the nets were so heavy with fish! We could barely pull them into our boats!" Peter was smiling, and Asa was too. His joy was contagious, and Asa was admittedly enraptured by the story, completely amazed. Suddenly, Peter sobered himself. "I left my boats and nets behind that day, and I've been following him ever since."

"But why? Why follow him?"

Asa understood the miracle. It was mind-boggling. But what he didn't understand was why Peter had continued to follow Jesus. Why didn't he just take the fish and go back to his home?

"I didn't want to at first. I wanted him to leave me alone. As soon as the fish swam into our nets, I knew exactly who he was. I can't explain it—I just knew. This man was a man of God. At once, I begged him to leave me. I didn't deserve him or his miracles. But he didn't leave me. He told me not to be afraid. He said my days catching fish were over. From now on, we'd all be fishers of men."

"Fishers of men?" Asa questioned this in his mind. Was this the revolutionary army that was being built?

"In ministry," said Peter. Asa thought he saw him wipe a tear from his eye before reaching for another piece of bread. "Jesus doesn't just preach the word of God. He preaches a message of love, a message of hope, and a message of forgiveness, based on the word of God. I was a terrible person before I met him, and I still have my faults, but he called me to be a part of his ministry. I'd never been 'called' to anything before. I'd made mistakes, put my foot in my mouth one too many times, turned more people away from me than I'd care to admit. But he called me and made me feel something. Love? Acceptance? I can't say. All I know is, if following him, learning from him, and helping him helps other people to experience what I've experienced and to feel what I feel, then it's all worth it."

"I think I can understand that," said Asa. "But... who is he to perform such miracles? Jesus of Nazareth?"

"I believe that he is the Son of God, the promised Messiah."

At this, Asa became very interested in knowing exactly what it was that made this man, and presumably everyone else in the room, declare Jesus as a Messiah. Asa had read almost every passage about the Messiah. He'd studied them all meticulously.

"The scriptures prophesy the Messiah will come from Judea,

not Nazareth in Galilee."

"He's not from Nazareth. He was born in Bethlehem during the census, but his family moved around a bit after that."

"Really?" Asa thought of Shamira's grandfather's account of the night in the field, but he kept his face straight. The story was astounding at the very least, but it could have just been a coincidence. Asa needed to know more. The student within him compelled him to keep searching.

"Yes," Peter confirmed. "Born in a stable, according to his mother and family."

Asa could barely breathe as his mind whirled, putting it all together. Jesus had been born in Bethlehem, in Judea. It was just as the scriptures foretold, and exactly as Shamira's own Sabba had remembered it. If he was the promised Messiah, he did not enter the world as Asa's father had interpreted the scriptures to declare, nor did he behave like the king that was anticipated by the zealots. He ate with the poor, the needy, the sinners. Asa had studied the scriptures for most of his life. Jesus of Nazareth certainly wasn't the Messiah he had expected, or that he had been taught to expect, but he fit so many of the prophecies. As he contemplated all these things, his thoughts trailed off into an indecipherable mess of scripture, testimony, knowledge, and belief.

"Ah, Asa! Come! Get up, there is someone I want you to meet."

Another man had entered the room, and Peter was rising to greet him.

"What? Who?" Asa asked as he also stood.

"This is Lazarus." Peter proclaimed this boldly, almost as if this should mean something to Asa.

"And this is?" Lazarus asked with curiosity.

"Excuse me, Lazarus. This is Asa, he's come from Jerusalem seeking answers about Jesus. I met him on the road and brought him here," Peter explained.

Asa smiled. "Pardon me, I didn't realize this was your home. My sincerest thanks for allowing me to visit and eat with you all. I truly didn't expect to meet anyone close to Jesus, let alone be in the same room with him or his followers. Your family's hospitality is truly appreciated." Asa bowed respectfully to the master of the house.

"Asa, it is a pleasure to meet you. I'd hope someone would do the same for myself and my family if we were weary travelers, but it is not me you should be thanking. This home belongs to a man called Simon. I am a guest here as well with my two sisters, Mary and Martha." Lazarus chuckled

"Ah, I see," said Asa respectfully. "My apologies."

"It's nothing. Besides, I'm just happy you're not here to see me. I've hardly been able to show my face in public as of late!"

"You?" asked Asa, puzzled. "Why you?"

Peter grinned, and Asa could tell there was something he had failed to mention about Lazarus, perhaps even on purpose.

"Asa, Jesus raised me from the dead," said Lazarus. Lazarus' face sobered, and his eyes grew intense, "Jesus said it best. He is the resurrection and the life. I was dead but now I live; anyone who believes in him can also live."

A story could be argued with—proven false or a lie. Asa had heard all sorts of stories from his father about the Nazarene teacher who'd been stirring up trouble in Galilee. He'd heard how Jesus had fed five-thousand people with only a few pieces of fish and some bread. He'd heard how people were claiming he'd healed the sick, the blind, the demon possessed. He'd heard of his power, what his father called trickery. But now, Asa had seen a man who had once been pronounced dead to be very much alive as he walked, talked, and dined before his very eyes. Asa could hardly argue with what he witnessed. He'd literally seen the face of Lazarus and heard his story first-hand.

It was a miracle.

He was a miracle.

At the very least, Jesus was a prophet sent by God at a time when Jerusalem was sorely in need of one. But could Asa call him Messiah? Could he ever follow him as Peter and so many others had clearly done before him? To do so would go against everything his father believed and everything his father had taught him. He'd seen the good Jesus could do, but he'd heard from his father the bad things that were happening. For many years Asa had questioned his father, maybe not outwardly, but inwardly. Why now was he leaning in on the values his father promoted and doubting the teachings and presence of the one who came in the name of the Lord?

The hospitality of these people was unending. Just as Asa had finished his food, another plate had been thrust into his hands, and it would be rude for him to refuse after all of their generosity. One of the disciples even had training in working with leather and was able to put Asa's broken sandal back together. It was a temporary fix, not perfect by any standards, but Asa and the other man were pretty certain it would hold up at least until he returned back to Jerusalem and could have it repaired properly.

"So, Asa, I'm curious to hear what you think after all of this. Have you gotten your answers?" asked Peter.

"Uh, well, I've gotten a lot of answers for a lot of questions." He tittered.

"But now you have more questions?" said Peter, chuckling.

"Yes, lots more questions."

Lazarus, who had been sitting on the other side of Asa, raised his voice to add to the conversation. "What questions do you have now? Perhaps I can help."

"Well, that's the thing. I don't know if any of you can help. It seems I've come to a precipice, and I must now decide what conclusion to draw from the evidence that has been presented to me."

"Ah, then I cannot help you there," said Lazarus. "I can give you some advice though: don't look so hard at the evidence that you miss the truth."

"No one can really help me," said Asa, callously. He had come all this way, and he was hardly better off than he was before. No real answers, only more problems. What good had this journey been? These feelings of defeat were foreign to Asa, who was used to having answers come easily to him.

"That's not true," said Peter.

"What do you mean?" Asa was sincere; he desperately wanted to understand.

"It's something Jesus said to me once before. People are always looking to label him. Prophet, lunatic, teacher, king, miracle worker, blasphemer. One night, Jesus asked us what we would label him if we had to. I told them the truth and said that I believed he was the Messiah. He replied that there was no way I could have known or believed that if it had not been made known to me by God in heaven.

"That's the way it must be for you, Asa. No one can tell you what to think about our teacher. I can't tell you what to believe about him. Lazarus can only tell you what he has done for him. The same with Simon, who used to be a Leper, and with everyone in this room. We can all tell you the facts, but only you can determine what you believe based on those facts. I urge you to pray, ask God for answers, and see what He speaks to your heart."

Asa was about to agree with him and thank him for the advice, but there was a loud commotion at the other end of the room where they were dining. A woman, the one called Mary, whom Asa had briefly met earlier, had entered the room carrying an alabaster jar of perfume. She had broken the jar, and small pieces of alabaster were all over the floor. As Jesus reclined in his seat, she began to pour perfume on his head, as if to anoint him. Asa's jaw dropped at the display.

"What is she doing?" whispered Asa.

"Mary! What are you doing? What a waste!" echoed the others in the room, in voices that were not even close to whispers.

"My sister," said Lazarus.

Some of the oil began to drip onto the floor, and Mary dropped to her knees anointing his feet with the remaining perfume. When she was done, rather than use a towel, she used her hair to dry his feet. Asa, like the rest, wondered why this woman would do such a thing.

"Why wasn't this perfume sold for three hundred denarii and given to the poor? *Hmm?* Would that not have been a better use for this perfume?" grumbled one man seated at the end of the table near Jesus. All the guests seemed to have this same sentiment. There was no lack of expression in this room.

"Oh, be quiet, Judas," Peter groaned, rolling his eyes.

Then Jesus stood at the head of the table. Asa bent forward, curious what he was about to say. He extended a hand toward Mary and helped her rise to her feet. "Leave her alone; she has kept it for the day of my burial. For you will always have the poor with you, but you will not always have me."

At this, everyone in the room fell silent again.

"What does he mean?" Asa whispered to Peter.

Peter shrugged his shoulders and opened his mouth to speak, but before he could, another loud noise drew his attention away. There was shouting in the streets. It could be heard all the way from the back room they were in, and from the sound of it, they were getting closer.

Martha entered the room quickly and approached Lazarus. "Lazarus, brother, the people know Jesus is here. They also know you are here as well. The crowds have come here to this house! They want to see proof that a man was raised from the dead!"

"This isn't even my home!" Lazarus exclaimed.

"It is our fault for imposing, not yours, Lazarus. They will follow Jesus wherever he goes," said Peter.

"I'm afraid I should be going as well. I've long overstayed my welcome, and if I don't leave now then I won't get home before dark," explained Asa as he rose from the table.

"Asa, wait," Peter said, standing up beside Asa. "Come back if you have questions, and I know you will. You won't regret following this man, if that is what you choose."

"Thank you, Peter." Asa was sincere, but he was also in a rush now; he must not be seen in this place.

"I'll be praying for you," said Peter, and then they parted ways.

It was late afternoon, just barely turning to evening. Perhaps Asa could sneak back into his house and his father might never notice just how long he'd really been gone. He ran up the steps toward his home and then very suddenly slowed his pace at the top of the staircase. Just before he opened the door, he paused to rest his hand on the mezuzah that hung beside the entryway. His fingers brushed up against the parchment where God's word had been carefully inscribed. He closed his eyes for a moment of meditation and thanks to God for His provision, and then prayed for more of His protection as he opened the door and tiptoed through the front room of his home.

All he had to do was make it to his room without being noticed by his father, mother, or younger brothers. A peculiar lamplight flickered in the distance, standing out. None of the lamps were lit and the rest of the house was overcome by the darkness that settled in their home when the sun began to make its journey to the western horizon. Usually, his mother would have had them lit by now. The only reason she wouldn't is if—

"He's a public nuisance, Avram! If we don't do something about him now, it will get out of control and all of us will be worse off for it!"

—His father had a guest. His mother would never disturb him if he had guests, even if it was getting dark. His father hated whenever his mother was near enough to hear private discussions. Better for the lamps to go unlit than to face his anger.

"I agree! More and more people are forgetting their sacrifices or foregoing them altogether in favor of following *him*. But what are you suggesting we do?" said Avram.

Asa shouldn't have been eavesdropping, but he couldn't help

himself. He could tell by his father's tone they were talking about Jesus of Nazareth. He followed the glow of the lamp to the room where his father typically conducted business. He crouched just outside the doorway to the room where his father was.

"We need to get the people to stop believing this man has any power, so what do we do? I say, we take away their so-called proof."

"What do you mean?"

"If there's no proof a miracle ever occurred…" the guest prompted.

"Then there's no proof this man is a Messiah!" said Avram, finishing the other man's thought. He hissed the words, and they echoed down the hall, bouncing off the darkened walls and haunting Asa like a ghost. "So, we kill the man they say he raised from the dead."

"He is called Lazarus of Bethany."

Asa lost all of his balance and tripped over himself, falling into the room. "What?!"

"Asa? What are you doing in here? This is none of your concern!" Avram shouted.

Asa could hardly believe what he was hearing. He knew what his father was capable of. He'd experienced his wrath first-hand on more occasions than he could count. But killing someone?

"You can't! I just saw—" Asa stopped himself just in time and hoped his father wouldn't notice.

"You just saw… *what?*"

"You can't kill a man just because of what other people say about him," said Asa firmly.

"And you have no business being in this room! Get out!" he ordered, walking toward Asa and forcing him out of the room. "This is priestly business. One day, you'll understand."

Once Asa was far enough out of the room, his father shut the door in his face.

"No, I won't," he whispered at the solid wood. He would never understand his father, and moreover he didn't want to. He could never follow in his father's footsteps if it meant becoming cold and heartless.

God could not be found in the temple where his father served, at least not for Asa. God was with Jesus of Nazareth, the Messiah. He had seen it with his own eyes and heard it in the accounts from Peter and Lazarus. At that, Asa ran to his own room and shut the door. If his father was up late talking, perhaps he would forget to discipline him.

Behind the closed door to his room, for the first time in a long time, Asa wept. His father would plot to have Lazarus and possibly even Jesus killed, and for whatever reason Asa felt like a guilty party in their ploy. At the same time, he felt utterly hopeless, and he cried for more than just Lazarus. Asa cried for every scar on his back, every wound his father had ever inflicted, every cruel word he'd ever said to him or to others. The weight of the world he lived in was heavy, and Asa had never felt so helpless.

He whispered a prayer, "God, please show me the way." In that moment, the burdens he carried began to lift.

A story could be argued with, proven false or a lie. Evidence could be tainted or destroyed by men who wanted to manipulate facts. Those who dared to disagree with the popular opinion could be killed or silenced by other means. But Asa couldn't argue with what he felt; he was certain now. His mind, heart, body, and soul were held captive by the conviction that Jesus of Nazareth was the answer to all the questions he had ever asked.

He could not ignore that; he would not ignore it. Not even if it cost him his life, as it may have cost Lazarus. He needed to tell this story to Shamira at once.

JERUSALEM'S DAUGHTER

10

"But the chief priests had decided to kill Lazarus also, because he was the reason many of the Jews were deserting them and believing in Jesus." - John 12:10-11 CSB

"Shamira, come and get the bread for dinner!" Shamira heard her mother calling from downstairs.

"Yes, Imma!" she pointed Libi toward the dinner table in the main room and gestured to her mouth to let her know it was time to eat.

Libi smiled and put her hand on her stomach.

"Oh, were you very hungry?" asked Shamira, only half-serious. Libi was growing so fast, and her appetite proved it. She smiled and nodded back and again pointed to the dinner table. "Go sit down so you're ready when we get started." She smiled as she watched Libi walk—no, run—into the adjacent room and slide onto a cushion in front of the table.

Shamira rushed around the corner toward the kitchen,

grabbing the basket of freshly baked loaves and pausing only a moment to breathe in all the scents from the delicious herbs and meats her mother and aunts had spent all day preparing.

"Hurry up and take those to the table, Shamira. We have a guest for dinner tonight—no doubt, he's very hungry."

"A guest, Imma? What guest? Who?" Shamira leaned forward, clumsily balancing the basket of bread on her hip. Her eyes darted from person to person, anxiously demanding a response.

"See for yourself. There's other work to be done here, and we don't have time to spend the whole evening answering questions while everyone else starves." Her mother's voice was teasing, but she didn't stop her work. She neatly arranged the food and handed it off to Devorah who hit Shamira with a knowing grin before heading back toward the main room of the house.

Shamira walked far faster than she should have. Not just because it was unladylike, but also because she was liable to drop the basket of bread on the floor. Hard-packed dirt was still dirt. It was a recipe for disaster.

When she finally reached the table and noticed who was sitting at the other end of it, she nearly dropped the basket despite her efforts to the contrary. She dropped her jaw instead and gasped.

"Asa? What are *you* doing here?"

"Asa is joining us for dinner, Shamira," said her father, suddenly standing behind her. "You should welcome him to our home and thank him for coming."

"Yes, Abba," said Shamira, turning bright red in the presence of Asa and all of her other family members. She could hear Beni and the other boys laughing. She jerked her head toward them and narrowed her gaze. They stopped laughing shortly thereafter.

Wise enough not to ask any more questions or embarrass herself further, Shamira carefully placed the basket on the table, and wiped up whatever was left of her pride off of the hard-packed floor. She took a seat next to Libi and waited for the other family members to gather around and for the meal to be served.

Her sabba prayed the traditional blessing and the food was passed from person to person. When the dishes came to Shamira, she served Libi before serving herself. Libi could do it very well on her own, but Shamira insisted, not even giving her the chance. The less idle time she had to endure Asa's penetrating stares and charming looks, the better. However, it became very difficult to focus as Asa's eyes seemed to burn deeper and deeper into her soul the longer he sat opposite of her. It had only been a few days since they had spoken. Why had no one mentioned to her that he would be sharing the evening meal with them? She might have tried harder to pull her unruly hair back just a little bit tighter into her braid if she had known.

"This is a delicious stew," said Asa, complimenting the ones who had made it.

Shamira's mother smiled at him, receiving the compliment gracefully and humbly. Everything in Shamira longed to speak out and to question Asa, but such bold conversation would have to wait until there were fewer pairs of ears around.

"It tastes the same as it always does," Benayahu shrugged, retreating a little within himself when Dodah Devorah gave him a pat on the back of his head.

"Well, if it's always this good, then I shall have to eat at your house more often. That is, if my presence does not test the limits of your generosity." He smiled as he spooned another bite of food into his mouth.

"You are a long-time friend and always welcome, Asa ben Avram. Our house is honored with the presence of the son of such a well-respected priest."

Shamira marveled at how her mother always knew exactly what to say, always managed such a graceful demeanor, and always appeared so kind and loving. Had her mother ever stumbled half as much as she did? Sometimes she wondered where her flightiness had come from. It seemed she was surrounded by near-perfect people all the time, and it was hard to live in the shadow of such grace and dignity.

"Someone remind me later that we need to talk about the hired shepherds. Two of them will no longer be with us by the time of the next shearing." said Shamira's Sabba Eliyahu. Meanwhile, dishes clanked together as eager mouths filled their stomachs with food; mainly Beni, Yuval, Gilad, and of course, Libi.

"Forgive me, Asa. I'm sure you don't want to hear about something as uninteresting as shepherding when you spend the day in the company of some of the finest minds of Jerusalem," Sabba smiled.

"On the contrary, I don't think it is uninteresting at all." Asa reached out with his hand as if he were searching for the right words to say. "My father teaches me from the Torah, and I spend hours learning and committing to memory all that I can of our holy texts. But it is my belief that there are some things which cannot be learned from reading alone. David was a shepherd before becoming a king and leader over Israel. We will never know for certain, but I would wager to say it was not simply memorizing what the Lord had said, but also studying what the Lord had done around him that made him a good leader."

"That which made him a man after the Lord's own heart!" Sabba smiled, his eyes lighting up. Shamira could see why. Not many people thought kindly of shepherds. Not many people thought on them at all after the smell hit them, but it would seem after what Asa had shared that he considered shepherding work fit for a king. Technically speaking, he wasn't wrong.

Shamira spent several moments pondering what the life of the young King David had been like before he had become king. She could almost resonate with it, relating so well to what Asa had shared. How many times had she felt so moved by the spirit of the Lord when she was outside of the city and among creation, that she had stopped everything to pray to God where she could be surrounded by his handiwork? She wondered if

David had been afraid before he battled Goliath, or if he never feared because he knew God would be with him. Shamira had already had to face many Goliaths in her life, and she was still learning about God's provision for her.

"But Abba," Benayahu interrupted and turned toward his own father, Binyamin. "Why can't I take the place of one of the hired shepherds and tend to the sheep in the fields? I am nearly the same age as you were when you began shepherding! I want to work!"

"Be patient, Beni. Your time will come soon enough," said Binyamin, dismissing him with a wave of his hand.

"Everyone else my age is already apprenticed to someone or working alongside their abba. It's not fair!"

Dodh Binyamin laughed, and Savta raised her voice to join the conversation. "He is your son, Binyamin! You couldn't have been more eager to grow up at that age if you tried!" She smiled and her eyes lit up at the memory.

"Yes, but I had much I needed to learn before I became a shepherd. So does Beni. He's not ready for the responsibility yet."

"Perhaps what Beni needs to learn he can only learn by doing," Sabba suggested. "He is right—every other boy his age works or will soon be working. He can't learn to be responsible without first being given the opportunity."

Ignoring Sabba and turning his attention back to his only son, Binyamin continued. "We will discuss this later, Benayahu."

Shamira was quite content with her daily life, the exact opposite of the young, ambitious, and sometimes pretentious Benayahu. She liked her routine and the predictability of it. Mornings were spent preparing and doing the daily chores, while evenings were spent with each other in reflection of the day's events. Of course, each day always began and ended with praise to the Lord. She was surrounded by the people she loved. Her life was so rich and full, how could she dare to ask for more?

Except, she could ask for more.

She could ask for the person sitting directly across the table from her. But fear of the unknown had kept her from pursuing the desires of her heart. She had promised herself she would try harder to let go of fear and leap into faith, but she still had her doubts.

"Since the topic of business seems to be unavoidable at this table," Shamira's own abba interjected. "Tell me, brother, how were things at the marketplace today? Did the livestock sell as expected?"

Binyamin stretched backward before responding. "We had a few hagglers, but the sheep sold at a good price."

"We'd make more money selling at the temple," Beni muttered, snatching up a piece of bread and shoving it in this mouth. He should've done that before he spoke at all.

"Do you have something you'd like to share with everyone, Beni?" Binyamin raised an eyebrow at his son. His gaze communicated what his words did not: if Beni wanted to keep eating at the table that night, he'd better not have anything else to share at all.

Shamira turned her head to her righthand side where Rut was seated. Rut looked at Shamira, communicating her annoyance with her eyes in a silent conversation spoken in a language only the two of them could understand. Beni may have wanted his father and the others to start seeing him as a man, but he wouldn't get very far if he continued to have such a disrespectful attitude.

"Father, why don't we sell our sheep in the temple? We could make a fortune there!" he said, dropping his bowl to the table. "Then we wouldn't have to live like this!"

"Like this? *Like this?*" Binyamin said. "You are fortunate to live in a home where you have a roof over your head, food to eat, and where everyone here loves you and supports you. I will not tolerate you speaking in this way!"

"Beni, we do not conduct business in the temple for a reason. The people who sell there conduct their business dishonestly and do so in the very presence of the Lord," Sabba explained.

"If *the Lord* cared, then He would stop them and drive more customers to our stall at the market instead!"

Even in the dim glow of the lamplight, Shamira could see her sabba's face had gone scarlet. "Understand this, *Benayahu*: this house does not conduct business in the temple. When I inherited my sheep from my father, I made a choice. I could have sold there, but what I knew of our God prevented me from doing so. The temple is His house. A place where we worship Him. We do not go there to make and to take. We go there to give back to the One who has chosen to give to us so generously. He gives to you every morning when you wake up and have one more day to live. He gives to you every hour of every day. It was my decision not to sell in the temple, but one day you will have to make your own decisions about the Lord and his teaching. Do you understand?"

Beni nodded. Shamira watched her grandfather's chest labor to rise and fall with each breath. Had she been blind to how her grandfather had been aging? She had seen him angry, but this was different somehow. His mind was strong, but his body seemed frail. She silently prayed that Beni would have the wisdom not to protest further, for she feared deeply that her grandfather's heart could not take any more of his brashness.

"As for you, Binyamin," he turned his head slowly toward his middle son, sighing deeply. "I trust you to teach your son as I once taught you. However, I caution you to make sure he is being equally educated in both the matters pertaining to the creatures of this earth as well as to their Creator." He coughed several times, and then after clearing his throat returned to his meal. The others surrounding the table seemed to stiffen some. In particular, Asa.

Shamira realized Asa would be highly uncomfortable with any negative conversation surrounding the temple where his father was a respected priest and valued member of the Sanhedrin. She turned to Asa, expecting him to be taking great offense at the subject. His head fell to his chest, not in anger, but in shame.

"Forgive us, Asa." Shamira's abba interrupted her thoughts, apologizing. "Our words must come across very harshly to you."

"Not at all, Aharon," he said, taking a deep breath. "In fact, I couldn't agree with Eliyahu more."

When the meal was finished, everyone got up to move about the house and resume their normal activities. Shamira's mother and Devorah began clearing the table and packing the leftover food and dishes back into storage. Normally Shamira would help, but tonight her mother had quietly told her she would not be needed. The younger boys began chasing each other in circles, Libi as well, and Chava tried to calm them and get them ready for bed. Most of the men remained reclined around the table, talking business, except for Beni who had gone up to bed early. Rut kept nudging Shamira's side in a not-so-subtle way.

"Ru-ut!" Shamira muttered through a fake smile, her back teeth grinding down on each other. "You're being ridiculous, and everyone can see you."

"No one even notices me. You're the one being ridiculous. Asa has always been your friend. It makes no sense for you to be acting so nervous and reserved all of a sudden. It isn't like you."

She paused. "Unless of course, you actually *want* everyone to know that you're wildly in love with him, in which case by all means, continue."

"Hush up, Rut! This is why I don't tell you things."

"Even if you hadn't told me, it's not that difficult to guess. Why don't you just go and talk to him?" She raised her eyebrows at Shamira.

"Regardless of any of this, Asa is still completely unattainable. It is not wise for me to entertain thoughts of a marriage which may never take place. I should be focusing on my housekeeping duties, so that I can learn to become a good wife for whomever my father chooses for me." Shamira crossed her arms in front of her, determined to be strong and not let her emotions get the better of her.

"How amusing," Rut said dryly. "You've never cared about any kind of housekeeping before."

"Well perhaps it's time that I started to care," Shamira sighed.

"He's not unattainable right now," said Rut, gesturing to Asa's strong, muscular frame standing in the main doorway of the house, silhouetted by the moonlight from the courtyard. "Just go, Mira. Everyone knows he's waiting for you. Besides, he is a guest in this household. It would be rude for you not to at least wish him well before he leaves. Remember what I said: trust in the Lord. Let your faith be stronger than your fear."

Shamira knew Rut was right, which was why she courageously took her cousin's advice and moved toward him, each step feeling like a thousand.

"Are you leaving so soon?" she said as she looked up at him, admiring the way the silver light of the moon danced in his wild, dark curls. She remembered how she had teased him over his hair when they were younger. Once she'd even compared it to a tree blossoming in the springtime. She felt somewhat remorseful now but justified herself with the memories of his own taunts and jokes about her fickle, up-turned nose.

"Why? Would you miss me if I left?" he quipped.

"I think I'd survive." She tried to say the words as if she meant them, but she was positive he could still hear the tremors in her voice. She wanted to pinch herself. When had she become so careless with her emotions?

It happened when she realized how much she cared about Asa.

He chuckled and said, "You did it again."

Perplexed, she replied, "Did what?"

"When you're confused, or anxious, or deep in thought— your nose wrinkles, or crinkles, or whatever you want to call it," he explained, pointing to his own nose, with a smirk spreading across the right side of his face. "You've done that since you were little."

Little.

She wasn't a little girl anymore though; she was a grown woman. A woman of marriageable age, and a woman deeply in love with Asa. But none of that mattered, whatever their feelings were. Her family was not one of wealth or power. They were simple, humble shepherds, and Asa was a descendent of the tribe of Levi. His past and future were at the temple. As such, he would need a far more dignified wife. Preferably, one who could do more than make bread.

Still, as she looked into his eyes, she could sense he felt the same way she did. Maybe their feelings did matter; maybe as long as they had each other they could overcome anything. He smiled down at her, not in a patronizing way, but in a way that seemed more like he was admiring her. Shamira realized that he hadn't been mocking her for her nose. He, too, had been remembering that time so long ago, when they were both littler and life had been so much less complicated.

Understanding dawned on her now that she knew how he'd been able to read her thoughts so easily all those years. It was all down to her tell-tale nose. Shamira turned things back around him with a quip of her own. "I thought I told you never to tease me about my nose again?"

Only this time, her voice was not the voice of a confused ten-year-old—it was full of endearment she couldn't hide.

He smiled and looked at the ground. "My humblest apologies. I didn't mean to tease."

"You didn't?"

He looked back up at her and their eyes met again.

His gaze startled her.

It was deep and intense.

"Why would I tease the most beautiful woman my eyes have ever beheld?" he whispered.

"Asa!" If his words hadn't taken her breath away, she might have scolded him. For him to say such a thing, even in jest, was incomprehensible for Shamira. She didn't know whether to look away or to keep looking back at him. Truthfully, she couldn't have looked away even if she tried.

As if reading her mind and sensing her doubt, he continued, "It's true, Shamira. You're everything to me."

Asa took a step backward, refocusing his gaze on the moon and stars above, and Shamira was grateful considering they were in full view of her entire family. Suddenly his eyes were darker. A serious expression took hold of his face.

"There's another reason I somewhat invited myself to dinner tonight—I needed to talk to you. I saw him today. The teacher we spoke of before in the fields—Jesus of Nazareth—he's in Bethany."

Forgetting herself, Shamira gasped and jumped—no—leaped forward with excitement and anticipation. "Asa! Have you found out any more about him?"

"He will be coming to Jerusalem for the Pesach celebration. It is likely you will be able to see him and hear him teach then."

"I don't just want to *hear* him, Asa. I want to ask him to heal Libi!"

"You don't know that he can do that," he cautioned. His tone was sharper than she'd expected. Almost the complete opposite of how he'd spoken just mere moments before.

"You don't know that he can't!" Shamira retorted and planted her feet even firmer on the ground beneath her. She would not waver on this matter. She had to get to this Jesus of Nazareth—she needed to see him. Something inside of her commanded her to do so, and she wanted Asa's support in this quest.

"Miracles can have a cost, Shamira."

Something in Asa's voice gave her pause. She had known him for nearly as long as she could remember. She knew he was keeping something from her. She relaxed her stance and stepped closer to him. "Asa, tell me. What's wrong?"

"There's nothing wrong with me, Shamira," he said, running his fingers through his hair.

"You can't hide things from me. I know when something is troubling you. I *always* know," she whispered.

"At least I know it's not because of my nose." He half-smiled at her.

"What's wrong? What happened to you?"

He sighed deeply, and then began. "I did what you asked, Shamira. I went out looking for answers about Jesus of Nazareth. As a matter of fact, I went all the way to Bethany, where I had heard he was staying."

"You did?"

Shamira was stunned. Curiosity seized her, taking over every part of her body and putting decorum to shame. She should have been more grateful to Asa; he'd walked to Bethany and back *for her*. How had he managed to get ahead of his studies? Did his father know?

"I did. I met some of his disciples. I heard him talk. I even met some people who say he healed them."

"The man—the one that was raised from the dead. You mentioned him before. Was he there?" Shamira couldn't help herself—she had to know, and she could tell he was holding back.

"Lazarus," said Asa, grimly. "Yes, he was there."

"Oh, Asa! I have to see Jesus. I have to meet him myself!"

"It's not that simple, Shamira! You don't know—" He stopped himself, and Shamira could tell he had more to say.

"I don't know what?"

He bit his lip, and then continued. "You don't know what could happen. I... I shouldn't even be telling you this."

"Telling me what?" she said, putting her hands on her hips.

"Swear, "Asa demanded. "Swear you will keep your oath and not repeat a word I am saying, not even in a moment of haste." Shamira nodded her agreement, and Asa continued quietly. "I overheard my father and some others talking. They were plotting to have Lazarus killed."

"Killed?" Shamira squeaked. "But... but why would they do such a thing?"

"People—devout people—are following Jesus because a man who was dead is alive. The leaders think... they think if they kill Lazarus then they'll kill the reason people are following Jesus. If no proof of his miracles exists, then maybe people will give up following him."

"That doesn't make any sense. Why would..." And then Shamira realized why Asa was so worried. Following Jesus put her in direct danger. If Libi was healed by a divine miracle, it put her in the line of fire. "Oh, Asa..." She could understand what made him worry, but she wasn't afraid. Strangely, although she was afraid of many things in her life, on this matter she was quite at peace.

His expression softened. The dim moonlight in combination

with the flickering candles seemed to be playing tricks on her mind. She thought she saw him smile, but only for a moment.

"Are you still so determined?"

"I am," she said without hesitation.

He nodded. "Very well then. The second I hear something I shall come for you. You have my word."

"Thank you, Asa!" she replied gratefully.

"Now I must thank your father and mother for extending the invitation to me for dinner, and then I must be on my way. I have already stayed too long, and my family will be expecting me." Shamira detected a hint of reluctance in his voice.

"Of course," she replied and watched him leave from a distance, taking time to contemplate everything that had just transpired between them and everything he had just said.

Later that night, Shamira and Rut talked in whispers. Careful not to break her trust to Asa, Shamira only shared the updates she was able to speak of. Rut was amazed to hear of Asa's journey and how quickly he had found Jesus.

"Shamira, we must stay devoted to prayer if it is true that he is coming to Jerusalem. If he is the Savior that our sabba witnessed, this could change our lives."

Shamira was breathless. "It has already changed mine."

"The next day, when the large crowd that had come to the festival heard that Jesus was coming to Jerusalem, they took palm branches and went out to meet him. They kept shouting: 'Hosanna! Blessed is he who comes in the name of the Lord — the King of Israel!'" - John 12:12-13 CSB

Shamira held Libi's hand tighter than usual that day. The crowds in the city were overwhelming. The marketplace was almost always crowded with people, but that day in particular the people seemed to be coming from all different directions, each in a rush to get somewhere else. Libi was small for her age, and Shamira didn't want to lose her in the crowd. If she did, she'd have no way of calling out to her, and Libi wouldn't be able to cry for help. Most days, Shamira could forget about Libi's hearing impairment, but on days like today she was forced to be keenly aware of any and all possible dangers.

"He's here! The teacher is here!" Shamira thought she heard

someone call.

Teacher.

The word made Shamira shudder with anticipation, wondering if they meant *the* teacher she had desperately asked Asa to search for. Shaking her head, she convinced herself that she'd misheard.

It was a logical explanation. People were shouting so loudly all the voices seemed to mix into one single unintelligible roar. It was entirely possible she'd made the whole thing up in her subconscious mind. Ever since Asa had surprised her at dinner and told her everything he had seen, she'd thought of little else than the miracle worker from Nazareth. The very idea of his existence sent shivers of excitement up and down her spine. She had yet to see him herself or even hear him teach or witness his alleged miracles, but she found herself fascinated and inexplicably drawn to him.

"Why do you think that there are so many people in the marketplace today?" said Rut, keeping a very impressive hold on Gilad, who was not at all amused at the idea of holding hands with his cousin in public.

"Perhaps it is merely the Pesach festivities. Certainly, travelers would need to get supplies and purchase things that they couldn't travel with," she answered.

She knew better though. While the crowds were certainly large enough for a Pesach crowd, or any other feast or celebration for that matter, there was something about their hurried state which seemed to suggest an out-of-the-ordinary sense of urgency. Briefly, Shamira turned her head to see if she could see what the source of all the commotion was; however, she quickly lost her footing and began to stumble. She felt the earth's pull dragging her down toward its hard surface, and she was already wincing from the pain she knew was just seconds away.

Before Shamira could hit the ground and pull Libi down with her, a young man caught her arm and steadied her. For all of the reasons she should have been surprised to see that particular man there at that time, not one stayed put in her mind. Asa had a habit of showing up in places he shouldn't be with impeccable timing ever since she had been a young girl.

"Asa," she gasped. "Thank you! The crowds today are horrendous!"

Once she was back on her feet, they walked in unison behind the other members of her family, pushing their way to their stall in the marketplace.

"I'd tell you not to be so careless, but then I wouldn't have nearly as many opportunities to help you," Asa said, smiling at Shamira. "Hello, Libi!" He waved to her.

Libi grinned and waved back, and then gave Shamira a very suspicious glance that made Shamira wonder if even her younger cousin could sense her feelings.

Looking at him, being with him, and walking together hand in hand with Libi made Shamira feel so hopeful for a future together. Asa had always been so kind and generous, as well as helpful wherever her family was concerned.

"My abba and dodh have some business to take care of, Rut has some more wool to sell, and there are still a few things we need before Pesach," said Shamira, explaining her family's presence at the marketplace.

She imagined briefly what it would be like to be married to him, fighting these crowds together on their way to pick out their own goods from the marketplace. Perhaps she would find some new herbs and spices to make a delicious meal for him, and he would surprise her by sneaking off to a nearby merchant to barter for a piece of jewelry for her. They would each carry a child in their arms as they walked home—one of *their* children. After the evening meal had been eaten, the dishes cleared, and the children tucked into their beds, he would give her the gift, she would smile at him, and…

She was snapped back to reality when she realized nothing like that could ever happen. Surprisingly, her reason for thinking so was not because she and Asa were "doomed" to be apart. She had given that over to God. No, the reason it could never happen that way was because Shamira had almost no natural ability or skill when it came to cooking. She burned almost everything except for bread, which was too simple for even a woman as notorious as Shamira was to mess up.

If she had gone to the market, she would've most likely knocked over the tray of spices not knowing what she was doing, and then Asa would have had to pay for all of them. The thought of the two of them having children together was not nearly as outlandish of a fantasy as being able to cook a delicious stew from scratch. However, as plausible as the idea was of them being together in comparison to the idea of her being able to handle herself and a pot of stew over an open fire, in that moment it was still just a dream. She was still just a shepherd's daughter. He was still a priest's son.

Shamira reminded herself that God was keeping watch over her, just as a shepherd kept watch over his flock. Those words, taken from the story Savta had shared with her, had stayed with her since she first heard them. Whenever anxiety threatened to lay claim to her heart, she would repeat them, and her fears would subside.

Her sabba had told her that words had power, and those words definitely had power over her heart. She had also become considerably more invested in her prayer life. Her prayers, when spoken to God, also became powerful, because she no longer asked for her will but for His. When she could do nothing, God would be at work answering the prayers and keeping watch over her heart.

"Shalom, Asa," Rut called out from ahead, keeping one hand on Gilad's shoulder and not even bothering to turn around.

"What brought you here today?" Shamira asked, legitimately curious to know if he had an excuse this time, as opposed to all of the other times that he had caught her by surprise.

"I had some shopping to do," he stated, matter-of-factly.

"No, really." She raised an eyebrow at him in disbelief.

Asa lowered his voice just enough so Shamira could hear him. "Have you seen the crowds today? How thick and heavy they are?"

"I would have to be blind not to." She laughed, still being rocked from side to side by the dozens of passersby.

"They're all here for Jesus of Nazareth," he said. "I was coming to tell you."

Shamira stopped in her tracks.

"He's here? The teacher is here?" Shamira's jaw dropped, and her mind whirled with possibility.

Libi tugged at Shamira's sleeve. She pointed ahead at the rest of the family, and looked back at Shamira, eyes wide with confusion—and possibly a little bit of irritation.

"Beni!" Rut called out and motioned for him to join them, which he did, bringing Yuval with him. "Shamira, what's wrong? Are you feeling ill?"

"Oh." She smiled. "No, no. I feel fine! Absolutely fine!"

She had to stop herself from cackling. Rut and the others were looking at her like she had lost her mind.

Libi kept on tugging at her sleeve, and Shamira bent down to Libi's level, taking both of her hands in her own. She wanted to shout for joy and tell her, *"This could be the day that you are healed!"* but she knew she couldn't do that in front of everyone else. She wouldn't dare voice those dreams aloud in front of her family, but she quickly realized she didn't need to use her voice to communicate these things to Libi. She gave Libi's hands a quick squeeze and smiled at her, and Libi smiled back.

"Would somebody please explain what is going on? Our parents are still moving ahead of us. We should be going soon, or we'll all get lost."

"I'm sorry, Beni," Rut began. "I thought something happened to Mira, but apparently the crowds and the heat have just made her lose her mind!"

"Imma and Abba will be wondering what's keeping us," Beni rolled his eyes, not caring a whit about what was happening. "You can't just stop every few minutes because the sun has made you sick in the head."

Before Shamira could even think of a response, Asa stepped in and said, "You go on, Benayahu. Take the boys with you, and tell the others I'm here with Shamira, Rut, and Libi, and we've just stopped to rest. I will make sure they catch up with the rest of you safely."

Benayahu nodded and turned around grunting and muttering about how annoying his sister was. Yuval and Gilad trailed behind him.

"Asa, what have you done to Shamira?" Rut asked.

"I didn't do anything. Jesus of Nazareth is approaching the city. Shamira had told me previously that she wanted to see him, so I came to tell her he is nearby," he announced.

Rut's jaw dropped, and Shamira wished Asa hadn't been so forthright, even if honesty was one of his best qualities.

Shamira tried to explain. "Rut, you've heard what they say of him. They say that he performs miracles in the name of God!"

"But do you not grasp the concept of how much trouble you could get in over this?"

"Sabba would believe me! He would!" Shamira retorted. "How can you have grown up in the same home, shared the same walls, heard the same stories, and still not believe as I do? You have heard Sabba's story. The Messiah is coming, and he may even be here today. Don't you want to be a part of that?"

"But what if you're wrong? What if this man is not the Messiah, as you so passionately believe that he is?"

Shamira released a long sigh. "Then I am no worse off than any other day, and in no less trouble than I've already been in," Shamira said softly, her eyes watering with tears. "Please, Rut."

"Please what?"

"Come with me, or at the very least, don't tell my parents or your parents where I've been or what I'm doing."

"Oh, I never said I wasn't coming with you," Rut stated, without even hesitating to answer. "I want to see too, Shamira. I truly want to believe every word. Imagine if Libi could be healed! I just want to make sure that you are certain of what you're doing."

Shamira was shocked. "Then you do believe!"

"I believe in having *hope*," she corrected. "You're fortunate Asa is here to watch out for you and vouch for you later on to our family. I certainly won't be able to defend us both."

Shamira smiled at Rut, who was always there and would always be there for her through good and bad. "Let's go," she said, and then turned to Asa. "Take us to him."

Shamira hoped this adventure would be good.

"We are getting close. Can you see him? He's just there." Asa gestured down the road, keeping one hand on Shamira's shoulder, steadying her. On any other day, Shamira could have easily navigated the uneven roads by herself without incident, but today she was grateful to have Asa watching out for her, as the swarm of people only grew more and more dense the closer they got to the main road.

"Why are the people carrying palms and rejoicing in song?" said Rut, craning her head to one side.

"Because he's here, Rut! The Messiah is here, I'm sure of it!" Shamira smiled, completely undeterred by the fact that her short stature made it impossible for her to see anything. Nevertheless, overcome with excitement, she called out, "*Hosanna!* Hosanna in the highest!" mimicking the calls of those she heard around her. "Blessed is he who comes in the name of the Lord—the King of Israel!"

"But you haven't even seen him yet," said Rut. Her cousin's logic seemed to wage war against Shamira's own impulsiveness, which Shamira felt was a perpetually losing battle.

"I don't need to see him. I already feel like I know him, as though I've always known him. I believe in him, and for whatever reason, I have faith in him." She had to believe in him.

The crowds kept moving as he moved, and Shamira realized she was running out of time. "I know it doesn't make sense, Rut, but I have this calling on my heart. I have to get Libi to him."

She tilted her head back and for just a moment marveled at what a beautiful day it was. The clouds floating overhead in the bright blue sky were white and fluffy, and the sunlight shone through them, making them look as brilliant and shiny as pure silver. To be so close to the Messiah, the deliverer sent by God; it was perhaps the closest she would ever come to knowing what heaven must feel like on earth.

Suddenly, palm branches began to fly above her head, making the sun's brilliant rays of light dance between their leaves. It was a glorious sight to behold. How much hope she felt in that moment beneath the palm branches, how much faith she had, was immeasurable. Shamira could feel the presence of the Lord, and it was just like her sabba had always described.

The people around her kept pushing her closer, and she moved with them like sheep move with their flock. They waved their branches in the air and tossed them into the road, parting to make way for Jesus of Nazareth. All around her they shouted, "Hosanna! Hosanna in the highest!"

"Shamira, I can see him! He is riding on a donkey accompanied by the twelve! Can you see?" Asa exclaimed.

She couldn't see anything from her vantage point, and she felt so left out of something so obviously momentous, but she could experience it through Asa's eyes. They gleamed in the sunlight and Shamira smiled at his smile. A woman about Shamira's size tapped her on the shoulder, stealing her attention.

"Excuse me, girl?"

She turned her head, coming face to face with the woman who was much older than herself, but whose eyes were filled with a joy that made her appear much younger. "Yes?" she answered.

"Would you like to toss this?" said the woman, holding out a palm frond to her. The woman reminded her of her savta.

Shamira stared at it for a moment. It was just a branch. They grew on trees everywhere. But this branch meant so much more to her. It meant everything: the coming of the Messiah, the faith she had in him that only a few people closest to her understood, her belief in redemption and a brighter future.

"Yes, thank you," said Shamira, nodding gratefully. She took the palm branch and held it tightly in her hand. Briefly, Shamira looked back to ask the woman if there was anything Shamira could do for her in return, not that she had much to give anyway, but the woman had already disappeared. She turned back toward the road. Shamira was pleased to see Rut and Libi both had a branch as well.

"Asa?" she called out, her eyebrows raised in question. "Will you help me? I'll never be able to reach the road."

"What do you want me to do?" he asked.

"Would you throw this for me? Onto the road?"

"Ours too!" added Rut. "Please?"

He reached for Shamira's palm branch, and for a moment they were both holding onto it. Their hands brushed up against each other's. Shamira knew she needed to let go, but she struggled to release her grip. It was as though her whole life she had been adrift in a river, and this branch, the physical manifestation of her hope and prayers for a Savior for her cousin and a Messiah for her people

, was all that had kept her afloat.

If she let go, what would happen next? She closed her eyes and breathed in. *"Lord, I am giving this branch to You. I am like a sheep that needs to be guided and taken care of, a tree that needs to be uprooted and replanted, a piece of driftwood at the mercy of the current of a river. I'm putting my worries in Your hands, my fears, my hopes... I surrender it all to You. My hope and my trust are in You."*

She looked up at Asa and slowly released her tight hold on the branch. His expression wasn't clear. Of course, he would have had no idea about the moment Shamira had just spent with God, the prayers she'd prayed, but she could tell he, too, was feeling moved by the moment. Asa turned the branch back and forth in his hands, studying it carefully. Shamira wondered what the branch represented to him. Briefly, she saw grief in his eyes, but it was quickly replaced by a look of hope, dedication, and determination.

"Asa?" she said.

He smiled and nodded at her, then raised the palm branch high above his head. "Hosanna!" he shouted, smiling back at Shamira just as he released the branch, throwing it at the road. He did the same with both Libi and Rut's branches.

Although she wanted to ask him about his feelings and beg him to divulge whatever thoughts had crossed his mind, she was too overcome by joy to speak.

She joined him in praise, singing, "Hosanna in the highest!" Her words had power, not just over others, but over herself. This was her declaration, her song, her battle-cry. There would be no going backward from this point, only forward.

Just then, Libi's hand slipped from Shamira's grasp. Shamira watched as she, so small for her age, seemed to fly backward and land hard on her back. The crowds were only getting more and more violent, turning the moment of praise into pure chaos. "Libi!" she screamed, her voice rattling.

Someone must have knocked into her and caused her to lose her balance. It wouldn't be hard to knock her down if she wasn't on her guard. Shamira leapt toward her younger cousin, covering her with her body to protect her from the crowds.

"Shamira!" Asa swooped down, helping them both up. "You both could have been crushed!"

Regaining her balance, Shamira looked first to Libi to make sure she was all right, and then to Rut, whose face was full of trepidation.

"I knew this was a dangerous idea!" cried Rut, clutching onto Asa's sleeve as the crowd became more ravenous, pushing and shoving in the direction of Jesus.

"No! We're so close!" said Shamira, lunging forward into the mass of people, keeping both of her arms wrapped around Libi.

"Oh no, you don't," commanded Asa, pulling her back. "I will not return to the house of Eliyahu to tell Aharon I allowed one of his daughters to be trampled. I am taking you back to your family, Shamira."

"But what about Libi? I know that if I could just see him, if I could only speak with him, he could help her!" She was almost screaming with emotion, her eyes just barely overflowing with tears. The crowds kept moving, and with every step, she knew Jesus was getting farther and farther away. Had she thrown away Libi's chance, as she'd thrown away that palm branch?

"I could do it, Asa! I could!" She kept fighting. Even though she knew in her heart Asa was right, she didn't want to believe it. What if another chance never came?

"Shamira, please." Asa's face hardened. "You know there is almost nothing on this earth you could ask of me that I would not give my own life to make possible, but right now you need to listen to me. I have no doubt you could reach him. You could probably convince this entire crowd to turn around if you tried. You've never let anyone stop you from getting what you want and speaking your mind, least of all me. You're strong, Shamira, but look at Libi. She's tired—frightened, even. Is this really what's best for her? A moment ago, she could've been terribly hurt. You have to wait, Shamira. Wait until a better time, when there are less people. Less danger."

Shamira's heart plummeted. She had given over everything to God. Why had He not immediately given to her what she'd asked for in return? She'd gone from the mountain top to the valley in a matter of minutes.

"Please, Shamira, let's go home," Rut begged.

Shamira was reminded of what her abba had told her not even a fortnight prior. He had asked her to consider whether or not her actions might hurt more people than just herself. His words repeated over and over again in her mind. She knew she would never be helping Libi if she wasn't first looking out for what was best for her, however pure her motives had been. God was simply telling her to wait.

"All right," Shamira sighed. "But Asa, you must promise me the next time you hear the name Jesus of Nazareth, you will come and find me at once. Promise me."

He smiled. "I've never broken a promise to you before."

She wanted to return his smile and affection, to get lost in the moment between them, but there was no time for that. She turned her attention away from him and said, "All right then, let's turn around and head back toward the market."

No sooner had she said the words and their party had begun moving, than Asa had stopped dead in his tracks.

"What's wrong?" Shamira asked naïvely. When he did not respond, she moved her head to see what he was looking at and what had caused him to stop so abruptly. Ahead of them, staring disapprovingly, was Asa's father.

"I, um…" Asa hesitated. "I have to go. Shamira, I'm *so* sorry. Tell your mother and father I am deeply sorry I did not see them today, and that I had to leave you so suddenly."

Shamira anxiously looked back and forth, from Avram and

back to Asa. Confused and overwhelmed with nervousness, she replied, "Asa, what is wrong? You don't have to go so soon." Even as she said it, she knew it was not the truth. Only wishful thinking.

She shuddered as she remembered each and every bruise she'd seen Asa try to hide from her, punishments for each minor deviation and alleged indiscretion. However, she realized there were far worse punishments his father could inflict now that he was older. Asa needed to go home and get out of this place. She hoped desperately that his father had not seen everything that had transpired on the road. What consequence could come from a single palm branch?

"I have to go, Shamira." His eyes locked with hers, and she only saw strength and resolve. The twinkle of mischief briefly lit those same dark, golden-specked eyes as he blinked in the sun. Bending his head down toward her one last time, he raised an eyebrow jovially and added, "Tell your savta to keep some of those dates set aside for me. I promise to return again sometime soon to make up for this short visit."

His ability to make her happy even in the most turbulent of times was one of the things she appreciated the most about him. How lovely it would be to live each and every day, climb every one of life's mountains, and cross every one of its valleys with such a man. No struggle they could ever face would be too great for the two of them together, with God as their guide.

"Mira?" Rut said with her lips pursed and eyebrows raised. Shamira was once again made aware of her surroundings and realized without Asa, the crowds seemed even more threatening and dangerous. Wherever he had disappeared to, she knew not, for she'd been too caught up in her thoughts to make any observation of use.

"Right, we must begin to make our way back. We just need to walk a little way—the crowds are heading in the opposite direction. We'll be going against the grain for a short time, but soon we'll be past them. Let's get going," she said. She tightened her grip on Libi's left hand, and Rut moved to her other side to clutch Libi's right.

"I will not even dignify this behavior with an explanation of why this is unacceptable, Asa."

"I'm sorry, Abba, I was just…" Asa began, trying to explain away why he'd been here on this street instead of at the temple where his father had left him like he'd done a dozen times before.

"Don't you understand? I do not care what your explanation is. Anyway, I don't have time to deal with this now," Avram sputtered in a rushed tone.

"My apologies," said Asa, his head hanging low. "I will return to the temple for the rest of the day."

"No, you will not!" his father commanded.

"What?" said Asa, taken aback by the sting of his father's order striking his heart. How could his father forbid him from the temple? Was that not God's house?

"You will go straight home. When I am finished here, I will return myself, and then we'll have a very lengthy discussion about this insubordination. I have business to attend to here, now go."

"Business?" asked Asa. His father was already walking away from him and the question did not stop him.

"Avram! I've just come this way from the other side of the street. The amount of people here is innumerable. Something must be done!"

Asa recognized the man approaching them as another one of the priests, the same one his father had been talking to when Asa overheard him plotting to have Lazarus killed. He briefly wondered if his father had been successful.

"Staying here is useless. Little can be done about these wayward worshippers. It is time we got to the center of the issue. We must find a way to get to the Nazarene."

Get to him? Something in his sinister voice made Asa suspicious. It was the same tone he'd used when he'd spoken about Lazarus. He wanted to believe his father's aim was strictly intellectual. Perhaps he was interested in Jesus' teachings or wanted to learn more about his abilities and where he'd come from. Maybe his heart was softening, and he, too, longed for a Messiah. But no matter how many times Asa repeated those explanations in his mind, his rational nature could not accept them. Not after the lifetime of wickedness he'd witnessed at his father's hand.

"I know one of his disciples who might be amenable to a meeting. They call him Iscariot, Judas Iscariot. Perhaps he would be willing to arrange an introduction to Jesus of Nazareth for us."

"Perfect. Then we can ask him all of the questions we want," said Avram.

That was all Asa needed to hear before leaving to go home. Despite what his mind told him, his heart still kept advocating for his father. Even if believing his father had good intentions was illogical, it was better than accepting the opposite. If Jesus had the power to bring Lazarus back from the dead, then maybe he could restore his father's hardened heart as well.

Maybe.

The three cousins formed an unbreakable chain as they forged a path through the jagged, narrow streets of Jerusalem. They pushed against the crowd, shuffling upward along the stone-paved alleys at a painfully slow pace. Several times, Shamira's own sandals got caught in the cracks of the earth, causing her to stumble forward a few paces. Her petite stature placed her at a distinct disadvantage as people pushed at her from all sides, seeming not to notice their small little group existed.

"Shamira, the crowds aren't getting any lighter." Rut's voice tremored with each step.

"I know," she replied, not wanting to add that she had no idea where they were.

Jerusalem had always been her home, but she would be the first to admit it could also be a dangerous city, especially if you ended up lost within its walls. She thought they would have reached the marketplace by now, or at least a familiar-looking street close to their home, but it wasn't so. The sun was setting rapidly and creating dark purple-hued shadows behind the tall buildings.

"Do you even know where we're going?" asked Rut, seemingly reading Shamira's mind.

Shamira did not answer her question. Rather, she gestured and said, "This way." Keeping moving was better than standing still and allowing her anxieties to take hold of her mind.

They turned onto a side street. Admittedly, there was no logical reason why Shamira had led her cousins down that way, but she figured anything was better than being on the crowded street they'd been travelling endlessly. She had seen the direction the sun was setting and knew that they needed to head south towards their home. At least, she thought it was south. She'd gotten so turned around that she couldn't tell left from right. They might have already passed the streets that would lead them home.

The farther they walked down the dark street, the more Shamira realized she'd been wrong to take them that way. She had wanted to get away from the crowds, but she hadn't meant to disappear completely. The dim and narrow alley didn't have a single other person in it that Shamira could see. The stench of it made her feel dizzy, and an ominous feeling slunk into the pit of her stomach. The sounds of the busy street faded into a murmur, which was soon replaced by the moaning sound of the breeze blowing between the buildings.

"Mira…" Rut whispered, moving a little bit closer to her cousins. "I have a bad feeling about this place."

"I know," she said. "But the end is just a little bit further." It wasn't a lie. She could see the horizon peeking through just a few yards ahead.

They were the longest yards she'd ever had to walk.

"Yes, but what if—"

At that moment, Rut was silenced. A hand around her face jerked her backward, and Shamira turned around and screamed, jumping backward in shock. There were two men behind Rut, one who was holding her back, and another who was smiling at Shamira in such a way that made her want to be sick. She tried to scream for help, but her throat seemed to close up. She could barely breathe.

"Well, well, well. What do we have here?" said the toothy one with a devilish grin. His eyes widened, and Shamira shrunk back. Libi clung to her side, shaking, and Shamira stretched out a protective arm in front of her.

"A couple of pretty ladies it would seem," hissed the one holding onto Rut.

"Please," Shamira started. "We don't want any trouble. We're just passing through." She held up her hands hoping they would be persuaded to leave them alone.

"Are you now? Well, we wouldn't want you to leave in a hurry just because of us," he sneered. Shamira observed that this man was clearly the leader of the two; the one holding Rut seemed like he was just following the taller man's lead.

"What should we do with them, Gershom?" said the follower, pulling Rut's hair and jerking her face closer to his. He laughed at her. Shamira felt bile rise into her throat. She forced herself to swallow it back.

Gershom. So that was the name of the man who was about to ruin their lives, steal their virtue, and maybe even kill them. The name meant *stranger, exiled, foreigner.* It was a fitting name for an attacker.

Gershom looked at Shamira with a piercing gaze. He looked stronger than the other one, and Shamira knew there was nothing she could do to stop him if he caught her. He pulled out a knife and pointed it at her. Shamira pushed Libi behind her.

"We don't have any money. Please, leave us alone and we'll be out of your way."

He raised an eyebrow at her, and then looked her up and down as though he were appraising her in his mind. "You may not have any money, but you might be worth something."

Gershom started toward Shamira, and she could only

imagine the possible horrors he was planning. Would he sell them as slaves? Hold them for a ransom? Or take their virtue and leave them for dead? She froze. She didn't know what to do. Her hands started fidgeting at her sides. Her lips quivered. Her pulse quickened.

"Ahh!" the other man screamed.

Shamira's eyes widened. Rut had kicked the man in his shin and caused him to fall to the ground.

"Nooo!!!" Rut screamed. "Leave us alone!"

In a force Shamira had never before seen Rut exhibit, she lunged at Gershom, who had already turned around in anticipation of her attack. He grabbed Rut and laughed again, as if this were all some kind of sport for him. A disgusting, horrific game, like a lion playing with its prey before finishing them off.

"Well, if you're going to make it so difficult, then maybe I'll just have to kill you."

"No!" Shamira gasped. "Please! I beg you!" She hated lowering herself and begging from this man, this scoundrel, but it seemed she had no choice. Her words were not as powerful of a weapon against Gershom and his accomplice as the knife he held in his hands.

He grabbed Rut by her shoulders and threw her at a wall. The other man fully recovered, and both he and Gershom now had their full attention on Shamira. Out of the corner of her eye, Shamira saw blood. Rut's blood. Rut had been wounded and now lay unconscious; Shamira feared the worst. She could never fight them both off, and what about Libi?

Libi!

Just as this thought crossed her mind, Libi shoved past her. "Libi!" Shamira's scream was piercing. She coughed as she fell onto the ground, the dust stinging her eyes.

Libi had started running down the alley back the way they'd come. Where was she going? Was she to be lost now too, and on her own? Shamira had always had a knack for finding trouble and she knew it, but it had never been as bad as this. This time, she had no excuse. None, except for her own stubbornness and carelessness.

Tears filled her eyes, and she could barely see. Why could

she never learn? Gershom and the other man's bodies faded into blurs, menacing blurs that grew in size each time they stepped nearer like the monsters she used to imagine as a child.

Shamira was backed into a corner, trapped. "Help! God, please help us!" She cried out her prayers, knowing that even when she was powerless, God would always have the power to protect her.

Just when she was about to give up hope, Gershom and the other man seemed to stop. Shamira's cries hadn't stopped them, so what had?

Shamira heard loud shouts from the other end of the alley that matched her own volume and urgent tone.

"Shamira! Rut!" said one voice.

"Rut! Shamira! Libi!" followed the other.

They were the voices of Shamira's own father, Aharon, and her uncle, Dodh Binyamin. They were saved!

"Abba! Abba! We're over here!" she answered their call, her voice hoarse and weak. She turned toward them and saw them begin to run with Libi in tow.

"What do we do now?" whispered Gershom's henchman.

"They're not worth it." He spat on Rut and slapped Shamira across her face. "Come on!"

At that, both of the men hurried away running in the opposite direction. The slap was a trivial wound in comparison to what might have been. She praised God for sparing her and protecting Libi, but a part of Shamira's innocence died simultaneously. She'd always been cautious in the city, but she'd never had reason to fear. Now she did. Now she knew exactly what kind of dangers awaited women alone. She crawled beside Rut, wrapping her arms around her knees and giving in to her sobs.

"Ahava sheli! Are you all right?" her abba said, crouching down, squeezing her in his protective embrace. "What happened? Did those men hurt you?"

Shamira couldn't open her eyes. "Rut... Rut..." was all she could manage. Her prayers for safety had only been half-answered. Rut's life still hung in the balance.

"Rut!" Binyamin's worried cry shocked Shamira's own father, as he loosened his grip on his own daughter to help examine his niece. Libi stayed close by Aharon. Shamira realized that Libi must have seen him in all of the confusion at the end of the alley and ran to him to get help. Libi, the smallest of them all, had in a way saved Shamira. Hopefully she had saved Rut as well.

"She is just asleep," said Aharon, placing a steadying hand on his brother's shoulder to draw him back to reality from his panicked state.

"She's... bleeding!" said Binyamin, his face drained of its color. His whole body started to shake. "If anything happens to her, Aharon... I'll kill the men who did this!"

"You know that won't help anything, brother. We have to get the girls home; that's what will help. The sooner we get them home, the sooner Rut's injuries can be attended to. We must be quick."

Binyamin nodded and bent down, quickly tearing off a piece of his clothing and wrapping Rut's head before carefully lifting her into his arms. Aharon turned to face Shamira again and hoisted her body to a standing position. "Shamira—can you walk? We have to get out of this part of the city."

She couldn't open her mouth to speak. She just kept trembling. Her breath quickened, and she suddenly felt as though her heart were about to burst out of her chest. What was wrong with her?

"You're in shock, Shamira. It's all right. I'm here now, but we have to go. Do you understand me?" Her father asked her in an imperative tone, and she knew they didn't have time to waste.

She nodded.

Keeping one arm around her and the other around Libi, her abba guided them home.

"Please, please let her be all right. Please!"

Shamira repeated the prayer over and over again in her mind. In that moment, she felt she would never be able to forgive herself for any of that day. Would her family ever forgive her?

When they arrived home, Shamira was ushered through the wooden gate. Her father sat her down on the bench in the courtyard, then he followed Binyamin inside with Rut's limp body. Chava ran toward Libi, wrapping her arms around her and taking her inside the house. Everyone was so busy, no one was even paying attention to her. Shamira felt so alone. She reminded herself that she had done this.

They had been just a two-minute walk from the marketplace, and a five-minute walk from home. They'd been so close.

"Do not fear, for I am with you; do not be afraid, for I am your God. I will strengthen you; I will help you; I will hold on to you with my righteous right hand." - Isaiah 41:10 CSB

"I wish I could have been there!" said Beni, arms crossed in front of his chest. "If I'd been there none of this would have happened."

"No, you don't, Beni! This isn't one of your childish games, this is serious!" Shamira didn't mean to shout, but judging by Beni's reaction, that's exactly what she had done. She had gotten ahead of herself and hurt someone close to her in the process. Another someone.

Sighing, Shamira tried to apologize. "I'm sorry, Beni. I am just worried about Rut."

"My name is Benayahu," he announced. "And I do *not* play childish games." He reeled around and stomped up the stairs.

"Beni! Benayahu, wait! That's not what I meant." Shamira hoped her words would calm him.

They didn't.

Benayahu may have been a thorn in Shamira's side on more occasions than one, but he was her cousin. No doubt Benayahu may have even thought the same of Shamira from time to time. Besides that, if Rut was like a sister to her, then Beni was surely her brother. She'd never had a real brother of her own anyway, and what was a brother compared to a cousin? Shamira would do anything for her cousins and wouldn't trade them for any relationship in the world. Her carelessness and inability to think about others before herself had already hurt Rut; she didn't want to hurt Beni too. She started to run up the stairs after him.

"Don't follow him, Shamira," her mother said ever so gently to her, appearing from out of nowhere.

Shamira felt like she should've been startled. How long had her mother been there listening? She didn't care. She was just glad to see her.

"Young men are not like young women. Sometimes they can be far more… delicate." Imma spoke with tact, enunciating each syllable with grace and dignity.

"Delicate?" Shamira asked, surprised. She even managed to crack a half-smile.

"Yes, delicate. Fragile. They can be so temperamental at times; it's best not to get them upset or hurt their pride, if you understand what I mean."

Shamira had never heard her mother say anything like that before, and the very thought, while somewhat truthful, made her smile in the midst of such a turbulent day. She understood the sentiment because Asa was like that too, strong on the outside and sensitive on the inside.

Shamira pondered what her mother had said in the context of her discussion with Benayahu. She knew she was wrong to have spoken to him the way she had, but he had also been the one to run away, refusing to give her a chance to explain and apologize. She looked up at her mother.

"And men say that we're the delicate ones!"

"Well, perhaps we let them think that." Shamira's mother smiled down at her as they shared their private joke. "In all seriousness, Shamira, it is important for you to know that men are complex. Strong, protectors, warriors—your abba is the strongest man I know. But I choose my words carefully because under my warrior's armor is a sensitive heart which I have been entrusted with. When a man loves you, he doesn't want to let you down, so always choose wisely and seek to offer support."

Shamira turned toward Elisheva, leaning into her open arms. If men, who were considered strong, could sometimes be called delicate, did that mean that women, who were considered delicate, could sometimes be called strong? Shamira tried to measure her mother's statement against what she knew to be factual. As a young woman, month after month she endured her timely pains. When she was older and married, she might be blessed with a child. She shuddered to think of all the pain childbirth entailed. A woman was also expected to cook and clean, run a house, support her husband and family emotionally; the list of tasks that would be expected of a woman was almost never-ending.

Then Shamira thought of the most difficult task of all for a woman: to become a mother, to raise and care for a child, to love them unconditionally, to be willing to sacrifice their own life for their child's benefit, only to have to give that child away. For when a child comes of age and a mother has done all she can for that child, she must let the child go to start a family of their own, and so the circle would continue. Shamira realized a woman would have to be very strong to do all of that. Stronger still to let go.

It was all too soon before Shamira remembered why they had been together in the first place. The feeling of sadness and worry took hold of her again.

"Imma, I am so worried for Rut. It is my fault! I should not have been so impulsive. You are always telling me to think before I act. Perhaps if I was more grounded like you are always telling me to be, instead of letting my head fly off into the clouds, I would not have dragged Rut and Libi with me into such a dangerous part of the marketplace and then we would not have gotten lost and then... and then... and then..." She gave way to her tears at last, unable to control herself.

"And then what? You would not have been saved from ruin? You are very fortunate this isn't more serious. We'll know the extent of Rut's injuries soon enough," Elisheva said. Then her back straightened and she lowered her voice. "Besides, I have half a mind to march right over to the house of Avram to tell him he should not let his son go around persuading young women to accompany him, only to leave them stranded. We are lucky you all aren't hurt, and that at least you and Libi escaped without any broken parts or worse. Asa let us all down today; I do not think your abba will forgive him anytime soon."

"Asa? What did he do...?" Shamira furrowed her brows as she considered what her mother had said.

Did Imma really blame Asa for what had happened to Rut? Of course, she did! They had all taken Benayahu's word for it when he told them that she, Rut, and Libi would walk the rest of the way with Asa. They could not have known it had been Shamira who had persuaded Asa to take her to that part of the city. No one really knew that what had happened to Rut was entirely Shamira's fault.

"Yes, Asa! Leading you to that horrid part of the city, on a day like today when the crowds were absolutely wild. Once Rut has been taken care of and is resting comfortably, your abba and your Dodh Binyamin will probably have to be forcibly restrained in order to keep them from taking justice into their own hands and going after him. Your father cares for Rut very much and is of course concerned for her, but I imagine he's just as furious with Asa. It could just as easily be you lying up there on that cot.

"With the amount of time you had been gone, we were all so worried. Now of course we know we should have been worried, seeing how irresponsible Asa has been. We always trusted him like our own son, that is, until today. Don't you worry about a thing, Shamira" —she patted Shamira's shoulder— "I'm sure none of us will be seeing him again for a very long time. We believed he might care for you differently—his actions have proved otherwise."

Shamira groaned as the sick feeling in her stomach once again grew worse. She feared she would retch if she remained silent any longer. The thought of her family blaming Asa when he had done nothing but try to protect her made her feel nauseous. She knew it would be easier to let them blame him, then she would not have to bear the brunt of another thoughtless action. Still, Asa's name did not deserve that mark. She could take it, even if it did make her feel ill.

"Imma, please listen to me. None of this was Asa's fault. It was all my doing, for it was I who—"

Before Shamira could finish her confession, they were interrupted by her abba who was standing in the doorway with a weary expression. His face had aged ten years in that one single day.

"Abba! Is everything all right?" Shamira rushed to her father's side, anxious of any news that pertained to her dearest cousin.

"Yes, Aharon, tell us if there is news of Rut. Shamira and I have been so concerned."

Aharon took a deep breath, wrapping one of his arms around his wife and the other around Shamira. "It is not as bad as it could have been. Just a flesh wound and a sore head. Binyamin and Devorah are with her now."

Shamira sighed, relieved. Then her father continued. "As for Asa, I always trusted him, but after today... tell me daughter, where did he go if he was not with you? What was so important to him that he could not be bothered to watch out for my daughter?"

Tears welled up in her eyes. She blinked back several times and swallowed down the bile rising in her throat. "Oh, Abba! It's not Asa's fault—please don't hold this against him. I am the one who wanted to go to that part of Jerusalem. People were shouting about a teacher who had just entered the city and I wanted to see him for myself. Asa tried to stop me, but I wouldn't listen. I am so sorry, Abba. Punish me, but do not blame it on Asa. He had to return to his father, and I foolishly made the choice to continue on without him, and without asking for any help."

Shamira's entire body started to tremble. She was grieving, but she wasn't entirely sure what she was grieving for, other than the punishment that was yet to come.

"Well," her father began. "This is unexpected, although I

can't say I'm surprised."

Shamira took two steps backward and waited for her father to decide what kind of punishment would be appropriate. "You are forbidden from leaving the house until after Pesach. The courtyard is as far as you may go without a guardian. Do you understand my orders?"

"Yes, abba," she whispered, keeping her head bowed. She could barely look at him, or anyone without thinking of all the trouble she had caused and the devastating consequences her actions had nearly brought.

"Shamira." He stepped toward her, placing a hand under her chin and forcing her eyes upward. "I am disappointed in you, and I can't understand why you did what you did, at least not right now, but that does not mean I have not forgiven you. I have, but there are others in this house whom you also need to receive forgiveness from. You must apologize to your Dodh Binyamin and Dodah Devorah for what happened to Rut.

"You must also apologize to your Dodh Tamir and Dodah Chava as well, for endangering their only daughter's life. Finally, you need to apologize to Rut, but you may wait until she is feeling more up to talking."

He finished his declaration with the most solemn frown plastered onto his face, and Shamira's heart broke a little. She hated seeing her father like this, and she prayed it would not last.

"I am deeply sorry, Abba. I just want everything to be all right again."

He sighed. "Shamira, I cannot tell you the depth of trust you have lost with your family today. This is something you will have to earn back. It will take time, and I cannot help you. Do you understand?"

"Yes, Abba. I am not permitted to leave the house unattended, and I am to apologize to Dodh Binyamin, Dodah Devorah, Dodh Tamir, Dodah Chava, Rut, and Benayahu." Shamira did not speak it out loud, but in her heart, she knew she owed Asa an apology too.

"Benayahu? What did you do to Benayahu?" her abba inquired. Her imma placed a hand on his arm and shook her head, and he relaxed. Shamira was grateful. "Never mind it then, you may go upstairs now."

"Yes, Abba…"

She hurried upstairs to her room, which was also Rut's room. She quickly felt out of place when she got there, because inside the small sleeping room was Rut, surrounded by her parents and an annoyed-looking Benayahu. Shamira had nowhere to go where she would not be in the way. If she could not leave her home, how would she get Libi to see the healer, Jesus of Nazareth? Had her actions taken away hope for Libi's future as well?

Darkness came to the house of Eliyahu like a mother coming to put her tired children to bed. It was welcomed by those who knew they needed the respite. One by one, the lamps were blown out as members of the family wished each other a good night's rest, parted with warm hugs that were just a little tighter than usual, and willingly wandered to their beds where they fell into a deep, peaceful sleep despite the day and all of the troubles it had wrought.

Shamira had been too lost in her thoughts to notice everyone else had gone to bed, and the only light she had to guide her were the small beams of moonlight that snuck between the curtains meant to keep them out.

Weary of the day, she crept up the stairs and around the corners, not wanting to wake any of her younger cousins who had already fallen asleep. When she reached her room, she was confronted by an image which reminded her more of her earlier distress than of the restful slumber she was supposed to be having. Her lips parted as she gasped, unprepared to see her dearest cousin in such a state. Her sleeping body appeared almost lifeless, and Shamira blinked away the nightmare.

Rut's eyes fluttered open, and she whispered, "Are you all right?"

"Me?" Shamira asked. "You've been attacked by ruffians, sustained a head wound, been carried halfway across Jerusalem, and you're worried if I'm all right?"

"Of course, I am. If I wasn't worried about you, you'd continue punishing yourself for what happened to me. In the end, you'd be hurt worse than I am."

Shamira smiled in the darkness and stepped over her cousin. She crawled onto her own mat, sprawling out on her back and resting her head on the pillow. It felt good to lie down, to let the cushion support her instead of carrying the weight of the world on her own shoulders. "Yes," she said. "I suppose you're right. I feel sick about the whole thing, and I don't think I will ever be able to forgive myself."

Rut sighed dramatically. "Well, I have already forgiven you, and I'm the one with a bandage wrapped around my forehead. I have certain rights you know! You are indebted to me. You have to do whatever I tell you to, now that I'm an invalid, and I'm telling you to forgive yourself."

"Are you sure that bandage isn't wrapped just a little too tightly?"

"Mira!"

"All right, all right."

Shamira struggled with forgiving herself a great deal. As a matter of fact, it was what she had been struggling with from the middle of the afternoon when the incident occurred all the way until sundown when everyone else had retired for the evening. She had put both her and her cousins' lives at risk by choosing to follow her selfish urges to see the teacher and healer she had heard so much about. After doing so, she still did not even get to see him, Libi had not been healed, and her other cousin had ended up wounded and worse off instead.

Then there was also Asa. She had seen for herself the bold risks he'd taken to try to help her; her demands on this dear man had put him in danger as well. If she did forgive herself, and if she did continue to pursue Jesus of Nazareth, just how high would the cost of following him be?

Above the silence, Rut's meek whisper could just barely be heard loud enough to interrupt Shamira's silent discourse. "I know what you're thinking right now."

"What?"

"You're wondering if it was worth it," said Rut somberly. She let out a long deep breath, either because she was deep in thought or deeply in pain.

"What do you mean?" Her mouth went dry and her palms began to sweat.

"Shamira, you must remember, hiding the truth about what you feel is not one of your gifts. If it were, you'd get into far less trouble. You know exactly what I mean. You are wondering if all of your efforts today were worth it, if it caused both myself and Libi to be exposed to such danger, without even the promise of success later on. You're wondering if it will still be worth it for you to continue to seek out Jesus of Nazareth, or if you should forget him and disregard him as so many others in our circle already have."

Rut's powerful words struck Shamira's heart, and she felt deeply convicted. She didn't know why she was caught off guard by the assessment, as she and Rut had been nearly inseparable since the day Rut had been born. If anyone knew the thoughts that went through her mind, it would be Rut.

"Look at yourself, Rut. I took those risks because I wanted Libi to be healed, and you've ended up here, in pain."

"I will heal in time, Shamira. It's just a cut."

"But it could have been worse!" Impassioned and caught up in the moment, Shamira's voice rose high above a whisper, and she heard other members of the house stirring. Neither of the girls moved. When the house had settled, Shamira took two or three deep breaths. She clasped her hands together and interlaced her fingers, then repeated in a much more reserved tone: "It could have been so much worse, Rut."

"But it wasn't. You're dwelling on something that did not even happen. My head is fine. It will heal quickly enough, and it doesn't even hurt that much. If it scars, then I'll be happy to bare a scar that may have saved us both. But Shamira, I am worried that your spirit will not escape this day so unscathed after today's events." Rut turned onto her side to face Shamira, who tried to hide her form in the darkness.

"Well then you tell me, Rut. You tell me if it was all worth it. If that scar is worth it."

There was a long period where neither of them spoke. For a bit of it, Shamira thought Rut may have either fallen asleep or was too gentle of a person to say what she really thought: that Shamira was lucky something worse hadn't happened and that her father and uncle had found them. Shamira had almost fallen asleep herself when Rut's ever-gentle and compassionate voice startled her from her trance-like state.

"I will admit, you have been acting peculiar lately, but who am I to judge? I had thought that perhaps it had something to do with Asa, that he was the reason you had lost your senses. In all fairness, he may have been a part of that breakdown, but I quickly realized he couldn't have been the only culprit. He's been stealing bits and pieces of your heart for years; there had to have been something else that had changed you."

"What do you mean?" asked Shamira.

"You have always had a strong spirit, challenging the opinions of others when you shouldn't, asking far too many questions when you know people don't want to answer them, and raising your voice in situations where women would never share an opinion normally, let alone shout one." Rut paused to laugh quietly, although her chuckles were uneven and cut short.

"However, our family is known for having somewhat controversial opinions, but only one other family member has been as outspoken about them as you are. Sabba. He has often told us stories of miracles so extravagant that they seem like fantasy. You have heard the way our abbas have talked, so how could I have taken them seriously? But I remember watching you when we were both such little girls, smaller than Libi even. You would hang on his every word as if your very life depended on it."

"I have always loved the way he tells that story," Shamira sighed.

"I know... When rumors spread that some teacher from Nazareth had been performing miracles, I knew it would not be long before you heard those rumors and undoubtedly believed them. It is dangerous to even gossip about such things, but why would that ever stop someone like you? Don't take that the wrong way, Shamira. I am not criticizing you. I am *admiring* you."

"Me?" Shamira questioned.

"I have always admired your strength and boldness. You possess qualities that I do not think I will ever have, and, admittedly, a small part of me envies you. Still, I would not envy the part of you that could be punished for testing limits of the Law. So, I remained skeptical, and I did not take what you said about a Messiah seriously."

Shamira grunted. "Well perhaps you were right to do so."

"No, Shamira, I was not! Let me finish, please." Rut paused a moment, then continued. "I was skeptical of you, just as I was skeptical of Sabba—until today. Today was a miserable day. The streets were crowded, the sun was at its highest point with almost no shade to be found, not even in the marketplace. I was irritated with you for wanting to follow Asa to see this teacher. When we finally got to where he was and none of us could see him, I wanted to chide you and tell you that perhaps you were wrong. I looked up at the sky and I saw the palm branches flying. I heard the rejoicing voices of the people, and I saw the look of hope on your own face. Never have I ever heard our people sing and praise in that way. It was so genuine, Shamira. Although I could not see the teacher that they were praising, something happened in my own heart, and I felt something unlike anything I've ever felt before. A hopeful feeling? A peaceful feeling? An exciting feeling? It was like all of those things rolled up into one. It was like... it was like I felt the presence of God. I don't think I have ever felt His presence so clearly, Shamira. Not even in the temple."

Shamira's breath hitched. Her eyes were already burning and stinging from the rivers of tears she had shed earlier, but she felt them watering even more. *Drip, drop, drip, drop* onto her mat, wetting her face and hair.

"I confronted you in the marketplace. I asked you what you would do if you were wrong, if you were found out, if you had to face consequences of grave value—and you did not waver. When you did not hesitate, even for a moment, about following a man whom you'd never met, I knew I couldn't question you about it anymore. You were firm in your beliefs, and I had no right to tear you down for it.

"Then I myself was confronted by dozens—hundreds of people whose convictions seemed just as firm and unwavering as your own. I realized, who am I to say Sabba's stories aren't true? Who am I to judge whether or not this man is the Messiah for which our people have prayed? If you're a raving lunatic for believing in this man, then they might as well call me one too. I believe in hope. I believe in God's promises and in His faithfulness at keeping them. If this man is the Messiah, then I believe in him too. And I believe in you."

Rut laughed carefree into the night, and Shamira shared with her all of the things that weighed so heavily on her heart. How she had been praying for this day ever since she was a little girl and how she had always believed the Messiah would come in their lifetime. Shamira told her cousin how she knew, just knew, if she could find a way to see the Messiah just once and bring Libi to him, she could convince him to heal her.

"Shamira, if this little cut does leave a scar, *make* my scar worth it."

"But I don't know how I can do any of that if I'm not allowed to leave the house," said Shamira.

"You have to trust in the Lord. Have you prayed about it?" asked Rut.

Shamira hated to admit it, but she hadn't thought much about praying for anything other than Rut's health since the incident.

"I see," said Rut. "We'll both pray about it then. If it's His will, nothing can stop it from being so, and if His will is even stronger than your own, I have no doubt that we will see the day come when Libi can speak, even sing His praises alongside of us."

Shamira smiled. "Rut, what would I do without you, my cousin by birth, sister by heart?"

"And what would I do without you?" she replied. "We will always have each other. When you or I fall, we will have each other to help us back up, and when one of us gets herself into trouble, the other will be right there alongside her making sure she's not alone. I will talk to my parents—they may be more forgiving of you if they know this was not all your fault. I went along; I would not have been struck if I had not fought back. This time you were the one who was trying to reason. You cannot take the blame completely."

Shamira nodded in wonder at Rut's words; she actually had been trying to find a voice of reason during those terrible moments. This was not typical for her, but perhaps there was hope. She was learning after all.

It was only when the dark black of the sky began to fade into the light purple hues of dawn that they finally fell asleep. Even though the hours Shamira slept that night were few in number, they were the most peaceful hours of sleep she had experienced in the past week. Her talk with Rut had revived her hope, and the uncertainty of what tomorrow would bring brought no fear to her dreams, only light.

"When he entered Jerusalem, the whole city was in an uproar, saying, 'Who is this?' The crowds were saying, 'This is the prophet Jesus from Nazareth in Galilee.'" - Matthew 21:10-11 CSB

"Thank you for sitting with me. My imma hasn't let me help with any chores since I was hurt, but it's just so boring having to sit alone in the dark upstairs, and I wanted to come outside," said Rut. An entire day had come and gone since their attack. An entire day since Jesus of Nazareth had entered Jerusalem. "It's nice to have company."

"Oh, it's all right. I'll happily take any excuse to be away from the kitchen," said Shamira, which was exactly the response she had given earlier when Rut had first asked her to sit with her in the courtyard.

Shamira leaned her head back to marvel at the clouds in the sky. The buildings in Jerusalem were tall and close together, so she could not see much between the roof of her home and the homes of their neighbors, but she relished what she could see. The clouds were particularly voluminous, and the sun shone brightly through them.

It had not been easy to get Dodah Devorah to allow Rut to go outside. She had it in her mind that Rut might faint or have a dizzy spell and had kept Rut inside since the injury. But with Shamira there to watch Rut and make sure nothing happened, her cautious aunt had allowed it.

It was for the best anyway. Although the flesh wound had mostly healed, Rut still lost her balance sometimes when she stood up or walked, and she had to move slower than usual.

Schwoop!

Something suddenly buzzed past Shamira's ear. She heard another whirring sound shortly thereafter, followed by a pronounced thud. Was she imagining things? She whirled her head around, perhaps there were some birds in the tree beside them that were causing the leaves to fall. Still, leaves would not fall with nearly so much force as to make a sound. She looked to the side of the courtyard where she had first heard the unnatural sound.

The gate.

Over it came a small pebble, which skidded to a landing right between her feet. She focused her ears. Outside of their gate, Shamira heard the familiar sounds of the city: voices in conversation, feet rushing up and down the street, and the rolling thuds of carts being wheeled to and from the marketplace. It was almost impossible to make anything out of all the hustle and bustle, but Shamira knew Asa's voice. She would not have missed it in a crowd of thousands of voices.

"Shamira? Shamira?"

She heard him calling for her, low and hushed, but loud enough.

Clearly, he was also loud enough for Rut to have heard him too, because she tilted her head suspiciously in the direction of the street.

"Your abba wouldn't think too kindly of you having visitors when you're supposed to be under firm restriction," said Rut, raising an eyebrow.

"No, he wouldn't…" she agreed slowly, biting her lip. But her abba was gone. What could she do?

She looked back at Rut and begged her with her eyes, hoping she would let her get away with it just this one time. She just wanted to know why he had come. That was all. Rut took a long, deep breath, and Shamira could tell she disapproved but looked the other way. Shamira smiled, relieved, and thanked her cousin.

"Thank you, Rut! I won't be long; I just want to find out what he wants."

"I won't say anything, but you can't blame me if somebody else notices, and if anyone asks, I won't lie to them," Rut declared, once again reminding Shamira of the risks she was taking.

Shamira nodded. "I won't blame you."

Asa peered through the cracks between the dark, worn wooden planks nailed together to make up the gate. Shamira's gate. Where was Shamira? Normally she and Rut would have been chasing the younger children all around the house and the courtyard. A shadowy figure obstructed his view. Was it Shamira? Or would he have to explain to Aharon why he was throwing rocks over their wall?

"Asa, what are you doing here?"

It was Shamira!

"Shamira, let me in! I have to talk to you!" he said. The sound of her voice alone was enough to take his breath away, and he could just breathe in the scent of sweet honey and tree sap he'd grown to associate with her. He couldn't wait to tell her Jesus of Nazareth was in the temple today. She would be thrilled once he told her, and he hoped she would be happy to see him as well. A few awkward moments passed, and then Asa realized she still had not unbolted the gate. What was keeping her? He knocked on the hard wood to see if she was still there.

"Asa, I can't... I can't let you in. I'm not allowed."

"What? Why not?" Worry filled his chest. He had seen her and her family just the other day. What could have changed for them in such a short time?

"Rut and I had a difficult time getting home after you left. We got lost and... and we were attacked."

Attacked? By whom? Did they touch Shamira? Every muscle in Asa's body tightened, and at that moment he had the strength in him to bust down the gate himself, just so he could see Shamira and confirm that she was all right.

"It was my fault for insisting that you take us to that part of the city. In the struggle—"

At the mention of struggle, Asa was ready to charge after whomever was responsible and give them a just punishment for even looking at Shamira with intent to harm.

"Rut was hurt. The man threw her against a wall, and the impact drew blood. Our fathers had come looking for us and had found us just in time, just before..." Shamira's voice trailed off again.

Before what? Again, she had left Asa hanging. What had those men intended to do to Shamira? He didn't even need to ask the question. He knew exactly what they would have wanted from her, a beautiful, radiant young woman. He tasted bile in his mouth just thinking of their sick thoughts and dastardly intentions.

"Nevertheless, I'm being punished for not telling anyone where I was going and endangering both Rut and Libi. I can't leave the house. Asa, I'm sorry, I know you were also punished for my request. I hope you can forgive me."

Asa's breathing became irregular. He wanted to say that none of it was Shamira's fault and place the blame solely on himself. He had left her. He had abandoned her. If he had been there, he could have protected her from those men. He loved his home city, but he was not blind to its flaws.

If he had been there, he could have seen to it that they never got lost in the first place! He was the one who had left them defenseless in the streets of Jerusalem. Of course, that could be blamed on his father. Or was his soured relationship with his father Asa's fault as well? Every move he made seemed to disappoint his father and only bring more and more trouble into his already non-existent family life, and all of those were his decisions. Maybe that was why he'd wandered into Shamira's courtyard so many times as a boy.

Asa had been enamored by Shamira's family and the way her parents so often seemed to enjoy one another whether in conversation, a telling smile, or an affectionate gesture. The manner in which they all spoke so freely with one another, completely unafraid of retaliation or offense intrigued him. The look of love in their eyes was what he had been most fascinated by. A small part of him, he supposed, would always wish he could have been born into their family instead of his own. That he could have seen his parents look at each other with something other than reproach. However, that part of him was largely ignored at present by the part of him which wished to one day start a family of his own with the love of his life: Shamira.

"Shamira, you have nothing to be sorry for as far as I am concerned, but if you must offer an apology then of course I forgive you. I should be asking you for the same forgiveness as well. I had offered to escort you, and I was the one who left you. But Shamira, that isn't why I am here. The reason I came can't wait—it's Jesus of Nazareth!"

He couldn't let her ignore this one chance to get what she'd always dreamed of getting: answers. Answers about who Jesus was, and if it was even possible for him to heal Libi. Answers to Asa's own questions. Asa had seen the man Jesus had raised from the dead. He'd dined in the home of a man who was once a leper. Surely, restoring a little girl's hearing would be just as noble.

"What about him?"

"He's at the temple! Today! Now!" He hurried his words, anxious to take her to him. This time, he would not leave her unattended.

"But I can't go!" Shamira said.

He could hear her warring with herself in her wavering tone. Even though he couldn't see her, he could tell she was in distress.

"Shamira, you may not get another chance like this again…"
He knew it was risky. He knew he was asking her to disobey her
family's command and to go against her father's wishes. He
knew she would be worried about disappointing them. He also
knew the fear of punishment. In fact, he dared to believe he
knew the fear of punishment better than she ever could. His own
father had not spared the rod but had used it liberally. Still, this
was all she'd talked of since they were children. He could not
let her miss this opportunity.

Shamira didn't answer immediately, but when she did, she
whispered through the gate, "All right, but Rut can't walk very
far. Do you think you could help me carry her?"

"Jesus went into the temple and threw out all those buying and selling. He overturned the tables of the money changers and the chairs of those selling doves. He said to them, 'It is written, my house will be called a house of prayer, but you are making it a den of thieves!'" - Matthew 21:12-13 CSB

Heat from the oven hit Shamira harder than the pungent aroma of whatever it was her mother, aunts, and grandmother were cooking for the evening meal. The sweetness from the fruits combined with the savory scent of the stew nearly made Shamira forget why she had gone to the kitchen in the first place, but she quickly remembered when she saw Libi's blank and bored face in the back corner behind her mother, Chava. She came to life again when she saw Shamira standing in the doorway.

"Dodah Chava," Shamira started, doing her best to sound pleasant and unassuming. After all, she did have good intentions, and she truly wanted to make things right between everyone in her family. "Rut is sitting in the sun and a small companion would be a sweet distraction. Could Rut oversee the care of Libi?"

Shamira had to focus her emotions in order to avoid stumbling over her words, for in truth she still felt very guilty about everything that had happened before. Still, she continued. She would not let the troubles of yesterday deter her from pursuing what could be the triumphs of today, and if they did triumph, then she could tell them everything.

Everything.

Then there would be no more lies. A guilty wave swept over her, but she concentrated on letting it pass.

Chava only stared back at her with an unreadable expression on her face. Out of the corner of her eye, Shamira saw her mother step forward. "Chava, it might be good for her to get outside today. Won't you consider it?"

Chava shook her head, and for a minute, Shamira doubted herself. Maybe it wouldn't be possible after all.

She shrugged her shoulders as if to shake off the betraying thoughts and continued in a tone even more commanding than before. "Dodah, I am terribly sorry for the incident before. I promise that it will not happen again. I know better than to go unattended anywhere. Please let me take Libi for a while. I am only trying to help make up for whatever trouble I've already caused." She paused, not sure what to say next. Then it came to her. "Of course, I could always help here. I'd do anything to ease the pain from what happened."

"Oh, we wouldn't want that, would we Chava?" Savta said, rising from her chair to wink at Shamira. "Let the girls go. What could possibly happen in the courtyard?"

Shamira wanted to laugh with her savta, but inside she was still too worried her plan would be found out to let her guard down even for a moment.

"All right," said Chava. "But just for a little while, do you understand?"

"Yes, Dodah," said Shamira, taking Libi's hand. She prayed God would forgive her for this sin in light of what she was trying to achieve. Only time would tell.

Shamira bent down to Libi's line of sight, looking deep into her eyes. How she wished she could communicate verbally what was about to occur, but alas, she just had to keep moving as if nothing out of the ordinary were happening. "Come with me, Libi. We're going outside for a little while."

She led Libi so quickly back out into the courtyard she almost felt she was dragging her. Still, she couldn't afford to waste a moment. They were almost out of the gate when Shamira heard a voice from behind.

"Where are you going?" said Benayahu.

"Nowhere, Beni," Shamira told him, hoping he would be disinterested. Her hopes were unfounded. He hadn't given her the time of day since their quarrel, and she doubted he was holding her back so he could accept her apology and grant forgiveness.

"You can't fool me, Shamira. I know you're up to something, and I also know you're not allowed to leave this courtyard. Tell me what it is, or I'm telling your mother and Dodah Chava."

"Beni, please," Shamira countered. "I can't tell you! But please, *please* don't get me in trouble. I'll be in enough trouble as it is. I'm sorry that I treated you poorly, and you can pay me back for it anytime, but not now, I beg of you."

Benayahu tilted his head backward, then replied, "Then let me come with you."

"What?! No!"

"Then I'll tell!" he said, crossing his arms. Shamira knew he wasn't kidding around this time. "Come on, Shamira. You need me to go with you. I can vouch for you later and protect you, as a man."

He was right. Her father had said she wasn't allowed to leave the house without a guardian. Shamira knew her father probably hadn't been referring to Benayahu, but he was better than no one at all. Seeing no other alternative, she nodded her head in agreement. "All right. But hurry up and be quiet!"

Benayahu hadn't heeded her request. He ran from behind her, brushed past her, and careened through the open gate.

Shamira followed closely behind. Asa, stealth as always, was there with Rut at his side, extending his arm to steady her on the journey. Finally, he looked to Shamira, who had just shut the gate behind them.

"Thank you, Asa," Rut whispered. "I wouldn't miss this for anything."

"Miss what?" asked Benayahu.

"You'll see," Rut assured him.

"Are you ready?" said Asa to Shamira.

"Yes." She had never been more ready for anything in her entire life.

"Where are we going?" said an exasperated Benayahu who trudged along beside Shamira. Both of them walked behind Asa, who led them toward the temple in Jerusalem with Rut in his arms.

"We're going to the temple," Shamira explained. "The teacher from Nazareth is there."

"The one that they say performs miracles?" Beni asked.

"Yes, the one they say is the Messiah."

"The Messiah?" he replied, his jaw gaping open at her.

"Don't shout like that! We're already in trouble with our family. I'd prefer not to get into trouble with anyone else while we're out." Shamira admonished her younger cousin.

"So, you're taking Libi there in the hopes that he will heal her?" asked Benayahu, putting the facts of their journey together.

Shamira nodded. "Yes, now you're catching on."

"It is nearly Pesach. The temple will be flooded with people buying animals for sacrifices. Are you sure this is a good idea?" he asked her. "This feels like yesterday all over again."

"I'm never sure that any of my ideas are good ideas, Beni. Why are you asking so many questions?"

"Because I'm a man! It's my job to know what's going on and to make sure that no harm comes to you!"

Shamira rolled her eyes and muttered, "Boys..."

"Stop saying that, Shamira. I'm not a boy. I'm almost old enough to go into the temple to witness the sacrifices with the other men, and old enough to work. In just a few years I'll be old enough to marry, *not* that I expect to find anyone I'd like to marry anytime soon."

He pronounced his age defiantly, and although Shamira felt somewhat offended by his attitude, she also felt ashamed. He deserved to be treated better, instead of like one of the other children she was so used to taking care of, except she didn't have to take care of them anymore either.

"I'm sorry, Beni—Benayahu," she stuttered as she corrected herself.

He chuckled to himself a little. His laugh was much deeper than Shamira remembered it being. It could almost be mistaken for his father's laugh.

"It's all right, Shamira," he began, speaking much more tenderly than he had before. He really was maturing, and Shamira was grateful for that. "You can still call me Beni if you want."

She smiled at him, in admiration of the young man he was becoming. "Some things will never change, Beni. You'll always be like a little brother to me, and I mean that in the best way possible."

"I understand," he said.

"And by the way," she added, "if by some chance a young woman ever does come along who absolutely captures your heart in every meaning of the phrase... she'll be very lucky to have you in her life."

Beni, for all of his pride, blushed at the sentiment. "Well, I'd be lucky to have any woman look at me the way you look at Asa," he said, before taking the first few steps up to the temple's entrance.

The rest of the conversation was stunted as Shamira helped Libi up the temple stairs, following closely behind the rest of their group. For that, Shamira was grateful. She had loved her conversation with Benayahu but didn't want to have to answer any questions about how she felt toward Asa. At least not from Beni.

The closer they got to the Court of Gentiles, the outermost court, the more Shamira felt as though they were approaching some kind of battle. The sounds of the people shouting and things crashing sent fear into her heart, and she prayed once again that her efforts would not be in vain. She couldn't afford to make another disastrous mistake. She prayed the Lord would give her the right words.

"Asa? What is going on?" She quickly moved to his side.

"Do you see that man there?" He gestured by turning his head in the general direction of a strong, rugged man in the center of the chaos. "That's him. That's Jesus." Asa helped Rut to sit down and then ran his fingers through his hair as he straightened his back. He angled his body toward Shamira and his nearness to her would have made her lose her breath, if she had not still been gasping for air from the climb they had taken to get to this spot.

The man, Jesus of Nazareth, thrashed violently about, overturning tables and breaking open the cages of animals meant for sacrifices. The coins that had belonged to the money changers and merchants were scattered across the stone floor of the temple complex. As he stumbled back and forth, throwing things and knocking over crates and carts, he began to shout with a voice so loud it could have shaken the very pillars holding the temple up. It shook Shamira to her very core.

"It is written, 'My house will be a house of prayer,' but you have made it a den of thieves!"

The crowd was quiet then, save a few people's shocked gasps, and Shamira's heart began to race as she wondered what would happen next. "He is... He is ridding the temple of the merchants!" Shamira whispered.

She had often overheard her father and uncles complaining about the practices of those who came to sell livestock and trade in the temple. They would say it was unfair to charge people such obscene amounts of money, just so they could worship their God, and she agreed wholeheartedly with their reasoning, but she never thought anything would be done about it. Her father and uncles were always in agreement on that matter, bleak as it was, that some things might never change, but that it was necessary to at least try to do what was right in spite of the ways of the world.

She looked from side to side to gauge the reactions of her companions. Asa watched the man's actions intently. Rut couldn't see anything from where she had sat down, unable to stand, but she was listening to what was happening, and she too appeared amazed, with her arms encircled around Libi. Shamira looked over to Beni, and strangely enough, Beni was quite solemn. She wondered why he would appear so despondent, as if he were personally convicted by Jesus' declaration, and then she remembered his earlier conversation, barely a week prior.

"Abba... Abba and Sabba were right," he whispered. "I... I feel so foolish."

Shamira looked at him and his guilt-ridden face. She placed a hand on his arm. "Beni, you can't trouble yourself over that."

"I should have listened... I should have understood."

"All that matters is that you understand now," she reminded him.

"Yes, and I really do this time."

Nobody in the temple moved, except for Jesus of Nazareth, who had begun to walk away from the mess made in his stand against the temple's hypocrisy. His shoulders heaved up and down as he breathed deeply, wiping the sweat from his brow.

A voice to Shamira's left called out, "Although I cannot see you, I know who you are. I have heard the stories and what other people have said about you." She turned to gaze upon the owner of the voice and realized at once that he was a blind man. "Please, forgive me of my sins."

Jesus, relaxing, went over to him and looked upon the man with such love. Softly, he said, "Your sins are forgiven." Jesus touched the man's face as if to wipe away the dirt from his eyes.

At once, the man's eyes began to focus, and instantly they filled with tears of gratitude. Shamira gasped. With a few words and a simple touch, a man's sight had been restored!

Another called out to him, one who was lame, and Jesus

helped them too. He pronounced their sins forgiven, just as he had done with the formerly blind man. The person used a stick to walk and support themselves, but Jesus took it from their hands, and suddenly their limbs straightened. They too had been healed!

"Go and sin no more," Jesus smiled.

Shamira realized that now was her only opportunity, as he continued to walk through the Temple, laying hands on those with afflictions and healing them. She didn't know how to greet him. How to get his attention. What words could she offer to the Messiah? What words would ever be fitting? But she remembered what Rut had said, about how they had felt so close to God when he'd ridden into Jerusalem and they'd all been singing his praises. Shamira felt just as close to God now as she'd witnessed Jesus' devotion to His commandments. As the money launderers and merchants were being driven out of the temple, it seemed the presence of God was making its way back in, and Shamira could do nothing but praise the one who had done it.

Shamira fell to her knees and cried out, "Hosanna to the Son of David!"

"Hosanna! Hosanna!"

Beni dropped down beside her, and Asa as well. Both bent their knees and repeated her words. "Hosanna to the Son of David." She heard Rut's voice from behind her as well, and Shamira hoped and prayed he would look favorably upon them.

"Hosanna! Hosanna to the Son of David!" they called in unison, all except for Libi, whose eyes remained affixed on the mysterious man at the center of attention.

All at once, Shamira's joyful countenance fell when she heard the bitter voices of the temple leaders and priests.

"Agh, what do the children know? See, Jesus of Nazareth, your work here has meant nothing to anyone, except for these children who should be with their parents. Surely they must be disciplined!"

"Yes, Jesus, do you hear what these children are saying? What do you have to say in response?"

Shamira wanted to stand up and shout at them all. However,

if she had learned anything in recent times, it was that shouting wasn't always the answer. She remained silent, and prayed instead, begging God to have mercy on them all. She whispered a prayer ever so softly, "Please Lord, have mercy on us."

Next, she heard the voice of Jesus of Nazareth, who did not sound nearly as full of wrath as he had earlier when he was overturning the tables. When he spoke this time, his voice was calm and full of love. He answered them: "Have you never read, 'You have prepared praise from the mouths of infants and nursing babies?'"

Shamira felt now was her chance. Keeping her head bowed, she cried out to Jesus to plead for Libi the only way she knew how to. Words had power, and she would use her words to beg for forgiveness for her family. "My Lord, my youngest cousin, Libi, has been deaf-mute since birth. If my family has committed any sin that has caused her to live with this affliction, then we are deeply ashamed, and I beg you to forgive it. She does not need to bear this burden for us."

She waited with bated breath for his reply, but what followed were only the objections and protests of the Pharisees and Sadducees who surrounded them on either side.

"She is a girl who does not know her place!" shouted one.

"Will you now rebuke this child?"

Shamira did not let their words affect her. She kept her eyes focused on the stone floor beneath her, listening only for the voice of Jesus. "Have I not already said, 'Let the children come to me?'"

Shamira did not know what to do next. She was at a loss for words, for perhaps one of the first times in her life she could recall, and she was too stunned to move. A shadow crossed her vision, and she raised her head up ever so slightly to see that it was Jesus himself, kneeling down in front of her. He took her hands and raised her up, and at his touch Shamira began to cry.

"Don't cry, daughter. Your faith has pleased my Father in heaven. Show me your cousin, the one you say is deaf-mute," he said gently.

Shamira thought in her mind that she should still be afraid and nervous, but her heart overflowed with a strange peace. This man had called her 'daughter,' and addressed her in love. There was no shame in his tone.

Shamira did as instructed. She turned around and took Libi's hand, pulling her forward and presenting her to Jesus. Libi looked back up at Shamira, and Shamira nodded that it was all right. "He is a friend, Libi, go on," she whispered. The little girl's hair fell in unruly locks that partially covered her face.

Shamira looked up expectantly at Jesus, wondering what he was about to do. When she looked at him, she felt as though she were looking at a great light. He was completely radiant, and to be so near to him took her breath away. She knew in her heart she could never forget what it felt like to be in his presence, and if this was what her sabba meant every time he spoke of that fateful night out in the fields of Bethlehem, she most certainly understood.

Jesus looked at Libi, smiled at her, and said, "Do not despise this girl nor any of these children, for their angels always see the face of my father who is in heaven." Then, in one swift motion, he tucked the strands of unkempt hair behind Libi's ears and spoke directly to her. "Daughter, you have seen much today. What have you to say about all that you have witnessed?"

Libi's sweet voice broke through the crowds like lightning through the night sky. The sound of her speech was like birdsong, and her laughter just as pleasant. She sang, shaky at first but stronger with each syllable. "Hosanna! *Hosanna!*"

*"The blind and the lame came to him in the temple, and he
healed them. When the chief priests and the scribes saw the
wonders that he did and the children shouting in the temple,
'Hosanna to the Son of David!' they were indignant and said
to him, 'Do you hear what these children are saying?' Jesus
replied, 'Yes, have you never read: You have prepared praise
from the mouths of infants and nursing babies?' Then he left
them, went out of the city to Bethany, and spent the night
there." - Matthew 21:14-17 CSB*

Asa couldn't help but laugh, the joy he felt overcame his reason.
He realized he probably sounded maniacal or insane, but that
didn't matter to him. They'd seen Jesus and his power right
before their eyes, in action! Libi, whom they had all long
believed would never hear or speak, whom his father had
practically condemned to a living death, was in fact, speaking,

and her voice was so, so pure.

"Say," said one of the temple leaders who had been watching the events unfold. "Isn't that your son, Avram?"

Asa squeezed his eyes shut. Of course, it had all been worth it. How could it not have been? But the mention of his father's name still filled him with dread, even if he had known all along that this kind of confrontation would be unavoidable.

From the back of the crowd Avram emerged in all of his priestly robes, instantly putting all rejoicing to a halt. Asa looked on at his father whose face burned with fire.

"Asa!" he roared. "How dare you disrespect me like this in a public setting. In the temple! Come here at once!"

Asa looked at his father, then at Shamira, then back at his father. He had an obligation to Shamira. He had to keep her safe. He would not let her out of his sight unprotected—not after what had happened the last time he let her go. Shamira deserved to be treasured in ways he had never seen his father treasure his mother. It always astounded Asa how his father could spend so much time engrossed in God's word, and still be so unfamiliar with love. Asa was convinced that love was written on every page. It was love that would keep Asa from parting with Shamira, even if it meant he himself would be hurt.

"Abba," he stuttered. "I cannot; I promised Aharon I would keep Shamira safe."

"I'm not going to ask again, son," he replied, tapping his foot on the hard, stone floor. The tension was thicker than the air on a hot, humid Jerusalem day.

Without breaking eye contact with his father, Asa saw Benayahu step toward Jesus and ask, "Please, come home with us!"

Shamira echoed the request. "Yes, no one will believe us if we say these things to them. You must come home with us and meet our abbas!"

Just then, the twelve disciples Asa had met in Bethany came up behind Jesus. "Teacher, the sun is setting. We must leave the city soon if we plan to make it back before dark," said one of them.

"Leave the city?" Benayahu asked.

"Yes," another one of the disciples answered. "We are staying in Bethany during the week of Pesach."

Shamira didn't seem to let that stop her. She continued her bargaining. "Our houses will be on the way for you then, since we live on the edge of the city ourselves. You can come with us!"

"Not you, Asa! You are going home." Avram once again interrupted them, sending a dagger into the heart of the conversation.

Asa bit his lip. With everyone standing around them and staring, it seemed Asa had little choice in the matter. How could he argue with his father without dishonoring him? Without breaking one of God's commandments?

Just then, Jesus of Nazareth raised his voice to speak again. "Your faith has rewarded you, daughter of Jerusalem. You could not have known these things about me were true by your own knowledge, yet you believed."

The disciples around him nodded in agreement, and Asa let the words wash over him. How many times now had he seen the proof of Jesus' miracles, and still struggled to believe?

Jesus continued, "However, because you have asked me with pure intentions, my disciples and I shall accompany you to your home."

"Asa? Is that you?" Asa heard his name being called from among the disciples. He turned his head and recognized the voice and the man who bore it immediately.

"Peter! Yes, it's me!"

"Teacher, I know this young man. We've met before," Peter explained to Jesus. Asa saw Peter make eye contact with his father, before turning back to Asa to add quietly, "We shall see to it that your friends are safely escorted back to their home. Be at peace and do as your abba says."

As much as Asa didn't want to leave, he prayed his thanks to God for providing a way out of the situation. Shamira would be safe, and hopefully, Asa would not anger his father anymore. He looked to Shamira, not knowing what to say or even if he could say anything to her with his father in such close proximity. Her warm brown eyes seemed to smile at him as she nodded, and he knew she would not hold any of this against him. She understood.

He returned her gaze with a half-smile, grateful that all was well—at least between them. Then, Shamira turned, breaking off the intimate moment of silence they shared.

"Oh!" she said. "This is my cousin, Rut. She was hurt recently and can't walk very well without assistance. It was Asa who helped carry her here, and I can't support her myself."

"Here, I will help," said Peter, offering an arm to Rut.

Then Shamira, her cousins, Jesus, and the disciples began the long descent down the temple steps toward their home. Asa watched his heart disappear on the horizon, and then he prepared himself for a stern lecture from his father. He knew he wouldn't be punished publicly. Not in front of all the other priests and Levites—that would only exacerbate the situation. But later on in the evening Asa knew the punishment would surely come. He just didn't know how hard of a blow he would receive.

Doubt flitted through his mind as he imagined what his father's reprimand would be. Was he in the wrong? No, he reminded himself, strengthening his resolve. Libi had been healed. The impossible had become possible in the blink of an eye. That was most certainly right, regardless of what his father said.

But did that mean that his father was the one who was wrong?

Even from outside of the gate, Shamira could imagine the scene beyond the wall. Her family must have been distraught, wondering where they had gone off to. But Shamira wasn't afraid. She had Jesus with her, and she couldn't wait to introduce him to her family, or for any of them to hear Libi's beautiful song. Shamira pushed open the gate, and held it open for their company to squeeze into the narrow courtyard. First

Benayahu, then Rut who was followed closely by Peter, then the disciples, and finally... Jesus, who still held Libi's hand.

Shamira watched Chava's expression change from fear to relief. "Libi, hamuda!" she cried, falling to the ground and opening her arms.

A nervous smile spread across Shamira's face, realizing that everyone, except her father and uncles, was present. Her father, Tamir, and Binyamin would have still been at work, of course, but her mother, aunts, and grandparents had clearly been upset by their disappearance. How would her family react?

Jesus bent down to Libi. "Go on, little girl, tell your imma you love her."

Letting go of Jesus' hand, Libi sprang into a run and nearly jumped into her mother's arms. "Imma! I'm home! Why are you crying?"

Chava's jaw dropped and sobs escaped her. "Can it be? Can it really be so?"

Shamira wanted to laugh, to affirm that Libi was indeed healed, to sing for joy with her mother and family, but her savta's screams interrupted them, and her screams were not the same joyful kind as Chava's.

Shamira diverted her attention to her grandparents. Her sabba had fallen to the ground, and his face now lay pressed into the dirt. Had he collapsed? Were all of Shamira's plans about to go wrong, again?

As her heart pounded, she heard whispering. Praying? Was he praying?

Raising his voice, her sabba began, "My Lord, my eyes are weak with age and my mind is not what it used to be, but I would not forget your face even if I were to live to be a hundred years old." Tears streamed down his face, creating small puddles on the ground. He barely lifted his head as he continued. "It is you, isn't it? Your eyes... they're exactly the same."

Jesus stepped between all of them and walked toward Eliyahu, holding out both of his hands to help him rise. "Eliyahu," he said, gesturing to Shamira and her cousins. "I have found your lost sheep."

"I worship you, my Lord! My Savior!" Eliyahu cried.

Shamira stepped forward on her toes, eagerly watching the events unfold and looking back and forth at the faces of each of her loved ones, trying to judge their thoughts and hearts.

"But, but how has this happened? We were told... We were told that..." Elisheva said, tripping over her words. It was the first time Shamira had heard her mother's voice tremor.

"Truly I say unto you," Jesus began, "this was done so that God's works might be displayed. We must do the works of him who sent me while it is still day. Night is coming when no one can work. As long as I am in the world, I am the light of the world. While you have the light, believe in the light so that you may become children of light."

His words were soft spoken, and his cadence was slow, but the meaning behind what he said resonated with all of those who heard it. They were powerful words.

"Now, we must be going," said Jesus, turning to leave.

Shamira jumped forward, ready to protest. "You cannot leave now! You must wait until my abba and uncles return so they can see you too!"

Her sabba placed a hand on her shoulder and continued in a way Shamira knew was much more polite and reasonable. "Please, forgive my granddaughter for her boldness, but it would mean a great deal to me—to all of us—if you would join us for dinner. You have given us Libi. Let us at the very least give you food for your empty stomachs!"

Jesus looked up at the sky, where the sun was rapidly setting, and then back to Eliyahu. "Don't trouble yourself, Eliyahu. I really must leave you all now, but you will see me again very soon. I promise."

Shamira saw tears fill her sabba's eyes as he took Jesus' hand between his own. "It is enough for me just to have seen you today," he said, then he continued to look at Jesus but spoke to the women behind him. "Elisheva, Devorah—please go and get some food and wrap it up for these men so they can take it with them on their journey."

Barely a moment had passed before they had returned with rounds of barley bread and cheese. The disciples thanked them for their generosity, and after a few more parting words were spoken, they left as quickly as they had come.

Shamira was left standing dazed and confused in the middle of the courtyard. It had all happened so fast. In one afternoon so much had changed, and now—was it over? What was she supposed to do next?

Chava began to exclaim her praises. "Blessed be the name of the Lord! Surely that man was the Messiah that Eliyahu has told us about so many times!"

"What is the meaning of this? Why have you all assembled here?" said Tamir, entering the courtyard from the front gate, followed by his two brothers, Aharon and Binyamin, who stood with mouths agape.

"Yes, tell us! What is all of this fuss about?" said Binyamin, scratching his forehead.

Chava ran to her husband, the first sign of closeness between them that Shamira had seen in years. "Libi. It's Libi! She has been healed by the teacher from Nazareth—the one whom everyone in the city has been talking about!"

"It is true," said Eliyahu. "He is the Messiah!"

"Father, how can you possibly know such a thing as fact? You could easily be mistaken and lose your life over a poor judgment of character," Binyamin objected.

His wife rushed over to him. "No, Binyamin! We saw him. He was here just moments ago. What they're saying is true!"

"Chava, what are you talking about?" questioned Tamir, pulling away from his wife. Chava never stopped smiling, even amid the doubts that whirled and circled around her. She reached out to Libi, who quickly skipped to her father.

"Abba! You're home!" she cheered.

He raised a hand to his face and stumbled backward. "Is it true? Is it really true? Am I really hearing…?"

"Abba!" she repeated.

Tamir picked her up in his arms and twirled her around in the air, bringing her back down to the ground and holding her tight against his chest, laughing heartily and speaking words that were unintelligible through his smile.

"How has this happened?" said Aharon. "When was the teacher here?"

Shamira anxiously tip-toed toward her father and made her confession. "It was me, Abba. I snuck out of the house earlier today with Libi, Rut, and Beni when I heard that Jesus of Nazareth was at the temple. Asa came to let me know Jesus was close."

"Shamira..." he sighed. His expression was unreadable, and Shamira couldn't tell if he was upset, confused, or angry. "Did you learn nothing from what happened yesterday?"

So that was it then. She was meant to be apologetic.

"Aharon, please," Elisheva pleaded, stepping between them.

"Don't scold her, brother," Tamir intervened, still smiling down at his daughter, who beamed with pride. "I do not know who this Jesus is or by what authority he acts, but Chava has told me he is responsible for my daughter's healing. Libi is living proof of his power. Shamira's faith and boldness played a role in giving our daughter a voice, and I will vouch for both her and Jesus of Nazareth. Surely God was in this, for He protected them all and returned Libi restored."

"I am very happy for you, truly I am, but that's not what this is about. Shamira needs to realize her actions could have had detrimental consequences." Aharon's voice was low but firm.

"How can you say you would follow this teacher you've never met, Tamir?" asked Binyamin.

"Do you not see the miracle before you? Have you so little faith?"

"I have faith, brother, but that doesn't mean there couldn't be more than one explanation..."

The three brothers continued to bicker, and Shamira's head began to hurt at the continued back-and-forth of her emotions until Eliyahu raised his voice over all of them and shouted, "Silence! I have said it before, and I shall say it again: I knew this man as an infant in Bethlehem. I recognized him at once— he was radiant and full of light. My eyes have only ever beheld such glory once before in my life. Surely, this was the work of the Messiah, for he called me by my name and knew what was in my heart!"

Binyamin replied, "Abba, he could have learned your name from any one of the children. You have no way of knowing his knowledge was divine. Now, I agree that we should praise God for Libi's healing, but we are still uncertain if this man is the Messiah. You can't simply throw that title around."

Aharon added, "You're tired. Perhaps you should rest until tomorrow, then you might have more clarity."

Eliyahu shouted, "No! I won't! I am not tired, nor crazy, nor mad! I am an old man, but I am still of sound mind. That man is the Messiah! He was the one whose birth was proclaimed by angels. He was... He was..."

Shamira noticed how her grandfather began to teeter-back-and-forth. His breathing became ragged and unsteady. Sabba Eliyahu raised his hand and clutched his chest, wheezing sounds coming from his throat.

"My husband!" Savta cried. Before anyone else could react, Savta rushed to his side, and as he collapsed onto the ground, she fell with him, refusing to let go.

While her family moved around her in a frenzy, Shamira froze in place, petrified by fear. Would her beloved Sabba be taken from them, just as easily as Libi's voice had been given?

16

*"Even though he had performed so many signs in their
presence, they did not believe in him." - John 12:37 CSB*

The lamps remained lit all through the night as Shamira's Savta
Hodiyah maintained her vigilant watch over Sabba, who was not
recovering as well as the rest of the family had hoped. He had
remained unconscious since his earlier collapse, and Savta had
remained lost in her prayers ever since. Even now, in the early
hours of the morning, Shamira could hear the quiet murmurings
of her conversation with the Almighty from her upstairs
bedroom. It wasn't keeping her awake; Shamira's own heart
was too troubled to sleep.

The previous night, after Sabba's collapse, no one brought
up Jesus again, although his name continued to echo in
Shamira's thoughts. He had acknowledged her, a young woman,
in front of a whole crowd of others. He had not reprimanded her
or punished her for her outspokenness or presumptuousness.

Instead, he had listened to her and answered her with grace. He had not turned away from Libi or ignored her but had embraced her with love. He was not repulsed by her, nor did he accuse their family of hiding their sins from God. He was compassionate to each and every one of them. He was everything the priests were not, and that excited Shamira.

Furthermore, she knew something her father and uncles did not. She knew no one had told Jesus what Eliyahu's name was. He had known it without asking. Even if they did not believe it, Shamira knew it in her heart: Jesus was the Messiah.

Shamira wanted to scream and shout at the world that on the day of such a blessing, such a tragedy had also occurred. In the face of irrefutable evidence, her family still seemed to disagree. The evidence was literally speaking to them through Libi. She prayed God would open the eyes of her precious family so that they, too, would know their Messiah.

Rut groaned and rolled onto her side. Shamira turned to see if her cousin was awake, but she was still sleeping soundly. Sighing, Shamira quickly tossed aside her own coverings and rose to her feet. The light of day was already shining bright enough that she figured more of her family would be rising soon.

She crept around Rut's still body and walked barefoot out of her own room, making her way through the rest of the house. She pulled her arms close to her chest, the chill of the floor beneath her feet numbing her toes and giving her goosebumps all over. She didn't know where to go. Downstairs where Savta lay at Sabba's side? Upstairs where her family slept?

She could no longer run to her mother and father's arms every time she woke up from a nightmare, especially because she was now living the nightmare. Just a few weeks before, Shamira didn't think it was possible for her grandfather to die, but the harsh realities of the world were quickly catching up to her. Everybody died, and her sabba was not as young as he used to be, nor as she liked to think he was.

She puttered down the stairs, passing the lower room where her sabba was resting under careful watch of her savta. She peered at them for a moment and smiled when she saw her savta cradling her husband in her arms, keeping him close to her heart.

She was still singing, ever so softly, and Shamira found the moment too beautiful to disturb. She continued her walk through the house and found herself in the courtyard.

She had always enjoyed sitting under their tree and reflecting on life's many blessings and its many challenges. The tree, the little bit of God's creation, made her feel calm. She was surprised to see her father was already sitting underneath it in her usual spot.

"I see why you like coming out here, Shamira," he said, his morning voice hoarse and unpracticed. "It's quite peaceful."

"Only when I'm in trouble," she quipped, heat rising to her face. "It's the best place to sort out my thoughts."

"Oh, my star…" he sighed. Shamira hated seeing him so weary and grief stricken. "I think it is me who has done something wrong this time."

Shamira blinked several times, both because of how tired she was, and because of how surprised his statement made her feel. "You? Abba, you have not done anything wrong at all. It was I who disobeyed orders and left the house without permission when I was forbidden to do so at all. Don't blame yourself. It was me who was in the wrong."

"Well, yes, Shamira. You were wrong for disobeying me, but I was more wrong for not listening to you in the first place. I understand it was similar motivations that caused you to make the choices you did in the marketplace just the other day. While they were wrong choices, I can only assume you made them because you didn't feel you could trust me. And I'm ashamed to say I think you were right. Furthermore, I was wrong for not listening to my own abba, and I regret that so very much now." Aharon paused. "Tell me, ahava sheli, my bright shining star, how did you ever come to have such a reckless belief in someone you could not see?"

He motioned for her to sit by him, and she obliged, happy to sit close to him where she would be warm and protected from the bitter morning air. She rested her head on his shoulder and watched the sun slowly rise over the Jerusalem buildings.

"I'm… I'm not really sure, Abba. When Sabba would tell his stories, when I would hear the scriptures read in the temple and listen to you and Sabba explain them to me, I never believed anything different. It all seemed so clear to me, and I felt so strongly in my heart that it was true. It just had to be true, Abba. I have clung to that hope for so long. Not nearly as long as Sabba, of course, but as long as I can remember. I always believed the Messiah would come. I knew it in my heart."

Her father chuckled to himself. "You surpass even me with your depth of faith, Shamira. How did I ever get so blessed to have such a daughter?" He ran his hands through his hair, which was the same shade as Shamira's naturally, but had been dusted by a bit of gray throughout. Shamira thought it made him look courtly, noble even.

"How did I ever get so blessed to have such an abba?" she countered, smiling.

She loved her father so much. Whenever she felt like a failure, whether she'd ruined something for dinner, broken something valuable, made a mess, or gotten herself into trouble, she could always count on her father's wisdom to guide her path.

She heard her father's breathing hitch and listened to the shaky and unsteady words he spoke next. "I wish I had felt the same way about my abba when I was your age. The way he raved about a Messiah—I thought he was a lunatic. The whole village did! That's why we settled here, in Jerusalem. A large city where one man's ravings can go unnoticed among the masses. Now I fear I will never get the chance to tell him how wrong I was."

"You believe him? You believe that Jesus is the Messiah?" Shamira lunged forward, her eyes suddenly wide open with excitement and anticipation.

"I would seem like a lunatic if I didn't, wouldn't I? Libi is literally speaking and talking among us, when a week ago to even suggest such a thing would have been impossible. How could I be confronted with such evidence and still doubt?" he said to her, but Shamira knew him too well.

"And yet I still hear doubt in your voice."

He took a deep breath and answered, "To accept it—would change *everything.*"

"Abba, is that not what you have been hoping and praying

for? Day after day, night after night I hear you talk of oppression and hypocrisy, both in the temple and outside of it. You have prayed diligently that our God in heaven would see the frustrations of the people of Israel and bring about a great change. Why are you now refusing the gift He is offering you, that you have wanted so very much?"

"My father's zeal… it made us outcasts." Aharon, the man Shamira had always respected as a father and as a leader in their family, was afraid.

"But perhaps, coming to Jerusalem was not a way for you to hide from the world, but for Jesus to be revealed to the world through you. Through your family."

Aharon turned to face his daughter very slowly, tears welling up in his eyes, and said, "My little Shamira."

She clung to his arm and burrowed her face into his chest, breathing in the scent of earth and musk.

"I know, Abba."

"When did you become such a wise young woman? Here I thought it was my job to teach you. You have showed me a different path to walk entirely, and soon you'll be forging your own path in life. I underestimated you, Shamira."

Shamira wanted to object. To tell him she would never leave his side and that she would stay with her family in their house forever, but change no longer seemed so frightening. Shamira felt as though she could face any change with just as much confidence and hope as she had when she had come face to face with Jesus for the first time. She had always been bold and impulsive, but perhaps that boldness was propelling her toward something great.

She pondered all of these things silently, sitting next to her father as the two of them watched the sky turn from purple, to golden, to bright blue. A new day. Whatever challenges it presented, Shamira would face them.

But what if the next change was not a good change? What if she had to face it with one less family member?

"Oh, Shamira?" Her father's question pulled her out of the trenches of her own mind. "One last thing. Please, don't ever leave this house without telling me or one of your uncles again.

Is that understood?" She could tell the rule was not made out of reproach, but out of love, and she nodded in reply.

"My star, your faith shines like the light in the heavens. Even in the darkness, your passion for what you believe burns like candlelight in the black of night. Seeing your faith manifest itself in a miracle yesterday was…indescribable. But I want to caution you and say that the way your faith manifested the day before was not nearly as joyous or miraculous. You put both yourself and your cousins in danger. I am asking you—my beautiful, wise, and sometimes too impulsive for your own good, bright-shining star—to honor my request. You don't need to bear the weight of the world on your shoulders alone. I will always be here for you. Can I count on you to honor me in this way—to respect my authority as your father, heed my caution as your guardian, and understand how much I treasure you as your abba?"

"I promise, Abba. I will honor you, and I will listen to your voice as well as God's voice. No more relying on myself." No more lies, no more deceit. God would be with her.

"*Promise* is a powerful word." Her abba looked at her, beaming with pride. The gleam in his eyes threatened to outshine the morning sun as it crested the tops of the buildings surrounding them. Shamira bowed her head respectfully. *"Promise"* was a powerful word, and she intended to use the power of her words for good going forward.

She had learned the hard way how her words and the words of others had the power to tear down and destroy, but she was also learning that her words had the power to encourage and make things right. If she prayed her words to God, He might take them and use them for His glory. If she used her words to share His love, others might come to know Him and hear of Jesus' for themselves.

"There's something else still on your mind Shamira, I can see it in your eyes. Is it Asa?" Her father's question was direct and to the point.

Shamira didn't even try to hide her emotions, her eyes immediately filled with tears.

"Oh, Abba, I'm terribly worried!" she confirmed. "Asa came

to tell me that Jesus was here in the city and helped me get Libi to see him. But his father was there at the temple and saw everything and he... Well, the way things ended, I'm afraid of what he'll do to Asa. It's all my fault!" A sob erupted from her throat.

"Oh Shamira," he said, pulling her closer to him. "Tears are all right for now, but when you're ready, you must change those tears into prayers. God holds the future in His hands, there is nothing for you to be anxious about that he is not already taking care of. We shall pray for him together, all right?"

"All right, Abba," Shamira sniffed, "Thank you."

"What are you doing down here?" said Rut.

"I'm trying to make a stew," said Shamira, almost in tears. The top of her dress was covered in a variety of different herbs and spices. Rut looked down at the ingredients on the table, then back to Shamira, then back down at the ingredients, shaking her head.

"Here, let me help you," offered Rut, moving toward the table. She set some of the ingredients aside, and, taking a knife in her hand, focused on a much smaller selection of onions and carrots. "Lentils and barley will be added to the pot, and garlic, pepper, salt, and a few other herbs will season the mixture once it begins cooking over the fire."

"You shouldn't be helping me. You should be upstairs resting," said Shamira, although she was grateful for Rut's assistance.

"And you shouldn't be trying to cook, ever, but here we are." Rut smiled. "Why are you making a stew anyway? Shouldn't this room be busy with preparations for the Pesach meal?"

"No one is themselves today. And Sabba... Rut, I just feel so useless! I had to do something!"

"And preparing a stew was the best idea that you could come

up with?"

Shamira laughed a little, the nervous tension all throughout her body subsiding for just a moment. A day ago, Shamira had felt as though her whole world would be only laughs and smiles for the rest of her life, and in half that time, she wondered if she would ever smile again. Her whole family was in shock.

"Well, it might not have been my best idea, but it was my only idea."

"It is a wonderful idea, Shamira, truly. You are wanting to comfort our family."

"It's only a wonderful idea because you're helping me, otherwise my stew would have just made everyone feel worse than they already do."

"Stop that," chided Rut. "Stop talking about yourself like that, or I won't help you. Is Sabba really doing that poorly?"

"Has no one told you anything?"

"Imma had been watching me like a hawk you know, but ever since Sabba collapsed she seems to have forgotten that I even exist. I know I'm still technically supposed to be resting upstairs, but I was so lonely and bored. My head doesn't even hurt anymore, I'm not dizzy, and I don't feel faint. I feel like my old self again. Imma was just being overprotective."

Shamira felt sorry that Rut had been ignored all morning and wished she would have remembered to check on her cousin sooner, but no one had been in their right mind that day.

"Savta stayed awake all night with him, but he didn't wake. He's been in and out of consciousness all morning. Sabba's more than just tired—he's weakened like I've never seen. It's as if... I don't know. Never mind."

"No, Shamira. What is it? You've always had good instincts, even if you do tend to be impulsive about them."

"Yesterday... Did you hear what Jesus said to him?"

"Which part?"

"It was quiet, and very quick. I doubt anyone else even noticed, but as Jesus was leaving, I heard him tell Sabba that they would be together again very soon."

"That could have meant a number of things. Jesus is staying nearby in Bethany for the Pesach week. Perhaps he merely meant that our paths would cross again, or that he would return to our doorstep."

"But he didn't say it like that." Shamira bit her lip anxiously. She wondered if her words sounded irrational to her cousin.

Rut chopped the vegetables with increased diligence and continued. "And you think he was foretelling Sabba's death, don't you?"

"I don't know, Rut. It just sounded odd. I'm probably just hearing things in the tone of his voice, nothing more."

Shamira found herself wishing Asa was beside her at that moment, steadying her, comforting her. In fact, she wished he could always be beside her. It didn't make sense to her that when her family needed her most all she wanted was to be with him, until she realized Asa *was* family. Even if they weren't bound by a ketubah yet, they had grown up together. Her cousins loved him. Her savta had a special fondness for him. He was just as much a part of their family as any one of them. If their family was going through a hard time, she wanted him to be there with them.

"What has your thoughts so captivated now, Mira?"

One tear escaped her eye, then another. She whispered, more shrill than usual. "I just wish Asa was here."

Setting down her knife, Rut ran to the other side of the table and embraced her cousin. "It's all right, Mira. It's all right. Just let it out. You don't have to worry about anything or protect anyone, Shamira."

"No, no, Rut. This is my problem, not yours." Shamira straightened with determination.

"Shamira, it is all right to have feelings. You don't always need to be the strength of this family, the one who always has something to say, the one who will defend her family no matter the cost. It's all right just to be a woman, and a woman in love."

"Is it wrong for me to be so worried about Asa, when my own sabba lies in the next room, gravely ill?" she said, guilt still tugging at her stomach. She had prayed over the matter as her abba had counseled her to, but Asa still captivated her thoughts.

"No! It's not wrong at all. You're scared right now—we all are. It is only natural for you to want the one you love to be by your side. Asa is a part of this family. Even if you two weren't meant for each other, he stole Savta's heart the first day she saw him."

"You know I love you too, Rut. I am glad to have you by my side as well." Shamira wiped the rogue tears from her eyes.

"It is as we have always said. We will always be there for each other."

"Oh, wonderful, now I'll never get rid of you." Shamira feigned annoyance.

"You can't fool me, Shamira. I know your heart is too big for your own body. Admit it, you wouldn't want it any other way." Rut smiled impishly.

Shamira chuckled, giving herself away even if her words said otherwise. Waving a finger in the air, Shamira replied, "I think we should get back to making the stew!" And both of them filled the room with laughter.

Shamira quieted. "Do you want me to get you a chair? You must still be exhausted."

"Shamira, please. I'm fully recovered—unless you ask my mother. To her, I might as well never lift a finger again. Maybe I should have a chair ready if she comes this way—that way I can leap to it, and she'll never suspect a thing! That's a big *if* though. It always shocks me how even in such a small house where we're all so close together all of the time, we can still lose each other."

"I know what you mean. I once thought it would be a good idea to play a hiding game with the boys when they were younger. I was so worried that I'd lost them forever and that I'd never find them, but they came running quickly when Dodah Chava called for dinner."

"I remember that!" Rut grinned. "You had come running upstairs to find me, scared for your life!"

Rut bent over in a cackling fit. Shamira sighed, "You know, I meant it when I said we should get back to the stew, Rut…"

"Yes, of course…the stew…" she said between snickers. She turned to the table, now keeping her back to Shamira which still didn't hide the fact that she was shaking with laughter.

"Rut!"

"I'm sorry, Shamira, but it really was terribly amusing!"

Shamira let her laugh for a moment. The Lord knew they could use the respite from life's troubles. "Well, when you're done being so amused at my expense, perhaps you can show me how to actually prepare this stew properly!"

"Here, why don't you put these things away. These definitely don't belong in any kind of stew." She gestured to the pile of discarded ingredients. "Then when you come back you can help me finish chopping these, and we'll put this pot over the fire and let the heat do its work. All right?"

"All right," she said, still unable to completely ignore Rut's subdued but still-audible giggles in the background. She stared at the handful of vegetables and herbs she held and stood by her earlier assessment that these seemed like suitable stew ingredients. Although she was aware Rut knew what she was talking about, she wondered just how awful a stew with her ingredients would have tasted. "I really thought these would have made a good stew. They looked like the right ingredients to me."

"Really?" said Rut, side eyeing Shamira's stash. "Maybe I can teach you to pick them out by smell. I suppose they all do look sort of similar, and it's often dark in here. I could see how you might confuse them."

17

"Sacrifice to the Lord your God a Passover animal from the herd or flock in the place where the Lord chooses to have his name dwell." - Deuteronomy 16:2 CSB

Shamira turned the corner, clutching the bowl tightly between her hands and taking each and every step with care. Heel, toe. Heel, toe. Heel, toe.

"Sabba? Savta? May I come in?"

Savta rose from her seat and walked toward Shamira. "Your sabba is very tired, Shamira. Let me take that bowl; I will make sure he is fed."

Shamira almost gave it to her, and she would have if they had not been interrupted by her sabba. "Let her come in, Hodiyah. It is you who is tired." His voice was weak, but still had the same jovial, youthful life in it Shamira had always loved so much.

"Yes, Savta. You have not rested for even a moment. Let me

take this to Sabba, and you can get some much-needed sleep in another room." Shamira tried to smile, but on the inside, she was falling apart having been confronted with the image of Sabba's declining health.

"But I can't rest! I must take care of you until you get your strength back," Savta argued.

"And then what? Run out of strength yourself? Listen to the girl," said Sabba Eliyahu, half-smiling with the other half of his face riddled with pain.

Savta looked back and forth at both of them and finally raised her hands up in defeat. "All right, I'll go for a little while, but I won't be resting. I'm going to see what I can do to help Devorah and Elisheva with the Pesach meal preparations."

Savta stepped out of the room, albeit somewhat hesitantly, but it gave Shamira a much longed for moment alone with her sabba. She had not even had a moment to share with Sabba the joy she had felt at the miracle Jesus performed before his collapse. She always thought she would be celebrating with her sabba when that day came. She never imagined that day could be one of his last. She shunned the thought from her mind; she refused to imagine that any day would be her grandfather's last.

"Come sit by me, Shamira," her grandfather said, motioning ever so slightly with his hand, which he could barely raise. He tried to sit up more, but he only fell back again, sinking farther into the cushions that supported him.

She obeyed immediately. "Does it hurt, Sabba?"

"Don't worry about me." He smiled again. "My heart only hurts because it is so full! I have too much love for my family, and my heart is having trouble containing it. I will be fine."

She wanted to believe him, but as she watched him slowly raise his hand to his chest, she knew he was not as healthy as his chipper tone wanted her to believe. That speech may have worked on Yuval, Gilad, or even Libi, but not on Shamira.

She would still smile at him though. If he could keep smiling in as much pain as he was in, then so could she. Although she felt a different type of pain, her pain was in her heart just the same as his. Perhaps not quite so literally, but figuratively. Nothing hurt her worse than seeing her family hurting, and she had felt so certain all of their troubles were behind them.

"Sabba, I made a stew." Shamira took the spoon in one hand and stirred up the ingredients.

"Are you sure you are trying to make me feel better?" He arched his eyebrows, smirking.

"Rut did help me."

"Ah, well I can be certain Rut has my best interests at heart," he teased, scooting backward and adjusting his cushions for support. "And so do you. Thank you, Shamira."

"Here, let me help you." She set the bowl down beside her and straightened his cushions, helping him sit up. "There, now do you need help eating the stew?"

"I think I can still handle a spoon on my own." Sabba took the bowl from her, resting it on the blankets in his lap. "Although, if your savta comes back, you'd better take this bowl from me immediately and pretend to feed it to me yourself. I'm not supposed to move a muscle according to her." He winked at her, and she laughed softly.

She watched him blow into the bowl, which still had wisps of steam floating off of the top of it. She waited until he'd taken a few spoons full before allowing her heart to reveal her own grief. "Oh Sabba, is anything I do ever right?"

"This stew isn't *that* bad."

"Sabba, you know that's not what I meant."

"What did you mean then, ahava sheli?"

"The first time I sought out Jesus, Rut was hurt. Who knows what could have happened if our abbas hadn't shown up? The second time, well, the second time I did see him, we all did. But now you're here…is it my fault? Is our family cursed, like Asa's father suggests? Is there a secret sin that someone harbors, that results in one of us being forced to always suffer from an ailment? Sometimes I feel as though every time I try to do something good for the people I care about, they end up worse off than before."

"Worse? Shamira, the only thing which has brought me comfort as I lay in this sick bed all day has been the sound of a little girl's chattering from upstairs. That little girl couldn't even hear two days ago, let alone speak her own name. Is she worse

off than she was before?"

His words convicted her, and she could no longer look him in the eye. "No, Sabba, she is most definitely not."

"Then why are you still so somber? Have you already begun to mourn my life?"

"No, Sabba! Please, do not talk like that. You must think of regaining your strength and all the things that you will do with us and with Libi once you are feeling better!"

"Shamira, I did not mean to upset you. I am trying my best to recover, but you must know there is nothing to fear in me not getting better either. If I run out of strength in this life, I will have strength tenfold when I am in paradise. A strength that will never run out. There is no need to fret for me. Be hopeful of whatever is to come, in any outcome."

She took a deep breath, blinking back the tears burning her eyes. She had cried enough these past few days, and she was weary of it. "I will try, Sabba, but it is so very, very hard."

"Good," he said, relaxing his shoulders. "Now, you have still not answered my question. What is it that makes you so melancholy? Is it something to do with Asa or his father?"

Shamira bit her lip. "It's not Asa this time; though I am concerned and hope to hear from him soon."

"You love him, don't you, granddaughter?"

"Oh, Sabba, I do," she confessed. "I have for a very long time. I have always thought that due to his family and circumstances it would not be possible, but I am seeing that with Jesus, much is possible. Things are changing. At least, I hope things change regarding our relationship."

"I bless your union." Sabba's breath was a little more laborious. "I know it is not my blessing you need, but in addition to your abba, I want you to know that I believe God will make a way. Asa is a good man, and I consider him a grandson just as much as your cousins."

Shamira blinked tears back. "Can we keep this just between us?"

"Yes," he agreed. "But Shamira, I don't think one spilled secret is enough to make you shed tears. What else is weighing down your spirit?"

"I fully believe in Jesus as our Messiah, Sabba. But even after seeing his miracles, looking straight at Libi and seeing her eyes light up with understanding at every voice and sound, everyone else still has trouble believing in him. I had been convinced that once they saw his miracles, no one could deny him or doubt him. But now I feel as though I was wrong, and I am so sad that others do not share in the joy that I have. Ever since I spoke with him, I have felt so... so light! Am I making any kind of sense?

"Shamira... you are a strong young woman. I have told you before, and I'll tell you again, your words have power. God can use them in magnificent ways. I kept telling my story my entire life, repeating the same words over and over again even when people thought I had lost my mind. But I'm glad I did, because it led you to him. You found the Messiah. You never gave up. That is why you must keep telling your story, keep speaking the words only you can speak."

"But what about the rest of this family? Why doesn't everyone believe? Even my own abba still has his doubts. He wants to believe—I know he does, but he is worried. Should I be worried? People say I am outspoken and that it will get me into trouble someday. Should I continue to speak his name and praise him as the Messiah, whom I believe him to be? Or should I keep quiet to protect my family?" Shamira spoke her worries out loud.

"Quiet?" he nearly shouted. "Never!"

Eliyahu lunged forward, throwing himself into a coughing fit. "Ach, I can't get up. Shamira, Shamira," he heaved between breaths. "Go and get your abba and uncles. Get everyone. I must say something."

"Sabba, what is it?" she asked.

"Now!" he coughed.

"All right, all right!"

She jumped from the bed and gathered her skirts, scurrying to the other room with haste. Her feet scraped the floor in her hurry. "Abba! Imma! Everyone! Come at once!"

Her own abba was the first one to respond to her call, and the panic in his face made her worry. He ran toward her with his eyes wide open and grabbed her shoulders, bearing his fingers down into her arms so hard it almost hurt.

"What is it? What's wrong Shamira?"

"Eliyahu?" Savta called

"He says that he has something he must say to all of us," she explained, as breathless as everyone else in the room.

"It could not wait until he was well?" asked Savta, worry creating creases between her eyebrows.

"Aharon—is it father?" said Tamir, coming down the stairs with Libi and the boys, followed by Chava, Binyamin, and Devorah. Benayahu and Rut came into the house from the courtyard as well, and every one of them was bursting with more questions.

"Come this way. Sabba must speak to us." Shamira motioned for them all to follow her.

It was a tight fit in the small downstairs room Sabba and Savta had shared for as long as Shamira could remember. Somehow, the whole family managed to cram in, even if there was barely any room to move. Shamira watched with great concern as Sabba hoisted himself up with his arms, which were shaking, supporting his weight.

His face was scarlet red, and he was struggling to breathe. Savta knelt down beside him, nearly falling to her knees. "Eliyahu, my husband, could this not have waited until you are well? Why are you upsetting yourself?"

Savta placed a hand on his forearm, and he wrapped her hand up in his own, gently patting her hand as if to communicate his heartfelt gratitude and thanks to his wife. Words weren't necessary between them; the years they'd spent together were written on their faces in the silent conversation Shamira observed in their touch. Shamira could only hope she would share such a deep bond with Asa someday.

"Yes, Abba, now is not the time for upsetting yourself; it is for resting and recovering," said Tamir.

"I'm sorry, son. I know many of you have grown weary of my speeches and constant talking. You may even resent me for my outspokenness—"

"Never, Abba," said Aharon.

236

"Nevertheless, you shall have to endure one more speech from this old man. I will not be silenced, not this time. If I am to recover, then blessed be the name of the Lord, but if I am to die, I want to have said this, and even so bless His holy name."

"Abba," interrupted Binyamin.

"No more interruptions. I know what you're thinking, and I think it is important that I first clarify one thing—I am not crazy. I may have a weak heart, but that has not weakened my ability to think logically. Shamira has informed me there is still doubt among this family. Doubt of God's goodness, doubt in the man they call Jesus of Nazareth. Perhaps it is because you haven't all seen him, but I tell you all, you see his hand every time you look upon Libi. Every time you look at Tamir, Chava, Gilad, and Yuval. A month ago, that son of mine spent night after night in the fields with sheep. Chava, whom I have long considered a daughter, spent every day in quiet mourning for all the words she would never verbally be able to communicate to her daughter.

"Both of you are strong, stronger than either me or Hodiyah could have ever been as parents in your same situation. We watched you walk through those battles, helpless to do anything for you, except provide what love we could. Yuval, Gilad, and Libi have a wonderful mother, and a wonderful family supporting them, but they did not have a father.

"Now all of this day I have heard nothing but the sounds of children playing. Two headstrong young boys and a beautiful little girl laughing, playing, and talking with their father. I have heard Chava and Tamir express their love for each other, and the look in their eyes reminds me of so many looks I have shared with my own beloved wife. They endured a trial together and they are wiser for it. Their lives were made good— miraculous—by one man. One man! It is… it is my dying wish that you follow this man, this teacher from Nazareth."

"Abba," Shamira's own father pleaded. "You're not dying yet."

"Do not argue about whether or not I will die. It is not for you or me to decide! If I am going to die, then I want to have said all of these things clearly to all of you so I will return to dust with no regrets for my life. My wife, my sons, my daughters, follow Jesus! Believe in him! A day is coming when this world will fall, but following him will give you peace in this time. A peace beyond all understanding.

"When I was around Tamir's age and had the same youthful passion as Shamira, I saw a babe lying in a manger, and that sight changed my life. Certainly, Hodiyah had feared she had a mad man as a father to her children. But regardless of the doubt, regardless of what the world said—I knew what I saw that night. I left my sheep to see that child, and I knew who he was and what he would do for our people. I proclaimed my belief in the Messiah, that he was coming to restore brokenness, to heal, and to make things new. It wasn't always easy, but I always had peace. The Lord God was faithful, and I have lived long enough to see the fulfillment of the promise the angels gave that night.

"Look at your brother's family. His marriage was broken, their daughter deaf-mute. Look at where they are. See how they have been transformed because of their belief, not just on the outside, but on the inside. The angels said it to me so many years ago, and I have believed it is true all this time. He is the Savior born for all people, the Messiah. Believe. Do not lose heart, do not turn away, do not cower in fear. *Believe.*"

"I believe, Abba! I believe!" Aharon said, falling to his knees before his father and beside his mother, who still rested there herself.

"Oh, my son." Eliyahu reached out. "Oh..." His arms fell, and then the color began to fade from his face. The whole family was soon buzzing, with Hodiyah rising to her feet to aid her husband, who had fallen back out of consciousness. The children were ushered out of the room altogether, and Shamira followed, lingering just for a moment in the doorway.

"Oh, Sabba..." Shamira whispered, praying to God he would not slip away from her; she wasn't ready. Passover would begin in two days. She couldn't imagine the celebration led by anyone other than her sabba.

Then, remembering her grandfather's words, she prayed a second prayer, that God's will would be done, even if it wasn't what she wanted to happen. Shamira followed her sabba's advice and believed in Jesus' power with all of her heart, and she now waited for the peace of God to settle her soul.

The Pesach would officially begin that night at sundown, and the temple had never been busier. It was nearing dusk already, and Asa was surprised his father was nowhere to be found. Granted, the crowds were ferocious, but since it was so close to sundown, he thought his father would be preparing to return home for their own *Seder* and Pesach celebration.

Celebration seemed like a strange word to use. Pesach was one of their most revered holy days, but Asa didn't feel very much like celebrating. He scratched the top of his head as he remembered Shamira. It had now been three nights since he had last seen her. The last time they'd been together was when they had sought Jesus at the temple, and his father had been furious with him for that. It was a humiliation to his role as a priest; Asa recognized that. His father had every right to be upset and offended—his own son was seen showing support to a rival teacher. As much as he could see how his father's anger was justified, he still would have made the same decision again.

The only guilt he carried was that he hadn't been able to ensure Shamira and her cousins returned to their home safely. He trusted Jesus, Peter, and the other disciples, but it didn't make up for not being able to be there with her himself. When he'd left her before, she'd nearly been attacked! Just thinking about her admission of the event made his fingers curl into a fist.

She was a smart young woman and was more than capable of holding her own; he knew that fact all too well from personal experience during their childhood. That didn't mean he would ever stop worrying about her.

As Asa continued to wander the temple, his thoughts turned back to the Pesach. As the son of the priest, the history of the Pesach was one of the things Asa had studied most intensely.

He had been taught to remember God's almighty power, but he couldn't help but also feel compassion for those who had lived through that night so long ago. He could imagine waiting behind a closed door, the beams outside soaked with the fresh blood of the lamb, a sacrifice that would appease the angel of death. What were the Hebrew people thinking? Were they filled with trepidation as they waited to see what deliverance God would provide? Did they rest easily that night, trusting in God to be faithful in His promises?

He would never know what that felt like, but he certainly understood the visual. So many had come to the temple to slaughter lambs that day, ready to roast them for their Seder. The blood of the lamb bore the burden of death for them, and it was because of that blood their people had been spared all those years before. As a Levite, Asa had been called upon to serve that day and assist with the ritual sacrifices done in remembrance. The priests like his father would spend the day slaughtering the lambs, while Asa and other Levites would be ready with a bowl to catch the blood. The priest performing the sacrifice would take the blood and splash it upon the altar as a symbol. Levites would take the lamb, skin it, and return it to the family so it could be roasted in time for the meal at sundown.

Asa had seen many lambs that day and assisted many who had come to take part in the sacrifices, but he had not run into anyone from Shamira's family. It was a large temple, so it was plausible that he might have just missed them. Perhaps it was the uneasiness that still resided in the pit of his stomach after their last encounter had been cut so short, but something felt wrong to him. He did not know what troubled him, but he sensed something wasn't quite right.

Despite the nagging concern that pulled his stomach in all different directions, he continued to attend to his duties. This night was for Pesach, the night they remembered God's deliverance. It seemed ironic to him that his people would celebrate deliverance from slavery, when now hundreds of years later they were once again oppressed, this time by Romans rather than Egyptians.

Will Jesus be our deliverer?

Asa's mind drifted to Messianic prophecy. He was aware of many scriptural references that some thought could refer to the coming Savior whom God had promised. Opinions varied, but he had read enough and listened to enough of the debates of others to form opinions of his own. Many believed the Messiah would come as a prophet like Moses, and that he would speak and teach the words of God. Asa had only heard Jesus speak a few times, but he was certain his message was from God, even if his father did claim it was radical.

He cared for the poor and needy as the Psalmists had written. Asa had been told how he made the blind see, and he had seen firsthand how Jesus had made the deaf hear, just as Isaiah had written. He had entered the temple; he'd even ridden into Jerusalem riding on a donkey in a processional such as the prophet Zechariah had described. Asa was convinced, even if his father wasn't. How could he deny it when confronted with such evidence, the fulfillment of scripture written long ago? Evidence he had spent his entire life studying and memorizing? Asa was ready to witness to the whole world what had happened, and he would start with his father.

He turned a corner and there was Avram, lingering in the shadows. Asa halted in his tracks. He wondered why he was hiding, and even more so, why he had guards with him. Had his father taken to hiring his own personal patrol?

Although it wasn't likely, Asa wouldn't put it past him. Something made Asa back up farther behind the corner, peering around it with just one eye squinting at the figures distorted by the flames of torches. There was a figure who was almost completely in shadow. He was cloaked, but Asa recognized his form faintly as Judas Iscariot. He recalled that Judas had been one of the disciples he had encountered at Bethany, the one who had grumbled at Mary's gift to Jesus.

"I am sure of it. Tonight will be the night—there will be no crowds with him because they will all be in their own homes taking part in the Pesach meal," said Judas, hushed and quickly.

"Good, good. We don't want any witnesses. It could cause rioting, and that is something we *cannot* have." Asa heard his own father's words.

Asa's thoughts ran wild. What kind of witnesses? And to what? Usually, people only worried about witnesses if they were doing something wrong.

"The silver then?"

"Silver? The task isn't even completed."

Judas lowered his chin. "You want it completed, don't you?"

Avram nodded and reached into his white priestly robes, pulling from his sleeve a small sack that jingled with the sound of coin. "You may take these men as well to help you apprehend him. We want this done quickly and without incident."

Judas seemed to hesitate for a moment, and then began, "You just want to talk to him, right? See what he's all about?"

"Iscariot, you've already said he is a problem to you, and he's a problem for all of us as well. He will be dealt with. *All problems have a solution.*"

Asa recognized that tone. His father was cold and calculating, but not this cold. Could it really be true? Then Asa remembered with a sudden horror that flashed through him like a bolt of lightning, striking his heart and nearly sending him to his knees. There was one prophecy which Jesus of Nazareth had yet to fill.

He was going to die.

They were going to try to kill him. This Pesach, he would be their lamb.

"Abba?" Asa shouted in disbelief.

Avram didn't even flinch at the sound of his son's voice. Asa searched his mannerisms hoping for some sign of remorse, some sign of shame at the idea of conspiring like this in front of his own son. His firstborn son.

He found none.

"Go," said Avram, not bothering to turn around. "Get it done."

At that, Judas Iscariot nodded and turned to go, the troop of temple guards following closely behind.

"Get *what* done, Abba?" Asa said through gritted teeth.

"Asa, there are some things about this world which you still do not understand." Avram closed his eyes and shook his head, holding up his hand as if to stop Asa from protesting any further.

He would not stop.

"I understand conspiracy. Plotting in the darkness. Murder."

"No one here is going to murder anyone," Avram guffawed.

"Then what was that about? Blood money? Soldiers? You're going to arrest an innocent man?"

Avram's face reddened, enflamed with anger. "Innocent? That man is hardly innocent, Asa. He incites the people to danger and rebellion!"

"How? By teaching love? By teaching that God is a God of love, hope, mercy, *and* justice? That God is… is like a father to us?"

"Father? You think God is like a father to you?" His father sneered at him.

"You wouldn't know about that," Asa hissed. He rarely lost control of his temper, but this time his father had provoked him. "You've never been a father to me or to my brothers."

Avram struck Asa hard in his jaw, but he wouldn't back down.

"You will not speak to me with such disrespect." His voice was commanding.

It was true, and Asa felt a pang of remorse at speaking to his father in such a way, but he had not been able to stop himself. Not if his father was going to have Jesus, an innocent man, arrested and possibly killed for his own gain. "Father, look at the scriptures. It all points to him. You can't do this; you can't have his blood on your hands. Listen to me, to reason, to the writings of the prophets!"

"You don't get to tell me who to listen to. I can see now I've been far too lenient with you, letting you traipse about the city chasing after pathetic shepherd girls. You will marry and soon, but to a proper Levite woman. One who is worthy of your station and will provide you with many sons to carry on our family name and our divine purpose. But most importantly, you will not meddle in affairs that are above your understanding. Am I making myself clear, Asa?"

"You're clear, Father, but you are also wrong. I am saying these things because of what you taught me, not because of what I did not learn. How can you not see that?"

Asa ran a fist through his hair, frustrated. Tears stung his eyes. He didn't want to see his father like this. As cruel as he'd been to him, to his brothers, even to his mother, a part of him still loved his father. If God could love and forgive all the Hebrew people in Egypt so long ago, sparing their lives with a Pesach lamb, surely God could soften his father's heart as he had softened the Pharaoh's.

"Silence!" Avram roared.

Asa shook his head. "I'll stop them. I'll warn them—I swear I will!"

"You'll do no such thing."

Asa turned to go.

"If you walk away from me now," Avram began, "then you will never be welcome in our home again. You will no longer be my son. Do you hear me?"

Asa didn't walk. He ran. With each step he felt freer from the oppression that had held him back from chasing after God with all his heart. He ran with purpose; he ran toward his future.

"Then the chief priests and the elders of the people assembled in the courtyard of the high priest, who was named Caiaphas, and they conspired to arrest Jesus in a treacherous way and kill him. 'Not during the festival,' they said, 'so there won't be rioting among the people.'" - Matthew 26:3-5 CSB

Shamira was having a dream. She was ten years old again and a pebble had just flown through her window. She turned to see if Rut had noticed the rock too, and sure enough she had. It must have been that strange boy with the ridiculous hair from Eliana's wedding. Another small pebble whizzed past her ear. It was then Shamira realized she was not having a dream at all; a small rock really had flown through her window. But why were rocks flying through her window in the middle of the night? Her family had finally settled down to rest after a quiet Pesach celebration. Who could possibly be trying to get her attention at this hour?

The next pebble that came through the window hit her in her right side. "Ah!" she shouted, waking suddenly.

"What is going on?" said Rut, reacting to Shamira's cry.

Shamira lifted a finger to her lips to signal to Rut to quiet down. "I'm not sure," she whispered. *Thud!* Another rock. If these rocks got any larger, they could get injured.

"Shamira, look out the window and see what is happening before we get killed!" Rut tossed and turned on her mat.

Shamira did so, surprised to see a cloaked figure standing in her courtyard. Whoever it was must have seen her too, for the figure waved to her. She narrowed her eyes and wrinkled up her nose in confusion. She tried to make out a face, but her eyes refused to adjust to the darkness. She recalled a night years before when a certain young boy, of whom she'd just been dreaming, had surprised her in her kitchen. The gate to their home had been bolted, as it usually was after sundown, but he had climbed the wall.

Shamira knew only one man who was so agile.

The figure removed his hood, and she recognized him immediately. How could she ever forget his silhouette, which had been burned into her memory by the fiery embers of passion that blazed in her heart?

"It's Asa!" she whisper-shouted to Rut who was behind her, but kept her eyes forward, facing straight out the window.

"Asa? What on earth is he doing here, in the middle of the night?"

"I don't know, but he's motioning for me to join him," whispered Shamira, biting her lip.

Rut moaned. "What kind of woman does he think you are? I mean, truly, Shamira. You've been in a lot of trouble recently, and you need to consider very carefully what impact your actions might have. May I remind you that no good explanation ever began with, 'It all started when I ran out of the house to meet a young man in the middle of the night?'"

Shamira was too busy tying her sandals to consider the absurdity of it all. Rather, she countered, "Then you must come with me, Rut!"

Rut sat straight up on her mat. With her eyes suddenly wide

open, she argued, "No! You've gone mad!"

"No, I haven't! Something must be horribly wrong or otherwise he would not have come. Not cloaked and under the cover of darkness. Not like this." She paused. "He knows that the last time we spoke I was under restriction. He would not come here again without the invitation of our family if it was not something important. Especially not during the Pesach! Besides, I have this feeling, Rut..."

"A feeling? Do I also need to remind you of what happens whenever you act on your feelings?"

"Rut, this is different. Something isn't right, I know it. I've had an uneasy feeling all day and now Asa's here. He would only be here if something was wrong. Please come with me so we can hear what he has to say."

"Well, I don't have to do anything, Mira. This may not be safe for either of us."

Shamira cocked her head to one side and put her hands on her hips, "But somebody has to keep me out of trouble."

Rut rolled her eyes. "You always say that, yet I always end up in trouble *with* you."

However, even as she said it, Rut was already getting dressed and tying her belt around her outer garments. Shamira could always count on her cousin whenever she was in need, and she knew Rut would always be able to count on her to make her presence needed.

They climbed down the stairs and made it all the way to the doorway. Shamira was just about to open the door and step into the moonlight, until the echo of a promise, of powerful words, stopped her.

"What are you doing?" Rut questioned; her tone was grumpy with sleep.

"I made a promise to my father," Shamira responded. "I told him that I would seek out his help if I was ever to be in trouble. I have to wake Abba in order to keep my word." Shamira spoke the words aloud but almost wished she could ignore them, but she knew her father would never trust her unless she also trusted him.

Rut's frown turned to a wide smile. "Shamira! You have

changed!"

"I trust him, and I just want him to keep trusting me."

Rut waited at the bottom of the stairs while Shamira carefully and quietly retraced her steps, only this time instead of going back into her own room, she entered her parents' adjacent room.

"Abba," she whispered quietly. She had to touch him gently before he roused and looked at her through sleepy eyes. "Asa is here. Can you come with me? I think that there is trouble, and I need your help." No faster had his eyes blinked open than he had tied his sandals. He was up in a flash, stopping only to whisper something in Elisheva's ear before gesturing to the door. Together they hastened to the courtyard.

"Shamira!" Asa exclaimed when she and Rut appeared in the doorway, both cloaked in shadow. He straightened when he noticed Shamira's father, Aharon, was also behind them. How would he explain his presence in a way that seemed rational?

Shamira raised a hand, silencing him with a finger to her lips, and then motioning toward the gate. Four pairs of feet shuffled quickly across the dirt and sand; Shamira eased the wooden plank upward and unbolted the gate, pulling it open only as wide as her waist so they could squeeze through. Asa knew if the gate had been opened any farther, the entire house would be alerted to their activity by the betraying screech of the old hinges.

Once all four of them were a good distance down the eerily empty street, they stopped, forming a small circle.

"Aharon," Asa whispered, facing her father. "I would not have disturbed any of you if it was not a matter of urgency. I wasn't sure where else to turn—I don't normally make such late visits, especially during the Pesach."

Her father nodded and replied, "I understand. Shamira woke me because she thought there might be trouble, and I am happy she did. I want my daughter to know she can always come to me when there is a problem, and I hope you know the same. We are old friends, Asa, and you are a part of this family."

Asa noticed how Aharon scrunched up his nose in the same way Shamira did when she was deep in thought. "How did you get into our courtyard? Our gate was bolted shut." Aharon was suddenly deviating from the urgency that had brought Asa in the first place, and Asa didn't know how much time they had.

"Abba, please? Asa said this is an emergency."

Aharon nodded. "Yes, Asa, what has happened that is of such seriousness?"

"I was at the temple serving with the other Levites," he said, trying not to ramble. "It was near sundown, so I began to look for my father. That was when I saw him in a dark part of the temple, surrounded by guards and other angry men. They were talking to Judas Iscariot."

"Judas... You mean one of the disciples of Jesus?" Shamira's eyebrows were moving closer and closer together with each new piece of information Asa revealed.

"My father," said Asa, forcing himself to continue, "he paid Judas with a bag of silver and told him to take the guards."

"Guards? For what? The temple has never approved of Jesus. I doubt they'd protect him. And what would they be paying him for, unless..."

"They've arrested Jesus." There was no other way to say it.

"What?" she almost screamed.

"I am telling the truth," he replied.

Shamira's eyes searched his face, and then Asa noticed the way her gaze stopped on his cheek.

"Asa, what happened to you?" she sighed, taking a step closer to him but maintaining an appropriate distance.

"My father and I fought," he began, raising a hand to cover the worsening bruise on his face. "I doubt I will see him again."

"What do you mean? It can't be as bad as all of that."

"It is, Shamira, but never mind that right now—I ran from the temple in search of Jesus. I thought I could warn him—the disciples, all of them—that there was a traitor among their group, but when I found them it was too late. They had already taken Jesus, and his followers were running everywhere. It was insanity, there was no order to it at all, except on the part of Jesus himself. He went willingly, as if...as if he already knew what was going to happen. I went back to my father's house and peered through the windows. He was preparing to meet with the Sanhedrin at the high priest's house! They're going to put Jesus on trial!"

"But why? Why would they take him in the middle of the night? That doesn't make any sense," asked Aharon.

"And why would they arrest him at all? He hasn't done anything wrong," Rut added.

Asa continued to explain, his words slurring together. "He has performed so many miracles. You both know that, and in doing so he has claimed to have the authority to forgive sins. You've seen the effect he has on people. As soon as the sun comes up, he is followed in by droves of people begging him to speak and perform miracles. People all over the city are calling him Messiah..."

Asa knew the real reason they had taken Jesus in the middle of the night was because they wanted it to be done in secret—it was premeditated. The temple couldn't risk the public uproar that would occur if Jesus were to be arrested during the day, in full view of everyone. His father and the priests would never have approved of that. *The Romans* would have disapproved even more. Roman government would see any Jewish uproar—whether sanctioned by the temple or not—as a rebellion against Caesar. It was perfectly clear to Asa what the Sanhedrin had in mind for Jesus of Nazareth: a murderous plot cloaked in darkness and perpetrated in secrecy.

"But he *is* the Messiah, isn't he? He is! He healed Libi at the temple. You were there Asa; you saw him do it. This is nonsense and you know it!" Shamira said, her words tumbling out of her mouth in a hurried, haphazard way.

"That suggestion alone is enough to be considered blasphemous by the temple, Shamira!" said Asa. He hadn't meant to sound so harsh, but he could tell by the way she shrank back toward her abba that he had frightened her.

"But Asa...you know this is wrong," said Aharon.

"I do," he nodded. "I would not have let *this* happen if I

didn't think my father was making the biggest mistake of his life." He pointed to the bruise on his jawline.

"What are you saying then? What is there to do about it, except get yourself hurt?" Shamira questioned.

"I don't know, but I do know I'm going to the house of the high priest... I wanted to let you know what was happening in the event that something happens to me." He paused and then turned to face Shamira's abba directly. "I apologize, Aharon; I probably should not have come here. Clearly this is a matter of concern, but I was wrong to rouse you all. I just wasn't sure where to turn and I..." Asa stopped his rambling to catch a breath.

"I'm going with you," Aharon replied. A wave of relief washed over Asa. He turned to his niece. "Rut, I cannot in good conscience take you without consent from your father. I am truly sorry, but I cannot wrong my brother in this."

"This could be very dangerous," Rut reminded all of them in her hushed voice. "I understand your hesitancy. If you can let me in the courtyard, at least I can inform the family of what has happened when the sun breaks through. That way there might not be such alarm when the family rises and sees that you are gone."

They all turned and headed back toward the family home.

"Shamira, go inside with your cousin," Aharon said. "Your imma would feel the same way."

Shamira turned. "Abba, please! I honored you. I did as you asked and came to you first when I knew that there was trouble. But you told me you also would honor my faith. I must go to Jesus—*I must!* You cannot leave me behind now, not like this. Please."

"All right," he said, sighing. "For your faith, I will allow it, but you must listen to me if things become dangerous. If at any point I decide that it is no longer safe for us to go on..."

"I will keep my promise, Abba," Shamira let Rut in the family courtyard, and she and Rut exchanged a quick hug before she and her abba followed Asa away.

"The Lord bless and keep you," Rut whispered before disappearing back behind the gate.

"Wait, Asa—we cannot simply walk into the house of the high priest! That's mad!"

"I didn't say anything about going in," Asa assured. He had a plan. "If I could climb over your gate and enter your courtyard unseen and unheard, what makes you think I cannot get us to a place where we can hear what the high priest will rule? I'm afraid for Jesus' life. If I can just find out what is happening that will be enough."

"Your father is a part of the Sanhedrin?" Shamira asked.

Asa nodded grimly. "The words I exchanged with my father…they can never be taken back, not for me at least; I have to know if for once my father will do the right thing. I have to know if what happened between us had any impact on him at all. I believe firmly in the power of Jesus of Nazareth. I believe in his teachings, and I believe he has been sent from God. I also believe the misleading teachings and the misused power distributed so heavy handed by the priests and teachers in the temple come from man alone.

"I have spent all of my life studying the Lord. I have studied His laws backward and forward. I have spent countless hours pondering the writings of the prophets, the history recorded by those who witnessed His miracles firsthand. Perhaps my father wanted me to become like himself through this studying, but it has only opened my eyes to a God who is so much more than anything my father thinks. At this very moment my father and others are preparing to hold an audience with Jesus, to question him, and if necessary, maybe even sentence him to death. I must see for myself if my father will still deny Jesus, even when all the answers are laid at his feet." Asa took a deep breath. "More importantly, I must see Jesus."

Shamira was quiet for a moment as they continued to walk. The only sounds that could be heard in the usually loud city were their footsteps on the dirt. Then Shamira raised her voice to ask, "What if your father still does deny him? What will become of Jesus of Nazareth?"

Asa stared at her blankly, having no words. There was no way he could answer such a question. He didn't even want to think about what would happen if that were the case.

Aharon changed the subject, bringing Asa back to the more immediate matter at hand. "Lead the way, Asa."

It wasn't usual for the Sanhedrin to convene at the house of the high priest. While their business was usually private, for them to have gathered in the earliest hours of the morning meant they were attempting to keep the public from becoming aware of any part of this matter. From the looks of things, it was not working.

The closer they got to the high priest's mansion, the more the city seemed to join them in their search for Jesus. The streets were restless with people like themselves wandering about in similar fashion, searching for their teacher, whispering in dark corners, and shouting accusations in other parts of the street. Despite the Sanhedrin's best efforts, there would be some witnesses to this unlawful atrocity. People sleeping in the streets had gathered around small fires to gossip and spread rumors about what was happening. The crowds were not as thick as they had been at previous occasions which centered around Jesus of Nazareth, but Asa still could plainly see this part of the city was more congested than it should have been at that time of night.

"Asa, I am nervous. I don't have a good feeling about this," Shamira said, her teeth chattering.

Asa felt bad for dragging her out at such a late hour, but he also knew if she'd found out about this on her own, nothing could have stopped her from being here. At least this way, he and Aharon would make sure she was safe.

"Here," said Asa, offering his own cloak to her for extra warmth. He could do without it for a short time. "Shamira, look over there. I think I recognize that man. Perhaps he can help us find out what is happening."

Asa pointed toward a small group huddled around a fire. Peter seemed to hide among them, keeping close enough to the fire to benefit from its warmth, but far enough away to not be directly in its light.

"Yes, I recognize him too. His name is Peter, right? He was with Jesus."

"Let's go to him," said Asa, leading both Shamira and Aharon toward him.

He didn't wait a moment before asking, "Peter, have you been with Jesus all this night? Please, tell us what you know!"

"Leave me alone," the man muttered, pulling his cloak even tighter around his face.

"But wait," said Shamira. "We've seen you before."

Suddenly Peter arose, shoving them aside and shouting, "I said, leave me alone!"

"What was that about? Was that really the same man?" Shamira asked.

Asa shared her feelings of confusion and upset. If even Jesus' own disciples were too afraid to speak on his behalf, what treacherous fate loomed over them all?

"I'm not sure," said Asa. He swayed from side to side, keeping one hand protectively on Shamira's shoulder while he tried to decide what to do next.

"Never mind it then," said Aharon, matter-of-fact. "Perhaps he was not who you thought he was."

Asa knew that wasn't true.

"Or," Aharon continued, "perhaps he fears for his own life. Let's keep going."

All of a sudden, a great uproar sprang out not fifteen paces from where they were standing. Men and women began to cry out, "What is happening? Where are you taking him?"

Simultaneously, other more snarling voices howled, "Traitor! Blasphemer! Take him to Caiaphas!"

In the middle of them all was a group of temple guards escorting a prisoner inside the grand house. Asa recognized Jesus even at a distance. His heart sank.

Without warning, Shamira's own voice joined the few others who were already shouting, "Why are you arresting an innocent man? This man has done nothing wrong! Leave him alone!"

Asa pulled her backward. "Have you lost your mind, Shamira? This is dangerous—anyone could hear what you are saying and then you could end up on the other side of that wall on trial, just like Jesus!"

She lowered her gaze. "I—I'm sorry, Asa. I didn't think."

"I'm sorry too," said Asa, softening. He hadn't meant to hurt her feelings. He was just stressed by the grim situation, as she probably was as well.

"But," she added, "I can't deny him."

He smiled in the midst of the pain, admiring her passion, fire, and strength.

"I'm not asking you to deny him, Shamira. I'm just asking you to be careful," Asa explained. He would fight off a thousand or more men if they threatened Shamira, but what good was his strength? Jesus had the power to perform all kinds of miracles, but even he had been overtaken by a group of soldiers. Asa feared his father and men like him, realizing there were no limits to what they could do when determined.

"Asa is right, Shamira," Aharon chimed in with a voice of reason. "We both just want you to be safe. Let us try to listen and find out what is happening. Yelling as these others are doing will do us no more good than it has done them."

Asa changed the subject, pointing toward the grand door facing them. "That's the main entrance to Caiaphas' house. I've been here before, with my father."

"Do you know the high priest? Could you get us inside?" Shamira asked.

He shook his head. "No, I don't think I should be seen. My father will be inside as well. If someone alerts him that I am here... I do not think it would be wise to use my name and family connections in this instance."

"Oh," Shamira sighed.

Asa didn't want to disappoint her. Suddenly, a memory came into his mind, and that memory quickly turned into a plan. He pointed toward a path that went around the side of the house.

"Come this way, there is a side where the wall surrounding the courtyard is not as high. Our best chance of seeing anything is from there."

Turning the corner, he noticed some discarded crates on the other side of the street. Quickly, he pushed them up against the outer wall, stacking them up and creating a kind of ledge. He motioned for Shamira and Aharon to come closer, pressing a finger to his lips, reminding them they must remain quiet or risk being caught.

"How did you know about this place?" she asked him.

"I used to play here with the other priests' sons when I was very young. We would often eavesdrop on our fathers from here."

Beside him, Shamira stepped on top of her own crate, but the uneven ground beneath them nearly sent her to the ground. "Oh!" she exclaimed.

Asa reached out to steady her and she clung to his arm while moving to regain her balance. Even in the dark, he could tell she had corrected her footing and didn't need his support anymore, but he was reluctant to let go. What were they about to see? Would Asa truly have to confront his worst nightmare, the fear of his father directly denying Jesus? Denying him?

He gave Shamira's hand a tight squeeze. She smiled at him, and Asa felt comforted. Finally, he released his hold on her and prepared himself to watch the proceedings, for better or for worse. Beside him, Shamira also raised her head above the wall just high enough so she could see what was going on.

"From this vantage point, we should be able to see everything as it unfolds," Asa said to Aharon, who was perched on a crate on the other side of Shamira.

"This is a good place to watch from. You were right to take us here, Asa. We are far enough removed from the crowds, and as long as we stay in the shadows, we will not be spotted."

Asa nodded in agreement, and then turned his attention toward the reception hall. He recognized a few of the men in priestly robes, but he noticed the entire Sanhedrin was not present. Everything about this was wrong and went directly against the laws his father claimed to adhere to so vehemently. The faces of those who had gathered were lit only by the flames from torches and lamps, which seemed to flicker and flash and create all kinds of disturbing shadows.

People in the grand room were shouting accusations, each eager to tell their story with more dramatic flair and outlandish details than the speaker before them. At a certain point, none of them could agree on anything. The lies they were speaking had gotten out of control, and the narrative no longer made any sense. The leaders did nothing, however. They kept letting the farce of a trial go on, almost as if they had encouraged the uproar and exaggeration.

One of the Sanhedrin spoke out, pointing to Jesus and saying, "This man said, 'I can destroy the temple of God, and rebuild it in three days.'"

This incited loud shouting that resonated within the mansion walls and reverberated like thunder. On the left, Asa could just make out his father joining in the insanity with equal enthusiasm.

Why wasn't Jesus doing something? Why didn't he defend himself? This was his one chance! The only time the Sanhedrin and the leaders would truly listen to him.

Caiaphas, the man Asa knew as the high priest, stood up and spread out his hands demanding silence. When they had quieted down, he turned his attention toward Jesus and inquired, "Don't you have an answer to what these men are testifying against you?"

Still Jesus did not respond.

The crates beneath them creaked as Shamira lunged forward. She appeared to be just as desperately searching for answers as Asa, for some kind of sign to explain why this was happening.

The high priest continued. "I charge you under oath by the living God: Tell us if you are the Messiah, the Son of God."

At this, Jesus looked up at him and answered, "You have said it, but I tell you, in the future you will see the Son of Man seated at the right hand of Power and coming on the clouds of heaven."

The high priest shook violently with anger, yelled at the heavens, and, pulling at his garments, tore them in two. Shamira gasped quietly and quickly, turning away from the sight. Asa forced himself to look on, waiting for a confirmation, an absolution of some kind.

Caiaphas was red in the face as he shouted, "He has blasphemed! Why do we still need witnesses? See, now you've heard the blasphemy. What is your decision?" He turned to the remaining members of the Sanhedrin, beckoning them to give their answer.

One voice spoke up in the now silent room to condemn Jesus of Nazareth. Just one. It said, "He deserves death, Caiaphas."

It was none other than Asa's own father.

Shamira turned to Asa, eyes wide. He was breathing heavily, and she could tell he was upset. Every vein in his neck bulged outward, and she could see even in the shadows of the nearby flames how he repeatedly clenched and unclenched his jaw. They needed to get away, quickly, before Asa did something he would regret.

His father was no longer the only one calling for Jesus' execution. Soon, all of the people watching began to shout, repeating Avram's sentiments and drowning out Avram's own voice. Still, she could not have imagined what Asa must have been feeling, knowing his father had been the instigator of the ruling.

"Asa, come on," she said, pulling him away from the side of the house and down the street, not paying attention to which direction they were going. The so-called trial continued, but they would not stay to watch the rest.

Behind them, a number of voices shouted, "Yes, death! The punishment is death!" Shamira was heartbroken, but at that moment her only concern was for Asa, who had just witnessed his father declare the unthinkable.

"Abba!" she cried, glancing over her shoulder to make sure he followed behind, tripping in the process. "Asa! I'm sorry! I'm so, so sorry!" It was as if he'd forgotten she was there.

"Asa! Asa!" shouted her father, catching up to them and then passing her. "Stop!" he commanded, taking hold of Asa's shoulders. Shamira watched as Asa wrestled against him, but her father kept a strong hold on him.

Finally, Asa stopped his tugging and thrashing and fell to the ground between them. "Stop, son!" The pale moonlight slowly faded into the glow of the early morning sun. Shamira looked at the awakening world around her but could not recognize anything, upper city or lower city. She knelt down to take Asa's hand, but he jerked away from her.

Her apologies had come too late and tears already streamed down Asa's face. "I don't know what I was expecting. I don't know why I thought anything would be different," he choked out. "I would have liked to think my father was not the kind of man who would send an innocent man to his death. A man of God! But I was wrong, Shamira. I was wrong, and I hate him."

"No, Asa. No. You mustn't hate him." Shamira once again snatched his hands into hers. When she did that the second time, Asa relaxed. He even began to cling to her hands. He crushed her fingers in his grasp, as if she were the only thing tethering him to the ground. Their eyes locked, and Asa drew her closer to his own body. She shuddered, feeling the warmth of his breath. In this moment, they didn't need words. There were no words more powerful than the unspoken bond of their hearts, strengthened by the shared experience of whatever was happening on this night.

Shamira's father cleared his throat, and Shamira nodded up at him, slowly withdrawing her hands and pulling away to a more appropriate distance.

"Why mustn't I, Shamira?" Asa's shoulders rocked back and forth as he heaved rapid and uneven breaths.

"Why did you choose Jesus, Asa? Why did you choose him over your father? Because He preaches a message of love and forgiveness, and if you give into hate and anger, you will be just like your father and those whom you so readily condemn. Is that what you want?" Her voice grew stronger. "Asa!" She demanded he answer, even if it hurt.

He shook his head, and after a few breaths, rose to his feet again.

Just as Asa was opening his mouth to speak, a ravenous crowd started down the same path they had just trod, lighting their way with the bright orange light from their torches. Aharon yanked both of them out of the open and into the shadows. The crowd was pushing a blindfolded Jesus, mocking him and spitting upon him.

"Prophesy to us!"

"Prophesy, Messiah!"

"Who was it that hit you?"

It was vulgar, and it made Shamira sick. She had seen the healing power of Jesus' words, and she knew if he wanted to, he could bring down all of the men who surrounded him, so why didn't he?

"Out of the way!" someone muttered to a follower in the crowd. "This prisoner is to be taken to the governor!"

Just as quickly as they had come, they had passed, and once again Shamira and Asa were left bewildered and in the dark.

"They're taking him to the governor!" said Asa. Shock made his face turn white.

"To Pontius Pilate? Why?" asked Shamira.

"I know why," Asa responded reservedly. "They can't punish Jesus. Not during the Pesach, according to the Law. They're going to get Pilate to do their dirty work for them."

"Well, then we must go to the governor's palace! Jesus has not committed any crimes against Rome. Pilate won't be able to punish him, will he?" Shamira was reaching out, looking for answers.

"There's only one way to find out," Asa began. Turning toward Shamira's father, he continued, "That is, if you would permit it?"

Aharon nodded slowly. "We'd better hurry, soon the whole city will be awake."

"I know a shortcut from here. Follow me."

Shamira felt a glimmer of hope that maybe, just maybe, Pilate would release Jesus, and all would be well. It was a branch to hold onto during a terrible storm, like a palm tree with strong roots that could withstand even the worst winds, and she would cling to it. As dawn broke, she prayed that with the light from the sun would come clarity and peace for Jerusalem.

JERUSALEM'S DAUGHTER

"Then they led Jesus from Caiaphas to the governor's headquarters. It was early morning. They did not enter the headquarters themselves; otherwise they would be defiled and unable to eat the Passover." - John 18:28 CSB

Exactly what Asa had predicted was coming to pass. The higher the sun rose in the sky; the more people began filling the streets. There were the usual sounds of the morning: people loading their carts for another day at the marketplace, gates swinging back and forth, footsteps running in one direction or another, and the menacing rooster's crow that sounded every few minutes.

Some things were out of the ordinary though. For instance, the way groups of people had gathered in the streets to whisper gossip, some of it based in fact on what Asa and others had witnessed in the dark of the night, but much of it being based on nothing at all. He winced at the memory of his father's part in this chaos. There was also the added sound of metal clanking together, the armor of Roman soldiers who were patrolling the area—as if the tension wasn't high enough.

It had been hours since they had seen Jesus. Asa had found a place for them to sit and wait for news. Aharon had sat down and closed his eyes, probably exhausted from the night's events. Shamira looked just as weary, but she hadn't dared to rest for even a minute. He knew what she was thinking because it was the same thing on his own mind. What were they doing to Jesus? Asa knew Romans could be cruel, and he'd learned more than he would have liked to know about how far the leaders at the temple would go to maintain order and control. When they were working together, the consequences could be lethal. With no knowledge of what was happening, the three of them continued to linger near the governor's palace.

"Asa," said Shamira, reaching for his arm and bringing him back to the present. "What is happening? Is there any news?"

Asa gently pulled his hand from her grip, smiling down and promising to her with his eyes he would take care of her. "Let me go and see what I can find out. If your father wakes, let him know I'll be back with any news I hear."

"Please be careful, Asa," Shamira said, her eyes wide. "Please?"

Asa nodded. "I've told you before, I will always find a way back to you. Nothing could ever stop me."

Aharon roused ever so slightly and mumbled, "I'm just resting my eyes Asa; do hurry back though."

With that, he turned toward the masses and tried to see if he could extrapolate any information. Everyone Asa approached had a different answer than the next.

"I heard they were taking him to Herod," said one.

"I thought he was accused of treason," said another.

"Does it matter as long as he gets what he deserves?" said yet another. "All he's done is cause trouble for us and Rome!"

He turned around, defeated. This wouldn't do. He couldn't go back only to deliver such abysmal news. Shouting from the front of the crowd closest to the governor's palace halted Asa in his tracks. He turned his head in that direction to discover that Pontius Pilate had appeared surrounded by several guards, and

Jesus. Turning quickly, he ran to get Shamira and Aharon.

"Asa, what news do you bring?" asked Shamira, already back on her feet.

Aharon stood too and with a question of his own. "We heard shouting. What's happening?"

"Pilate is here, he has Jesus with him."

"Then we must go!" said Shamira. "Abba?"

Her father nodded his agreement. He added, "Yes, but we'll stay near the back of the crowds for safety."

Where the crowd had assembled, Pontius Pilate, the prefect of Judea, stood in a high-up place before them with soldiers on either side of him. He was also accompanied by two prisoners, Jesus being one of them.

"What have they done to him?" asked Shamira, who had clearly noticed the changes in Jesus' features. Asa could barely stand to look at him, yet he couldn't tear his eyes away. He was tired, weary, dirty, and by all accounts, he should have been writhing in pain, but he stood there as if he were at peace.

"Why don't they just let him go? A punishment has been served and now he needs help!" she added. Asa admired her compassionate heart, and wished he could provide a logical answer, but no such response existed.

"I think if we just listen, we will soon find out what Pilate's intentions are," suggested Asa. It was the only suggestion he could offer.

"But he hasn't broken any laws!" she repeated.

Aharon nodded in agreement. "Asa is right, Shamira; we need to listen now."

Pontius Pilate raised his hands in the air, signaling to the crowds to be quiet. When they did, Pilate began his oration, and Asa tuned his ear to the sound of Pilate's voice, ready to study his words like he'd studied his father's Torah lectures as a boy. "You have brought me this man as one who misleads the people. But in fact, after examining him in your presence, I have found no grounds to charge this man with those things you accuse him of. Neither has Herod, because he sent him back to us. Clearly, he has done nothing to deserve death. Therefore, I will have him whipped and release him."

For a moment, Asa was relieved. He felt Shamira relax beside him, and he, too, sighed and shifted on his feet. But those feelings only lasted so long.

"Take this man away!" cried someone.

"What?" said Shamira, turning her head.

"Crucify him!"

"Crucify?" she whimpered, turning to Asa and searching for understanding. Couldn't he explain what was happening? He'd always had the answers before.

He shook his head. "I don't understand what's happening, and it makes little sense. Pilate has ruled, and they can't overturn his ruling."

The shouts grew louder and multiplied in number. Pilate raised his hands again to try to address them, but it did little good. The crowds began to get violent, jostling Shamira, Asa, and Aharon around as they tried to pass. People wouldn't take matters into their own hands, would they?

Guards came to Pilate and escorted him away, along with Jesus. "Where are they going?" asked Shamira, although she no longer expected direct answers.

"I don't know. I assume to carry out the punishment."

"But what about the people? This is turning into madness!"

Shamira began to lose track of time. How long had they been standing there? A half hour? An hour? She leaned heavily on her abba, who held her tightly in the midst of the crowd that threatened them like a storm-tossed sea. Finally, Pilate re-emerged from the darkness of the palatial interior. Again, the people grew louder, deafeningly loud, until he raised his hands. When the people still refused to quiet down, his guards stepped forward, positioning their weapons. At this, the people were silenced. Then Pilate turned and whispered something to one of the guards.

Asa grabbed Shamira's shoulder. "Shamira, I don't think you should see this."

"What? What shouldn't I see?" His touch distracted her, until she remembered where they were.

"They'll have beaten him badly. I don't think you should watch," he said.

"I will see it, Asa. I will see what they have done to the man I know is our Messiah," she replied with resolve. A chill went up her spine and for a moment she considered covering her eyes, but no, she wouldn't do it. She couldn't. She would stand by Jesus no matter what, she would not turn away.

"It's all right, Asa," her abba confirmed. "Shamira is a strong young woman."

"Yes, sir. I know that to be very true," Asa replied.

Pilate spoke. "Look, I'm bringing him out to you to let you know I find no grounds for charging him. Here is the man," said Pilate, gesturing behind him.

A man stumbled forward out of the shadows, a man covered in blood and unrecognizable. Shamira gasped in horror at the image which had now been seared into her mind, piercing her heart and leaving a wound that was unlikely to ever heal. His head was covered in blood that trickled down his face from his forehead, which was wrapped in a crown of thorns. His clothes were equally bloodied. Shamira thought she saw one of his attending soldiers snicker. How could they make such a mockery of Jesus?

Shamira cried out and buried her face in her abba's shoulder, drenching his tunic with her tears. She began to pray, asking, no, *begging* God for answers. *"Deliver him! I know You can!"* She prayed the words over and over again with all of her might. Her words may have had power, but God had a power greater than anything on earth. She trusted in Him to do the miraculous, to hear her prayers and to answer them.

"Crucify! Crucify!" people shouted. Shamira saw it was the priests and temple servants who had gathered near the front of the crowd.

"No… No!" Shamira whispered, and then raising her voice as loud as she could, "Release him! Spare his life!"

"Release Barabbas to us!" the others yelled even louder.

"Barabbas?" said Shamira, turning to Asa.

"It's a custom. At the time of the Pesach, Pilate can release a prisoner if the people request it. Barabbas is a known agitator."

"Then we must request he release Jesus!" she said, then turned her body to face forward. "Spare Jesus! Spare the life of Jesus of Nazareth!"

Still, her voice was overpowered. "Crucify Jesus! Release Barabbas!"

"Which of the two do you want me to release for you?"

"Jesus!" Shamira, Asa, and her father shouted together. "Jesus of Nazareth! Release Jesus!"

Shamira's heart sank into her stomach. She was screaming, but compared to the rest of the crowds, her voice was a mere whisper. Her Sabba had told her that words and prayers were powerful when in the hands of God. If that was true, then why weren't they making a difference? Why wasn't anyone else taking a stand? Why wasn't God answering her prayers?

She was powerless.

They were powerless to do anything.

Shamira couldn't believe her ears when all around her people chanted Barabbas' name.

"Why is this happening?" she cried.

Fists punched the air in rhythm with the cheering and chanting. Aharon shook his head and said, "This is turning into a mob. We need to move on from this place."

Shamira tried to turn to follow him, but she couldn't. She felt weightless. Her father had to practically drag her behind them because she was no longer in control of her own limbs. Bile rose up from her stomach, and with every step they took, they still could not escape the shouting.

"Then what do you want me to do with the one you call King of the Jews?"

"Crucify! Crucify!"

Jesus was to be betrayed by the very ones who had sung his praises, and there was nothing Shamira could do to stop it.

Asa, Shamira, and Aharon all walked together in the painfully slow processional, following Jesus as he carried his cross down the streets that had, just a few days prior, been covered in palm branches and filled with people singing his praises. But now, rather than chasing a triumphant beginning, they were forcing themselves to walk toward an inevitable end. The heavy beam which would become Jesus' cross dragged on the ground every step of the way from the center of Jerusalem all the way to the hill where he would be crucified. Its weight thudded over every dip in the ground, every obtrusive stone. Asa couldn't help but wonder—was Jesus really to die on that day?

Too soon they reached the top of the hill, Golgotha, and the guards seized Jesus' body, throwing him onto the ground.

"No!" Shamira screamed, running forward.

"Shamira, stop!" Asa shouted. Together, he and Aharon leapt toward her, pulling her back from the foot of the cross and the threat of the Roman centurion's spears.

She wrestled against them, pulling at both of their arms. "Shamira, there is nothing we can do now," said Asa.

"But... But... But he can't die. Not like this," she said, overcome by sobs and unable to catch her breath. Asa and Aharon didn't have to hold her anymore. Instead, she sank to the ground, crumpled into a heap, and began to weep. Her cries joined the wails of the other women and mourners present, becoming like a sepulchral choir singing dissonant, eerie harmonies.

Asa could do nothing to ease Shamira's grief, which magnified his own pain. All he could do was stand beside her and watch the fruits of his father's scheming flower. The first nail dug through Jesus' wrist with alarming ease. Asa watched as Shamira's body shuddered with each strike of the mallet. One more, and then another. It seemed that, for the Romans, three nails were all it took to kill a man.

For his father, it took only a few words.

He continued to watch as the soldiers heaved his cross upward so that all of his weight rested on those nails, with his body contorting in unnatural directions as he gasped for air. One soldier climbed up on a ladder and hung a sign over Jesus, reading, *"The King of the Jews."*

"Father, forgive them, because they do not know what they are doing," spoke Jesus. Even as his hours of suffering were only just beginning, he turned to God. Where was He in all of this? Where was God's love and mercy that Asa had always trusted?

At noon when the sun should have been at its highest, an unnatural darkness settled over the land. It appeared as though even the heavens had turned away in shame. Shrouded in shadow, Jesus cried, *"Eloi, Eloi, lemá sabachtháni?* My God, my God! Why have you abandoned me?"

"Asa, why is this happening? He doesn't deserve this!" Shamira wept.

Words came to Asa's mind, words he'd spent countless hours studying and committing to memory. *"They will look at me whom they pierced. They will mourn for him as one mourns for an only child and weep bitterly for him as one weeps for a firstborn."* He heard words from Zechariah, Isaiah, and all the other prophets echo in his mind over and over again. All of them explained what was happening, yet none of them explained why. At least not in a way that could comfort them, or that would comfort Shamira.

"I... I don't know," said Asa finally. "I can't understand it, even with everything I've been taught—I can't understand."

Tears welled up in his own eyes. Tears for Jesus' life, for the life Asa would never have with his father. Tears he should have cried long ago. As he watched the unjust punishment of a good man, a righteous man, before him, years of pain made their way to the surface, and Asa couldn't hold it in any longer. In the span of a day, Asa had lost his home. He'd lost his father. And now he'd lost his Savior. What did he have left?

"It isn't right!" she shouted. "If God is a God of love, then how could He allow this to happen? Wasn't that what Jesus preached? A good God? A loving God? What kind of love is this? What justice?"

"You don't mean that." Asa fell to his knees beside her, his feet sinking into the dirt and his legs being cut by the jagged edges of the rocks mixed with the sediment. He ignored the pain. Being there for Shamira, as she had been there for him when he was at his lowest in the early hours of that very morning which now felt like days ago, was all that mattered. He would always have his love for Shamira. Even if he wasn't sure at present how he would ever be able to marry her without a job, a family name, or anything to call his own, he would find a way to be with her. He always had before, and he always would.

"Yes, I do," she replied coldly.

"No," he said, stiffening. His eyes were affixed on Jesus, his gaze affixed to the wooden beams suspending him. "You don't. Just as I didn't mean what I said about my father. If you mean that, Shamira, then you mean that you have already given up on everything Jesus stood for."

He knew how stubborn Shamira was. How fiercely loyal she had always been to everyone she loved, her parents, her cousins, her family, him—he hoped. She would never give up on them or anything she believed in. He wouldn't let her give up on this, even if it was the most painful thing either of them would ever have to endure.

They would endure it together.

Shamira wanted to scream. She had not given up! She would never give up, but for the first time in her life, she had difficulty believing in what she could not see. Like the rays of sunlight that vanished behind the curtain-like clouds, her faith dwindled. With every coarse breath Jesus expelled, another piece of her died right alongside him.

His words came like whispers, and between the haughty

laughs of the soldiers, the insults of the priests and teachers of the Law, and the weeping of the onlookers, Shamira could hardly hear anything. That was when Jesus heaved himself up, taking one final breath.

He shouted out, "Father, into Your hands, I commit my spirit."

Shamira wanted to object, to say something, to do anything, but she found herself incapable of forming words. Every thought she had came out in cries and in tears.

At last, Jesus raised his eyes up to the sky and added, "It is finished." As he said it, his entire body went limp. He hung lifeless from the cross, no longer exuding the hope and light Shamira had seen in him before. He, too, had been claimed by that day's strange and unusual darkness. Shrill screams were heard from every direction, followed by a great rumbling from the earth.

The rocks on the ground began to fly into the air. The earth began to shake beneath them, as if it was ready to toss them off of its shoulders at any moment. Shamira screamed in terror as did others in the crowd. Her abba reached out to her and Asa. The three huddled closely together.

"What's happening?" Shamira yelled desperately.

"It's an earthquake!" Asa shouted back.

"Stay down!" Abba ordered and he threw himself across both of them. "We must not be separated."

All they could do was hold tight and wait for it to stop. Shamira wondered if it would ever stop, or if God had finally decided to intervene and was now going to punish all the earth for their hands in Jesus' death.

"Aharon! Shamira! Asa!"

Two male voices came from behind their little huddle. Feet stumbled forward until they fell beside the group. Shamira couldn't see anything, but she could feel their presence. It was her father's brothers, her dear uncles. Rut would have informed them of their whereabouts, and they must have come to find them upon hearing the news. Shamira leaned into the now bigger group, the tremors of her sobs matching the rhythm of the shocks beneath them.

Binyamin shouted over the screams of the crowd, "Even the rocks cry out at this man's death!"

With her father so close to her, she just barely heard him whisper, "What have we done?"

Shamira feared the worst. If even the mountains mourned for this man, he surely was the son of God. He surely was the Messiah, and now he was gone. She closed her eyes tight, not wanting to see Jesus' lifeless body suspended in the air. Her father picked her up in his arms, and she let him carry her home, still refusing to open her eyes.

When they finally arrived home, they were only met with more sobbing and crying. Shamira's eyes briefly fluttered open to see images of oil and carefully crafted jars, strips of cloth lying haphazardly, and fingers boring into the ground and then beating the dirt into their own clothes. Women could be heard wailing, joined by the shrill cries of frightened children.

Imma met them, her eyes red with tears.

"I'm so sorry, Aharon," she eked out the words. "We tried to keep him with us, if you'd just been a few moments sooner. Just a few moments…"

Eliyahu was dead.

JERUSALEM'S DAUGHTER

"All the crowds that had gathered for this spectacle, when they saw what had taken place, went home, striking their chests." -
Luke 23:48 CSB

Shamira's grandfather had to be very quickly anointed and wrapped in linen so he could be buried before sundown as their law dictated. It seemed like such a slight to a man who had made such a magnanimous impact on her own life. Was a rushed burial truly all they could afford him? According to the Law, they had no other choice. When she was told it was time to return to their house, she wanted to protest. She was not ready to begin a day of rest. She still needed time with her sabba, time to process everything that had happened. Time she would never get.

It was almost as if Sabba had waited for his Savior to breathe his last breath so he could follow. Had he known somehow?

"Shamira?" Rut whispered from beside her.

Shamira pretended not to hear her. In truth, she'd forgotten

Rut was even in the room. She'd been so lost in her thoughts, staring out the window at the sky and the quiet Jerusalem streets. Where was Asa out there, and would he be all right? In the confusion and chaos, she had not realized what had happened to him after the crucifixion; her mind had blocked those hours from her memory. Was he safe? Warm? Fed? She thought of his love for Sabba, and she was sorry for the pain she knew he would feel. She wanted to say so many things and ask so many questions, but she couldn't open her mouth. She was hungry but couldn't eat. She was thirsty but refused to drink. She wanted to sleep but rest would not come to her.

"Shamira?" Rut whispered again.

Shamira couldn't answer. She was still reeling from the loss of everything that had been taken from her in just one afternoon. Her hope in the future, and her link to the past. And what about her present? Asa was her present, but she didn't even know where he was or how he would fare, without a home of his own and a roof over his head.

"Shamira, I know you can hear me."

Her heart tugged at her, reminding her she was being unfair to Rut. Rut was grieving too; they just had different ways of processing pain.

"I lost a lot today too, you know. You weren't the only one who loved Sabba, who had special conversations with him, memories that you shared which can never be replicated. You weren't the only one who had loved and chosen and staked everything on Jesus."

She had staked everything on Jesus, but what had come of it? Shamira twitched her nose at the moisture in the air. Water started to drip from the sky and the stars began to disappear. Sprinkles of rain turned to showers, and Shamira drew the curtain covering their window. She turned to sit on her mat, leaning her body toward her cousin.

"I know," she whispered, barely audible.

"Oh!" Rut exclaimed, wrapping her arms around her cousin. "I thought I would never hear you speak again! Don't do that to me, Mira. I need you right now more than ever. You are the only person in this house who can tell me what happened through the night and this day. I know probably not now, but in time—Shamira, it broke my heart to stay behind. He was my Messiah too. The things happening around us make no sense at all. I could not—cannot bear it without you by my side."

"I need you too, Rut." She smiled in spite of her sorrow, being grateful for just a moment of respite from her pain. "I want to talk to you, but I just feel so…numb."

Her cousin's nearness brought her some semblance of comfort, and she began to relax. She reminded herself she was not alone, and she had never been alone. She prayed Asa would feel that same comfort—the comfort God could surely provide him.

"Shamira?" small voices from around the corner whispered.

"Children?" she called out, waiting for them to show themselves. She would never get used to hearing the sound of Libi's voice, that beautiful pure sound. "Come in!"

Shamira and Rut sat curled up in the corner of their room on the same mat. They motioned for their younger cousins to come and join them. Yuval, Gilad, and Libi piled in until each one had a place beside the other somewhere between Rut and Shamira's arms.

Libi's lips quivered. "Where did Sabba go? What happened to him?"

Shamira took a deep breath. She wasn't even sure she understood the answers to those questions, let alone how she could relay them to children in a way they would be able to understand.

"He was a very old man, Libi. And in a great deal of pain," she began.

"Sick like me?" she said, pointing to her ears. "Sick" wasn't the word Shamira would have used to describe Libi's affliction, but she nodded a reply to Libi anyway.

"His body was very weak. He wasn't strong anymore, and we all need to be strong in order to live. God saw his pain and weakness, and so He took it away. Now he is at rest forever," Rut said.

"You see, God is a God of love; when you are with Him, you cannot feel any pain. Sabba ran out of strength in this life, but

God has given him strength tenfold in the next," Shamira echoed some of the last words her sabba had spoken to her. He had believed them, and Shamira needed to believe them as well.

"Now he is with God feeling no more pain, only joy," finished Rut. "You know what joy is don't you?"

The children nodded in a variety of different directions and Shamira realized this would require more of an explanation. "Yuval, how do you feel when you are playing outside with your toys, make-believing that you are conquering lands and collecting treasure?"

"I love doing that!"

"Yes!" replied Rut. "And Gilad, do you remember how you feel each time your abba takes you out to the fields to see the sheep?"

"That's fun!" replied Gilad.

"Lots of fun!" echoed his twin brother.

"And Libi," Shamira began, "what do you enjoy doing?"

"I like cooking with you and Imma and Savta, and playing with my brothers, and listening to the birds singing!" she said, proudly listing off one thing after another. Shamira took Libi's hand in hers and swung it back and forth, giving her hand a little squeeze.

"When you do all of those things, you are all experiencing happiness. Joy is like happiness, but you feel it all the time. It never ends. When you are with God in heaven, there are no chores to be done. You will never get too tired to run or to play. You will never have work to do. You will never be hungry. Only joy. Try to remember your Sabba like that, full of joy, because that's how he is going to be all the time from now on. One day you will get to go to heaven too and feel that same kind of joy."

"We will?" Libi's eyes widened.

"Yes, indeed!" replied Shamira.

"But why does Sabba have to experience it all without us? Why couldn't we all go to heaven? Or why couldn't Sabba have just stayed here, and Jesus could have made him not sick anymore like he did for me?"

Shamira understood Libi's confusion more than she knew. A part of her was jealous of her sabba, angry even that God would take him from their family. In her heart she was distraught, but in her head, she knew it was wrong of her to feel that way. How could she explain that to a child?

"Well," she sighed. Then Shamira remembered something she had heard her Imma say before, the last time Eliana had visited. "Sometimes God does things that we don't understand for reasons that are far beyond us. I know you are sad now; I am sad too! But God will use this experience to teach us something. That is His way. All right?" Shamira prayed it was true, and that she would see God's purpose in the pain sooner rather than later. In the meantime, she would petition for peace. Peace for her family, peace for her heart, and peace regarding the unknown future she was to face, hopefully with Asa by her side.

They all nodded at her, and she kissed the tops of their heads. "Now get to your own beds before your parents find you in here!" she teased.

They scurried off to their own beds, but not before bumping into Benayahu just around the corner. He may have thought he was hidden, but Shamira had seen his shadow appear in the entry long before she'd finished talking to the younger children.

"Beni! What are you doing out here?" Libi exclaimed.

"Never you mind. Go to bed like Shamira told you to," he said, half-smiling.

"Do you want to come play with us?" asked Yuval.

Beni smiled and replied, "It is late, Yuval. Ask me again tomorrow, all right?"

"Good. I thought you were a grown-up now and didn't want to play anymore."

Benayahu chuckled. "No, I'm still child enough to play with you, but none of us will have the energy to play at all unless you get to sleep."

"All right," said Yuval.

When Shamira could tell all the children had passed into the other room, she called to Beni, "You can come out from your hiding place now."

Beni turned into the doorway, facing his sister and cousin.

"Not a grown-up yet?"

"No, I don't think so." His voice sounded tired. "Growing up doesn't seem as desirable to me as it used to, not after today. I thought I was so smart and that I knew everything. But...but Sabba..." Benayahu's voice trailed off into a few deep breaths. Tears fell one by one from his eyes, and he wiped them away with the back of his hand, brushing the pain off his face. "I want to make him proud. I want to spend more time listening and learning from my father, practicing what he tells me, working hard in the fields when he believes that I am ready. Anyway, I just wanted to say that what you said to the children was, well...it was pretty good."

"Thank you." Shamira smiled, for real this time. Her family warmed her heart and removed the chill from her body.

"I would say it was *powerful,*" Rut added, dropping her head on Shamira's shoulder.

He nodded. "You know, I wasn't meaning to spy on your conversation. The adults were all downstairs, and you were all up here... I just didn't know what to do..."

"It's all right, Beni. There's nothing to apologize for."

"Beni?" said Rut, standing up and stepping toward her younger brother. "You know that I love you, don't you?"

He poked her shoulder ever so slightly. "Of course, even if you are an annoying older sister."

"Even if you are a pesky younger brother!" she joked and wrapped her arms around him to hug him just the way they used to when they played together as small children.

Feigning a yawn, he pulled away. "Well, I think I'll go to sleep now. Goodnight, Rut, Shamira."

"Goodnight," the girls said in unison.

"And Beni?" said Shamira. He halted on his way out. "I think you're wiser than you know."

"Thanks, Shamira. I appreciate you saying that, but if you don't mind, I'd rather you didn't say it too often. I don't want to ever fool myself into thinking I know everything. I always want to be learning," he replied.

"All right," she agreed as he left the room.

Shamira fell back on her mat, exhausted and weary. She stretched out her spine and closed her eyes, keeping them closed to avoid the sting from all the salty tears she had cried throughout the day. Her family had been broken today, but they would heal.

Her mind wandered a little further, replaying memories, scenes, words, emotions, and faces. She thought of Jesus and how even in the most difficult moment His heart had been drawn to His Father in Heaven. She realized that in her own uncertainty and pain, she too needed to draw closer to God.

If she could believe in a Savior who would reconcile her people and heal dear Libi, if she believed God could work miracles like making the deaf hear and the mute speak, she could believe He had a plan for her life and for Asa's. Following His leading before had always led her to miraculous results, whether or not she'd realized them at the time. Why then, shouldn't she believe it was equally as possible for God to create a future where she and Asa could be together, and be happy? Whatever God's plan was, she could always count on Him to have a plan. That was the constant she could cling to.

Asa was growing more and more concerned with each drop of water that fell from the sky. He had slept on the street the night before, confused and guilt-ridden. By the time he'd woken up, he was surrounded by a large, muddy puddle. Should he have stayed with Shamira? Was it his place to mourn with her family, or had he been right to leave them to their own grief? What about *his* grief? He pulled his cloak over his head to cover himself from the rain, but it did little good and the cloth quickly became soaked.

He was cold and hungry. Very, very hungry. He'd had nothing to eat for quite some time, save a loaf of stale bread someone had thrown at him. Whether it had been thrown out of pity or out of disgust for the wandering vagrant he appeared to be, he couldn't decide. All he knew was he was incredibly grateful for their kindness. It was bread from God as far as he was concerned.

Still, his stomach rumbled for more, echoed by the rolling thunder. He needed to find better shelter than he'd had the night before, or he wouldn't last long at all. Despite the cold air, he was sweating. He knew he was weak from the night he'd spent watching the events of Jesus' last hours unfold and the lack of sleep he'd had the night after, in combination with the effects of the earth's elements.

Asa was overcome by the realization that he was homeless; he had nowhere to go for help. He couldn't impose on Shamira's family; it wouldn't be appropriate, and now he had absolutely nothing to offer. He couldn't go home; his father had made it very clear that was no longer his home. He wondered if they were worried about him or even noticed he was gone. The thought was too depressing to ponder long; Asa just kept walking.

And walking.

And walking.

His eyelids were getting heavy. He needed rest. Proper rest. But instead, he found himself in a part of Jerusalem he'd never been before, or at least that he couldn't recognize in the storm. *"God, if you're listening, please help me,"* he prayed.

He approached the door to a home and knocked. "Hello? Is anyone there?"

"Who's there?" a voice called out from behind it.

"Please, I need somewhere to stay." He could barely even say the words. He was shaking so severely.

A short pause gave him hope, but his request was denied. "There's no room here. I'm sorry."

That was it then; he had to move on.

He tried another door.

Did he even knock? Or had he just been standing there for an indeterminable amount of time? He wasn't sure.

The door swung open and an angry man bellowed at him, "Who are you and what are you doing here?"

Either Asa had knocked, and this man was very unwelcoming, or he'd been loitering, and the owner of this home had grown suspicious and wary. "Please," he begged, "I need somewhere to stay."

"Does this look like an inn?" the man growled. Asa had already started to walk away. "Don't come back here!"

One more door.

That's all he would try.

Just one more.

He dragged his feet each and every step, getting mud and rocks stuck between his toes. His sandals had worn out much earlier in the day, and he'd been cutting his feet ever since. The dirt had the odd sensation of stinging his wounds, while the mud cooled them at the same time. Neither sensation was pleasant. While the coolness of the moist earth provided him temporary relief, it only reminded him of how truly cold the rest of his body was. He was coughing, hunched halfway over as he approached the next door.

He raised his hands to knock but couldn't make it.

He felt his legs give way from under him. "Please…" he called as he fell, landing with a thud against the door.

"Help me, please…" he called again. Still there was no answer.

He kept coughing. *"God, please let this household answer me,"* he prayed.

More time passed, enough for Asa to take three shaky breaths. His throat burned, and he knew he couldn't yell anymore. If these people didn't open their door, he would just sleep right beside it. His eyelids weighed heavy and his legs and arms even more so.

Maybe he was dreaming or hallucinating, but he thought he heard whispering from behind the door. It was whispering! Was someone there?

Just then, the door crept open and a man said, "We have to help him."

"I know this man!" said another voice. The owner of the second voice bent down, and Asa opened his eyes just wide enough to see him. "Asa, Asa, it's me, Peter."

It was Peter, the disciple! Asa tried to call out for help, but he couldn't make his mouth form words.

"He's sick. John, help me get him inside," said Peter.

Again, he tried but failed to force sounds into something intelligible. He wanted to explain, to tell them what he had seen, to thank them, but all he could manage was a few hoarse syllables.

"He's trying to say something, Peter," said John, leaning closer over Asa.

"He's delirious. We'll warm him up inside and get him some broth, then see what he says."

He had to try again. Swallowing back hard, he groaned, "Wait…"

"It's all right," said Peter. "We'll help you."

Asa nodded in understanding and surrendered.

21

"On the first day of the week Mary Magdalene came to the tomb early, while it was still dark. She saw that the stone had been removed from the tomb." - John 20:1 CSB

There was a pleasant smell in the room. Bread? Soup? Asa's eyes fluttered open. They were met by the morning sunlight peeking through the curtains that covered the windows in the room. He looked around and saw Peter sitting beside him. "Peter!" he exclaimed.

"You were very ill last night. Are you feeling better today?"

"Yes, much," said Asa, assessing himself. The burning sensation in his throat had disappeared, and it felt good to be in dry clothes again.

"Good. We tried talking to you last night, but you wouldn't answer. What happened to you?"

"My father...he... He disowned me after I told him I wanted to follow Jesus. That was...two days ago... I think, maybe three." He was still dazed and confused. It would take him a while to regain his sense of time.

"During Pesach?"

"Yes, I was at the temple serving with him."

"Three days then. And you said your father was a priest?"

Asa nodded. Shame suddenly flooded him. "I saw him exchanging coin with one of the men who was with you."

Peter sighed. "We already know about Judas, Asa."

He bowed his head, unable to look Peter in the eye. It was his father who had done this. His father had been involved in the conspiracy to kill Jesus. His father was one of the Sanhedrin who had called for his death. His father had been among those who cheered for and demanded his execution. Even if his father carried no shame, Asa would bear that burden for the rest of his life.

"My father...He...He wanted Jesus to die?" Asa said the statement like a question, still shrouded in disbelief. Peter, who had been listening to him, handed him a bowl with stew and some bread on the side. He was starving, yet the realization of the past few day's events made him want to wretch.

"I abandoned him. What does that say about me?" said Peter gruffly. "I know you saw it."

His bluntness made Asa turn white.

Peter grunted. "Nobody here will hold the actions of your father against you. Least of all me."

"That's right... We saw you—"

"At the house of the high priest," Peter finished. "I... I am sorry about that."

"As am I."

Neither of them said anything else. Asa did his best to nibble at the food he'd been given, and after a few bites his hunger had been reawakened. He finished the first bowl ravenously, then the second, then the third very slowly, until he was full.

"What do you all plan to do?" asked Asa, curious about where the disciples would go next.

"Some of us are leaving, some of us plan to stay in Jerusalem a while longer until things calm down." One of them Asa hadn't met confirmed this plan.

"What about you? What will *you* do?" Asa asked again, this

time to Peter specifically.

Just then, a woman burst through the door. "They've taken the Lord out of the tomb, and we don't know where they've put him!"

The disciple Asa recognized as John approached her. "Mary, you're talking nonsense."

"Who is that?" Asa whispered.

"Mary of Magdala," said Peter aside to him, then rose to join John. Other women followed in behind Mary, none of whom Asa recognized beyond being followers of Jesus he'd seen in Bethany but had never actually been properly introduced to. "What did you say?"

"They've taken the Lord! The tomb is empty!" said Mary to Peter, grabbing his arms. Her eyes were wide, and she looked petrified.

"The tomb... The tomb..." Peter repeated the words in a state of shock. The very next moment he took off running out the door, nearly knocking over the other women behind Mary. John followed Peter, and Asa jumped up to follow John.

The tomb is empty! thought Asa. *Empty!*

"Could it really be?" said Asa, panting for air and trying desperately to catch up to the other disciples. *"Could he have risen from the dead?"*

There was only one way to find out.

It was now the third day since her grandfather had passed away. The third day since Shamira had witnessed the cruel injustice of her people and the subsequent crucifixion of Jesus, her Messiah. The world seemed to go on turning as though nothing unusual had happened. People returned to the streets after the Shabbat was over and business resumed. Shamira marveled at how her entire life could change in the course of just a week, but everything around her remained the same. The sun still rose and fell over Jerusalem, the streets still came alive with the gentle hum of conversation and footsteps, and the same air filled her lungs. It didn't seem right to have endured so much, but to still be living in the same world where nothing outside of her had changed in the slightest.

Resting her hand on the mezuzah, Shamira looked out into their courtyard and was happy to see at least some things had been changed for the better. Although the family was dressed according to the tradition for those who were in mourning, they were together in their grief. Her entire family gathered around each other talking and smiling as much as they could under the circumstances. Gilad, Yuval, and Libi ran in circles around the courtyard as Benayahu chased them and Rut cheered. Chava and Tamir held hands under the shade of the tree. Even her own parents seemed particularly close to one another. She wanted to ask her abba if he could help her find Asa that day; it had been so long, and she worried about where he was.

It had been a difficult, traumatic few days to say the least, but Shamira couldn't say she was altogether unhappy. Being this close to her family filled her with a sense of peace, more so than she had ever remembered feeling before. As Shamira stepped outside of her home, she instantly recognized two things. The first was the feeling of the sun on her skin, the way it enveloped her in its heat and made her feel safe and warm. The second was the shouting in the streets.

"Do you hear that?" she said, not really speaking to anyone directly.

"What is it?" replied her savta, who was standing nearby her.

Her father stepped forward, and his voice sounded weary. "What could be happening now?"

Her father approached the gate, and Shamira ran to his side, along with the rest of her family. Her curiosity was piqued by the commotion.

The people had already taken Jesus, and the Pesach had passed. What more could cause such chaos? Such pain? Shamira attempted to ease her anxious heart, and trust in God even when she didn't understand the purpose in suffering. Instead, she tried her best to believe perhaps that day would be the day God revealed His grand design to them all.

Her father unbolted the gate and pulled it back, and the whole family stared outside, watching people run past in intermediate intervals. None of them could catch what they were saying. Finally, a familiar face skidded to a halt right in front of her gate.

"Asa!" Shamira cried out with joy. "Asa! You're all right!" Relief swept over her soul. "What is happening?" She should have greeted him properly, but she couldn't help herself.

"It's…the…tomb." He heaved ragged breaths in between the words. "Jesus' tomb was empty. Mary Magdalene, one of Jesus' followers went there this morning."

Shamira wrinkled up her nose, not understanding.

"What do you mean, son? We saw the man die."

Asa sighed, gasping for his next breath. "But he is not dead! At least, not anymore. He is alive! He is risen!"

At this, Shamira screamed excitedly and replied, "Alive? But how?"

"I have been with the disciples. Mary Magdalene is just one witness! I've been to the tomb where they laid him myself, and it truly is empty."

"We must join them!" She would give anything to see Jesus just one more time. Shamira stepped toward him, realizing her family was not following her. She turned in surprise and said expectantly, "Abba? Aren't you going to come?"

Her father stared at her blankly. For a moment, she was filled with worry. He had said he believed, but that was before. Was doubt still holding him back?

"I will go," Savta announced.

"But mother," Binyamin objected.

"Do not tell me I am too old! I have been 'too old' for many years now. It does not stop me from getting around! Without my husband here, there is nothing left for me to do in this house. I will go and see this miracle for him. I will witness what he could not. I will carry on his legacy. I will tell them how my beloved husband was summoned to welcome the newborn Savior. I will tell them the whole story if they want to hear it, and I will see how the story ends."

Shamira had seen her grandmother cry many tears, but she'd also seen her grandmother when she was determined and stubborn. This was one of those times. She would be going, and no one could stop her.

"We cannot go," said Shamira's mother. "Devorah, Chava, and I. We cannot travel or leave the house while we are still unclean from preparing the body for burial."

"Neither can we," said Binyamin, gesturing to himself and Tamir.

"All right, Shamira," said Shamira's father. She waited on bated breath for his pronouncement. "I will go with you and your Savta to see if these things are true."

"Thank you, Abba!" said Shamira, her heart soaring.

"Quickly then," said Asa. "I will take you to where the disciples are staying."

"May I go, also?" said Rut, asking her own abba for permission. He nodded.

Shamira, her abba, Rut, and her savta took flight behind him, eager to see proof of the resurrected Savior. The farther they travelled, the thicker the crowds got, which was to be expected in that part of Jerusalem late in the afternoon. The sun was at its brightest and hottest, and even though their group moved with urgency, the people of Jerusalem moved slower and became more sluggish under its intense glare. They were forced to move at a painfully slow pace, having no real idea of where they were going. Asa was the only one who knew the whereabouts of the disciples.

"This morning," Asa explained to Shamira who had not left his side. "A woman named Mary Magdalene said she had seen Jesus alive and heard him speak. The news was shocking to say the least. Others are gathering now."

"Others?" said Shamira.

"His followers! They all fled for safety after the crucifixion, afraid they would be next. The disciples and many others have already gathered in secret to discuss what has happened. That's where we're going, to join them."

As they walked on and she listened to Asa's every word, Shamira accidentally rammed into a man just in front of her.

"Oh, I am so sorry. I beg your forgiveness," she said, bowing her head respectfully.

"It is given," said the mysterious man, his face hidden by the shadow of his cloak which protected him from the sun. "Where are you all trying to go in such a hurry?"

Her abba answered the stranger, saying, "We are looking for the man who goes by Jesus of Nazareth, whom they say has risen from the grave."

"He was crucified just three days ago," Shamira explained. "Have you not heard?"

The man nodded, following them as they walked. Shamira would have been concerned by the stranger's presence, but something about him seemed almost...familiar. If she did know him, then why couldn't she recognize him?

"It seems as though you have cause for great joy and excitement, although I see you are also in mourning. Who is it that you have lost?"

"It was my Sabba," said Shamira.

"My father," added Aharon. "He was very old and very ill, but he believed firmly in the power of the Messiah. It was his last wish that we would take up and follow Jesus."

Shamira tried to turn to face him but the glare of the sun was too blinding. She kept her eyes on the ground in front of her as she walked.

"Do not worry," said the man. "Eliyahu resides in my father's house. Believe in me, and you will see him again."

"Eliyahu resides in my father's house." Shamira repeated the words in her mind, unable to comprehend them. *"In my father's house."* It was as if all of her thoughts were hitting an imaginary wall in her mind and bouncing back, repeating over and over again trying to breakthrough. It was then Shamira realized why the voice seemed so familiar. It was the voice of Jesus! He had appeared to them!

"Jesus!" she exclaimed, but he had already gone from them. "Where did he go?"

"That was him!" said Savta.

"Yes, I recognized his voice!" added Rut.

"That was Jesus of Nazareth," Shamira repeated. Then, she turned to Asa and excitedly asked, "Did you hear him? Did you hear what he said?"

"Let's hurry," said Asa. "We must tell the disciples what we have witnessed."

*"When it was evening of that first day of the week, the
disciples were gathered together with the doors locked
because they feared the Jews. Jesus came, stood among them,
and said to them, 'Peace be with you.'" - John 20:19 CSB*

When they arrived at the disciples' hiding place, Shamira
quickly assessed the location. It was a small room high above
the street, with the entrance well removed from the main road.
Asa knocked several times in a very specific rhythm and a man
cracked open the door just barely. Shamira recognized his eyes
as Peter, the one who had denied Jesus that fateful night. If she
had not seen Jesus already, she would have still been angry at
him for giving up so quickly. Now however, she could not
blame him for being scared, nor could she deny him the
forgiveness Jesus had so freely given.

Peter opened the door just wide enough for the five of them
to squeeze in. The room was already overflowing with people,
somber and quiet. She recognized some of them as the disciples,

and she presumed the others were also followers of Jesus. In the middle stood one woman who was pacing back and forth.

"I'm telling you; I saw him! He was alive! I have seen the Lord!" she said to them.

"Mary, sit down," someone groaned.

"Who are all of these people?" Shamira whispered to Asa.

He leaned toward her ear. "That's Mary of Magdala. She is the one whom Jesus appeared to. You know Peter and the other disciples. Everyone else here is another follower of Jesus."

"How did you find this place?"

"After…after Jesus was crucified, I followed you and your family home. I had nowhere else to go and I couldn't go back to my father's house. But when we got to your home and I realized… Everyone was in mourning, and I knew it wasn't my place to be there. I'm sorry I couldn't be there for you. I wandered all over the city, sleeping on the street without food or shelter—I had lost my strength, even my wits. I knocked on some doors but was turned away. I collapsed in front of a house, and eventually Peter and John found me. I stayed here last night, and this morning we heard the news. I came to you as quickly as possible." Shamira marveled at his declaration. She could not have imagined sleeping on the streets without a place to call home.

"Oh Asa, I'm so very sorry."

"Don't pity me, Shamira. I can already tell that you are. My father had several chances to redeem himself and make things right between us. I cannot deny my belief in Jesus as the Messiah, and my father cannot deny his belief that to suggest such a thing is blasphemy. It is what it is, and while I am saddened, I feel no regret. Peter and the others are good men. They gave me food, drink and dry clothes—they have little, but they have shared much. They had no reason to trust me, the son of one of the men who convicted their teacher, but they did anyway. They are living the way I want to live, not by legalities or obligation, but because they love God with all their hearts. I have learned a great deal here in such a short time."

As much as he said it with resolve, her heart still broke for him. She wondered where he would go and how he would live.

Shamira couldn't imagine a rift so great, a chasm so wide, it would separate her from the love of her father. She didn't believe such a thing existed between herself and her abba, nor that such a thing could ever exist between them. She supposed though that after a lifetime of harsh treatment, perhaps this shift was a gift of freedom more than a curse of shame for Asa. Even knowing this, Shamira still felt her heart splinter into a thousand pieces on Asa's behalf. If it didn't bother him, it bothered her.

"I'm telling you; I saw him! He was alive, and he called me by name and gave me a message to tell you: that we should go to Galilee!" More shouting from the center of the room drew Shamira's attention away from Asa. The way the Magdalene woman spoke with such passion reminded Shamira of herself. Outspoken, but firm. "Other women went to the tomb as well. Joanna, Mary…ask them! They will also tell you the tomb is empty!"

"It's true, his body is gone! John and I have seen it," confirmed Peter. "He is risen!"

Someone asked, "Did you see Jesus, Peter? Did you actually see him for yourself? Alive?"

"No, I didn't. But Mary did! And I can't deny the tomb is empty. He has to be alive! He has to!" Peter argued.

Another disciple spoke up. "Even if everything you are saying is true, soldiers will be on high alert with the events that have taken place these past few days. It is too dangerous to try to get out of the city now!"

Just then, the door burst open behind them with a loud boom, nearly stopping the hearts of everyone in the room. Two men pushed their way forward in great haste, one of them stepping on Shamira's open toes in the rush. They were both speaking so fast no one could understand them.

Peter's eyes lit with recognition. "Cleopas! What has happened?"

"We thought you were on your way to Emmaus," questioned John.

"Were you in danger?" said another.

"Danger? Ha!" the one called Cleopas laughed heartily. "No danger! We have witnessed a miracle! A miracle!"

"Yes," began the other. "We were on our way to Emmaus, and as we walked, another man joined us. We were arguing, you see, about what had happened to Jesus. The man shocked us both when he asked us what we were arguing about!"

Cleopas interrupted, "Indeed, he made it seem as though he had no idea what had transpired in Jerusalem. So, we told him, 'The things concerning Jesus of Nazareth, who was a prophet powerful in action and speech before God and all the people, and how our chief priests and leaders handed him over to be sentenced to death and crucified him. But we were hoping he was the one who was about to redeem Israel. Besides all this, it's the third day since these things happened. Moreover, some women from our group astounded us. They arrived early at the tomb, and when they didn't find his body, they came and reported they had seen a vision of angels who said he was alive. Some of those who were with us went to the tomb and found it just as the women had said, but they didn't see him.'"

"He listened to all we had to say, and then he called us foolish!" said the second one, now also in a fit of giddy laughter. "He said to us, 'Wasn't it necessary for the Messiah to suffer these things and enter into his glory?' And he began to explain to us and interpret the scriptures. All the way back to the writings of Moses! He interpreted all the things concerning the Messiah in all of the scriptures!"

Cleopas cut in again, saying, "We were so intrigued by what he had said that we were not ready to part with him once we reached our destination. So, we invited him in to break bread with us. He agreed and we all went inside and bowed our heads as he blessed the meal. He took the bread, blessed it, broke it, and then distributed it among us. It was as he was praying that we suddenly realized who he was!"

"It was Jesus, himself!"

"Jesus?" said another one of the voices in the crowd. "How?"

"I do not know, but we are telling the truth. Once we realized who he was, he disappeared. It became so clear as we remembered how our hearts burned from within us when he was explaining the Scriptures to us on the road. Instantly we grabbed our things and got back on the road to return to you!"

Shamira's jaw dropped and without thinking she jumped forward and proclaimed, "The same thing happened to us!"

"Shamira, do not interrupt," her father whispered from behind her.

"Wait," commanded Peter. "I want to hear this."

Shamira turned bright red and looked side to side, expecting her father or Asa to tell the story.

"He's talking to you, Shamira," Asa whispered.

She had never been *asked* to speak in public like this before. Asked to be quiet, yes, many times, but asked to speak because a larger group cared about what she had to say? It was an unusual feeling, but Shamira reveled in it. Asa gave her another nod of approval, encouraging her to speak.

She swallowed back and began, "My family and I were on our way here after Asa—" she gestured to the tall, handsome love of her life standing beside her "—told us that there had been a sighting of Jesus. We were followers of his and his message and were eager to see if the story was true. As we walked, a man came up alongside us and we all thought that he seemed familiar to us, but none of us could place where we knew his voice from. He asked us where we were going and why we were in such a hurry, and we told him we were anxious to hear news of our Lord, who had been crucified just three days ago! He noticed our garments and our weary appearance and asked us why we were in mourning.

"I told him that my grandfather had also died just a few days prior. My grandfather had believed in the Messiah's coming for his whole life, and if Jesus was alive and had conquered death, then we just had to find him. It is what our grandfather would have wanted. Then the man spoke with authority and told us, 'Do not worry. Eliyahu resides in my father's house.' He knew our grandfather by name. That was when I was truly convinced it was him, it was Jesus. We all realized it then, but as quickly as he appeared, he vanished."

Peter smiled, his smile slowly turning into joyous laughter. "It is true! He is alive!"

"It just seems impossible to me," doubted one man.

"I agree. We saw him die!" spoke up another.

"But he lives! We have heard multiple testimonies now that prove it is so."

"If he's alive, then where is he now?"

More voices arose in the confusion, each of them positing their own theory to break apart the testimonies presented to them by Mary Magdalene, the travelers, and now Shamira. Some picked arguments or poked holes in the narratives of Shamira and the two other witnesses, while others rebuked their doubts.

"But... But..." Shamira whispered, unable to come up with a reply that would either solidify her testimony, convince the naysayers of the truth, or both.

"Peace be with you," said a voice that seemed to resonate and echo off all the walls surrounding them. Shamira recognized the voice this time, and she knew she would never forget it again.

Peter turned around and fell to his knees. "My Lord."

There Jesus stood, reaching out to Peter with the marks from the nails still present in his wrists. Peter didn't look up, but remained with his face pressed toward the ground, shaking his head. "I can't... I can't..." he cried.

Those who had been bickering recoiled in fear, silenced in the presence of what they had deemed impossible. Everyone was quiet, but all Shamira wanted to do was burst into song at the sight of him, her Lord and Savior.

"Peter," said Jesus, bending over to help him stand. Shamira remembered how Peter had hid during the trial. He had done all of that hiding, and Jesus was still reaching out to him.

Then Jesus turned to the others crowded in the too-small annex and said, "Why are you troubled? And why do doubts arise in your hearts? Look at my hands and my feet, that it is I myself! Touch me and see, because a ghost does not have flesh and bones as you can see, I have." Those in the room relaxed and approached him to measure the truth of his word, which could not be refuted.

"It is you... It really is you!" said Peter.

He stretched out his hands, and many of the people did as he told them to. They broke bread with him once more as he taught them and made known to them all of the ways in which he had fulfilled the Scriptures which had prophesied his coming, his death, and even his resurrection. Shamira and her family were witnesses to all of this, and as much as Shamira wished her sabba could be with them to witness the glory that came from the fulfillment of God's ultimate promise to his people and to all the world, she took even greater delight in the knowledge that he would be witnessing things immeasurably and unimaginably greater in God's kingdom in heaven, just as Jesus had told them he was.

Shamira and her family were eager to spend time with Jesus again, having last seen him that day in Jerusalem, the day of his resurrection. They had listened for word from the disciples about where he would be next, and when they heard he would be nearby, Shamira, her parents, her Dodh Binyamin and his family all travelled to meet him the day before.

It was early in the morning on the fortieth day when Jesus had taken them all out to a high place near Bethany called the Mount of Olives. Selfishly, Shamira was also excited to be spending time with Asa again, who had been travelling with the disciples. She enjoyed watching Asa from a distance and hearing his stories about studying and debating with the disciples and other men who were a part of the caravan. His knowledge of the word of God with his father at the temple had perfectly equipped him now to study and apply the teachings of Jesus. She found she loved that part of him, the way his mind worked to understand things and commit them not only to his memory, but to his heart.

Most people were still arising and getting ready for the day, breaking their fast and pulling down their tents from the night before. Some children still stumbled around with sleep hanging over their eyelids. People started to gather near Jesus as he began to speak. Shamira pushed herself nearer to the front of the crowd, eager to hear what he was about to say.

Jesus said to them, "I will be leaving you, but I urge you to stay in Jerusalem. The Father's promise is coming soon, which you have heard me speak about."

Rut, who had come up behind Shamira, asked her, "What does he mean?"

"I do not know," Shamira whispered, crossing her arms in front of her.

Jesus opened his mouth to speak again and continued, "For John baptized with water, but you will be baptized with the Holy Spirit in a few days."

One of those among the crowd called out, "Lord are you restoring the kingdom to Israel at this time?"

"It is not for you to know the times or periods that the Father has set by his own authority. But you will receive power when the Holy Spirit has come on you, and you will be my witnesses in Jerusalem, in all Judea and Samaria, and to the end of the earth."

As soon as he said it, a bright, white cloud overcame him. When the cloud was gone, so was Jesus. There was confusion and whispering among the followers, and people began looking all around, wondering what had happened to their risen Messiah.

"He's gone!" exclaimed Rut. "Jesus is gone!"

Shamira leaned her head back and dropped her arms to her sides, astonished. Suddenly two men dressed in white appeared beside them, saying, "Men of Galilee. Why do you stand looking up into heaven? This same Jesus, who has been taken from you into heaven, will come in the same way that you have seen him going into heaven."

They disappeared along with Jesus, and Shamira could only assume they may have been angels. She could scarcely think. She was so short of breath, equally overtaken by the wonder of the miracle that had just taken place before her very eyes, but also by the fear and sadness that came with the realization that Jesus was no longer with them.

"He's not gone," said Asa, joining them and gently placing Shamira's hand in his own. "He will never be gone from us, not really. He is with us in our hearts, forever."

"What will we do now?" said Shamira, turning around to see her family.

"Go back to Jerusalem. That's what Jesus commanded," said her uncle, Binyamin.

"We will, but there is something else I think we should do first," added Aharon.

That very day, Shamira and all of the family who was with her went with the disciples to a nearby body of water and each of them were baptized, including Asa. When Shamira came up from the water she experienced a sensation of rejuvenation and rebirth. She felt the presence of Jesus within her very heart, so strong that it was becoming a part of her. She was a new person, washed by the water of her baptism and ready to go forth and be a witness as Jesus had commanded. Shamira witnessed similar changes in each of her family members after they had arisen.

She had moved to a sunny area to dry herself, when her father approached her. "Shamira, I want to say something to you."

Briefly, she recoiled in fear she had done something wrong, but the fearfulness did not last. The days of fear were behind her. "Yes, father?" she replied.

"I never truly understood my own father until after he was gone," her father began.

"Oh, Abba. Sabba loved you and all of us! You mustn't feel regret now, especially after all that we have witnessed. He would be so proud of you." Every day she had her moments of grief. She was certain everyone in the family did, but the time and encouragement from others and from Jesus' teachings had made it easier.

"Thank you for saying that, Shamira, but I think you misunderstand," her father cooed. "I never understood my father, the way he acted, the way he, for reasons beyond my understanding, always made claims which any other person would have called outrageous, even putting his own livelihood at risk in certain instances. Even when it would have been easier for him to just let it go—he faced so much persecution all throughout his life for his perceived madness. His blind faith drove me to such anger. At times, your actions made me angry too—the way you would act so impulsively and speak so fearlessly. It's not that I was angry at you for being who you are, but I was angry because I couldn't protect you. Sometimes your actions were dangerous and reckless, and as your father all I have ever wanted is to protect you from harm. It's very hard to do that, however, when you were always running headfirst into trouble," he teased.

"When he was gone, I felt so remorseful for everything that had happened and everything that hadn't happened between us, and then I saw you. You were, are, and always have been my *bright shining star,* Shamira. Without you, our family would not be here. Libi would not have a voice. I never would have taken up my father's faith. We never would have been baptized as followers of Jesus.

"Because of you, I discovered faith. I discovered what it was that made my father so passionate about his beliefs, and what in turn made you so passionate about everything. I have seen the miracles of the Lord, I have heard the teachings of the Messiah, and I have experienced the feeling of being in his presence. I cannot deny it anymore. I have received salvation all because of you, my bright shining star, who has always guided me in this. I hope you know that Shamira. The whole family is grateful to you for the healing you helped bring into our lives. God has used you in great and mighty ways."

Crying, he held onto Shamira for several minutes, and Shamira began to cry also. She blushed at her father's words, embarrassed by his praise and not used to hearing so many compliments from him. She had always known her father to be a man of few words, but when he poured his heart to her, she knew he meant it. All of her wrongs had finally made a right, although she knew she could not really take credit for what had taken place. It had belonged to God alone, and to His son, Jesus.

"Go, therefore, and make disciples of all nations, baptizing them in the name of the Father and of the Son and of the Holy Spirit, teaching them to observe everything I have commanded you. And remember, I am with you always, to the end of the age." - Matthew 28:19-20 CSB

"Shamira," Elisheva called. She turned to see her imma standing in the doorway that led to the kitchen. Shamira had just been clearing the leftovers from their breakfast before her mother had startled her, taking her breath away. "Would you and Rut go fetch some water from the well?"

"Yes, Imma," she said half-smiling, half-shaking from the surprise.

Her mother turned to leave and then stopped and smiled back at her mid-turn. "Oh! And take Benayahu with you! I don't want the two of you wandering through the city on your own, two beautiful young women such as yourselves." Although life had very much returned to normal in Jerusalem, in many ways it was different.

Shamira finished her task bringing the remains of their meal into the kitchen to be preserved for another time, and then marched through the house and up the stairs to get Rut. She could hear her laughing with Libi from the bottom of the steps. That was another thing that was different about life—Libi's perfect voice. She paused for a moment to praise Jesus and once again thank God for the miracle of Libi's healing, her songs, her laughter.

"Rut?" she said, turning the corner into their shared living space. "Our mothers want us to go get water from the well. Are you able to go with me now?"

"Yes," said Rut, smiling and laughing with Libi who was close beside her. "I was just helping Libi move her things into our room! She has decided that she would like to sleep with us tonight. What do you think?"

Shamira giggled. "I think this room is going to get very crowded, very quickly! The real question is, what does Libi think?" Shamira bent down on her knees to hear her cousin's answer in the sweet, sing-song voice that was all her own.

"I think," Libi said, taking her time. "If Shamira thinks it's going to be too crowded that she should marry Asa and move out!"

Shamira turned her face away so Libi would not get the satisfaction of knowing how she'd embarrassed her. She cleared her throat. "Libi! Don't be silly and say such things." She tried to be nonchalant before addressing her other cousin. "Well then, Rut, I'll let you get your sandals on. Meet me downstairs in the courtyard?"

"My sandals are already on," Rut chortled. "I'll come with you now!"

Shamira didn't acknowledge Rut but kept walking. "Benayahu?" called Shamira when they reached the tiny courtyard. "He must still be inside somewhere."

For a moment she thought she would have to turn around and go back upstairs. Then she saw one hand rise up and flail about from underneath a pile of two playful and mischievous boys.

"Here!" he said, the sound of his voice unusually muffled as though he were being crushed. "I'm down here!"

"Gilad! Yuval!" exclaimed Shamira, laughing, but quickly coming to his aid.

"Play time is over," Rut instructed. "Benayahu has to help us with some chores."

Still the children did not relent. Shamira heard their front gate swing open and turned to see who it was. "Asa, what are you doing here?" she gasped, feigning shock but at the same time not at all surprised. Asa had a way of appearing just when he could be most helpful.

"Apparently, stopping a war!" he laughed heartily, then only added to the chaos by jumping into the pile with the others. "I officially declare the prisoner conquered and captured! All soldiers return to camp! I want this prisoner kept alive and unharmed for interrogation!" Asa commanded it as though he were a proper warrior, and the little boys stood straight up and played along. Benayahu rose to his feet, covered in dirt and dust

"I'm sorry, soldier, but before you can interrogate this young rogue, he must complete the manual labor necessary to absolve him of his crimes!" Shamira said ruefully.

"I never thought that I would be so glad to have to do chores!" Beni joked. "Thanks for the help, Asa; two on one is hardly fair."

"That's commander to you, prisoner!" he kidded.

"What about her?" said Beni, pointing to Shamira.

"No, she'll always outrank me." Asa winked.

"Ehem—" Shamira cleared her throat "—you never did answer me, Asa. What are you doing here—that is, if you're done playing like a child? Rut, Beni, and I were just about to go and fetch some water from the well if you'd like to join us..."

Asa stepped around Shamira and continued to walk past her, which made Shamira wrinkle her nose up at him. He had never turned down an opportunity to spend time with her before. "Actually, I have some business to talk about with your father."

"Business? What business could you possibly have with my father?"

"Uh, well now that I'm back in Jerusalem, I'm going to need a steady job. I know the sheep and the pastures well, and I've come to see if he could use another shepherd."

"I'm sure he could. Come with us to get the water now, and when we return you can ask him about it over supper!" Shamira suggested.

"I would rather talk to your father alone, if you don't mind. I'll stay a while though if all goes well, and I'll be here when you get back. Is that all right?" he asked, his voice wavering with uncertainty.

"Of course, it is," said Shamira, blushing. "I didn't mean to be so forward. Surely it is up to you, I apologize..."

Whatever it was that was making him nervous made her nervous as well. Perhaps she had been too bold as had often been the case. Still, she didn't think that after all she and Asa had been through together such formality was necessary. Maybe she was mistaken. She grabbed the water jars from the side of the house, said her goodbyes politely, and proceeded out of the gate and onto the main road with her two cousins beside her. Despite the brush-off from Asa, a sense of relief flooded her knowing he was planning to stay nearby.

Rut snickered beside her and Shamira immediately turned her head to look at her with a cross expression. "What, *dear* Rut, is so amusing?"

"Oh, nothing! Just how clearly upset you are!" she continued to smile.

"I'm not upset!" Or maybe she was.

"If you're not upset now," remarked Beni, "I would hate to see what you are like when you are really upset!"

"What's that supposed to mean?" Shamira grunted, grateful in that moment she didn't have any actual younger brothers of her own.

"Nothing, Shamira, but if you're trying to hide that you're bothered by Asa's rejection then you're not doing a very good job." Benayahu's confession was brutally honest.

"What's more amusing," added his sister, "is how oblivious you are!"

"Oblivious?" Shamira squeaked. What could she be oblivious about? She had asked Asa to come with her, and he had said no. She had every right to feel at least a little bit dejected.

"You really think that the only thing Asa wants to talk to your father about is business? Sheep?" probed Rut, with an obvious secondary meaning Shamira still didn't understand. "Didn't you hear how he talked, like he was avoiding something? Or not telling the full story?"

"Never mind it," Shamira replied, not wanting to get her hopes up. "If it's all right with all of you, I would like to add a stop to our journey."

"Where did you want to go?" Benayahu asked.

"I want to visit Eliana; it's been too long." Shamira looked off in the direction of her older sister's home longingly.

Taking a deep breath in, she was reminded of the deep breath she'd taken after she'd been baptized. She was gasping for air, her first breath in her new life. Once again, she was refreshed and refilled with that indescribable feeling of joy she'd had in her heart every day since Jesus appeared to them all after his crucifixion. She was reminded of his words and all he'd taught while he was on earth, and specifically, what he had said at the Mount of Olives just before he had ascended into heaven. They were meant to proclaim his message in Jerusalem, Judea, and all the earth. Shamira would start with her sister.

"I know it's out of the way, but…"

"It's all right by me," said Benayahu, shrugging his shoulders. "As long as I'm with you, I know our abba and Dodh Aharon do not mind. They instructed me that this is my job now."

"And me," agreed Rut, seemingly understanding what Shamira had not said out loud but had only felt in her heart. "But we only have mere hours before the evening meal. We'd best be going."

Over the course of the past six years, Asa had probably become more comfortable in Shamira's home than he'd ever been in his own. Because of that, he felt so foolish over the way he was acting, pacing back and forth and creating trails in the dirt as though he had not known this family for years and come to love them like his own kin.

"Asa?" said Shamira's Savta, coming around the corner. "What are you doing here?" Concern showed in her eyes and Asa's face reddened just a bit when he realized she'd been watching him.

Asa's hands dropped to his sides at once. "Hodiyah! How lovely it is to see you."

"I'm Savta to all of my grandchildren and that includes you." She winked. "But you haven't answered my question. Have you perhaps come by for some of my dates?"

Asa tittered. "Actually, I came to see Aharon. I wanted to talk to him about, uh, business of sorts."

"Ah, yes, 'business,'" she said with a knowing tone. "From the looks of you, it's the same 'business' my Eliyahu once discussed with my own abba. Am I right? Don't bother answering—I will see where my son has gone."

She smiled at him, and at once Asa felt slightly more relaxed. "Thank you, Savta."

"It is nothing. Afterwards, come and find me and I will get some food for you. You need more meat on those bones!" She laughed as she walked away from him.

"Yes, Savta," he called. He had never known his own grandparents. To a certain extent, he supposed he never really knew his parents either. He knew his mother was fragile and timid, and it was his father's fault that she had become that way. The same could be said of his brothers. They were all taught to keep quiet and avoid causing trouble, and by their father's definition of trouble, that meant avoiding nearly everything. If the conversations he planned to have with Aharon today went well, he would make sure his life with Shamira would be nothing like the way he had grown up.

"Asa," said Aharon from behind him. "It is good to see you. How have you been faring since your return to Jerusalem?"

"Very well, actually. The disciples have been very kind to me. Travelling and staying with them has taught me so much more about our Lord. I found that I'm learning about things I have studied my whole life, but in new and exciting ways..." Asa cleared his throat as he realized the conversation was digressing. "It's good though to be back with their encouragement to build a life of my own. Since I suddenly have so much time on my hands, I was wondering if you still had room in your employ for another shepherd? I remember you discussing that you were going to have two positions to fill. I know the trade, I've picked up enough from observing you all over the years, and what I don't know well enough, I can keep learning..." Asa's voice trailed off into a ramble and Aharon chuckled. He must have sensed how Asa was feeling.

"Asa, you know we have always been fond of you and of course we trust you. You don't have to convince me you'll work hard. The job is absolutely yours for the taking."

Asa could not contain his smile of relief. The conversation was off to a perfect start. "Thank you, Aharon. Truly!"

"No, thank you! It is perfect timing. My brother and his wife have finally consented to allowing Benayahu to fill the other position. Both of them will rest easier knowing you'll be with him," Aharon took a moment to pause. "Although, I feel as though it is not only the matter of your employment that has you here today. Would I be right?"

"I—that is… I'm not sure how to say it," Asa admitted. "It is times like this when I wish I had a relationship with my own father to ask for advice."

Aharon smiled. "It was not so easy for me when I first approached Elisheva's father either. I will try not to make it too difficult for you."

Asa took a deep breath and straightened his spine. "Aharon, it would be an incredible honor to… That is, I would like it very much if… I want to marry your daughter."

"I see," he replied. If this was him trying to make it easy, then it didn't help very much. Asa was completely unsure of how to proceed.

"I don't come with much—anymore, that is. I only have my

own savings, and what little I earned taking odd jobs as I travelled with the disciples. I'm prepared to put every last shekel and towards Shamira's mohar, but I'm well aware that it is not enough. I don't even think such an amount of money exists. She's priceless to me."

He held out his satchel of coins and extended it to Aharon, giving it to him to count. Shame colored Asa's cheeks, wishing he could offer so much more to and for Shamira.

"Asa, clearly you must see that none of us here have very much either. Please do not be embarrassed, but have confidence that God will continue to provide for all of our needs. We've known you long enough to know your character, and it's more important to me that my daughter marries a man I know I can trust, a man who I know loves her and cares for her. I know that is how you feel. I've known it for years, but I've seen it especially in these past months. I cannot tell you how much it would mean to Elisheva and me to have you officially become a part of our family as a son-in-law. You bring out the best in my daughter, and I know you will be better together than apart."

Suddenly, Asa felt like he couldn't catch his breath. A colossal weight had been lifted off of his shoulders. He had never doubted that he had a good relationship with Shamira's family, but he had doubted they would accept him.

"But" —Aharon wrinkled up his nose— "there is still the matter of the mohar."

"I expected that," said Asa. "I'm willing to do whatever it takes."

"Good." He scratched the beard growing at his jawline. "Let's talk about your pay as a shepherd. Would you be agreeable to foregoing a portion of your earnings each month, setting it aside to pay for your new life together with Shamira?"

Asa's jaw dropped. He couldn't have wished for a better arrangement. "Yes, absolutely!"

"Very well then. Assuming you work hard, which I have no doubt you will, get the job done, and do not let me down, after at least six months you should have enough saved in addition to what you've shown me here to become formally betrothed to Shamira. That all, of course, depends on how strictly you save your wages."

"You have my word. I will do exactly as you ask. I have learned to live on very little as of late, and while it can be hard, it will not be so hard knowing that I am doing so for Shamira." Asa had never meant a promise more sincerely.

"Of course, after that, there will be a formal betrothal period before the wedding can actually take place, as is the custom. During that time, you can continue to earn a wage and set up a home for yourself and Shamira. That seems like adequate time, don't you think?"

Asa nodded eagerly. The months would feel like nothing after all of the time he'd already waited to make Shamira his. Asa paused for a moment to reflect on his life up until this point. He was grateful that despite his own father's flaws, he would always have a father in God. He also thanked God for putting Shamira in his life and for allowing him to become a part of her family. He looked forward to when they would one day, if they continued to be so blessed by God, start a family of their own.

"If it's possible, can we keep this a secret from Shamira?" Asa asked.

"I should assume so, but she might be concerned when you start working long hours and disappearing for days at a time," said Aharon, raising an eyebrow.

"Of course, I don't want to keep her in the dark completely. I will certainly tell her I'm working for you, but I just don't want to tell her all of my plans yet. I'd like to keep it a surprise and, when the time comes and if it's all right with you, I'd like to be the one to tell her. I'd like to ask her myself," said Asa, sharing his plan with ease.

"Hm—" Aharon smiled, a twinkle lighting up his eyes "—I understand. That will be quite a challenge for you though. My daughter is not easy to surprise."

He outstretched his hand, and Asa took it firmly, shaking it and sealing their arrangement.

"Are discussions complete, then?" said Savta, entering the room so quietly that if she hadn't spoken, they would not have known she was there. Asa laughed, although this time he was not anxious. He was just too happy to keep silent.

"Well, I think there's still some more details to work out, but—" Aharon began.

"But," Savta interrupted. "You can discuss those details over cool water and some of my special dates." She held out a bowl full of the sweet fruit, and Asa graciously accepted.

He could hardly wait to tell Shamira about this conversation, this wonderful news, but he would wait six months just as he'd said to Aharon. And every second would be worth it.

Shamira knocked a few times on the large, heavy, and ornate wooden door. She hadn't been to this house since Eliana's wedding, and it still felt just as strange and surreal to be there.

"Shamira?!" Eliana gasped as she opened the door.

The distance between them was always unintended, but also unavoidable. Their lives had moved in opposite directions, with Eliana's duties to her husband and Shamira's role in her family, it was natural they had so little time together. Still, even when they were far away from each other it would always feel like no time had passed when they were reunited.

"Eliana!" said Shamira, embracing her sister.

"What are you doing here? Did you come alone?"

"No, Benayahu and Rut are waiting for me. I told them I would not be long. We are on an errand for Imma, but I couldn't resist the opportunity to visit my sister!"

"Of course not. Please, come inside. There is a place we can talk," said Eliana, leading Shamira through the door and into the large, open courtyard area that had once been the site of Eliana's wedding feast. How different it looked in the daylight without all the people, musicians, and tables upon tables of food.

Eliana led her even farther into the home where she had never before been. The rooms were much larger than she was used to, furnished with fine rugs on every floor. Despite

Shamira's obvious feelings of being out of place, Eliana moved around so comfortably as though she had always lived there. She belonged in this home, and Shamira could see it now. She was clothed in soft, luxurious fabrics in a myriad of bright and bold colors, the likes of which Shamira had never seen in clothing. The blush pink and deep purple fabric seemed to flutter as she glided through the grand hallways, and she reminded Shamira of a gentle breeze passing through during a vivid Jerusalem summer sunset.

"Are you happy here?" asked Shamira, wondering if she herself could ever be happy in such a place as this.

"I know it is much larger than our own home, but it's not so scary once you've gotten used to it, and as I have always said, I am happy with Matthan." Eliana smiled, but even with her graceful countenance, Shamira could still sense Eliana's longing for more.

"I don't know if I could ever be happy without Imma and Abba and the others nearby," Shamira sighed.

"You sound as though you're contemplating it... Has Asa spoken to father about a betrothal?" Eliana asked, sinking down onto a cushion and gesturing to Shamira to do the same.

"Asa? How would he... How do you... Why would you bring up Asa?" she stuttered.

Eliana laughed and the melodic sound of her laughter filled the house like sweet music. "Whenever I have visited the house, Asa has always been present, whether physically present or only present in your mind. You haven't stopped talking about him since you were ten years old. I didn't even live with you then and I know that much!"

"Well, he hasn't. At least not that I am aware of. A lot has happened you know," Shamira said, diverting Eliana's attention and trying to distract her own thoughts. Could a proposal be what was on Asa's mind?

"I know." Eliana spoke softly, pausing momentarily to wipe the tears from her eyes. "Imma told me about Sabba, but I'm afraid that between the Pesach and everything that has been happening in the city, I was unable to visit so I could mourn with you all."

"Don't worry, Eliana. Nobody blames you for not being there. I daresay it was a chaotic time for all of Jerusalem!"

"I came to visit a few days ago, but only Savta, Dodh Tamir, Dodah Chava, and their children were there. They said you, our parents, and Binyamin's family had gone out to meet the teacher called Jesus of Nazareth, but I thought he had been crucified? I'm afraid I didn't understand most of what they were saying. They also told me how this teacher had performed miracles... He'd healed Libi! I wouldn't have believed it if I hadn't heard her speak myself."

"It's true, Eliana. All of it! The man called Jesus of Nazareth is the Messiah!"

"I thought he was crucified... Matthan had told me..."

"Yes! That is true also." Shamira's breathing quickened. "We watched him die, but three days later he rose from the grave! Eliana, he was—he is so much more than just a teacher. He is the Messiah that Sabba had always told us had been promised. I can't explain it to you in any logical way, but I'm telling you it is true. We met Jesus at the temple. I'd heard of his abilities, and I wanted to see them for myself, so I took Libi to see him. Oh Eliana, I wish I could describe it and what it was like, but truthfully, I still feel the same feelings I felt that day every time I hear Libi talk or sing. And trust me, she sings nearly all day long!"

"But the priests said that Libi could never be healed. Physicians said the same."

"The priests were wrong, Eliana. Jesus was—is—the Son of God. He was sent by God to be our Messiah just as it had been proclaimed to Sabba all those years ago. He performed miracles, he even knew Sabba by name, and he was crucified although he was blameless. When he rose again, we saw the marks of the nails used to crucify him in his wrists and his feet..."

Shamira's voice trailed off as she once again became lost in her own thoughts. Sometimes, she was still caught off guard by the wonder of it all. Had it all really happened, and in just such a short time? She smiled recalling Jesus' words to her and to all of his followers, and how she would never forget their power. She would also never forget the power of his healing words to

Libi. The effects of that day seemed to reach farther than just Libi's life. They had touched the lives of everyone in her family, and although it had been what she'd wanted all of her life, she did not feel empty now that it had been achieved. That surprised her most of all. She felt fuller than she'd ever been. Her life felt complete, which was another reason to praise Jesus' name.

Well, her life was complete, except for Asa. She had to think of him in all of this as well. While Jesus had changed her life and brought them all even closer together, Shamira never would have been able to meet Jesus on her own without Asa's help. He had played an irreplaceable role in Libi's healing, in the restoration of peace in her family, in her own life up until this point. The only thing she didn't have yet, at least truly have, was him. What were his plans? Did he intend to marry her, and if so, when?

"That sounds like a very interesting story Shamira, but…" said Eliana, pulling Shamira back to the present.

"It's not a story, it's the truth. You could ask Abba, Imma, Tamir, Chava, Savta, Rut, Beni, Binyamin, Devorah, even the youngest children! They are also witnesses to what I am telling you now. He was crucified without any just cause, and on the third day He rose back to life and appeared to his followers, staying with them for forty days until He ascended into the heavens. Please believe me Eliana, we saw this with our own eyes."

"Shamira—" Eliana held up a hand to silence her "—if anyone else were telling me what you are telling me now, I would say they had gone mad. But my real question is, why are you telling me this?"

"Because Eliana—" Shamira closed her eyes, praying to God her words would not fall on deaf ears "—because I want you to experience what I feel every day. A joy that never runs out, a peace that surpasses all understanding, and an overwhelming love that can never be broken. You say you're happy, but I know you're not. Not completely."

"And how would I acquire such joy? Such love? Such peace?"

Shamira took Eliana's hands in her own and leaned forward

toward her sister, saying, "Believe. All you have to do is believe in Jesus, believe in his power. Acknowledge Him as your Savior, and your life will be transformed."

"This is preposterous," said Eliana, withdrawing her hands and shaking her head. "I'm an ordinary woman living an ordinary life. How could believing in the power of this teacher transform me? What you're saying sounds too good to be true."

"Perhaps it is like Imma said. Perhaps sometimes God doesn't answer our prayers the way we think or expect that he should. Maybe you think that you need one thing, but God wants to show you another way. Please Eliana, for me, believe in Jesus, and pray to God in Jesus' name. I will be praying for you also. What harm can possibly come from praying?"

"I have never stopped praying, Shamira," she said, taking a deep breath. "But perhaps I have not been expecting God to answer, as you have said."

"He always answers our prayers, Eliana."

Eliana nodded. "I will try to believe in all you have said about Jesus of Nazareth… But it will be hard to have faith that would rival your own."

Shamira smiled. "Then my faith will have to be enough for both of us! You will see the wonders of God, Eliana, just as the rest of us have. You will experience the feeling of knowing Jesus, I promise. Just look to God for guidance."

"I will."

"Well, you certainly took your time," said Benayahu. "Our mothers are probably worried sick by now!"

"Now Benayahu, how could they be worried sick when we have *you* as our protector?"

"Having a man around has never stopped you from getting into trouble before, Shamira," Benayahu quipped.

"It just took longer than I expected, that's all. I wanted to tell her about everything that has happened. Everything. Sabba, Jesus, Libi, and the change that has happened in all of our lives. I want her to experience that too," Shamira explained.

Rut went very quiet, and so did Benayahu.

"What's gotten the two of you so tongue-tied all of a sudden?" asked Shamira, picking up the jars and making her way back to the well near their own home.

"Don't you worry about what people will say? It's like the disciples said before. This city is dangerous for followers of Jesus. They will all think that we are heretics and treat us like criminals," warned Rut.

"If everyone in this city could believe what we believe and know what we know, then they would have no room to imprison all of us. Isn't this exactly what Jesus commanded us to do? To spread the good news about his resurrection, and the offering of new life that came with it?"

"But aren't you scared of what people might think?" Rut asked again.

This time it was Benayahu who answered, saying, "When has Shamira ever been scared of anything, least of all her reputation? Besides, she's right. We're not true followers of Jesus if we don't do what he asks of us. He has already laid down his life for us, surely we should be willing to lay down even a part of our own."

"In my heart I know that you are right, both of you. But the thought of putting it all into practice frightens me," confessed Rut.

"I understand, Rut, but you have nothing to fear. Jesus is with us." Shamira paused. "But you could be right—there may be risks and I think that is a question we have to ask ourselves. Is it worth it? Are we willing to lay down our lives for him as he did for us?"

"If you two are done talking, we might actually be able to make it to the well and back before the evening meal." Benayahu guided them, leading the way.

"Don't be such a killjoy," said Rut to her younger brother, "The sun is still high in the sky."

"It is for now! Let's get going," Shamira said, smiling.

The trio plodded along until they reached the well where Shamira and Rut waited their turn to fill up their jars with water. They arrived home in a timely fashion, and no one even bothered to ask why a simple errand had seemed to detain them. Asa and her father were so deep in conversation, Shamira wondered if either of them had even noticed how long she had been gone at all. In the old days, Asa would have been searching for her; now she wondered what could have captivated his attention so fully.

Supper was served and, after the meal was enjoyed, Asa said a quick farewell to the family and was on his way. As she and Rut were settling down with Libi before bed, she paused to look at the wondrous sight outside of her window. Shamira never tired of watching the sun rise and set, and this sunset would hold a particularly special place in her memory. It was pink and purple, just like the dress Eliana had been wearing earlier. She prayed it was a sign of God's faithfulness. It was the sunset on their first full week as baptized believers in Jesus. Shamira knew it wouldn't always be easy, just as Rut had said, but nothing ever was.

Regardless, she was mesmerized by the way the colors of light streaked through the clouds that stretched across the horizon. The sunset, calm and serene as it was, was just a sliver of what God could do. No matter how many clouds darkened her skies, no matter how many storms she had to endure, no matter how dark the long nights were, there would always be brilliant rays of light at the end of the day. They were, to Shamira, a promise from God for all the good things yet to be, that were just waiting behind the clouds to be revealed.

PART THREE — SIX MONTHS LATER

"They devoted themselves to the apostles' teaching, to the fellowship, to the breaking of bread, and to prayer. Everyone was filled with awe, and many wonders and signs were being performed through the apostles." - Acts 2:42-43 CSB

"Now all the believers were together and held all things in common. They sold their possessions and property and distributed the proceeds to all, as any had need. Every day they devoted themselves to meeting together in the temple, and broke bread from house to house. They ate their food with joyful and sincere hearts, praising God and enjoying the favor of all the people. Every day the Lord added to their number those who were being saved." - Acts 2:44-47 CSB

In the summer months, Shamira's family sheared the sheep for wool and the women went to work spinning and dying it, creating an array of yarn to be sold for a profit at the marketplace during the harvest time. Asa lived among the sheep with the other hired shepherds, applying himself as diligently and wholeheartedly as he did to nearly every task to which he set himself. Asa never did anything halfway, but only with all of his heart. He set out each day with unparalleled perseverance to master any new skill and conquer any new challenge presented to him, a trait Shamira deeply admired. Sometimes, Shamira would go days and even weeks without seeing him when he was driving the sheep to new and fresh pastures some distance away from the city walls and sleeping under the stars among them.

The weather cooled significantly during the harvest months. Asa visited for dinner often as the season changed, the chill of the night air only increasing the value of a warm meal. Of course, he was always welcome at their house. In those six months since he had begun working for her father, he had turned into a rugged young man. Judging by his appearance, it would be easy to believe he was the most experienced shepherd of all those employed by her family. She smiled each time he appeared in their doorway with his hair a little longer, and his face a little more worn from the light of the sun.

Before he left on the nights he visited, Shamira would be sure to fill his scrip, the satchel he carried over his shoulders, with all kinds of food from their supply to keep him well fed as he journeyed on. Bread, cheese, dried fruit, and anything else that could be spared, especially the dates he favored so much. After meals as the sun would set, she would sit by her upstairs window and watch the silhouette of him and his shepherd's rod disappear into the darkness of the city. He was usually accompanied by Benayahu, who was preparing to take over much of the business from his father when the time came.

Shamira and her family did not visit the temple as they used to, but they did go when the disciples were speaking. However, with increased tension between the priesthood and the growing members of "The Way" as the believers in Jesus were now called, Shamira wasn't sure how much longer peaceable meetings could last.

Nevertheless, Shamira was happy the disciples, now known as apostles, and even their new member to make twelve, had returned to Jerusalem after the ascension. With them close by, she could continue to witness how God was establishing His new covenant with the people. The promise of the Holy Spirit had come to fruition, just as Jesus had said it would, and they had all been empowered by it. They were building a new movement led by God. They didn't give offerings at the temple but instead gave any surplus of money in addition to their tithing directly to the disciples and to those in need. When they wanted to pray to God they prayed, and when they wanted to worship him, they worshipped.

Shamira asked Asa once if he had seen his father since they last spoke, when it did not end on good terms. Asa told her he had tried to contact him, but that Avram continued to refuse him. She felt very grieved whenever she heard this, but Asa would insist she not trouble herself, saying, "I pray for him every day and every night, but I cannot open his eyes. If things were to change, the only way it could happen would be between him and God. Beyond my prayers, there is nothing else I can do. It is in the Lord's hands. Don't worry about me though, I am doing very well, and I'm very happy where I am. If the shepherd's fields were good enough for King David, then they are more than good enough for me."

Often times, Shamira would confide in Rut about her feelings concerning Asa's difficult and unfortunate situation. She felt horrible about what Asa had to endure. She had even heard that his own brothers refused to speak to him, probably for fear of retribution from their father.

"Now he works everyday as a shepherd. A shepherd! Can you imagine, the well-educated Levite and son of chief priest and member of the Sanhedrin, reduced to shepherding?"

"Do you think so little of shepherds?" Rut would say. "Because I would hate to remind you that you do in fact come from a very, very long line of them."

"Of course not, but it breaks my heart that Asa's family has turned him away so many times."

"Somehow I don't think he's that heartbroken about it."

"What's that supposed to mean?" Shamira would retort, her face reddening at the suggestion. She didn't dare to presume Asa had plans for their future; that would have been tempting fate. It didn't stop her from keeping the matter in her prayers, however. After all, with God, all things were possible, just as she had told Eliana.

"It just means that I know something that you don't know about Asa's arrangements with your father," she would say anytime Shamira brought the subject up, much to Shamira's annoyance.

Scoffing and pointing her chin at the sky, she would reply, "I haven't the slightest idea to what you are referring. Besides, we're not supposed to concern ourselves with the unknown. That is up to God!"

After one such similar conversation, Shamira and Rut heard a commotion from the main part of the house.

"Eliana and Matthan must be here for dinner. Let's go down and greet them." Shamira was already on her feet and halfway down the stairs.

She exclaimed joyously when she saw her sister waiting in the doorway, "Eliana! You're here!"

"Oh, Shamira, I'm so happy to see you!" Eliana was beaming, dressed in brilliant blues. Bits of her hair flowed down past her waist like a waterfall from underneath her veil.

"How are you? I have been praying for you every day without ceasing! Is all well?" questioned Shamira, not wasting any time.

"Very well, thank you for asking," she said, smiling and giving Matthan a cheeky grin. Shamira was filled with amazement but not surprised as she saw the way they exchanged glances with each other. They reminded her of the way they had acted when they were first married, betrothed even.

"Shalom, Matthan," Shamira added, also greeting her brother-in-law.

Just as they moved into the house toward the table another figure appeared in the entryway. "Greetings, everyone!"

Shamira's heart swelled. "Asa! It is so good to see you." She walked toward him while Rut, Matthan, and Eliana took their seats. He now wore the clothes of a shepherd, which were a simple tunic, brown in color, tied with leather, and finished with a camel-hair outer garment to keep him warm when he slept.

"It is better to see you, I assure you. The company of sheep could never compare to being in your presence," he said. Shamira blushed at his forwardness. Although his new profession was more solitary than his yeshiva studies had been, he had not lost his poetic abilities.

"I wish we could spend more time together," Shamira whispered, prodding him to keep showering her with words of affection. Would he ever tell her why he spent so much time in the fields? Why he was more devoted to his work now than he ever had been when studying at the temple?

Asa only smirked, and then replied, "Someday soon, but right now, I'm famished. Let's sit with your family and eat! You know how much I look forward to your savta's cooking."

With a teasing wink, he moved around her and went to sit with the others, seamlessly joining their conversation. After everyone had been assembled, Shamira's own abba led them in their prayers, and together they began to break their fast.

"Tell us, Eliana," said Elisheva, "how have things been for you and Matthan since Pesach?"

"Well," Eliana began, serving herself a helping of lentil stew, "a few months ago, around the time the sheep would have been sheared, Shamira came to visit me."

"She did?" Shamira's imma said somewhat disapprovingly. It was another thing she probably should have told her mother about, but it was too late now—or maybe it wasn't.

"Imma," Shamira said under her breath. "I did not disobey; I had an escort just as I promised Abba."

Eliana went on. "Yes, she came to tell me all about Jesus and his teachings—the way He had changed all of your lives. I suppose I wanted some of that for myself, so I began praying to God, believing in the power of Jesus as the Messiah. I gave him control over my life. Whatever the cost, I knew I wanted to believe and follow him."

"Eliana, I'm so happy for you!" Elisheva's tears of joy were falling.

"I suppose Matthan noticed the change in me first," Eliana continued, blushing at her husband. "He said I was happier than he'd ever seen me. That I seemed to him to be so much more 'alive' than I used to be. He described it as though I used to walk around with weight on my shoulders but could now walk upright without anything holding me down."

Matthan cut in, adding his own side to the story. "She told me what you had told her about Jesus, how she believed that she was saved through him and not through anything anyone could ever do in this world."

Eliana nodded. "We hope to be baptized soon into our new faith, but we are extraordinarily grateful to God for the peace he has given us. Imma, I am truly content, no matter what."

"Shamira, may I speak to you privately?" Asa asked. Not everyone had finished their meal yet. She worried this would be an interruption.

"Oh, well, I suppose," she replied, looking to her own mother and father for approval. "Will you need my help clearing dinner, Imma?"

"Go on, Shamira. We can manage without you," Elisheva replied. Shamira felt awkward now. Asa's request had silenced everyone at the table, and they all seemed to be staring at her, watching her every move.

Trying to ignore the peculiar feelings rising up in her stomach, she led Asa out through the front door, and immediately a gentle breeze passed by and calmed her uneasy nerves. As her hand brushed up against the mezuzah, another wave of peace fell upon her, and she silently thanked God for steadying the rhythm of her heartbeat. The leaves rustled in the nearby tree, intermixing with the sounds of the birds chirping in the air as they flew overhead and the steady murmur of conversation in the streets beyond the wall surrounding their small but full abode.

"Have you been well?" Shamira asked, crossing her arms around her middle and hoping he could not sense the tension pulling her apart inside. "We didn't have time to talk much before dinner was served. Is everything all right?"

"Yes, I've been very well, thank you." He hit her again with a smile. The way his dark brown eyes glimmered at her made Shamira blush. She also took note of the beard beginning to grow around Asa's chin. She liked the change and let her eyes linger on him for a moment longer. "And I trust you have been the same?"

"Oh, yes," she replied. "I couldn't be happier. God has blessed my family beyond measure, taking what was broken and restoring it for His purpose. And…it wouldn't have been possible without you."

"I don't know about that," he said, laughing. "You're very determined, you know."

"No, really, none of this could have happened without you. From the day you saved Libi when we were just children, to the day at the temple when Libi was healed. You have always looked out for my wellbeing. Now it's not just Libi who is healed, but Dodah Chava, Dodh Tamir, even Eliana and Matthan's relationship has been restored because of Jesus and the part you played in helping me to find Him."

Asa shook his head in understanding. "We were both so young when Eliana and Matthan were wed, when we first met. Who could have thought where we'd be now?"

Shamira smiled at the memory. That night seemed like only mere months ago, but in reality, the time had spanned years, and the bond between Asa and Shamira had developed with the passage of that time. That journey had led them from young, spirited individuals to spirit-filled believers in Jesus.

"I was ten years old."

"And just as big-headed as you are now!" Asa teased.

"Who are you calling big-headed? You were the one with a mountain of curls atop your head!" she said back to him, joining in their fun.

Then Asa's expression changed from teasing to something more serious. "I remember watching you from a distance that night. I thought you were so peculiar, the way nothing seemed to please you. You didn't play like the other children, but just stayed put in your corner, watching the events unfold with such a serious expression on your face. You didn't care about the music, the food, none of it. Certainly not a typical ten-year-old. Even then, you were a deep thinker."

"Well, I don't think I was very pleased that Matthan was taking my sister away from me," Shamira said, still smiling and remembering how quizzical she had been at that age. She couldn't understand Eliana's romantic relationship with Matthan at all. Besides that, Shamira didn't know him all that well, and in truth she still didn't know him like she knew members of her own family, but he made Eliana happy. All she knew back then was that he had made her sister act so strangely for reasons she could not then comprehend. Now she knew those feelings all too well.

"But there was something more to it than that, Shamira. Even after the wedding when I visited you and your family in your own home, you were never afraid to let others know what was going on in that head of yours. You were confident and thoughtful. You were extremely protective of your cousins, so much so that sometimes I was afraid to go near any of them for fear your inner lioness might come out and attack me should I inadvertently cause any of them harm!"

"Asa!" she exclaimed. "I wasn't as bad as all of that, was I?"

"Well, probably not, but I was a twelve-year-old boy, and you were the most enigmatic and frightening obstacle I'd ever come across."

"Why was that?" she asked coyly.

"You were a girl, or 'nearly-a-woman,'" he chuckled. "But more importantly, you had a mind of your own. The other girls your age were always busy playing with little dolls, pretending to serve meals and be mothers of children. You on the other hand like to entertain conversations about the coming savior, Messianic prophecies, spiritual matters, the difference between right and wrong. You would not be so easily satisfied."

"You do know that you're making me sound like a dreadfully dull child?"

"My apologies, Shamira, that is the very opposite of my intentions." Asa looked at his feet and shuffled around, shrugging his shoulders as his ears turned bright red. She could see them scorching in embarrassment even through the wisps of his dark hair, which had relaxed over the years into tousled waves. "You captivated me with your words and your passion for everything you loved. Your family, your faith, your beliefs. Anything you loved, you would remain fiercely loyal to."

Asa paused again. Taking a deep breath, he turned and took Shamira's hand, causing her to shudder. Although he had held her hand before, this time, the sensation of his touch was unlike anything she had ever felt, sending waves of shock through her body. The strength in her legs began to fail, making her feel as though she had travelled back in time to the earthquake at Golgotha on the afternoon of Jesus' crucifixion. She held tightly onto Asa's hand to steady herself, and with the physical connection between them, she suddenly felt more whole and surer of herself than she ever had in her life. With Asa by her side, she could face anything.

"Shamira, it was then I decided I wanted some of that love for myself. I wanted you to look at me with that same passion, that same loyalty, and that same strength each and every day for the rest of my life."

"Oh," she said, gasping for air. The thoughts and desires she had dreamed of in the most secret parts of her heart were now within reach. Although she had always believed that Asa had feelings for her, hearing him admit it out loud was an entirely different matter.

"Shamira, these past few months I haven't been working for your father just to earn meals and a livelihood. I have been working to pay your bride price with your father's knowledge and blessing of my plans. I've spoken to him on the matter, and if you agree... Well, what I'm trying to say is... is..." He laughed anxiously, scratching his head. "Funny, despite the fact that I've been practicing this on the sheep in the fields for days now, I can't seem to put my words in the right order. When I spoke to your father, I asked him if I could ask you personally, rather than have it announced to you. You always said you wanted it to be your choice, after all."

He cleared his throat and began again. "Shamira, will you be my wife? Will you marry me and have me as your husband?"

Shamira felt weightless, breathless. The words she was about to say were powerful words to wield that would quite literally change the course and trajectory of her entire life, but the fear of that power and that change wouldn't stop her from saying them. Not anymore. That kind of fear no longer existed in the aftermath of her Savior.

"Yes," she cried. "Yes, yes, yes! I will marry you, Asa!"

"Shamira!" he began before excitedly continuing, "I love you, Shamira. I love you so very much. I love your hair, the way your curls move so wildly and untamed, just like the fire of passion that burns within your heart. I love your eyes, and the way they look at me and make me feel as though you are seeing right into my heart and soul. I love your thoughts and the way you're not afraid to stand up for what you believe."

Shamira could only smile and laugh. Joy abounded all around her. She pondered all the many ways God, through Jesus, had made His glory known to them in the past few months. Though they had not always understood the paths they were directed to take, God had been at work all the time. Miracles, big and small, had followed ever since. Peace had been restored in her family. Libi had been given a voice and the ability to hear. Marriage to Asa had always seemed like a beautiful dream, an impossibility, and God had made a way for that too.

"Shamira," Asa's voice was low and put a sudden pause on her rejoicing. "When my father and my family cut me off, it was hard. One of the hardest things I have ever had to endure, knowing that those relationships, which had always been broken, were now severed completely was difficult. Although it might have been even more difficult for you than it was for me."

"Asa," she whispered.

"I know your heart grieved for me and for my loss," he continued. "With your closeness to your family, the idea of something like that happening would be unbearable. Yet in so many ways, I feel as though I have been set free."

Shamira nodded. "I understand."

"Sometimes I struggle to admit that I don't feel great loss or pain, but your family has always made me feel as though I belong, long before this."

"Because you do belong!" She raised her voice, quick to confirm the truth in his speech. "You've always belonged. The Lord takes away *and* He gives, Asa, and we always praise His name for it. I'm not the only one in my family who thanks God for your presence in our lives."

He smiled wide, "I am convinced that I thank Him ten times as much for you. Shamira, you told me when you were ten years old that you never wanted to leave your family, and now, well, now we don't have to. As I have no family home of my own, I will be working here to build an addition onto the house during the days when I am not working in the fields. Your father has agreed to this."

"Asa, that's wonderful news, truly..." She wrinkled her nose and Asa looked back at her with a questioning expression.

"Shamira, I know you and your nose well enough to know that there is something you want to say. What is wrong? Does this not please you?"

"No, that's not it," she exclaimed. "Asa, I am the happiest I've ever been! This is all so much more good news than I ever thought possible, but I want you to know... I love my family, but I don't have to stay here."

"But Shamira," he began to object.

"Please let me finish. It's very important to me to be able to say this out loud after all this time." She waited for his nod of approval before she went on, "All my life, I thought *this* was my life. That gate, these walls, the people within them—my family. But then I met Jesus and I found so much more. My family, which will soon be our family, is so much greater than just the people within these walls. My life, my purpose is so much more than just this household. It's about Jesus too, and the love He has called us all to share. Asa, what I really mean is that I look forward to starting our marriage here. You've made me feel so very loved and treasured, but should God ever call us to take another path... In that case, you should know that wherever you go, I will be there too. You are my family. My home is wherever you are. It always has been since the day we met."

"Truly?" said Asa.

"I was afraid before, but I no longer carry that burden, and I will not carry it with me into our marriage."

He smiled. "Then let me hear it one more time, Shamira. You really are agreeing to marry me? Knowing all the uncertainties we may face? Knowing that I come with so little?"

She wrinkled up her nose at him, blushing as she opened her mouth to speak. "Yes, Asa, always, yes. I'll say it every day if it helps you to know how much I mean it—and never think that you come with little. You have given me your heart, and that is more than enough."

He tilted her chin upward so that she was forced to look him in the eye. He smiled and then he surprised her, letting out the cheer of a bridegroom-to-be as he lifted Shamira in his arms, spinning her around so fast her feet flew above the ground. Within seconds, the courtyard filled with her entire family who all gathered around and offered their congratulations and blessings.

Shamira's heart had never been so full. In that moment, she had everything she could ever want. Her whole family was united, her betrothed stood before her, and the spirit of God dwelled inside of her. She looked forward to fearlessly following His leading with Asa.

A dainty hand tugged at her sleeve. "Are you getting married now?" asked Libi.

"Yes." Shamira smiled. "Well, soon!"

"Oh, at last!" Libi sighed happily, and the girl was soon enveloped with the roaring laughter of all of her family.

"At last," was only the beginning of the hope God had given to Shamira's family through Jesus, and that He was giving to the whole world.

EPILOGUE

"I rejoice greatly in the Lord, I exult in my God; for he has clothed me with the garments of salvation and wrapped me in a robe of righteousness, as a groom wears a turban and as a bride adorns herself with her jewels." - Isaiah 61:10 CSB

34 A.D.

"What are you doing?" called Benayahu to Asa, who was leaning over the stream staring at his own reflection.

"I'm getting ready for my wedding day," Asa replied calmly. "What does it look like I'm doing?"

"Admiring yourself too much," Benayahu joked. Ignoring him, Asa dunked his head in the water and then, as he rose, tried to smooth out his hair. He looked down at the reflection again once the water and the dirt beneath it had settled, making sure it was satisfactory.

"I still can't see why you'd want to marry Shamira,"

Benayahu joked.

"Maybe you can't, but someday you will. I've loved Shamira for a very long time, but now it is so much more than I could ever have imagined. It is an honor to marry a woman who not only loves me but fears the Lord. You'll see Benayahu, it can happen when you least expect it. I was close to your age when Shamira and I first met. Looking back, it is as if God wrote her name on my heart. In bringing us together, we've both been brought closer to Him through Jesus."

Benayahu grimaced and turned red. "Well, I am certainly not falling in love."

"Ha," said Asa, smiling. "Just you wait. One day a girl may come along who will turn your head in a way you won't be able to understand. Then you'll know what it's like."

"Not anytime soon, I don't think," said Benayahu, crossing his arms.

"Never mind it then." Asa shook his head. His mind turned to his mental list of things to do. Asa wanted to make sure everything had been done perfectly for this special day. "Did you blow the shofar?"

"Yes," sighed Benayahu.

"Near the house?"

"Yes."

"And you're sure they heard it?"

"Yes, Asa! Everything is ready. We just have to go!" Benayahu threw his arms up in the air. "Whenever you're ready, that is…"

Asa chuckled, only partly anxious, but not because he was nervous. He just couldn't wait for the minutes to pass. He finished washing and then dressed in the attire of the bridegroom, wrapping the turban around his head and making sure he had everything with him.

"Are you ready now?" said Benayahu.

Asa took one last look at the fields of sheep. After the wedding feast today, he would have two weeks alone with Shamira. Weeks he had been waiting for and thinking about every single lonely night since their betrothal had officially begun. Apart from loving glances and stolen touches, he had never had time truly alone with Shamira. Time to hold her in his arms, to kiss her, to love her... The next time he set foot in these fields, it wouldn't be just him anymore. Shamira would be a part of him, as two became one in marriage. He would no longer be just Asa; he would be husband and provider to Shamira. She, in turn, would be his wife; the thought of it made his heart swell with pride.

"Yes, I think I am ready now," he announced.

"Good," said Benayahu, leaping from the place where he had been reclining in the sun. "I'm getting hungry!"

Asa laughed again, picking up his bundle as they both started toward the city. Toward what would soon be his home, a real home, full of love like he'd never had before.

"I don't think I'll ever get married," Benayahu continued. "Not if it makes you act so crazy."

Asa remembered how he'd thought the same thing seven years ago, but that was before he'd met Shamira. Every day since then he'd spent in pursuit of a life with her, and it wasn't until they both met Jesus and began to seek Him that everything finally fell into place. His pulse quickened and with each step toward her, he gave thanks to God that their union was finally about to begin.

Shamira was running out of time. But how could that be? She'd spent every day since the betrothal preparing, waiting for Asa to come as a bridegroom. And yet even now, it all still felt as though it were happening too fast for her to keep up with. If only time would slow down, she might be able to savor and reflect on every last moment with her family before Asa arrived. Of course, they wouldn't be going very far. Asa, Beni, and her father had worked together every spare moment to build an addition to the house on the rooftop. It may have been many stairs and a long climb to the top, but at least it would afford them more privacy as a married couple than they would have had otherwise. But even if she wouldn't be going far and things wouldn't be changing too drastically, these were her last moments before she became a wife.

Asa's wife.

"The veil! The veil! We must hurry," said Eliana, who had come to attend the wedding feast.

They all had an idea of when Asa would finally come to claim Shamira as his bride, officially. It had been days since their rooftop annex had been completed, and that had been the last requirement Asa needed to meet before they could formally be married. After it had been completed, he'd set out for the pastures once again with Benayahu. They all had the feeling that when he next returned, it would be for a wedding. In the later part of that day, they heard the sound of the shofar from the street, followed by Benayahu's pronouncement which told them that Asa was on his way. From that moment onward, her family had sent for Eliana, and the rest of the women in the household set about to the task of making sure Shamira was ready to become Asa's bride.

Her heart hadn't stopped racing since.

Smells from the kitchen downstairs had begun to waft and drift upward as her savta and aunts prepared the wedding feast for their family. Because Asa no longer had a family of his own, her relatives would step in their place and host the feast themselves in their own courtyard. Shamira was glad, because she wouldn't have wanted it any other way. Meanwhile, upstairs her imma, Eliana, and Rut tried to spoil her in every possible way, combing and plaiting her hair for her and helping her dress. Shamira had never been so formal in all of her life.

"Eliana, this is all too beautiful for me," said Shamira, suddenly feeling out of place. It had been just a few years prior that their positions were reversed, with Eliana being the beautiful bride and Shamira being one of the casual observers. She reached down and fingered the smooth fabric of her dress that had been painstakingly made just for this occasion. What if she tripped and it tore?

"Shamira, you are a sight to behold. You look exquisite, and

I for one cannot wait to see Asa's face when he sees you," Eliana replied.

"Thank you, Eliana." Shamira was surprised at the emotion she heard in her own voice, not realizing her own eyes had filled with teardrops of joy. She prayed her thanks to God for what may have been the thousandth time that day.

"Now please," she continued, "let me help you with your veil before he gets here."

"Imma?" said Shamira, looking at her mother whose eyes were also filling up with tears. "Imma, will you help me also?"

"Oh," said Elisheva. "Of course! I'm just so thankful to God for giving me two wonderful daughters."

"Imma," said Eliana. "If you start crying then both Shamira and I will have no choice but to join you! We must have only smiles and laughter today."

"Yes, I'll try not to," Elisheva agreed, wiping her face with a cloth.

Together, Shamira's sister and mother pulled the veil over her, completely concealing her face. From this point forward, no one would look upon her until Asa removed the veil himself, as was the custom. As the fabric settled over her, so did a strange calm. Her breathing became regular for the first time since the sound of the shofar in the distance told her that Asa was finally coming, not as a friend to the family, but as a bridegroom.

"I think you look perfect," Libi sighed. "It's all so romantic!"

Shamira giggled, "Thank you, Libi. I think so too."

"I agree with her," said Rut. "You make the most beautiful bride, and I couldn't be happier to be a part of this day with you, my cousin by birth and sister of my heart!"

"Oh, Rut, thank you so much," said Shamira, opening her arms to Rut for one last embrace before she was married.

As they were holding onto each other, a sudden knock came at the door. Though she knew Asa was coming, somehow the knock still surprised her, coming when she least expected it. She was grateful the veil obscured her face so others would not try to read the myriad of emotions she likely displayed.

"I'll get it!" said Libi, already running toward the stairs. Shamira couldn't help but laugh, thinking about how just a few years before, it had been herself running down to greet Matthan on Eliana's wedding day. Now it was Libi's turn. "I'll bet it's Asa!"

Carefully and with the help of Rut and Eliana, Shamira made her descent downward. Behind her veil, she could just make out Asa's silhouetted form standing in the doorway, but she knew it was him instantly. A chill ran down her spine and she shivered, pausing at the bottom of the stairs.

Slowly, the shadowy figure stepped toward her, one step at a time.

Closer...

And closer...

And closer... Until he was right in front of her. Her pulse raced in excitement as she waited. Time seemed to stand still.

Finally, Asa reached out and took her veil in his hands, and she moved with the weight of it. In one swift motion, he lifted it over her head, revealing her face to him. She lost herself in his deep brown eyes and all the emotions behind them. He was good, he was loyal, he was honorable—he was a man who chased after God with all of his heart. The only man she could ever see herself with. For a moment, the rest of the room faded away and it was just the two of them standing there, with his hand reaching out for hers.

His chest swelled as he breathed in and said to her, "My beloved, my Mira... Are you ready?"

She looked down at the open hand before her and back up into Asa's loving eyes. Then, taking his hand, she whispered, "Yes," as she'd promised to do every day when she'd first accepted his proposal.

"Yes," she said again, only a little more loudly for all to hear. He accepted her hand and placed on top of her veil a headband of coins and flowers. Then, when he was finished, she let him lead her out to the wedding feast, and from there to the rest of their lives.

THE END.

AUTHOR'S NOTE

Dear reader,

The Triumphal Entry has always been one of my favorite pictures painted for us in scripture. As a child I loved thinking about the bright, glittering sun shining down from such a pure blue sky, which would have been full of palm branches waving in the air and creating cool shade below. I knew I would love to read about characters who actually got to live through this event and experience this moment through their eyes. After some deliberation, I decided to write that story myself.

But first I had to come up with "my family." I already knew Shamira was going to be headstrong and that she had a fierce loyalty and passion for what she believed in. But how did she know who Jesus was? What made her believe so vehemently in the Savior?

As I read through the scriptures searching for answers about what the lives of the people who encountered Jesus might have been like, I remember reading in Luke about the shepherds. I thought to myself, "How amazing to have received such a message!" and then I wondered... What happened to them afterward? Did they carry this knowledge with them throughout their whole life? When they went home and told their families, how would they have been received? That was when I learned that Shamira came from shepherds, but not just any shepherds. Her grandfather would have been a shepherd at the time of Christ's birth. Other story details fell into place from there.

After I discovered where Shamira came from, I had to learn how she would have interacted with Jesus. Would she have been an observer? Did she herself experience one of Christ's miracles? Was someone close to her in desperate need of a Savior, and is that what propelled her forward in her journey with such urgency? My studies of the gospels continued. I had read through these passages countless times, having been raised in the church since I was a child myself. It was as if I'd read them for the first time when I read the passage in Matthew which described the cleansing of the temple. After Jesus cleansed the temple, Matthew writes that the blind and lame came to be healed by Him and even children began to praise his name, much to the frustration of the chief priests. It seems like such an afterthought to include that detail, but nothing in the Bible is an afterthought. It is all incorporated intentionally. That is where the climactic moment in Shamira's story comes from. I imagined her going there with her cousins, witnessing such a monumental event, and praising Jesus for it. This is where the inspiration for the pivotal scene of Libi's healing came from. Of course, Libi is deaf-mute, not blind or lame as Matthew writes. This is one of the only stretches of my imagination as an author, and one I hope you will forgive in light of the message of the story as a whole. This is a work of historical fiction, and only the Bible itself can be taken as fact, but the Bible tells us, "And there are also many other things that Jesus did, which, if every one of them were written down, I suppose not even the world itself could contain the books that would be written" (John 21:25 CSB). Who is to say that there were not those like Libi who experienced the healing power of Jesus?

I used many different resources when doing my research for this book. Some of my late grandmother's Bible study tools became invaluable to me, such as her chronological study Bible, her many commentaries and concordances, and other books that she had about daily life in Bible times. The tool I used most was the *CSB Christ Chronological*, which is a version of the gospel that organizes the scriptures in chronological order, placing each account side-by-side for easy comparison. The commentary notes for each section that discussed the differences between each account and the reasoning behind their placement within the book were highly useful and helped me determine how I would place the events of Christ's ministry on earth within my story.

One specific instance where I struggled to plot a Biblical event within my story was Jesus' anointing. Scripture and scholarly opinions vary on when and where this event took place. Furthermore, they also disagree on who it was that actually anointed Jesus. Matthew, Mark, and John place the event in Bethany, while Luke places it somewhere else. Within Bethany, Matthew and Mark write that the event occurred in the home of Simon the Leper, while John highlights Mary, Martha, and Lazarus' presence at the event. After much research and for story purposes, I placed this event chronologically just before Jesus' triumphal entry into Jerusalem. While I have Lazarus and his sisters present at the event, ultimately, I wrote it taking place in the house of Simon the Leper. I made these and other similar choices to have as much synergy between the Gospel accounts as possible, while also trying to ensure that the fictional story of Asa and Shamira was well-structured.

You may notice that after the scene of Jesus' anointing, Asa overhears his father plotting against Lazarus. Did this really happen? The only gospel to include references to such an event is John, who wrote in John 12:10-11 (CSB), "But the chief priests had decided to kill Lazarus also, because he was the reason many of the Jews were deserting them and believing in Jesus." How this passage has been interpreted by different scholars and churches has varied. The outcome of the priests' decision is never explicitly stated, although it is implied.

Because of this conjecture, I also left this point in my story open to debate. Asa overhears his father and another priest discussing it, which breaks his own heart, but he never finds out if his father went through with it.

When it came to writing about Jesus Christ, I decided I wanted to be mostly ambiguous. In other words, I wanted readers to care more about the message of Christ and less about His physical appearance, which we have no way of knowing. I used different passages of scripture for nearly all of His dialogue, except for a few scenes where I tried to write based on how He spoke in scripture. There are certain things I wrote Him saying that may not have occurred, or did occur but in different parts of the Gospels, but who is to say He didn't say the same thing twice? He repeatedly told the disciples that He would rise again, after all. More than anything though, I focused on the people who would have been around Him at the time. If there are any inaccuracies or inconsistencies, all I can do is ask for your forgiveness. It was of course not my intention. There are so many questions I would love to ask God in heaven about how things really played out! It is ultimately my hope that people who wish to hear more of Jesus' words will turn to their own Bibles to encounter His teachings for themselves.

I'd like to thank a few people in particular for helping to make this book possible. First, to God who is the ultimate author of stories. He has authored my own story in ways I never expected; indeed, if you had told me just five years ago that I would be writing and publishing a Biblical fiction novel, I would not have believed you. Looking back, I can now see how He so clearly orchestrated each and every moment to bring me to this point. Our God is an awesome God!

Next, I'd like to thank my family. Brandon, my husband, has always been there for me. Even when he didn't understand what I was doing, he would try to help me in any way he could, whether that was by being a shoulder to cry on, an ear to listen, or a voice of encouragement when I was at my lowest points. The same could be said of many people on this list, but he really deserves a medal of honor.

Thank you to my parents. Your names are Nancy and Steve, but you'll always be Mama and Daddy to me. The first to hold me. The first to pick me up. The first to push me to try new things. The first to encourage me to try them again. From the time I was born until now, you've always been there for me.

Thank you to my Grandpa and Grandma Graves. Although Grandma is no longer with us, I am positive I would not be here without her. She is the linchpin in my story. If I were to share an abridged version of my testimony, many details might be omitted or passed over, but not her. Her impact on my life through her actions and her prayers cannot be ignored. She encouraged me to read my Bible, watch documentaries, study history, and be a woman who chased after God with all of her heart. Even now, some of her old books and Bibles sit on my desk as I type this, full of her notes. I know we both miss her, Grandpa, but without either of you, I would not be who I am today. I feel blessed by your prayers every single day.

Thank you to Charissa, my cousin and best friend, who has always been the alpha reader for everything I've ever written. Thank you to all of my aunts, uncles, and cousins that I haven't named. Thank you to Audrey; God knew I needed a friend as sweet as you to get me through this crazy journey called life. Thank you to Alysha; you've been wanting me to write the sequel to this book since before I even finished this one. That's commitment! Thank you to my editor, Martha, and the M. K. Editing Team who helped me find my own voice and style as a writer.

Finally, thank you to you, the readers. You give my writing purpose. Asa, Shamira, and her entire family are all entirely fictional characters, whose stories stemmed only from my own imagination. The events that they experience however, such as the anointing at Bethany, the Triumphal Entry, the crucifixion, and the resurrection are from the true words of the Bible. It is my prayer that this story will inspire you to also take a deeper look at the gospels and see how Christ's sacrifice on the cross was for all people, including you.

"For God loved the world in this way: He gave his one and only Son, so that everyone who believes in him will not perish but have eternal life." - John 3:16 CSB

—Jenna Van Mourik

DISCUSSION QUESTIONS

1. Shamira and her family lived with many extended family members, which, even for a reader, takes a little getting used to. If you were in a situation like this, what do you think would be your biggest challenges?

2. In the introductory chapters, Shamira was a fiercely loyal and loving young girl, and very content with things just the way they are. She was grieved that her older sister was leaving home, and as a child, she wanted things to stay the same. Change is hard; what are some of the hardest changes you have been through, and what scriptures have helped you navigate transitions?

3. Weddings varied throughout Biblical times, from the Old Testament to the New Testament. A lower or even upper middle-class family may not have accommodations to host a gathering that might last several days. Times were changing, especially in the crowded city areas where less space was available, and after the feast, guests (other than visiting out-of-town family) might return to their own home. What type of wedding celebration do you think you would prefer if you lived in this time period?

4. Because of Asa's heroic actions, his whole family was invited to a special dinner to honor him. Shamira's family was not upper class, but despite this their guests still came. Do you think Asa's father had ulterior motives? If so, what would they have been? (Consider Luke 20:45-47)

5. It is explained that, at first, not many people noticed Libi's disability when she was very young. However, when she grew older, her limitations became more noticeable. As a parent in a difficult time when those with disabilities or sicknesses were often judged quite harshly, what do you think the biggest fears would be as the child

grew closer to becoming of age and more noticed by society? (Consider the assumptions of the disciples in John 9:2-3)

6. Asa was following in his father's footsteps by preparing for his future role, but at a time of political and spiritual unrest, especially as Jesus was becoming more known. What factors do you think caused Asa to wrestle inside with his future duty versus his heart's desires? From a personal perspective, think about the desires of your heart and reflect on Psalm 37:4. Do you have examples of how God has worked in your life or are you in a season of waiting for Him to provide clarity?

7. When Asa encountered Peter, he is taken to a home where Asa witnesses Jesus being anointed with expensive perfume. As an author, I based my story mostly on the account provided in John 12:1-8. Would you have chosen another gospel account? Why or why not?

8. Jesus healed deaf and mute individuals. When Libi was healed, not only could she hear but she could understand language and engage in conversation and even song. Did this surprise you, or did you believe that was part of the miracle?

9. At a turning point in the story, Shamira sought out her father to ask for his help and permission. Did it surprise you that Shamira honored her father's wishes in this way? In what other ways did you observe Shamira grow and mature, and what do you admire most?

10. When Shamira's grandfather passed away, her family told her if they'd arrived just a few minutes earlier they could have been there before his last breath had been taken. Did you wonder if perhaps he had passed earlier, then a miracle could have happened, and he would still be with them? (Consider Matthew 27:51-54)

11. Asa was disowned by his father because he went directly against his wishes. Do you think this was a price of

following Jesus that could still happen today? Have you ever experienced a serious loss because of a decision to stand for Jesus? (Consider the words of Jesus, Luke 14:24-26 and Matthew 6:33)

12. In the Old Testament, some of the most known names (such as Jacob, Moses and David) watched over their flocks; it was very common for families to shepherd their flocks. Shamira's family made ends meet by not only raising and trading livestock, but also by spinning and selling wool and using the milk from the sheep to make other goods. Had you ever thought of the business end of sheep herding in biblical times? Were you surprised that a family could be so enterprising?

13. In the Bible, Jesus talks about sheep and calls himself a "Good Shepherd." What traits does Jesus portray that are similar to a good shepherd in the fields? (Consider Psalm 23 and John 10)

14. Why do you think it was so hard for Shamira's family to trust her grandfather in his account of the night Christ was born? In all other matters as head of the household, the family business, and clearly the spiritual leader, he seemed to excel and be trusted. Have you ever been in a situation where you had to trust someone and believe in them even when you had doubt inside? How did you overcome this?

15. Throughout the story, Shamira wrestled with both the fear of change and the desire for change. She did not want to let go of her family, but at the same time, she wanted things to be better for them. Have you ever been in (or can you imagine) a situation where your needs and wants are in conflict with each other? What about a situation where your wants have conflicted with the will of God? (Think of Biblical figures like Jonah or Moses who were both called by God for specific purposes, but struggled with their callings)

16. By the end of the story, Shamira was able to let go of her

fear and replace it with faith in God. The narrative tells us, "That kind of fear no longer existed in the aftermath of her Savior." Once she put her faith in God, she was freed from the burden of fear. In what moments have you had to give over your fears to God and learn to live in faith? What feelings did you experience? (Consider 2 Corinthians 5:7)

ABOUT THE AUTHOR

Jenna Van Mourik is an author of Biblical fiction whose debut novel, *Jerusalem's Daughter*, was published in 2021. She graduated *magna cum laude* in 2020 from California Baptist University with a Bachelor of Arts degree in English.

Jenna is passionate about books, storytelling, and using the art of fiction to portray the truth of God's love. She enjoys sharing Christian fiction recommendations on her YouTube channel, and sharing all about her writing and personal life on Instagram and on her blog. She currently lives in Northern California with her husband, Brandon, and her toy Australian shepherd, Piper. She tries to live every day according to God's purpose, with what she calls a "Now Go!" mindset, in reference to her favorite passage of scripture, Exodus 4:11-12.

Connect with her at www.authorjennavanmourik.com or on social media at @jennavanmourik.